Bones
like
Bridges

Previous works include

When the Sea is Rising Red

House of Sand and Secrets
Empty Monsters

Beastkeeper
Charm

Bones like Bridges

Cat Hellisen

First Printing, 2020

ISBN: 9798648596351

For the broken and the free

One

The Grinningtommy

THERE'S GOING TO be a burning down on Lander's Common.

Burning days don't come along often. Here in the Digs outside MallenIve city – well it's a bit of entertainment to go watch someone die. Better'n picking over the rubbish the Lams throw out from their fancy houses, at any road. Better still than sitting on my own, feeling all sorry for myself because Prue went an let herself die.

I'm cutting through the Digs to get to The Scrivver's Hole where Oncle will be throwing back a pint, stone dust still in his hair. The old brick pub is squeezed twixt a pawn shop an a butcher's; the edges of the bricks crumbled an turning black from the mine smoke. I turn down a dirt street, dodging nilly shit an beggars. The reek of blood an inners from the meat-house near smothers the sour-porridge smell of the brewery behind the Hole. The sun beats down, high an far away.

Speaking strict, I ain't allowed in the Scrivver's Hole 'til I turn eighteen, but I'm so close that old Lyman never stops me coming in if I'm alone. It's my pack he won't put up with.

"Your lot'll rob me blind and then spit in the beer," he says, which is mostly true, 'cept for the spitting part. The pack would just drink it. No sense wasting a good high.

But I'm alone – most of the Digs's pack has already headed down to the common to go watch the burning, so Lyman pays no mind when I slip in to the dark pub. He's serving Oncle, who has his back to me.

"The lad's not going to like it much," says Lyman, polishing a murky glass with a rag that's near as black as the bar counter.

Oncle leans forward, all tired-like. "It's not that I like it myself. But I've no power in this; the law's on that bastard Lam's side. Besides," he says and sighs into his pint. "Might be that he could do a better job with Jek than me or Prue ever did. Lad runs wild, an there's no denying it."

"Firm hand is all he needs – Jek." Lyman's spotted me, an the conversation stops. Oncle shifts on his stool, an nods me over. I'm wary now, wondering just what the old codger has up his sleeves.

The bar counter is full of tired old Hobs, backs bent from years working underground. All the scrivvers are up from the mines, cooling their burnt hands on the glass, their iron picks put up for the day. They drink slow, sipping to make the ale last. Oncle's near the end, so I slip over to him an sit, pretending we're all chummy-like.

"You gonna buy us one then?" I says.

Oncle just laughs into his bitter. He's been working longer an longer these days, trying to make his quota in Deep Black. Said he'd try an get me a job working scriv, but there's more'n more old Hobs laid off recent. The chance of Oncle having a spare bit to buy me a pint is about as likely as our scrounger shitting silver nuggets.

Then he says, "Might do," which surprises me, 'cause we play this game all the time, an the answer is always no. May be that he's feeling bad for me 'cause of Prue. Been less than a week, an it still don't feel real.

Even now she's gone I can't call her mam. She never did like it.

Oncle waves the keep back. "A half Rusty Black for the lad – on second thoughts, make it a pint, Lyman."

Lyman lifts an eyebrow, well he only has one – a huge thing that crawls over his eyes like a windle-grub. Still, he pours me a bitter an pushes the glass over to me.

The faint tang of scriv an hops wraps round my face, heady as magic, before I take a sip.

Scriv is what gives the Lams their power – what they use to tap their magic, an it's more precious than air. It's what they use to protect the city from the Mekekana and the like. So we owe the bastards at least that much. Without them we'd have been churned under iron wheels a long time ago. So we mine their scriv an clean their houses an say yes-sir, no-sir, whatever-you-say-sir. An in return, they get all addled on scriv and keep the city mostly safe.

There's hardly more than a grain or two of scriv powder in a bitter – least-wise, not in Hob-bitter – but it's enough that I can feel it prickling my skin. The rush shivers over me, an I close my eyes for a moment an remember why it is I came here in the first place. "They caught a bat down the Wend, was still feeding when they found it." I stick my tongue in the creamy foam.

We all knew there was a feral vamp somewhere, drinking the little Hoblings dry. All those small corpses, paled an empty, turning up on the Wend-side heaps while the mothers cried an sobbed so hard that even we packs didn't bother them none.

First time in a long while there's been a vamp breaking MallenIve law and feeding off've anything more than a knacker yard nilly. Don't think no one believed it at first, but there's no explaining those bite marks away. I saw one of the bodies – found it, in fact, an had to chase the jackals away from their feasting. It was still easy enough to see where the bat had gone an torn the poor mite's throat out.

Still an all, it took the sharif long enough to go after the damn thing. Typical of them police-bastards. Course it was only so long before the bat moved on to better feeding grounds an got the Gris-damned Lammers involved. The Hob-council had to send sharif packs in to hunt it down before things got worse.

I heard Marlon said they took so long 'cause no one believed a bat would be dumb enough to start hunting here, so close to MallenIve. Once, long ago, when I was still playing second to that damn Hob, Marlon told me there's tame bats in MallenIve proper, but I don't believe a word that bastard says no more.

Vampires are lower even than street dogs, an there's no way I'm gonna believe that MallenIve's Lams let them walk the street just like they was people. Not when the buggers drink blood an all that crap. Besides, Marlon will tell anyone anything long as he has their attention.

"They gonna burn it?" Oncle says, an he tears his attention from his pint to peer side-long at me.

"Looks like. They're setting up a stake on Lander's." I drink a little more, letting the scriv settle strong in my veins. I feel like I could take on Marlon's Wend pack with one hand tied an smash that shite bastard down into the ground so hard he won't see straight for a month. Ah now, there's a dream to relish. "Was thinking you might want to go see it."

"Hmm." Oncle drains the last of his bitter. "Drink up smart, before we go an miss the whole deal."

Looks like it's a good day for me – a free drink an a bit of entertainment. It's the best day I had since Prue died, anyway. I drink quick even though I've no head for scriv an follow Oncle out into the last of the sunshine, my mind wobbly an too big for my skull.

By the time we reach Lander's Common, the sharif have already built a pyramid stake: black saplings stripped bare an lashed into place with scraps of red silk ribbon. A crowd is gathering – word spreads fast down our way – an the working-ladies have even come out from their dark rooms in their thin slips an petticoats.

Everywhere the Hobs are gathered, burned darkest brown by the desert sun, eyes squinted, sharp ears ready. As usual down our way, everyone looks too thin an tired: the Wend Hoblings with their pot bellies an woeful faces; my own pack, lean and sharp. Even the older Hobs are hunger-stunted, kept like this by the damned Lammers.

I keep a sharp eye for Marlon or any of his scavs, but a few of my own see me an nod; let me know it's all clear – that Marlon's keeping to his side of the common. Good. Last thing I need is an out-an-out war twixt the two of us. Best we just keep skirting each other, the way the blasted magicless Mekekana in their iron ships do with the Lammers.

I'm a good head taller than most Hobs, but I still want a decent view, so me an Oncle push through right to the front where the sharif have the bat tight in iron. Those chains must burn the fucker's skin something awful. The sharif hold the ends of the chains, hands carefully bound in leather strips so that the iron don't touch them.

I'm right near the front now. The bat is close to my height; just a little taller than the sharif around it. It's frightened, crying gobbets of blood. It looks almost like a Hob, only white as chalk dust and the skin on its face already blistering in the late noon sun. Damn thing's not like I was expecting. I thought it would look like a beast, all hungry-like, but it's thin and shaking, an its black hair hangs in its face like it were trying to hide.

4

"Well now, would you look at that," says Oncle. "It's not even full grown."

It does look young, but then I've never seen one up close-like, so I take Oncle's word on it. Best I can tell is that it's not all that much younger than me – may be just seen its sixteenth year. Then again, with bats, who knows right anyway?

The nearest sharif strikes it across the face with a length of iron chain, an the crowd whistles. The bat raises its white face. It's stopped crying. May be that it realises how useless its tears are here. Instead it shivers; shivers so hard I think it's gonna shiver right out of its skin. You never think of them wearing clothes an boots – they're just tales to scare children – but the bat is in a neat suit, a worn one with the knees darned an the sleeves an trousers too short. The bat's white ankles an bony wrists are on display, an there're red weals where the iron touched it.

The beer sits strange in my belly. I've done a bit of work with Oncle's pick before, an I know just how much iron hurts. I almost feel kinda bad for the damn bat.

"Please," it says when the sharif light their torches. We fall back a little from the heat.

The crowd goes still, an the bat knows. I can see on its face it understands – there's no one gonna feel sorry for it, child or no. It killed their babes, an it understands that much at least. We Hobs don't take kind to those that hurt our own. It tries to curl into a ball, but the sharif just kick it an drag it up to the stake, pulling the chains tight.

It's gibbering now, calling for its mam, but all we do is watch as the torches are put to the dry grass an kindle-sticks.

Black smoke an screams pour over Lander's Common, an tonight they'll be getting high down on the Wend. Celebrating. The air smells of wood ash an pork, near heavy enough to drown out the reeking shite stench from the Lam-heaps. The winds turn, an it blows the smell up the hillside to where MallenIve proper squats with its spires an gables. I hope the fuckers up there choke on it. This far from the city, I can just make out the nearest of the seven thin bell towers the Lams call the Widows.

"A bat that young, means it'll have a dam out there," Oncle says, as the firelight bounces across the faces of the crowd. "Stupid bint, letting its young go off hunting like that." He shakes his head. "Come on, Jek, we'd best leave."

5

"So quick?"

"Best, 'fore the crowd turns ugly."

He's in a rush to get home. This past week he hasn't wanted to spend much time in the house. Fair enough – neither have I. For starters, it's too damned empty.

We trip through the Digs, taking the long route back to ours. It's best I don't cut through Marlon's territory, even though he's probably up on the Common, spitting in the ashes. He runs Wend with an iron hand, an he'll burn anyone what crosses him. Far as he thinks, the Wend brats are his own to do with what he wants. He's not the forgiving sort neither, an he took my move to running the Digs pack like a slap to the face.

The Digs are quiet, the little sandy roads bare. No sign of anyone 'fore we turn up the low hill to where Oncle's hut leans in the shade of a cone-tree.

Most of the houses down this way are built of whatever junk we can get off the Lam-filth heaps – the crap that the Lammers cart here, as far from their precious city as possible. But Oncle's a dab hand with stone an bone, so his hut, while it might be all stolen planks an broken brick, is one of the biggest – two rooms: one for us, one for the pig. The old scrounger raises his snout when we come in. He's been rooting in the filth, an his whiskered face is red with mud.

I stop to give the pig a scratch behind his hairy ears, making him grunt an rub his head 'gainst my leg, leaving a smear of spit. Pig-kisses. The pig is long past his killing-day, an though Oncle says nothing, I know he's keeping the old bugger alive a bit longer because of Prue. Every year, it's the same thing. We get ourselves a little squealer for the bacon, an I get too attached to the damn thing. Killing day, I always head as far from home as I can get. Most-times I go down as far as the irthe orchards an sit watching the windle-silk tents flap in the hot wind.

Pigs scream when they die.

Of course, I don't tell no one about it, an I'm happy for the bacon an the sausages, but it still wouldn't do if Hobs knew Jek Grinningtommy got all sentimental over breakfast. I thump the scrounger's back quick-like, an step up to our room.

There's still three cots up here, although Prue's stuff has mostly been sold off already. The thatch is looking ragged, and mice are scritching in the low ceiling. Come summer, I'll have to head down to the banks of the Casabi to see what good reeds I can bring back, an help Oncle mend the roof.

"Here." Oncle's digging through a small kist what he's drug out from under his bed. "This'll see you." He stands an drops two bits in my hand. They're bright as moons in the dark room. I stare at him – that's more money than I ever seen in my life – two silver bits – you could buy half the pub with this.

"It's your mam's," he says. "It's what the Lammer paid her."

I don't right understand, an Oncle must see it, 'cause he claps one iron-scarred hand on my shoulder. It's heavy enough that I just 'bout buckle under the weight. Working with iron makes the scrivvers strong, an not in ways the Lams with their heads stuffed full of magic dust would ever understand. "You keep that tight, Jek. One day may be that you can buy your way free out of this mess."

His words don't make no sense, but they're making my chest feel prickly with nerves, an all my muscles tighten, readying me to run.

Someone raps on the wooden door frame, just before the scrounger squeals below. I follow Oncle through the mud an pig-shit, my fingers tight around those coins as I slip them into a sneak's pocket inside my jacket. At any minute now I'm gonna have to fly, I can feel it in my bones. There's summat not right in the air. No one in the Digs would bother knocking, an my heart stops-an-starts, because the sharif might, but there's no way they can know about that barrow me an Mik cleaned out, less the little worm turned tattle.

Outside stands a wooden cart, two shaggy dun nillies shifting in their traces, glaring about with slitted yellow eyes. A tall Lam's standing at their heads, one hand on the nearest one's ruff. He's just a low-Lam, but he stares down at us like we was no more than shite on his spit-shiny shoes.

Well, at least it's not a sharif pack. I breathe slow, watching the Lam careful-like, in case he makes any kind of move. Though why a low-Lam's out here in the Digs is anyone's guess. He best run that cart back home 'fore my pack rumbles him.

The cart's a simple thing fit only for a servant. Although there's a thistle crest on the side, so he's working for money. Stupid low-Lam, should've covered that up.

Oncle clamps one hand down on my shoulder again, holding me fast.

"Is that the boy then?" The low-Lam talks through his nose. He's round-shouldered in the way that tall an skinny people get from stooping all the time, an he squints at me over a nose that would do a carrion-crow proud.

"So he is."

"Doesn't he even have decent shoes?"

"Oncle?" I try pull out from his grip, but he holds me still an tight with his hard miner's hands.

"You're going with this one, hear," says my Oncle. "He's taking you to your da."

I wriggle free, but he catches me at the wrist, an it don't matter how fast I am, Oncle's scriv-sharp an strong.

"I've got no da," I says again. "Prue said."

The low-Lam sniggers. The sound makes the nillies skittish-like, an they roll their yellow eyes, dancing up on their cloven hooves. Like this, with their single horns gone, they look just like big raw-boned goats, nowt magical about them.

"'Course you do. Your mam came back from that fancy Lam-House fat with you, an two silver bits for her troubles. Now she's dead, so your da has rightful claim." Oncle don't let go of me.

"Nillyshit," I says, but it's useless. I've always been taller than the other Hobs, an though I've darkish hair an slant-eyes, they was ever the wrong colour, dark-green where most Hobs' are brown. If there's a Lam somewhere who thinks he's my da, well, there's no one to prove him wrong, an MallenIve law means the Lammers can kill me if I run. There's nowhere I can go, not unless I want to be burned like that skinny little bat.

"The boy will come quietly," says that spit-sucking low-Lam, his voice sharp an clean like a new razor. "Or there will be consequences."

"He'll give you no trouble." Oncle clips my ear for good measure. "Get in the back then, lad."

"Of course he won't give me any trouble," the low-Lam says, an quicker than I ever expected a Lam to move, he collars me. "I can't leave that sort of thing to chance." Pain runs in a sharp line, fire around my throat.

It's iron, a thin collar like you sometimes see prisoners wearing when they're leading them off to the courts, an it burns worse than I expect, like a brand. I try get a good kick in at the low-Lam 'cause there's no way I'm giving in an going all quiet-like – let the fuckers burn me. I'm not afraid of no low-Lammer.

But my Oncle pulls me up sharp by my jacket, forcing me still while the low-Lammer ties me to the iron ring in the back of the cart. "Do what they tell you, Jek," says Oncle, speaking just for me, his breath in my ear. "There's good that can come of this; you've more future in MallenIve than here, sure enough," He lets go, an I push at him. He just looks at me once then turns away to walk back into the house. I pull at the collar, but the thin chain has me fast, an my fingers are blistering. That's nothing. My own family just fucking sold me over, an there ain't no salve that will make that right.

An that's it. No more Digs, no more fighting with Marlon and his pack, or hanging around the mines seeing if we can cop scriv-dust. It'll be off to the towers an streets of MallenIve's Lam rookeries where the only Hobs are beggars or servants. Or worse.

I don't want to look at Oncle when the low-Lam hops up onto his seat an clicks at the nillies, so I turn my back an pull my knees up. It must be how a nilly feels when the bonesaw cuts through its horn an steals the magic. Empty, filling up the leftover space with hate.

I scrunch my shoulders an let the jerk an rattle of the cart take me away. My ear throbs where Oncle clipped me proper. I try push all my thoughts on that spot instead of the collar burning me. I'm reeling still – no one turns family in – that's stronger than law. But Oncle did it.

Prue did it too in her own way, by not telling me the truth. The hate fills up in me so tight I feel like I'm choking. I want to yell back at the Digs, about how this ain't right, but there's now way I'm speaking now, caught between the burn of iron an anger. I swallow it all down, promising myself that no matter what comes in my life, I will never become like Oncle. I'll hate him; I'll hate this da of mine. He'll never buy my loyalty. I'll even hate Prue for being weak, but I won't ever be like them an turn on my own.

All I got now is those two coins in my jacket pocket. I slip them out an hold them tight as we clop past the heaps of rubbish, past the first of the Seven Widows, all the way through the alleys an streets, the narrow apartments of the low-Lams, an then on to where the rich live in their shiny houses, up to where the bone finger of MallenIve University jabs the darkening sky.

From far away, I hear the thin scream of the scrounger.

Two

A Game of Wasps

"SWEET GRIS! WHERE was it living? In a pig sty?" The cook's voice is a squeal that could call the dead from their graves.

I raise my head from where I've been using one of Father's precious monographs as a cushion, and shut the thin leather-bound book, keeping my place with a green silk ribband. I've sucked the end, a dreadful habit for a girl to have, Mother says, and it's dark and wrinkled.

Cook's voice carries up the stairs, followed by Trone's long drawl. The words themselves are hard to make out, even though I sit with my head cocked, still as a little grey mouse.

It's stuffy in the library, and I'm feeling rumpled and bothered and out of sorts. Mother's been in hiding all day, and Father is away at the Mata court, so I've not had lessons, just sat in here waiting for Trone to bring the boy. Father's precious little mistake.

I leave my shoes under the long day-couch and set off in white-stockinged feet, creeping down until the kitchen door is just in view. The back stairs creak, the wood old and polished black, and the sound makes my heart flutter for a moment like a trapped moth, tickling against my ribs. I'm not supposed to use the Hob-stairs. What Mother doesn't know won't hurt her. I've been doing it since I was a child.

I peer around the corner.

Cook is brandishing a cleaver as he talks. The man not only sounds like a pig, he also resembles one, red-jowled and sweaty. He flails the broad knife towards the skinny thing that I can only assume must be my half-brother. Gris. What was Father thinking? Resentment flares in my chest.

"A pig sty is about the measure of it," Trone says.

The mistake is barefoot and filthy, with muddy hair down to his shoulders, matted with sticks and thorns. A thin red burn mars his throat. Cook is right – I wrinkle my nose. The smell crawls up the stairs, a solid presence.

"Well, I don't want it in my kitchen."

"And where am I supposed to take it, Dray? To the master's bath chambers perhaps? It's not using ours, for certain."

"Gris be a stone-shitting goat. You!" Cook snaps at a serving Hob, a stick-like girl who never looks up from the floor. "Get some sodding buckets of water, and be quick about it, mind!" He folds his meaty arms across his chest and stares down at the half-Hob.

The mistake's back is to me, so I can't get a good look at his face. I want to see if he looks even the slightest like Father. I sidle down a few more steps, praying that any noise I make will be attributed to the kitchen cats and ignored.

"Strip off that filth, boy," says Cook.

"Shan't"

"You puling little fucker. Take them off or I'll take them off for you."

The mistake says nothing, and I hold my breath. I want to see Cook beat him – this cuckoo fledgling that my father has shunted into our house – but just as Cook's face is turning raw-steak red, the boy unbuttons his jacket. "I'll want 'em back," he says. He has a dark brown voice, like garden loam.

Trone laughs, a whinnying sound that Father once said was like listening to a nilly being slaughtered, only not quite as pleasant. "Whatever for? These rags are best burned."

"Cause they're mine, you daft cunt."

Trone backhands him so fast the boy ends up on the floor. He stays there, unbuttoning the last of his clothes, holding them in front of him in a tight bundle. His neck and hands are brown as cone-tree bark. The rest of his skin is sallow under the dirt. I can't believe this is supposed to be my half-brother – no wonder Mother took to her room with smelling salts and a carafe of vai.

Whatever possessed Father to bed a Hob and worse still, to bring its filthy progeny here? Perhaps he thinks House Ives can stand his bouts of mawkish sentimentality. He's a fool. Even trapped in the house I've heard the whispered comments – House Casabi they mockingly call us, when they think we cannot hear. And like the river, we swell and grow fat and then with no more than a season's change of wind, we sink again, until we are nothing more than a dusty, silty mess down which the sewage floats.

I'll have to write to Iliana, telling her everything about this turn of events. Cloistered as she is in the Chalice, it's probable she hasn't yet heard of this latest scandal of Father claiming the Hob-boy as his own. She was at least was old enough to read the letters when we found them; all I remember was Mother crying, Father shouting. Letters from a Hob, in a simple round hand; answers to words my own father had dotingly sent her.

I wonder what to write to Illy, what information I should feed to keep her off-kilter and worrying about her place in Father's hierarchy of love. It might just be kinder to let my sister carry on in blissful ignorance and enjoy her last days of term. We owe each other some measure of sororal love, and I can give up my iron control for that.

The Hob-girl comes back, lugging two buckets of icy water from the outside pump.

Cook has already produced a yellow brick of soap and a rag, and he shoves them in the mistake's face. "Get yourself clean. And do it proper mind, unless you want me showing you how it's done." He leers.

At that, one of the dish-boys looks up from the sink where he's been keeping quiet, and scowls at the new arrival.

Interesting. I stare at him, carefully marking the way his expression twists with nervous jealousy. With his face committed to memory, now all I need is to find out his name – it'll be something to bribe Cook with. Low-Lammers aren't officially allowed catamites.

"I know how to wash," says the mistake as he takes the soap.

"Don't look like it to me."

"Nor indeed does it smell that way," adds Trone.

Murmurs drift down from above, and I glance up. It sounds like my mother is awake, calling a maid to look for me. Quick as I can, I race back to the library, set myself before the writing desk and lay my head down, pretending to have fallen asleep on *The Limitations of Powdered Unicorn Horn in Substitute Workings; Excessive Exposure and the risk of Alchemic Exsanguination*. The edges of the tooled leather presses against my cheek, hard enough that it will leave a faint fading mark of a unicorn on my skin.

My mad dash back to the library-room came not a minute too soon, because I've just closed my eyes when someone knocks softly against the door. "Miss," says a girl in a hushed voice. "Your mother is asking for you."

In order to keep up the pretence, I let her call me one more time, her voice rising a little with nerves, then I flutter my eyes open and cover my mouth as I yawn a splendid, jaw-cracking yawn. I'm quite proud of that. It manages to go from fake to real, so thoroughly do I fool even myself.

The servant has found my shoes under the chair, and she slips them on to my feet, lacing the silver ribbons neatly up my gossamer stockings. The only servants that make front-of-house are low-Lammers, and this girl is one, with dirty-blond hair tucked behind her pointed ears, and a wide, earnest face that looks like she's scrubbed it raw in an attempt to clear it of the dappling of acne that scars her cheeks. I look down at her parting, at her pale scalp. She smells of polish and soap and old cotton and sweat, but never of scriven. Never of magic. She'll know the dish boy, most likely. Probably shares her favours with him like any common servant.

"There's a boy who works in the kitchen," I say.

The maid starts, pulling too tight on the lace.

"Quite tall, has a skew nose, brown hair cut in that awful bowl-fashion you people fancy." I stand, point my toes to check the tension on the laces. "What's his name?"

"Sharpshins, Miss." She curtsies quickly.

I roll the name on my tongue, tucking the knowledge away as I walk to my mother's suite. "Sharpshins."

Mother's room is decorated in shades of cloud and pearl, and everything is sleek and polished, with a minimum of fluff or ornamentation. She's lying on her day bed with a white cloth pressed to her brow. Her golden hair is tied back in what looks like an effortless twist of curls but has in fact taken a half hour of pinning and coiling to achieve. She raises one limp hand, beckoning me in. On her smallest finger, the wedding ring binding House Eline to Ives flashes. She wears no other rings. Her silk dress is the colour of fish scales, and the material glimmers with rainbow undercurrents as she moves. The colour makes her pale thin face look haggard, the lines across her forehead cut deep with shadows.

"Mother?"

"Oh, Calissa. Trone tells me that your father's youthful little indiscretion has arrived."

I nod, because I'm supposed to know nothing.

"He'll be below stairs for now, but when your father gets back. . . ." She sighs. We all know. Father is going to want to do right by him, or some nonsense. At the very least give him a decent job in the front of house. He can be so very sentimental. "The boy is no part of your future. I want you to stay away from him, do we understand each other?"

It's not really a question; Mother doesn't deal with questions and requests. She expects to be obeyed, and everyone lets her keep her illusion of authority. She knows I've been bored since Iliana left to go to the Chalice, and this is just her way of warning me off the half-Hob as some kind of playmate. Sometimes, I wonder how old she thinks I am, if in her head I'm still five instead of fifteen.

"Of course, Mother." On her dressing table is a carafe and glass cut from desert quartz, soft pink and almost opaque. Next to it, scriven powder thick as chalk dust is piled in a little mound on a silver hand-mirror. The carafe is half-full, scenting the air with juniper and sage. Over that, boiled cherry sweets, too sweet and antiseptic. She's been trying for a Vision. Maybe she's decided to look into my future, to see what glory I can possibly bring to our soiled name. If she knew, she'd make her schemes without hesitation, just as she already has with Iliana. A little stiletto of jealous sadness pricks at my belly. Iliana is on a path I wanted, set there by Mother and fate.

The maid is clearing away the dirty glasses, subtle and quick. She stoppers the crystal vai container, putting spring water out in its place, and a plate of fruit and biscuits. She takes care not to touch the powder, lest my mother accuse her of stealing even a single grain

Mother sits up, the white cloth dropping to the floor. "How do your studies go?"

Obviously, she's remembered to take more than a passing interest in me. I always thought the youngest child was supposed to get the sphynx's share of the love, but if you're me, held up against the shining light of my sister, well, it stands to reason that you'll go unnoticed. Mostly I find it suits me. There's so much one sees and hears when people pay you about as much attention as they do a Hob.

"Well, thank you." It's easy enough to bore her, so I rattle off the latest discoveries regarding magical matter and the weakened nilly-strains that have been occurring in some of the hybrids. Her eyes flutter, and she turns to run one finger through the scriven dust, and lazily rubs it along her gums. Such a waste, really. Mother has never had a Vision worth her family name.

Only another two more years in this mausoleum of a house before I go join Iliana at the Chalice. We've Father's natural flair for magic, and a name, that while it's no longer good, was once great. The University practically salivates over people like us, like Iliana with her easy command over the air. Even my own simple talents as a Reader ensure my place at the University.

Mother's already lost interest, I can see, gone into the headspace where she sees futures and prophecies. Mother's gift – even enhanced by scriven, is still weak – all she ever gets are vague allusions to things that Could Be. It's why she married down, as she constantly likes to point out to us. House Eline having risen in the ranks while Ives fell. Her eternal shame is that she was never ranked a full Saint.

When her eyes have closed, I slip from the room and go back to my spying.

Downstairs the kitchen is in turmoil – Cook is booming orders and conducting chaos with his outstretched cleaver. Around him the kitchen staff whirl, dancing the arcane steps of cut and roast and dice and broil. Standing at one of the chopping boards, scowl plastered across his sharp rat-face, is the half-Hob mistake. There's something about his forehead and narrow nose that hold a little of Father's high bearing, but otherwise, he is no more remarkable than if he was any low-Lammer servant from a long-fallen family.

Trone has found him clean clothes that don't fit. The shirtsleeves are rolled up over and over. He keeps pushing the sleeves up in irritation, as they slip down again. Even after being scrubbed down like a child he looks ill-kempt, and his disposition has certainly seen no improvement.

Sharpshins keeps staring over at him, his brow furrowed in anger. My interest sparks again. What to do about the cook and his catamite, I wonder. It will be a few hours yet before dinner, and I have time to kill.

Three

Singing for the Dead

OH FIRE. IT hurts. Licking my dream-skin, these sharp-headed monsters.

Mother sleeps, her heart broken by Dae's death; by Dae's burning. There's only me left.

I'm hungry, but the Hobs are still out, dancing over the fields and burning burning burning. I need to keep my head down. I'm the wray now, the first fledgling. I am all that is left of my twin-soul.

I'll wait for night, for the pricking of the stars. The smell of meat and skin drifts on the smoke, but the fires must go out. Sooner or later. Until then, I lie close to mother, and wrap her long skirts over me. They smell like dust. She's crumbling. Crumbling. But her face is still white and clean. I kept it wet, carrying the water in my hands, splashing her face. The blue has faded from her eyes, sunk into her skin. Something black wriggles from her ear and drops to the ground. Scuttles.

Oh mother, oh wray. Oh why did you choose to die?

Sleep.

I'm wrapped in her skirts.

Sleep.

THE STARS WAKE me far far later. Mother is real-dead now, all dust and ashes. The fire is gone, the night still.

Now it's real.

We were meant to leave, to find another nest, find Dae a feyn for a mate. Dae who's all burnt away now, ash under the stars. Mother was going to take us back to the citadel, back to family.

I don't know the way.

I need to get away from the Hobs and the stink of death, go into the city, into MallenIve. There's bound to be other vampires there, someone to tell me the way home. Sing sing me home.

Careful as can be, I cover our mother with her red skirts, shake out the dust. I take her white seed-pearls. She can't wear them, and they are pieces of her to sell. I do not know how far it is to the Citadel.

Outside the cave, the mirror-stars of the city look far, far away. So I start to walk, keeping low, staying away from Hobs and scriven-stink. I will walk till morning, sniffing the air, looking for the right smell.

When the sun comes, making me blink back red tears, I'm in a white road, lost. The caves are tall, made of stones cut square, not like Hob-wood. I can smell others.

Vampires, mother says. Not bats, never bats.

Thinking about them means they come; a woman first, all wrapped in power. The tall Feyn steps in front of me, dark hair, blue eyes, so white and old and strong, so I bow low low, like mother says to.

"Saints. This one of yours, Mikal?"

Another one, also strong. Smell of blood and power. A Wray, a real one, not a fledgling like Dae at all. He wears soft clothes, dark.

"You insult me." He steps close, sniffs at me. "Where's your nest, wray?"

"You're frightening it."

"Stop going soft on me, Riam. It's a street-rat, must be from the other rookery – one of Glassclaw's brats."

"It smells wrong."

The Wray sniffs again.

My voice, I've lost it. I scrabble through my thoughts, looking for the right words."Mother's dead," I say. "And the other wray. Hobs burned him in a field."

"Sweet blood of the Alerion. A feral. We've gone and found us a fucking feral." The Wray looks up at the sky, laughs a thick bitter sound, like old blood.

The Feyn comes close close. "Heads or tails?"

He laughs again. "Neither. You can have it. I've no time for training up ferals. Damn thing probably doesn't even know what cutlery is. Besides – your line of business, you could always use a few more wrays. He's old enough to work, and young enough to keep some Lammer pervert happy."

"For a year, if that. Not that I like it when they're too young, I hate the look in their eyes the next day." The Feyn sighs. "Fine, then." She holds out one hand, white, clean. "Up you get, wray. We've a nest, a nice one, for you to come to. Come along, sweet. You'll be safe with Us."

Mother told me you always listen to Feyn, always obey. I stare, what does a Feyn want with me?

"I don't have the whole morning. Up."

I stand and give Her mother's seed-stones.

"This was your mother's?"

Nod. This means yes. I remember.

She clutches the white stones on their thread and looks up at the Wray. "Those fucking Hobs. We hate them." She turns back to me. "This way, sweet." Her sadness swims in the river of her voice, rising and sinking.

I walk after Her into one of the square stone caves. Glass squares let in light, steps go high, high, and we go up the steps, all the way to the top.

"What's your name, wray?"

"Sel."

"It's a good old name. Your mother was from Urlin, then? Ansel's a common name there."

Not a nod, not a head shake. "Don't know. She came from the citadel." I want to ask her if she can show me the way but all that comes out are the flapping of my hands and the twisting of my tongue.

"No one calls it that anymore, sweet Sel. Don't use that word here, understand?" She grabs my hands and stills them. These are both orders.

Nod. I look at my hands and wait for them to burn in hers. They don't.

"You will sleep here." She shows me a bed, soft-soft. It has no stone floor. No bones and ashes. "We'll start your training tomorrow."

Oh safe, I think, finally. Somewhere Hobs can't get me.

I curl up tight and try to remember all the pieces in my head, put them in some kind of order. Everything slips away, like trying to catch water.

I stare at my hands. Why aren't they burnt, and why is Dae ash, and I am not? My head is full of clouds and glass.

Why did Mother do this to me?

Four

The Grinningtommy

WELL, NO LIES, it's been about as crap a day as I can remember, but least-wise it's over. That low-Lam bastard Trone has shown me a room an says I'll be sharing with some other poor sod. There's two beds pushed into a hole even Oncle wouldn't call a cupboard. It stinks of socks an spunk. The other lad's already in here, I can hear him breathing, snoring so loud it's going to be a wonder if I ever get to sleep myself.

At least they've given me my tat back, with the two bit still safe in the little pocket of the jacket. Guess they didn't think a Hob would have anything worth stealing.

That fat cook in the kitchen made me work just about 'til my fingers dropped off. Bastard had me scrubbing plates until the moon was ready to set.

I kick off my shoes an crawl under covers that smell of must an that same yellow soap they scrubbed me down with. The other lad's snores seem to get louder an louder, practically shaking the dust from the roof timbers.

Don't like to say it, but I miss the scrounger's noise. My eyes get used to the dark, an I count the low beams of the ceiling, the dove-tail joints held together with magic an careful carpentry. No thatch. No scritching mice.

If I'm to be right honest with myself – I even miss Oncle talking scrivver-nonsense in his sleep. I knew my place in the Digs. Here – here, well I'm about as out of place as the scrounger would be in a uni herd, for all they've dressed me up in old clothes that smell like Lam, like that gritty yellow soap, an made me wash in cold water so I'll probably die now of the Lung the way Prue did.

How Marlon'd laugh if he found out. Jek the Digsman dead of cold water. An who's running the Digs pack now, is what I'd like to know. If it's that little Hob-punk Kray, then the Digsmen might as well walk into Wend right now, hands up, an turn out their pockets, start working the Lam-filth heaps like orphans.

I punch the pillow they've left me, an turn so that I face the wall with its paint peeling in long strips. Got to try get some sleep through all that snoring going on. I'll have a few choice things to say to my da, for sure, when I see that Lammer bastard.

"Get up, ya half-Hob," says a man the next morning, his voice sour as old milk. Least-wise, I think it's morning, although it's black as a scriv-mine in this little pokey room. No windows nor birds to tell me the time.

That pansy low-Lam I'm sharing the room with rips the rough wool cover from me. "Stop laying about. Trone wants you downstairs first thing."

"I'll get there early-like," I says. "Don't need you going off like a bantam."

He's watching me, the poncey git – Sharpshins, someone called him yesterday. I remember him from the kitchens – his face is all angles and a long nose like a pickaxe, bent skew from a good bashing.

"What's that low-Lam want me for?"

"How should I know? Do I look like a blasted Saint to you?"

No, but you look like a right little turd. So I get up, tie the laces on the shoes they gave me to wear, an tramp downstairs, loud as I can. If I gotta be up before the birds, then the rest of the house can suffer with me.

Turns out Trone's waiting for me in a little room off the kitchen. His study, he calls it. There's an old desk in the middle, near as big as the room itself, an two chairs; both as has seen better days. The desktop is scratched an scoured, the chair backs snapped, but they look like good pieces. If I saw them on the heap I'd take them straight to Oncle to patch. They're made of red wood, well turned, an the fabric – what's left of it – is all fancy patterns and details that let me know it's high value. No one's bothered to fix these, an the stuffing seeps through the worn cloth. Figures, that a Lam has no idea on how to take care of nothing.

Trone's sitting behind the desk, hands clenched together on the scarred wood. The light from the hissing gas lamps makes him look all yellow an sour as a little lemon from Pelimburg. Sometimes the barge-boys would toss us the fruit as we ran along the Casabi, splashing through the mud an ducking twixt the reeds. They always threw us the ones gone to mush, but Prue would use them in mint-tea anyway.

"Can you read?" the low-Lam asks.

"And a jolly good morning to you," I says. I won't think about Prue again today, I promise myself.

He's got a cold look, this one, just stares at me. "No? Can you make your mark?"

"I can write my name, an my family name."

There's a scrap of yellow paper next to his hands, an he pushes this over to me, along with a smooth painted pen-grip with a split-sharp nib. A pot of ink is already waiting. "Show me."

So I pull up that other rotten chair an take a seat. It's good paper this, heavy an thick. I dip the nib, watch the ink gather an drop. Ain't never used one before, just a stick in the dirt as how Prue taught me. Already my promise is broken an because of that an also just because the bugger's watching me an waiting for me to fail, I fuck the paper up good an proper, ink everywhere.

"Less ink, perhaps," he says, an his voice is like an old bone.

Still, I do use less ink, an I press careful-like on the paper an make the shapes for my name, an then Prue's. Then I put my family name, Grinningtommy, which is as old a Hob-name as you can get, although we're not like Lams with their love of names an who's who. Finished, I push the paper back to him.

He picks it up with his long fingers, his face all twisted. "What's this?" Trone jabs at the paper.

"It's me mam's family name."

"She's dead," he says. "Your family name is Ives. You will write it Ives Jek, like this." The low-Lam prints the letters neat under my scrawl.

Ives. An you could've knocked me over with a goose feather at that, because that's old blood, old House power. Even in the Digs we've heard that name. They're strong magic weavers, an one of the founding lines. Maybe not as strong as Mallen-as-was, or Pelim or even Mata, but it was an Ives that held the lamp high as Mallen Gris struck the ground with his walk-stick, an showed the Lams where to find their precious scriv.

No wonder my da paid Prue off with a two bit. There must have been some right scandal in the Lam-Houses when she turned up fat as a melon with a little halfbreed in her belly. Everyone knows Lammers with their magic an their scriv thinks they're better than any of us – thinks us Hobs are nowt but dogs at their heels.

"Is this all you know?"

"Well," I says. "I know how to kill a Lam so that there's not a mark on his body."

"Hob-boasts." He waves one hand. "Don't bother with them here. No one cares." Then he fixes me with those two ice blue eyes. "Your work starts at six every morning, in the kitchens. Cook will show you what to do. Before that you're to come here at five, so we can teach you to read and write before the master – your father –" An he grins this sphinx grin, all teeth an no laughter. "– gets back."

"So where's he at now?"

"In the Mata court. He's the head War-singer for the royal family."

Means he's strong, an I'm impressed despite myself. Defensive magic is complicated shite, even for the best of Lammers.

"He's due back at the end of Ames, which gives us less than three weeks to have you a step above illiteracy." He sighs, an pulls open a drawer, before thumping three thin old books on the desk.

He hands me a fresh sheet of paper an the first of the books. I flick through it – it's a child's workbook, full of letters. Each page has got one letter printed neat an straight, an then the letter copied over an over, in a wobbly hand. The ink is bright.

"Copy each of the letters on to your paper. The first is *ah*, draw the round shape first, then the little snip below..." An so I start lessons under Trone, with his sheep-bleat voice, with a full hour of this ahead of me 'fore my day has even started proper.

Five

Singing for the Dead

"YOU CAN CALL me Riam," the Feyn says in her snow voice.

Her building is cold and white. Too much light, too many wrays. I've never seen so many wrays before.

"Hob got your tongue?"

I check. "No, Riam."

"Good." She nods. "You need to lose that appalling accent. Didn't your mother teach you to speak properly?"

I shake head my head, then remember to talk, to hunt down words. "She didn't like talking."

"Well, we've no time here for fancies like that. Everyone here has to work, to earn a living, and I can't have you sounding like you're brain-damaged."

I stare. There are no words inside me. Nothing to say.

She sits down, leans close. Power is all around her, sweet-sweet like blood and white sand. It's licking my skin; and I hold my fingers out to touch power, to touch the magic.

"You know what Splinterfist does? My people?" Nervousness pulses around her.

"No, Riam."

"We earn our keep on our backs." She sits back, watches me, laughs like glass. "You're confused. The Splinterfist are whores. A good whore can buy his freedom in under twenty years. And if my boys train you, sweet wray, you will be good."

It's not a word I know. I hunt for it, but it has left no tracks. Freedom – this I know. I concentrate on the sound of it. "Freedom?"

"The right to walk MallenIve's streets without a pass, the right to claim citizenship. *Bats,*" she spits it out like a rotten tooth, "pay House Mata for this right. You understand this?"

Nod.

"Good." She stands, sweeps up power with her skirts. Like all feyn, she is spilling over with power. Mother taught me this, that the feyn are power and right, and the wrays like me and Dae, we must always do as they say. "We'll start off working with Mal. He's good, and he's kind. You're to do everything he tells you, little wray. No complaints."

She beckons. I follow her out from the white room, into a passage. Four doors down, and she knocks one two three.

The door cracks open, just a split to see a face, an older wray than me. He's not quite in his twenties, but his eyes are hundreds of years. "Riam." He grins "And what can I do for my illustrious lady?"

"Here." Her hands on my shoulder, pushing me forward. "I need you to work with him, show him the ropes."

"Oh, I heard about this – feral, huh. Is it for me?" He arches a brow, laughs.

"Sweet Mal." She drops one hand to his head, fingers curl in his hair. Like mother did with me, with Dae. Once. "Be good to him. Looks like he has all the brains of a nilly-foal."

"I'm to teach him?"

"Kindly."

The smile is gone from Mal's face. "Poor bloody bastard. Does he have any idea?"

"I'm not certain. See if you can at the very least encourage him to speak in complete sentences."

"Come on in then, little wray," he says. "What's your name?"

I step into the room, clean like the other one, white, neat. A bed raised from the floor. Windows. Hundreds of them, small as eyes. "Sel," I say, and the window eyes blink with sun and shadow.

The door shuts. Riam is gone.

"You want a bite to eat, Sel? We've got milk and nilly-blood, and then we can get started."

Nod. Then I remember I'm supposed to use words. "Eat, yes.

Then start."

"Eager, are we? Well it's one way to get out of here, I guess. Hope you have a taste for fucking Lams. Or you know how to snare one like a little dumb rabbit." He laughs.

The food is a glass of milk, yellow. It is a strange taste, thick and bland. I put the empty glass down carefully. It is so easy to shatter, so cold.

"I'm Mal – Mallen, like in the old stories, you know? A Blackcoat."

Mother didn't like the stories, never told me and Dae much.

He stops talking, sighs. Watches his hands as he undoes my shirt. As he shivers. "You've done this before?"

I shake my head, find my voice. "No." Mother always told me and Dae that when we are frightened, we must count our deep slow breaths, until we are quiet inside and the fear is gone.

"Fuck." He drops his hands, raises them again.

Why is he shaking?

"Don't worry, little wray. It won't be so bad, you'll see," he whispers. Strokes my skin. He has hard fingers for such a soft touch. I close my eyes, lie back and let it be not so bad. I can count my breaths, time them to Mal's. Perhaps he will lose his fear too.

Six

A Game of Wasps

TWELVE DAYS PASS in a flurry of boredom before I catch another glimpse of my half-brother. In the meantime, I've managed to liberate a pouchful of scriven from my mother's little ivory dream-box, the one with her old House crest – a leaf blown before the storm – carved into the lid. It even has the Eline motto inscribed beneath the image: Only We Know Where The Leaf Will Fall. Such hubris – as if they were the only House with Saints.

Mother beat a maid for the theft until the girl could hardly walk, then turned her out into the street. Of course she'd never suspect me.

I watched the girl leave. It's all I could do. I held the stolen scriv tight and pretended that it didn't matter. Then she turned the corner and was gone.

In my room, I open the little suede pouch and dip my finger into the dust. It's smooth, gliding over my skin like tiny grains; seeds of dream, opener of doors. I rub my finger across my gums, and scriven – the sweetest, purest uncut high – settles into me, under my skin. I take a deep, shuddering breath, fill my lungs with wonder.

I'm not like Iliana or Father, who can use scriven to shape the air – War-singers – or a Saint like Mother, who can catch flashes of the future. My talent lies in discovery, in spying, not to put too fine a point on it. I can Read people; tell if they're lying, see their moods.

Normally, I'll only pick up the bare edges of auras if the mood is intense. Passion or terror work well. However, with my talents scriven-buffered I can read people as easily as a child's primer.

And today, with the high running through me, I'm going to hunt down this older half-brother of mine, this sudden sibling, and Read him. Once I know him, I'll know how to use him. Simple.

I hide the rest of the scriven away in a little knothole on one leg of my writing desk and step out into my mother's realm. The passages are silent. The maids are trained to walk softly, to speak only when absolutely necessary, and then only in whispers. My Sainted mother, given to bad heads and attacks of nervous dementia, demands it.

Quick and quiet, I slip down the empty passages, my feet barely making the slightest thumps in the plush carpets with their swirling patterns of leaves in autumn gold and copper, to the back stairs with its dark wood rail polished black by the hands of hundreds of grimy servants.

Trone has the mistake working in the kitchens. He takes his tea outside, near the laundry lines. I've seen him from my bedroom windows, sitting on an upturned bucket, eating his bread and meat, drinking the cupful of weak cider that the staff get with their meal. He eats quickly, like a street-dog with a stolen bone.

The back door is open, and the sun shines through a veil of dull grey clouds. The washing is white and luminous in the half-light, and a chill breeze plucks at the sheets, making them flap like the silk irthe-tents in a sandstorm.

It's quiet out here. Only the birds trilling at each other in the leafless roadside trees, Father's sleek, narrow hounds barking from the kennels, and the distant sounds of MallenIve. Here on Ive's Mound we are far enough from the centre for it to be peaceful, almost provincial.

After I've checked that there's no one out, I walk between the lines of pegged sheets, my fingers brushing the wet fabric as it billows around me. I twirl through the white maze, dancing between the lines, humming to myself. The scriven is here, hard. I may have taken more than I should, when I can see the calm white auras of sheets and clean laundry. The cloth glows, content.

The kitchen door grates on its old hinges, and in my sheets and shadows, I pause.

Two voices, then silence as the other leaves. The scrape of a bucket, the rattle of wooden platters. I press through the sheets and come back out into the open. The sun has split through the clouds. Cold gold light leaves the wet cobbles black and treacherous as oiled glass.

The boy is sitting by the kitchen door.

My good feelings fade a little.

"Oi," he says. "And who are you?" His hand is halfway to his mouth, last night's leftover meat between two slices of heavy black bread. Around him the colours flicker, a bronze sort of bone-tired slump, flashes of steel – wariness. The mistake – my half-brother – is out of place here, and it shows.

"I'm talking to you," he says.

"Are you? I heard nothing."

"Oh, a smart-arse." He shoves the bread in his mouth, tearing off a huge bite. The curious sun-brown of his skin glows like heartwood.

"Where are you from?" I ask, to see what answer he will give me.

Instead of swallowing and answering, he chews with a bovine steadiness, watching me. He's amused now, little eddies of sunshine yellow swirling at the edges. He washes down the bite with a slug of cider. "You should know," he says. "I've placed you – in that pretty dress. I'm guessing you're supposed to be my sister sweet, or one of them anyway."

"I'm no sister of yours," I snap. "You're bred in the gutter, and I in the turret."

"Well, guess our da had no problems wallowing in the gutter then," he says as he stands, brushes crumbs from his shirt. "Why don't you fly back up to your tower then, if you think you're so wonderful. Fucking Lam," he mutters, "your shit stinks just like anyone else's."

"Is Trone going to start teaching you big words soon?" I say, sweet as I can.

Instead of taking the bait, he just stares at me. "Which one are you? Calissa or Iliana?"

He's startled it out of me. "Calissa."

"Calissa, ey? Well let me tell you summat chummy-like, Ives Calissa. You can't add numbers no better than me, you dot all your i's with little hearts, an you were once in love with one of the Mata – a boy called Trey. Enough that you wrote his name an yours all over

your learning books." He mock swoons. "Now, I know all about
you, darling, an you still know shite about me." He gathers his plate
and cup and swaggers back to the kitchen door.

"I know all about you too," I yell after him. "You – you –
illiterate Hob!"

His aura laughs orange and yellow and red, like he's caught on
fire.

The door swings shut. I stand still long enough that the black-
headed sparrows come down from the dry, grey-skinned boughs to
peck at the fallen crumbs. They shine of blue skies, silver wind
freedom. A headache is starting up behind my eyes, and I squeeze
them shut, trying to will it away.

On my way up to my room I see Sharpshins, and I call the
gangly thing over. He looks frightened, keeps twisting his hands as
he follows me up to my chamber.

Of course he's scared – what kitchen-filth wouldn't be? He's not
allowed here, and he dogs me with furtive steps.

"Close the door," I say, and he shuts it quietly then watches me
from under his shaggy fringe, the way a dragon-dog will when it's
not sure if it's been called for a beating or a twist of dried meat.

"How well do you know Dray?" I say.

"I work for him, miss."

He doesn't even realise how he shuffles back, ducks his head
lower. Fear. I don't need this high to pick it up, although it snakes
about him, a sick green churning the air.

"I'm not fooled," I say, as dry as the winter reeds outside by the
banks of the Casabi, the way they slice at each other, rattling their
blades. I know how to use my voice to flay, to stroke. I learnt it all
from watching my dear mother.

"Please, miss." Now the fear is in his voice. I haven't even had to
make any accusations, and this idiot is mine.

"Oh," I say, and wave my one hand before my face. "It's no great
thing to me who you choose to whore yourself to."

He's white now, blanched. He could lose his job. Dray will lose
his. Only High Lammers are allowed catamites. It's a right of birth.

"I'll turn my face." I smile at him. "That's kind of me, isn't it?"

He's nodding, furiously. It almost looks as if his head could
come off his shoulders. The whiteness hasn't faded from his face.
Clever boy, clever enough to know that all kindness must have its
price.

"And for my little favour to you, it's only fair you extend the same to me?"

"What miss, t-turn my face?"

Perhaps not so clever then. I'm losing patience. "No." I sit at my writing desk and watch him, hardly blinking as I do. It's unnerving, I know. I've practised it in the mirror, that cat's look of disdain. "You know the new boy, the Hob?"

"Jek," he says, eagerly reaching for the straw I've thrown him. "Yeah, yeah, I do. We share a room."

Better and better. A Saint couldn't have predicted such a smooth path. I smirk. "I do not like him."

Understanding dawns on Sharpshins's thin face, pocked with the scars of neglect and poverty.

"Perhaps you could make his life a little more interesting."

And the lout understands. I speak his language, sly and underhanded. I frown, because to think that Sharpshins and I are even a little alike. . . . The jealousy, the greed, the oily swirl of emotion that taints the air around him – I know these are echoed around me, and the thought makes me a little ill.

"You may go."

He ducks his head and leaves, his footsteps rushing away from my room. I drop my head into my hands and massage my temples. The last of the scriven is leaving my body, replaced by the headache. I turn and look at myself in the mirror of my dressing table. The faint eddies of guilt and jealousy are swirling away, fading into the cold air. Was I always like this? It used to be that I was my father's child, dandled on his knee. I was bright like him, a little sun.

And now?

Now he's tired and full of storms, bringing Jek into my world to take my place.

I press my hand between my breasts to where two fine keys are hidden on a silver chain. They are the keys to the heart of my father. One to his study, and one to a fine, panelled box that he keeps there.

It is the only way I know to understand him.

I release the keys and pull a fresh sheet of writing paper towards me. With the headache still beating at my temples, I write a letter of recommendation before sealing it with a wax-stamp stolen from my mother's table. When I am done, I pull a bell and wait for a servant to come to me.

"The girl who was fired, for theft," I snap at the Hob-girl who arrives, puffing and out of breath a bare moment later. She has the look of someone who has drawn the shortest bone pin. "You know where she lives now?"

The Hob nods, wary.

"Take this to her." I hold out the letter, and as soon as the girl has taken it, I turn away and stare at my reflection again. It annoys me that there is no way to make my father proud of me, that even the charity I show must be underhanded.

Seven

The Grinningtommy

SO THAT'S MY sister, the ikey bitch. She's darker than she should be, like a shadow. Slips about all furtive-like, full of secrets. I known people like that down the Low-walk. Some are quiet 'cause they're scared of life, an some because they're stealing secrets an learning everything they can about everyone. I don't think my sister's one of them as scared of living – just biding her time.

Back in the kitchen, Sharpshins is all good mood, grins an elbow-jabbing whenever a pretty maid comes in with dishes or baskets of winter kale an turnips. Bastard won't stop rattling his chops about this an that, while I keep smacking my head on the strings of onions knotted from the low beams. It's starting to piss me right off.

"Your da will be back here soon enough," Sharp says, all sly-like.

I just chop faster, turning my mound of carrots into slivers that the rich can shove in their tight little mouths. Trone says there's some crisis, so that's why my da's been holed up at the Mata palace. He won't say what it is, but then, may be that he doesn't know hisself, an he's just trying to look like he's in the loop when the rest of us ain't.

"Maybe he'll tell you some news," Sharp says. "There's rumours flying this way an that, an none of us knows what's what."

"I don't know nothing about rumours," I says.

"Word from the wherrymen is that there's been Meke ships out in the water round Pelimburg."

I shrug.

"Not that it matters none, not while we got the War-singers an all their bluster." Sharp jabs me with his elbow. "Just blow the bugs away, like that." He puffs out.

War-singers – an just how will War-singers save us from any Gris-damned Meke ship if they don't have no scriv, eh? But I don't say it, because maybe it's not as bad as all that.

I'm hoping that it was just Oncle's work – Deep Black, the third mine out past the Wend – that was having troubles. He muttered about it some, with his face all creased at the thought. More rock, less scriv. Had to delve deeper, work longer just to make his quota. Add in them other rumours about the Mekekana coming up cross the seas to Pelimburg, an you got yourself a nice fuck-up just waiting to happen.

It's why Oncle never noticed how bad Prue was getting – too jiggered by sun-down to do more than drink his bitter an sit quiet. I knew, but she told me not to say nothing, an like an idiot, I listened to her. I always listened to Prue, even when she was puddled as a newborn nilly. Wish I hadn't, wish I hadn't wanted to make her happy, pleased, so that one day she'd turn around an call me her boy, or let me call her mam.

Prue could read. She used to get letters when I was just a Hobling, an she'd make the messenger stand fast an wait while she read them through, then penned her replies on the backs. She would crack the red wax, an give me the shiny beads to play with, an I would pretend that it were jewels an riches an I was top Hob in the Low-Walk. Once, I remember, when I was no higher than an yearling irthe sapling, I asked her to teach me to write proper-like.

She showed me my name in the dust, made me write it over an over, till I got all the sizes right, an all the shapes. Then she said. "An that's it, Jek. There's no sense learning more than that." When I asked her why, she turned away an said it weren't worth the trouble it got you.

The next time she got a letter, she sent the messenger back without cracking the seal. Made me right angered, 'cause I wanted the wax. That messenger came three times more, an each time Prue sent him on his way an never once took the letters he brought her. Then he stopped coming.

Not long after that, I got took in as Marlon's second, an then I learnt all the stuff that was worth the trouble.

Now here I am, an it's Prue in the dust, an I have to learn more than my name. Press ink onto white paper, like I was a Lammer myself.

"Hey, Jek." Sharpshins snaps his fingers at my face. "Wash this lot up for me, will ye?" He jerks his head over to a pile of sloppy dishes that I can swear I washed not ten minutes back. Bastard. He's nodding over to where Dray is eyeing him across the tables, eyes glinting in his wide face. "I got myself a little extra activity, you understand."

I nod an pull the first of the dishes across to dip in the heated water. Steam hisses in copper pipes somewhere, an wood pops as a scrawn Hobling feeds logs near as big as hisself into the furnace.

"Cheers, mate. I'll owe you one. Show you some of the town when we get off?"

I'd forgot. It's the first proper half-day I'll be having since I got here. Last one I missed 'cause they figured I'd do a runner straight back to the Digs. I ain't that daft. I've seen people burn – there's no fun in dying. An shite as my life can get, I'll still prefer what I got here to if I got caught running away.

"THE MASTER WILL be back next week," says Trone while we queue by that little office of his, waiting. I'm last in line, as is natural, being the new Hob in the kitchens an all. "So if you've any high spirits, best get them out of your system now."

"These are your fortnightly wages," he says when I'm finally alone in his cramped office. "I'd suggest you use them to buy yourself a decent set of clothes." He drops a small envelope on the desk. It lands with a solid thunk, brass bits clanking. "You've the rest of the afternoon off, although you're to return in time to prep the kitchen."

Suits me. Gives me near six hours of time that's all my own. An enough money to buy a scriv-bitter.

There's comfort in the bottom of a glass, as Oncle says. Oncle. I grit my teeth. He'll have hung up the pig-meat to cure, smoked rashers of bacon. I'm glad that for once I weren't nowhere near him when he clucked for the pig to follow him out, bribing it with a turnip or something.

I'm still pissed at him, but it's fading a bit. He did what he had to in turning me over to my da, just like every year he has to kill a damn pig. Life on the Digs. There's no point holding it all against him.

"You're heading out, Jek?" Old Sharpshins is waiting outside the door, leaning 'gainst the wall. He stands up straight as I leave Trone's office.

"Might do."

"You can join us, if you want to. I'm meeting a few lads down the Sphynx's Laugh."

Well, I've been here lessen three weeks, with not a chance to get out, an for all he's a low-Lam, Sharpshins has turned out to be friendly enough. Also, I know nowt about greater MallenIve, outside of the Digs an Wend of the Hob-quarter. "Sure," says I. "Long as there's a shiny girl or two down the Sphynx." Now I'm hoping I don't sound lonely as I feel, so I grin, all rakish-like.

"Oh, always," he says, laughing. "You'll see."

I follow him down the narrow passage out into the afternoon sun in the little cobbled yard where the ladies hang the washing. There's linens there now, all sun-bleached an clean, like pinned-up wings. There's no sign of my sister-half this time, thank Gris. Girl's too full of herself for my liking.

We walk between the wet flapping sheets, out a little back door that leads into the maze of the city.

The Sphynx is out near the Chalice, an that bone tower looms overhead, bells ringing midday, joining the glass tongues of the Widows. Pigeons swoop about, beshitting the streets an the roofs. It's a longish trot, but we walk right fast, so fast that I hardly have time enough to mark the way.

The Ives's house is in a clean area, as expected. All the walls of the houses are stone washed pale, the soot from the factories not reaching this high up the hill. We trip down Ives's Mound an cut through a rougher part of town. A few Hobs, dirty as if they just fell off the heaps, are running through the shadows, watching us. Fox-sharp faces pinched all thin with hunger.

"Never mind them," says Sharpshins. "They won't try anything in broad light."

"So you says. I known buggers like this my whole life. They'll soon as steal your clothes as spit on you."

"We won't be here long, we're taking a short cut." He turns down a cobble alley, where the houses are narrower an close together. "They're old – used to be some Low Houses what lived here, but they're all gone now. All of them houses are chopped up inside – apartment buildings."

The houses are quiet, sleeping. Weeds grow up through the cracks in the stone pavings, but there's no rubbish in the gutters like you expect. It's clean an strange. There's writing on the walls, but none of it that I can read.

"What's this then?"

"Bat's rookery"

"What?" I stop. "You're shitting me? Bats – here?" So Marlon was right about the bats being allowed in MallenIve proper. Who'd have believed it.

The windows are all blank an shiny, an I can't see nothing inside, but I think of all them bats lying in their rooms, so fast asleep they might as well be corpses.

"Come on, they're most of them sleeping now anyway – or hard at work –" An here he winks, all sly-like, though I'm missing something. "Any how, this is the quickest way."

"I din't know bats was really allowed in MallenIve." So much for Marlon telling me a lie. I wonder what other truths he told me that I should have caught.

Sharpshins laughs low. "Well, as long as they stay in their rookery. If they want to travel outside, they need passes."

"An kills?"

"They've meat merchants – old nillies and pig's blood mostly. If any of them kill Lammers then we burn them. So far, not one of them's been stupid enough to try." He grins. "We're not all soft over them like in Pelimburg, letting the bats do what they please an set up bleeding Houses, like they was as good as Hobs an Lams."

It seems safe enough, although I don't want to let on to Sharpshins that the thought of all them bats packed around us makes my bones feel watery. I shiver an walk faster, wanting out of the bat ghetto. We pass under an archway made of wood an junk nailed together, an I see words I can read, scrawled across the top of the arch like a sign post. Splinterfist, it says in Lammic, the words broken-glass spiky.

Up ahead, I can make out the bone tower of the Chalice, and behind that, the palace all grey an glittery. A huge, blue-ish shape like a blown-up pig's bladder with a ridged fin on its back moves slow across the sky. Summat that looks like hundreds of dark ribbons hangs from its belly.

"What's that?"

Sharpshins cocks his head an squints. "The Mata."

"Not the bloody palace, chum. That."

"Oh, that's a blaas."

"A what?"

"A by-the-wind. Means one of the Mata is out. Only they can use 'em."

I'm more confused than ever, but I ain't telling Sharpshins that an making myself look daft as a Hob at a Lammer's wedding. I've never seen one before, not all the way out in the Digs. May be that I did once but thought it no more than a faraway kite.

The by-the-wind flashes silvery in the sun, an drifts slow as a cloud. The ribbons below it pulse an shift, the colour changing from deepest red to indigo. There's a small dark shape stuck to its belly, like it's feeding on summat. Gris-damned thing gives me the creeps – must be some other bastard creature what got turned in the Well's magic. Then the by-the-wind drifts behind a tower, an it's gone.

We leave the bats' rookery behind, an the lanes get narrower an narrower. There's hawkers on the pavements, so we walk in the roads, the smell of grilled meat an soup an smoke follows us.

We pass a tattoo parlour with a painted flame border around a grey window, an next to that is a dirty three-storey public house, squashed an black. The sign lifts an blows on its rope. There's a gold Sphynx with blood on its jaws grinning on the sign. Rebel pub, or old enough that it was around when the Mata wiped out House Mallen for opening the Well. Which, like the song goes, is an old, old tale.

Inside is about as far from The Scrivver's Hole as you can get. The wood is polished-cherry dark. They're using gas lamps instead of fatcandles, an it mixes with the smell of beer an pipe smoke.

"Flash place," I say, looking at the rows of pumps, bitters with names I've never even heard. There's no Rusty Black, so I order same as Sharpshins – a Wobbly Cob.

It's darker an thicker than what I'm used to, an heavy on scriv. It also costs a sight more than I wanted to spend, an I sip it slow to make it last the afternoon. Just one taste, an already I can feel the scriv rushing to my head an making my arms an legs all heavy.

"Ay, Sharps! This way, mate." A group of lads has staked out a lean-table, an they're waving us over. Place is packed, so we hustle through the crowd to put our pints down. Sharpshins rolls a fag quick as a blink, an one for me too. We lean our elbows on the little round table an blow smoke rings.

"This the new lad, then?" You can see they don't think much of me, but I'm tall enough to pass, so I just nod an keep myself staring at them until they back down.

"Jek," says Sharpshins. "He's all right."

They nod at that, an I relax, let my guard down a little an look around the bar to see if there's any pretty things worth eyeballing.

The Sphynx pulls a bit of a mixed crowd. Servants an Chalice kids slumming it before they go off to be good House Lams. Mostly though, everyone's young an loud.

A crowd of girls bursts in through the door, chattering an laughing like the flocks of ibises that come down over the river to hunt for greyshrimp – ticklers – in the mud. They're dressed in black skirts an red petticoats an carrying black parasols, all dressed up like windle-workers but their hands are clean an they don't stink of spit an shit. University girls trying to play at poverty. I snort, turn my attention back to my bitter.

"Looks like you're in luck," says Sharpshins.

"How d'you mean?"

"Chalice girls looking for a bit of rough," he says an nods at the girls. I give them another once over. They got their backs to us, crowded at the bar all clamouring for drinks.

Well true enough, there's no other reason for their type to be down here, away from their wine-bars an poetry-rooms an theatre-halls or whatever it is that Lammers do for fun.

"So go have a bit of a chat." Sharps grins. "There's one on the right looks a good catch."

Good call. I take a deep swallow of the Wobbly, an bow to the table. "I'll see you later. Hopefully much later," I says, an wink.

Sharps laughs, raises his pint. "Luck."

His mates chime in, glass chinking. I push through the crowd of lollygaggers, to squeeze myself twixt a fat greaser an the closest girl.

She's dyed her hair black, coiled it up under a hat an veil, so I get a good look at her neck. It's a neck made for kissing an biting, bleached clean as Lam-sheets.

She's just taken her pint from the keep, an she turns, knocking my elbow so that my drink goes flying, spraying dark brown bitter and cream foam all over the counter.

"Oh Saints. What were you drinking?" She's not smiling, but she's painted her lips very red, an against her Chalice-room skin it makes her look like a bat.

I take a step back.

"Wobbly Cob," I says, when I find my voice. She raps out an order to the keep, who pulls me another – full – pint. Well, I sure ain't complaining.

"It's too crowded in here," she says. "Place is like Marshall Square on month market."

"I've a lean-table," I says. "Bit less people, an least-wise a place to put your beer. Without knocking it over."

She smiles then, an her teeth are straight an neat. Good. Was worrying for a minute that she might have filed them sharp. There's some strange fashions in the heart of MallenIve. "A lean-table, you say? Well lead us on then."

I look back, to see if the lads won't mind, but they're gone, an Sharpshins with them. No one's noticed the empty table yet, so I make a quick grab for it, an she follows me, bustling past everyone in her crins an corsets.

The lean-table's in a dark corner of the pub, so I squash up next to her chummy-like. Now that she's smiling, I can see that she's shiny enough under the white powder an heavy paint. Her eyes are blue, but they're bright an clear, not the indigo colour of a bat's. She's got smudged ink on her right fingers. A scholar then, for sure. A Lam all dressed up to shock.

Now that I got her alone, I don't right know what to say. If she was one of the Wend girls, I could just make a few lewd comments about her, laughing, an she'd get the drift quick enough, but this is a Lam, even if she's tarted down. Lucky for me, she's forward enough.

"So," she says. "You've dragged me off to this intimate little nook. At what point are you planning to tell me your name?"

"It's Jek," an I take a chance, if the girl's slumming. "Jek Grinningtommy."

"Ia." She looks at me careful, up an down. "You're tall for a Hob."

"An you're a mite clean for a windle-worker, Chalice girl," I says. She sips from her drink, smiles thin. "It's obvious?"

"Well, you ain't fooling no one as ever seen the inside of a factory."

"Shit." She's drunk half her bitter in the time I've just had a few sips, but she's not getting all scriv-slow or nothing. Magic-worker for sure then.

"An you drink too fast. More money as sense, as we say in the Digs."

"Oh Digs Hob, are you?" She leans forward, her eyes glinting in the yellow gaslight. "What's it like there?"

An I could show her just what a Digs Hob can do. I grin, drink faster.

Three hours later, we're in the alley round behind the tattoo parlour, her skirts hiked up an her back to the wall. She may be a Lam, but she sweats just like anyone else, an I can smell it on her, pouring scriv from her skin sweet as oranges. Magic plucks at the air, an I wonder how high she is – high enough to go bed a Hob in a back alley.

"Oh Gris, yes," she hisses against me, an I haven't been laid since – well, in a while – an I try think about anything but the smell an taste of her.

Burning, nillyshit, the bat on fire.

Anything else.

She doesn't make much noise, grits her teeth instead, an buries her face against my shoulder.

Around us, now that I'm able to notice stuff like this again, around us, dirt falls, raining rubbish back down to the slime-slick cobbles. High as a paper Hob-kite, then, if she's doing accidental magic.

"I'll see you again?" She straightens her layers of petticoats an pulls her skirt neat-like over it.

"Maybe, got another half day in two weeks." I lean against the wall, trying for casual, but really, my legs feel like they're made of liver.

"I've got to get back now, anyway," she says, as she glances up at the bone tower. "Next fortnight it is then, Jek Grinningtommy."

Eight

A Game of Wasps

MY HAND IS poised over the fine paper. Ink dripped once, spoiled it, and still I haven't written a thing.

What do I say to Iliana? Of course, it might be better to tell her nothing and to keep the knowledge of our new sibling to myself. After all, in a house of Saints, secrets hold power. There in her ivory tower, so removed from the reality of our lives, it's not likely that Iliana's heard yet. We've kept it out of the Courants, by some miraculous feat.

In the end I write nothing about Jek, just inconsequential nonsense about Mother's heads and what little House gossip I know. And I skirt carefully around her impending marriage. Iliana with her War-singer's magic will be married off to Trey, my Trey, as soon as she's passed her time at the Chalice. Mata and Ives joined again to make a war machine. Blending what power there is left in the old lines.

Anything to keep the Mekekana's iron armies at bay.

I sign off with a *miss you, love you, your sister* and fold the paper, sealing it in an envelope. The first post will have gone out already, but I'll leave it on the silver tray downstairs in the entrance hall, and Trone can take it this afternoon.

On the stairs, I pause when I hear voices. First, Trone's pompous drone, and occasionally interrupting him, the coarse Hob speech of my unwanted brother. The sound comes from Trone's little broom cupboard that he calls an office. I creep down to the landing and put my ear to the door.

"– it's all just shite."

"You will be expected to take your place in the House of Ives. If you've any talent for magic at all –"

"– which I don't an I just told you that –"

"Any talent at all, you'll need to know how to read."

"What, his majesty's going to send me on down the Chalice – is that it? Let me mingle with my betters?"

There's a pause, and I can picture Trone's nervous frown, the look he gets when you've asked him an uncomfortable question.

"The master of the house will most likely want to personally oversee any training of his son."

Jek snorts. "You daft fucker. You can always just say no. No need to pretend."

"It's true." Trone sighs, and his boot-soles slap and squeak as he paces the small room. "That while your status would be raised if it were discovered that you held some magical talent, the gift being rare as it is, even if society accepted you as a low-Lammer – rather doubtful – you would still have no right to study at the University of Bone."

"You have any talent, then?"

"That's an impertinent question."

"So . . . no."

"My mother was a War-singer, my father a Reader. It was a great disappointment to them when I displayed no signs of any gift by the time I reached my majority. Are you satisfied?"

There's scriv in minute amounts in everything we drink, in every morsel we taste. If a Lammer is going to manifest a talent, there will be signs, little trickles of unintentional magic. With me, I was eight, and I always knew what to say to mollify my father's mood. He noticed, I suppose, and took me to his study, gave me a pipette of scriv and showed me how to take it.

Luckily for me, I saw auras and instinctively understood what the colours meant, and how to shift them; what to say, what expression to hold.

If I'd not shown any talent there is no doubt my father would have had me set up in some low-Lammer household, had my name changed and my status ruined.

We don't keep our mistakes.

We certainly don't leave their memories on our family trees.

Jek is still talking. "So, your mam an da were both Lammers. High House?"

"Read your Gris-damned book, Hob."

I step back from the door and creep down the last flight of stairs.

In the entrance hall, two letters addressed to my mother are waiting on the silver tray. The one is thick, the paper stiff under my fingers. An invitation then. I hold the envelope up to the light that streams through the glass panes on the door, but I can't make out anything – who it's from, or what it's for. I drop it back and pick up the other.

Father's handwriting, stiff and spiky. He addresses the letter to Lady Ives Miria. I wonder if they ever loved each other, these two unyielding people. They are like dawn and dusk; my mother filled with mysteries and dreams, and my father brisk, jolly, and quick to temper. He is the sun around which our house revolves. I put my letter to the side, trusting that Trone will see to it, and quickly tuck my father's letter into an inner pocket of my lined windle-silk jacket. Mother retired straight after breakfast; she barely touched her eggs and toast. There are visions wanting to be seen, and my mother, slave as she is, must bear witness. She won't come down for hours. I have time to see what it is my father says to her.

A maid has opened the curtains in my room, something I always tell them not to do, but at least this way there's light by which to read. My ink is still out on my writing desk, and I cap the bottle, then take a paper knife from the stationery box and slide it neatly under the red wax of my father's seal. It cracks easily, leaving an oily stain on the paper. Gingerly, I slide the thin letter out and stare at it for a few moments, my fingertips just barely pressing the edges of the paper.

A few scratched lines, no salutation, no signature. No are-thee-wells?

He wants Mother to be more careful with her scriven consumption. It seems the price is rising again. Another mine closed, the vein run out.

I shiver, close the letter and slip it back into its envelope. In the flotsam of my stationery box, there, next to my collection of duplicated keys, is a small half-candle of sealing wax, and I melt it carefully onto the envelope and press my stolen seal into the wax. A thistle, garlanded with smoke. Ives. The fallen House. A name as old as Guyin, as Mallen – and here we are begging for the scraps from the Mata table.

Quickly, before anyone can notice that the letter is gone, I run downstairs and drop it back in place, slipping it under the heavy invitation.

If the scriven really is running that low, we will fall – the whole of Oreyn from coastal Pelimburg to MallenIve herself – Hob and Lammer alike. We don't have the physical power to hold off an outright attack from the Mekekana and their great ships, their cannons and guns. It's only by the magic of the War-singers that we can keep the red desert clear from their iron taint.

We've known for a while that the scriven was failing, fading away. It's why we turned to the unis in the first place: the single-horned giant goats that range the Oreyn desert. The horn, ground down and powdered, makes for a substitute for scriven. Not a great one; not even a decent one, if we are to be honest, but anything is better than nothing. The dealers have been cutting scriv with horn for years now, it's an open secret.

Even my mother must have seen something of this – caught a glimpse of it on the edge of some inconsequential vision. Or is she that weak?

And the Mata, they will know. It's possible they've been stockpiling scriven for decades. In which case, my father will want Iliana bound to them before the news goes public.

Two more weeks, and then my Father will return from court; two weeks before he'll start making any formal public commitments.

I need to see Trey before I lose him.

"YOU."

The servant stops, keeps his head lowered and his eyes to the ground.

"I'll want a nilly ready to ride. In under five minutes."

He doesn't make a sound, merely nods his acquiescence and speeds away. It's been three days since I read Mother's letter. She's withdrawn completely, probably counting every grain of scriven in the house. And now, today, she's finally emerged, clad in layers of black windle-silk, her waist cinched in with a hand-flossed corset, and wearing an immaculate overdress with black-on-black embroidery, the buttons small as the eyes of a rat.

She left in the Ives's carriage. Off to the invitation, no doubt. Gone to do her duty as an almost-Saint. To tell the future for whoever will throw her enough magic dust. She'll be gone for most of the day, for there's no rushing these ceremonies.

It gives me time to escape. For a while, at least.

"Miss Calissa?" The servant is back, shoulders slumped, eyes down. "Your nilly is ready."

I rush down to the cobbled area behind the house where they'll have my mount waiting, but before I make it out of the laundry area, a familiar and hateful voice stops me.

"Well, well. Aren't you dressed down a bit? Did our da run out of money or something?"

Jek. I spin around to face him, aware that I look guilty in my messenger's cloak, my silver scroll pinned to my shoulder.

He flicks the pin with one grimy finger. "I won't tell."

"And why should I believe you?"

"Because I like to save up my favours."

We have something in common then, although I don't admit that to him. I jerk away then settle the wide-brimmed riding hat over my pinned-up hair. "Tell whomever you like." I let my voice stay steady, the nonchalance practised, easy. "I don't care."

"Of course you do." But he drops his hand just the same.

I can feel the burn of his gaze as I push through the day's laundry, beaten clean and smelling of soap. The sheets fall closed behind me, hiding me, and then I run, needing to get to Trey as quickly as possible, to get away from my half-brother's unknown plans.

The Hob has tethered the saddled nilly to a post, and the animal rolls its yellow eyes at me as I approach, lowering its head with unmistakeable bad temper.

"There, there." I rub the coarse hair around the stump of its horn and offer it a sugar cube stolen from the kitchens. "Don't be like that." The crooning stills it, and it slobbers over my hand as it lips the sugar cube. There's a crunch as it enjoys its treat, spitting gritty sugary saliva all over my hand. Quickly, I untie the reins. The nilly stamps, excitement jumping under its skin as I drag my hand down its fur to wipe off the worst of the spit. Nillies are rough and take ill to training, but their size and sure-footedness makes them serviceable enough mounts.

"Come on." I click at it, and the nilly trots off, sharp cloven hooves ringing on the stone.

Once I'm out into the streets, I turn my nilly through a dark alleyway, out to the houses that back onto the Casabi. There's a bridle-path worn up on the higher banks, a muddy red trail that ducks between the dead winter reeds. They rattle as the wind blows through them. It's a longer route to the palace, but one unlikely to have anyone else on it. I don't want to be spotted.

The Casabi is broad and slow. Sometimes, in summer, you can see the younger boys out on rafts, poling their lashed-together logs down her deceptive turns. Mostly though, it's the realm of the huge barges.

The wherries are wide, shallow-bottomed; like river-horses they nose their way slowly through the silty water, each one painted brighter than the last, their little flags rippling along the lines. The flags are code; they tell those in the know what they're loaded with, who owns them, who captains.

The Casabi touches all things. She's the lifeblood running through MallenIve; she cuts through the red desert, her edges thick with scrubby trees. As long as I follow her, she'll take me straight to the bustling heart of MallenIve. There's a bridge there – one of many – that spans her, connecting the old town to the newer, wilder part of MallenIve. The Mata, the destroyers of the House of Mallen, have their roots there. The new palace was built on the ruins of the old, and it's a glittering monster of glass and mirrors.

As Father says of his masters – "All flash and fire, and no heart."

I urge the sour nilly faster, wanting to arrive before the weather turns. The nilly flicks its ears and whip-like tail in irritation.

The rush of stalks and the chitter of the last of the marsh-birds hum around us as the nilly's hooves thud in the dirt. We race down the empty bridle path, my stolen cloak flapping and cracking. The smell of brackish water, rotting branches, and silty mud roils off the river, and soon the path forks, so I nudge the nilly to the right, up towards the bridge and away from the river's stench.

We slow here, waiting behind other legitimate messengers in their silver scrolls and russet cloaks, behind merchants with their carts, foot traffic. All trudge along the wide bridge. I guide my mount as quickly as I can, side-stepping the larger vehicles and squeezing between the crowd.

There, in the distance, the Mata spires glint like cold blades.

There's no blaas to be seen floating among the low clouds, and the residential flag is at the top of the pole. All the Mata are in the halls. Including Trey.

I should have sent him a note, but he'll be glad to see me, regardless.

The roads leading towards the palace become wider, cleaner, planted with avenues of shivering trees whose dry leaves flicker in the wind. These wide pavements are clear of hawkers and traffic, and the only merchants who come up the slopes are in fine coaches, with House or guild crests.

There's a guard at the gates. More for show than anything else, and he lets me in when he sees my coat and pin. I nod as I pass him, and the timbre of the hoof beats changes as we leave the cobbled road and step onto a paved entrance.

"Good day," says a uniformed low-Lammer as he runs to me to hold the nilly's head as I dismount.

The high doors are open onto a marble lobby, silent except for the echo of my footsteps.

"Personal message?" says the burly secretary when he sees my scroll. "Who for?"

"The Prince Trey."

"He won't be available. The Mata are in a meeting." He peers over his vast appointment book, brows raised.

"A long meeting?"

"Perhaps. Who knows? Do you want to leave the message with me?"

I sigh, pretend inconvenience. Which isn't all that hard actually, because I don't have time to waste; more time stood here means less time with Trey. But we've worked this out, he's told me what I should do. "I'll wait," I say. "But if it's at all possible, would you inform the prince that the message comes from a good friend from the Chalice?"

The secretary shrugs one shoulder then nods.

It's a lie. Trey had no friends at the Chalice – too elite to be treated with any modicum of normality. We only met because my father has been courting the Mata since my sister was born. We've met at garden teas, at uncomfortable dinners, at the rare unicorn hunts out on the deserts. I've known him all my life, and yet, to all appearances, we've never said a word to each other.

Like me, Trey knows how to go unnoticed. We think it's a side-trait of soul-reading. But I noticed him – the red-haired boy, sitting cross-legged and silent, hidden behind his long fringe. He was lurking behind a pedestal, watching the adults stab each other with pointed words. It's the clearest memory I have of him, and when he noticed me, he grinned slyly and beckoned me over. Together we watched them building their little alliances. It was a good way to learn.

The burly secretary scribbles a note, and sends it flying down a chute, and I smile to myself. Trey won't take long to worm his way out of some boring family meeting. Even so, I find myself chewing my thumbnail ragged. I drop my hand when I hear the tap of boots, clipping fast down one of the corridors.

He enters, pale red hair swinging about his shoulders as he moves. The secretary stands, and I stifle a smile, shuffling, with my head bowed.

"What is it?" The question isn't directed at me but is snapped to the secretary instead.

"A personal messenger, wouldn't leave a note." He nods at me, passing any blame.

Trey feigns irritation, shaking hair from his eyes. "This way," he says, even as he turns and marches off. I cock the secretary a conspiratorial grin, and follow the prince from the lobby, deep into the white belly of the palace.

Even though he's the youngest of the three sons, Trey still has a private office. As the only one of the Mata who is not a Saint, he holds lowest status, and so his stateroom reflects that. The opulence is muted, the upholstery last year's fashion, the paintings by minor artists. The only true luxury is the wide bank of windows that gaze down over the hills that fall towards the Casabi. She winks and glints between the reeds.

The door closes. The key grates before the old lock snaps into place as Trey makes certain that we will not be disturbed.

"I was beginning to worry I wouldn't see you before this blasted wedding," he says, and folds his arms around me, resting his chin against my shoulder. Together we watch the barges crawl down the river.

I close my eyes; breathe him in – citrus, sweet scriven, redmint. His chest is warm against my back, and I want to hold this moment forever. "It's official?"

"Well, they're hashing out details, but it's as good as done. Your sister graduates in less than a month, and your father wants the Houses joined as soon as possible after that." His voice gives nothing away – not anger, resignation – he could be talking about posting a letter, rather than being bound to my sister for all eternity.

"Gris," I say, and twist away from him, turning around so I can see his face.

He smiles weakly. "You look...

"Sweaty?"

"Thirsty." He goes to a glass table set with iced glasses, well-water in crystal jugs, and pours me a watered-down vai.

I take it from him, and we watch each other over our glasses. Drinking to fill the silence.

The drink is sharp, flavoured with some herb I can't place, and it burns my throat. Father doesn't allow me to drink – says I'm still a bit too young. It's only with Trey that I drop the childish shell I occupy in my own house. "Do you think you'll be happy?"

"Don't be stupid. It's not about happiness, you know that." He puts his drink down, carefully, and I realise he's had more to drink before this. Trey reaches into his breast pocket and pulls out a thin silver case embossed with Mata's eight-armed sun. Mint flavours the air, and he takes a few crisp leaves from within to chew, offers the case to me.

"Let's not waste time," he says. "Iliana will move in here soon enough, and there'll be no place for us to see each other again."

"I could find a place –"

He laughs bitterly. "I won't."

I swallow down the redmint, the dry leaves gone prickly in my throat. "You won't what?"

"Make a mockery of a House binding. And if anyone were to find out . . . ."

"You're just scared of your father," I snap.

"With reason."

"This is why you have no status, not because you're the youngest – because you have no spine."

He steps away from me. "My father is not a man to cross. And this wedding was decided years ago. You've known it was coming."

I go back to the window. Funny how the Casabi looks clean and shiny from here, and when you get close, you smell the rot, see its dust-brown depths, the river-weeds on the edges. "Why couldn't I be born the eldest?" I ask, more to myself than as a real question, but

Trey hears me.

"Have you ever asked a Saint?"

"I live with one, and it's bad enough with the way she tries not to look at me, without going to find out exactly what it is she's seen in my future that's so damned awful."

"Your mother's not a real Saint – go to a Guyin, their Saints –"

"And would you pay for the invitation?" I glance back at him. The Guyin Saints are second only to the Mata, despite the fact that their line will end with the current Lord, who if rumour is to believed, can no longer use scriven anyway. They will not tell me visions for a golden bit.

The room with its airy white walls and pale paintings in gilded frames seems suddenly close and dark. "Not that it matters. The visions aren't truth. I won't base my life on might be's and could have beens."

He looks down. It's exactly what his family does, after all.

"You know about the scriven?" I say.

"Of course. Although, more interestingly, how do you?"

I crook one corner of my mouth up in a humourless smile. "I have my means."

"Don't worry about it. It's bound to be only a temporary shortage." He moves back to me, closing his hands around my arms, leaning in to nibble at my neck. He smells of vai and the underlying burnt citrus tang of scriven common to the Mata, who practically bathe in the stuff.

I let him do that for a while, knowing he's only trying to distract me, which means the scriven is running out, probably faster than even my father realises. Then, when his mouth has reached my ear, I turn and press against him, putting my mouth to his, and tasting the distant tingle of magic on his tongue. I want to hold him closer, hold him so tightly that he becomes a part of me, and I will never lose him to my sister. I do not let myself blink, so that the membranes dry and the winter desert air licks away the tears I will not shed.

Around us the shadows stretch out like comfortable cats, the sun sinking towards late afternoon. Dressing back into my messenger's uniform, I coil up my hair, hiding it beneath the sweeping gallant brim of my hat.

"Was this the last time?" Trey says, as he pins the messenger's scroll to my lapel. His fingers, if I didn't know better, look like they're trembling, and for a moment, I want to throw away this whole stupid political dance and just hug him tightly, like people our age do in the streets. Like low-Lammers out watching the jugglers and fire breathers and spinners on Long Night, holding hands, laughing. I want to be normal. And then it's gone, quick as a summer butterfly, and just as useless.

Pretty things, they have no meaning. House Ives, House Mata – they've made us into parodies of our parents, old before our time. I'm almost sixteen, I should be enjoying my life instead of losing every damn thing I hold dear. I kiss Trey for the last time, keeping my eyes wide, dry, and inside I nurse the little flame of pointless hatred I have for my sister. She always gets what I can't have.

We take a different route outside. Trey leads me to a door, triple locked, singing with magic. One of the private entrances, telling your gaze to slide past, there's nothing of interest here, just blank stone wall, oh yes. It leads out to a small courtyard off the main stables, where my nilly will be waiting.

I don't let myself look back, just leave, moving blankly, and I when I arrive home, it's without a memory of the journey back. A ghost in my own world.

Mother is still out, and there are ways to make myself feel better. I search through my box for the collection of purloined keys, and slip off one – a small thing, almost insignificant, then call a maid to bring Sharpshins to me.

He arrives, sweaty and rumpled. He won't look me in the face, but he does grin slyly when I ask him what progress he's made with Jek.

"I took him out for a drink an set him up with some shiny Chalice-girl," Sharpshins says.

I blink. "And this is supposed to accomplish what, exactly?"

"A Chalice-girl all dressed as a windle worker, so that there'd be no one as could spot her being a daughter of a certain House."

"Oh?" There are possibilities there, and depending what House, I could have just been handed some wonderful blackmail material. "And just which House would that be?" I flip a brass bit on the writing table, and he watches it hungrily.

"Your own, miss."

I drop my hand over the coin, to cover the little gasp that escapes me. It seems my dear friend Sharpshins has a potential for cruelty to rival my own. "How interesting," I say, my voice faint. I lift the coin and toss it into his out-held palm. "You're to mention it to no one, of course."

"'Course not."

I shake my head, smiling, and fold the little key in a slip of paper. Sharpshins watches in silence as I seal the paper with wax, then drop it into my bureau drawer. Here's a game I can save for another day. I wasn't expecting such a welcome gift from my little sneak. "Iliana," I muse, and tap my fingers on the curved edge of my bureau.

"That's right, miss."

I will have that damned Hob out of this house, one way or another. Pinning a theft on him will have him out on the street as quickly as my mother turned that maid out. Jek won't even know what force moved him; he'll be so dizzy from the fall. But before that, I can make him suffer.

And I can punish my sister for her part in my unhappiness.

"He trusts you?"

Sharpshins nods. "Mostly."

"Arrange for him to have another meeting with his new acquaintance," I say. "You've a mind for amusing deceits – think of something. And when you're done, come back to me."

When Sharpshins has left again, I throw my messenger's hat on the bed and open my wardrobe so that I can dress myself in my mother's expectations.

Nine

The Grinningtommy

SHARPSHINS CATCHES ME just as I'm about to go back to work in that stinking kitchen. As always, I've eaten lunch outside, an he grabs my shoulder before I can stand.

"Feeling ill, Jek?" he says.

"Not exactly, though having to look at cook's face does give my stomach a nasty turn."

Sharpshins laughs. "I think you're looking more'n a little off colour." He's grinning wider than a sphynx, sharp teeth smiles.

I dunno what's got old Sharps all humoured up, an I frown. "What's happening?"

"Nothing." He winks at me, sly-like. "Just heard a sparrer spreading rumours. Seems there's some girl down the Sphynx who wouldn't mind seeing your ugly old rat-face again. Been hanging around the bar counter watching for you."

Ia. An I can't right help the warm feeling spreading over my face, like walking out of shadows into sunlight. "She wants to see me?" Blast having to muck about in my da's kitchens. "What's this about being ill?" I says.

"It's what I'm going to tell Cook when you don't show up in the kitchens in the next five minutes. I'm going to tell him you're puking up your guts and you've gone and turned yellow as a lemon."

"Oho, are you now." I stand an clap his shoulder. "An how am I to repay such a generous medical opinion?"

"We'll work that out some other day," says Sharps, "'Til then, I suggest you get on shank's nilly and trot down the Sphynx before someone spots you."

So I give him a bow, an click my fingers. "Seems I feel a sudden illness taking. An the only medicine that will cure it is waiting for me far from this shitehole." Before anyone can see me leaving, I duck under the laundry lines, an run for the little back gate, leaving Sharps to cover for me.

WHEN I'M ABOUT a block from the Sphynx, I slow down, drag my fingers through my hair, an ease back into breathing normal. So by the time I push open the pub door, I'm suave as a grey cat an sleeker than fur. Sure enough, Ia's there, sitting at the bar counter, in the midst of all her schoolmates.

She doesn't turn around at the sound of the door, just keeps chattering with the girl next to her, their heads all bowed close.

"All right?" I say as I pull out the nearest seat and slide in close to her.

"Jek?" Her eyes go wide. "Fancy."

"Thought you wouldn't see me again so soon?"

"Well, I –" She frowns, the marks pinching her face. "No matter. You're here."

Now I'm feeling a little like a wherry-sail with no wind. "Pub's quiet today."

"Hmmm." She's chewing at her lower lip, worrying it. "Look –" She glances at her friend, an goes red. "I'll be back in a moment," she says to the girl an hops from her barstool. She hurtles off, plain meaning me to follow her. Well sour as her welcome's been, I still go on an make my way to the back of the Spyhnx, where she's standing with her arms folded.

"What are you doing here – I thought you only had a day off every two weeks?"

"Hey now –"

"Not that it matters. It's too late now, Alys has seen you already. She's going to be spreading this all around the Chalice before the next bell rings." She huffs. The black dye is fading from her hair, an now it's a softer colour, coppery. "We can't stay here." She grabs my hand an leads me through the little warren rooms, to a side door that lets out into the alleyway.

I grin. There's good memories that go with these alley walls.

Hand in hand, we twist an turn down the narrow back roads, 'til Ia leads me to a small white-washed pub with a green sign of a little bird. "No one important comes here," she says. "Greenfinch."

More like no one at all comes here. The place is dull as paint, an emptier'n a bucket. Ia buys us drinks an we stare at each other across the foam.

This shite was much easier when my head was full of bitter.

I drink fast an say little. Seems to be a good enough way to go about conversation, an Ia looks glum an laps at her foam all kitten-like.

"Summat wrong then?"

She sighs an pushes her glass a little way across the table. "My family. The usual nonsense that comes with being part of the system."

"What system is that – the one where serving girls dress you an Hobs cook your food an everyone kisses your arse an tells you you're the biggest turd on the midden-heap?"

"Oh!" She growls a little at her glass, an I can't help laughing at her. "What would you know – you think it's all sunshine and roses because you don't know any better. Do you think you're the only person in the world who has troubles – that being rich means never having anything go wrong, or never feeling trapped?"

An I'm trapped right enough, in one of the highest Houses left. She's right, not that I'm going to admit it.

"So what's happened, your da refuse to buy you a dress you want? One too many parties this week?" I stand up an go buy us another round, even though Ia's barely touched hers.

When I get back, she's got her elbows on the table, an she's holding her head, her hair pushed back away from her face. Her mouth is all tight, worried. Even looking down, she's shinier than she has a right to be. So I feel kinda sorry for baiting her.

"What's wrong, love?"

"I have to get married."

Well, that weren't exactly what I was expecting, though the way Lammers are about girls, I guess I should have seen it coming from far. An it's not like I thought her an me had any kind of future. But I was hoping there'd be time enough for a bit of fun before we took our own paths. I set my drink down careful as I can. "Have to?"

"It's been arranged since I was two, just . . . somehow . . . ." Ia sighs an leans her head on her elbows, an talks to the table. "Somehow I never thought it would actually happen." Her bright voice is all muffled. She looks up at me. "I just thought it would be years still, that –" She curls her fingers. "– that somehow everyone would forget about it."

"So run away."

She snorts then takes a long drink from her half-pint. "I'm not insane. Besides, the marriage is necessary. My father's been drumming in the idea of damage control for as long as I can remember."

"Damage control?"

"The House I'm in – we, well, you won't understand, being a Hob, but we used to have respect and honour, and thanks to a string of idiotic ancestors making idiotic choices, we've rather lost face."

This House nillyshite about face never made sense to me; it always seemed like lots of interesting ways to make excuses to do things you hated. "So what's it all got to do with you?"

Ia don't answer me. Instead, she finishes the last bit of her drink, downs the second half-pint, an then reaches over for mine. She does it so quick that I stop her only after she's slopped most of my pint down her chin. I pry her fingers off the glass an set it out of her reach. I'm actually feeling sorry for the poor chit. She's crying, blinking so that I can't tell.

"One of those idiots was my father," she says, in between hiccoughs.

"So you're his price for face?"

"Something like that. Shit, I'm drunk." She stares miserably at the table. "I hate this. Take me somewhere else."

I know what she means, 'course, but it's not like I've a room to take her to, or money to pay for one neither. An even if I had, I'm not that much of a bastard. Instead I take her out to the alleyway.

"Again?" she says. "I feel like I'm making a habit of this."

But all I do is hug her tight until she cries for real, an then I walk her back to the Sphynx after she's fixed her face in the toilets of the Greenfinch. I let her tell me how unfair everything is, an I say nothing back.

It's not like I don't know how she feels, being used to pay for someone else's fuck-ups. Still, I'm not really sure how I'd go about explaining that bit of foolery, especially when I said naught about it last time.

"I really would like to see you again," she says, when we're standing outside the Sphynx. Ia's got a damp kerchief in one tight fist, an mostly it seems like she's talking to it, an not me. "I know it's stupid, and it's not like anything can come of it, but it's –" She waves her hand a bit, like she's looking for the right words.

"Better'n nothing?"

She goes an smiles thin, an it makes her eyes look less puffy an red. "That's it exactly, Jek. Better than nothing." Then she kisses me goodbye, an I don't give shit who might see us.

Ten

Singing for the Dead

THE ROOKERY ROOMS are dark even when they're light. So full of shadows, half-things, whispers, other wrays. They are not like me; they see me differently to how I see them. Even with everything in pieces I know the sourness of pity.

"Mal?" I'm standing outside his door, watching night fall all down the passages. He has been working. Soon I will be too and because of this Mal tastes like guilt. He keeps telling Riam to wait a little longer. Another day.

The door opens for me, because Mal wants me here. I can smell tiredness on him like dirt. He is clean, scrubbed, but under the skin the dirt is still there, waiting for something, for someone to wash it away.

"Stay – can I?" Whole thoughts. I need these. Learn to use them again, to remember. Otherwise no one understands what it is I want. But it's hard to focus on making them come out right. I try for Mal, though.

"I'm tired, Ansel." But he looks up from his bed, and the tiredness slips back under his skin, out of sight. Maybe I'm the someone he needs.

"Don't like that name," I tell him. How to explain? That it is so twisted up with someone I am not, that what I used to be is gone, burned away as clean as fat and firesmoke.

"Little Sel, then." He smiles soft in the darkness, and the room is made lighter just because of him. "What is it you want?" He sits up, pats at the covers, and it is an invitation. I hold on to that thought and follow it down.

Now that I'm here, the things I meant to tell him are gone. I sit quietly, and wait for them to come back, see if I can trap them in my fingers and keep them ready. The stars come out, and blood swishes in my ears. I listen to the sound of it, soft as a river.

I think Mal is talking to me, but the words are caught up in my blood, hard to hear. I concentrate, lose the beat of blood, and try make the words into sounds I recognise.

"– something upsetting you?"

Yes, but I do not want him to know this. He upsets me. When I am near him everything goes out of place, and the world is a strange shape, hard to hold. But it is a good shape, exciting in its newness. I mean to say nothing, and instead the words fly out of my mouth. I watch them circle, like little wrens, lost. "You did this to me," I tell him.

He sighs, and the guilt makes him dirtier than even the tiredness did. I did this. Perhaps I am wrong, and none of this is Mal's doing. He reaches out to touch my wrist, and I watch his fingers, wonder if I feel the same things he does.

"Riam wants you working as soon as possible. No room for freeloaders in the rookery. Even her own son pulled his weight before he found a way to get out."

I look up at his face. My mother looked at me like this once. She hated doing what she did, because it was wrong. But it was the best thing she could think of.

I wish I could remember what it was she did.

It wasn't like this.

"I'm sorry," he says. This time the words match his face. "I couldn't think of how to do this that wouldn't hurt you more than was necessary. And now –" He laughs. "You should probably stay away from me, before things get worse than they already are. In Urlin, we could work this out, make it right, bond, I suppose. You can't do that here, and all this isn't helping."

He doesn't understand me, or why I'm here.

"Not worse." I look back down at his fingers, and touch them with my own, to see if they will join together, the way I suppose bonds grow. "Feel safe with you."

"Sweet fucking Alerion's blood, Sel! That's exactly the problem." He pulls his hand away. "You have no idea just what it is I've done to you, do you?"

He doesn't give me time to find answers.

"I should have hurt you," he says, and his voice sounds all tight, like someone is choking him. "Everyone else will." Suddenly he pulls me close, and warmth touches me where our skin meets. It fills me, and my heart beats faster to match the heat. "I'm an idiot."

"This isn't bad," I try tell him, but I think the words come out wrong because he pushes me away and looks at me with wide eyes, filled with my mother's horror.

"One day," he says. "I'm going to pay for this." He starts laughing. "It's the very least I deserve. Lie down, Sel."

I do as he says, and fold our bodies close, so I can listen to his blood instead of my own. It sounds like tears.

There is something here that I do not understand. Why does he not know that he makes me happy?

"Enjoy this while you can," he says. "Because it's all going to be taken away from you, and I'm going to see it in your face and feel like the fucking shite I am."

This thing I feel for Mal, this new thing, I do not think it is allowed in Riam's rookery. "We could go away." It seems simple. That's what mother and Dae and I were doing. Going away.

"No we couldn't, idiot," he says, but the word is laughing softly at me. "There're laws against running away. I guess you don't know that – don't know any of the problems we're causing." He thinks quietly, arms shivering around me. "Who am I calling an idiot anyway? I'm the fool here." He holds me tighter, and I relax, even if I can't really tell if he's happy or sad. We stay like that while the stars spin higher, and I fall asleep for a while.

I wake when he tells me about how he cannot leave, not now. Because of me.

"Even if I could," he says. "Even if I had the strength of purpose that someone like Isidro had, all it means is that I swap this slavery for another. There's really no such thing as a free vampire in this city."

I will remember this. This dream where someone is scared of losing me.

"I don't know what I want anymore," he says, very softly.

I hold his face in my hands, wait for him to work it out.

"You're starting tomorrow," he says. "You can hate me all you like then. For now though," he closes his eyes, "I'm going to pretend you don't."

Mallen kisses me, and I remember that this is why I came here.

Eleven

The Grinningtommy

IT'S BEEN A few days since I spent that weepy afternoon with Ia, an even though I know she's bought an paid for, it don't mean I have to stop thinking about her. Girl even manages to look shiny when she cries, an I'm going all soft over her. This is worse than getting sentimental over the scrounger.

"The ladyship's out," Sharp says to me as he passes, holding a grimy wicker basket filled with old potatoes sprouting eyes. He knocks me out of my day-dreaming, an I drop the potato I'm trying to peel, an slice my thumb.

I suck the blood off my thumb an raise an eyebrow. "What's that to me?"

"I know she keeps a good bit of scriven – also happen to know where she stashes it. Old hag won't miss a pinch or two." He nudges me with his elbow. "You've got a break coming up. An you owe one for that story I spun Cook."

Best to keep my silence on this for a bit. He's right – I do owe him. An while I wouldn't mind a scriv high, today's the day my da comes back home, an I don't want to do nothing that's going to stop me from taking my half day next week. I'm looking forward to seeing Ia again. For all her being a Lam, an her House troubles, I can't stop thinking about her. An she wants me. I grin; it's always good to be wanted. I'm thinking I'll bring her something – buy her whatever it is that Lam girls like. I don't mind spending a bit of brass to see her. Maybe cheer her up a bit.

"There a flower market in MallenIve?"

"You going daft on me, mate?" Sharp clicks his tongue an laughs. "You got a look on your face that better suits a spring-nilly."

"That's just your imaginings," I say, but I can feel my skin heat. Gris, caught dreaming about a girl like a mumbler. "So," I says to cover up. "Where's this stash then?"

"In her Ladyship's rooms."

My skin prickles. May be that it's too hot in this kitchen. Sharpshins slips something down onto the cutting table, casual-like. Small an silver. A key. I pocket it with an easy move, like I was doing nothing more than brushing a sod of earth from the potatoes.

"Dressing table, right drawer. There's a small box, ivory, with a leaf or summat-such on it."

"Yeah?" An like that I'm caught up in the trade again. It's been too long since I felt like I was doing something normal. Gris, Jek – wanting to go an buy the chit flowers – you are going soft.

When I take my break, I slip upstairs, quick as can be. I'm not meant to be here, an I'm sure that any moment, someone's going to see me an call me out.

"Jek!"

I freeze: my heart's going so fast it's about ready to leap out my body, an I turn slow on the wooden steps.

Trone's looking up at me, all sour-like. "Your father will be here this afternoon," he snaps. "In case you've forgotten."

"No. Just gone to scrub up," I says. "Throw on a spot of lace an perfume, like."

"Don't get smart," he says, but there ain't no bite to it. He sighs an brushes one hand over his slicked-back hair. "There's a suit put out for you in your rooms. It should fit. Don't embarrass me." Then he's gone, rushing off to bark orders at whatever hapless sod crosses his path.

Well fuck me, that had me certain I was rumbled. I go the rest of the way quick an quiet, keeping to the shadows.

I've never been in this clean cold room. It's dull as the lady herself – all grey an white an silver, dead as rock. I catch a sideways look at myself in a huge polished mirror on the dressing table – first time I've ever seen my reflection proper an I stop 'fore it a moment.

I'm all out of place. Too tall for a Hob, too dark an sour-looking for a Lammer. An if I saw me in the streets, I wouldn't think I'd spent near eighteen years in this life.

Even all the decent meals in the world don't make a body lose that hungry look. I snarl at the reflection an rifle through the top drawer of the lady's table, trying not watch myself snaffling her stuff. It's a bit like being caught red-handed.

An there it is. Just where old Sharp said. The box opens easy, the little key sweet in the lock. Inside there's more scriv powder than I've seen in one place before. I take in a deep breath, an scrape a thimbleful out, packing it into a fold of dirty paper Sharp gave me.

One quick look about the room to make sure that everything's put back as it was. There's not a sign I've been here at all.

Back in mine an Sharp's room, there's a suit of neat brown clothes waiting for me folded on my bed. Normal-like I don't pay fashion much mind, but even I can see this shite is ugly. Trone's also gone an put a pitcher of water an a wash-bowl on a small table. Bastard ain't subtle, for sure. I sigh to the empty room, an splash water on my hands an face so's to wash off the the dirt. That mirror gave me a pretty good idea of how third rate I look, so I even dig out a comb an get the worst of the tangles out of my hair.

All this, an it ain't even for Ia.

The suit actually fits all right, better than the other hand-me-downs they've been making me wear. Just as I finish buttoning the fitted jacket closed over a new white shirt, Trone comes barrelling in without so much as a by your leave. I shove the folded paper full of scriv deep in my pocket.

"Hmm," he says, an looks me over down his long nose. "I thought it might fit."

When I say nothing, he adds, "It was your father's when he was about your age."

"Laying it on a bit thick, ain't ya?"

"It doesn't hurt to remind people of themselves," he says, an for the first time Trone gives me a little smile. Quick an awkward as someone who don't smile often, true, but it was there. "Now. Scrape that mess out of your face or I'll cut it off for you." He pulls silver sithers from his pocket an snips them once in my direction.

Trone has me gussied up in my father's old suit, made me spit-shine my boots an braid back my hair. They keep trying to get me to cut it, but Hobs know there's strength in hair, an I won't cut it just to please some stupid Lam. Even if it's my da. Well especially, in this case.

So now we're standing in that front hall, turned out like we're going to the races. That high-toned bitch what my da married is standing ahead of me, Calissa at her side. They're both kitted out in their finest, an there's seed-pearls about the wife's neck. That's flash money, that is. Worth near as much as those two bits Prue saved. A lifetime's money on one neck. Makes you sick. Or maybe that's just the thought of finally meeting this bastard da of mine.

From the street comes the sound of hooves on stone. The rattle of wheels. Trone opens the door with a sweep, ready to help the master of the house down from his coach. I can see the coach from here – it's a grand thing, painted black with the silver ribbon an thistle that I've come to know as the Ives crest. Strange that it's supposed to be mine too now.

The coach door opens, an out steps my da. He's wiry an tall, with thinning hair an a crooked smile. "Sorry we're late," he says. "Stopped to pick up a little surprise." Behind him I see the figure of a girl, a shadow-shape leaning over.

"Mother," she says. "Calissa."

An my heart stops, dead in my chest. Sweet fucking Saints.

"Iliana?" says my da's wife, starting forward. "Oh my sweet, you're home early!"

The girl reaches out a hand, an my da helps her out. She's all blond now, dressed in neat pleats an gloves. She's washed out the last of the dye, toned down the face-paint an outfits.

"Now, you must be Prue's boy?" my da says, nodding to me. "I'm sure we'll have much to talk about." Just behind him, Ia's seen me, an her face has taken on a nervous frown.

"Who's this then," she says. "A new servant?"

My da looks uncomfortable. "We'll talk inside, and I'll explain."

His wife snorts, a little sound, but loud enough to carry.

Ia presses her lips thin an stalks into the house, her blue eyes flicking to me. Outside, the coachman clicks to the nillies as the coach rattles away to the stables. Trone closes the door. No sunshine spills into the house now, just the dim light that comes through the curtains. There's a curious tight pain in my belly, an I remember it well from the day I got dragged into this whole mess, when Oncle turned me over. There's no good coming my way, I can tell.

Everyone looks all eager an nervous, shifting on their feet. My da clears his throat. "Perhaps, if we could all move to the study." Meaning, where the servants won't hear, 'cept he's forgotten that for all he's claimed my blood, I still live back-stairs.

We file into his office, an my da shuts the door, glances at us all then clears his throat again.

"Well," he says. "This is a bit awkward."

"A small understatement," says his wife. "I wish to be excused from this meeting. And Calissa already knows, there's no need for her to hear it again." She grabs the little rat's hand an leads her out the door, gone before my da can say yea or nay.

He looks at the closed door then gives his head a little shake, like there's no point chasing her down like he should. My da turns back to us both. "Take a seat then." He points to the black leather chairs, an Ia an I sit down, like trained dogs. We don't look straight at each other, but I can see her a little out the corner of my eye.

I've never been in here before. It has a dusty look to it like no one comes here but my da. The room smells like leather an scriv, spices an wood. There's more books in here than I can count on both hands, an it don't matter how many letters I've learned so far, I don't think I'll be reading an understanding any of these right soon.

My da stands at a black stone mantelpiece over a dead fireplace, leaning there for a minute, like he's lost an getting his bearings, an then he strides to a sideboard to lift a bottle from the tray of glasses there.

Instead of opening the closed, heavy curtains, my da lights candles – seven of them, a sacred number, like you use for important meetings.

Glass chinks, the sound of pouring, the smell of spice an nose-itching sting of vai. He hands us both a full glass. Vai is clear like water but it smells strong enough to fell a scrivver. I sniff at it, 'cause I ain't never actually had vai before. I hope it'll do something about the churning in my gut.

Ia's my sister then – half-sister, an Hob law is strict as sharif on that. Well, under Hob law it would still be almost all right 'cause she ain't my ma's child, but Lam law is stricter still, an they put all their store in the sires, not the dams. If my da finds out about this I'll be burned at the stake for sure.

"So," he says. "Where do I begin?"

I gulp at my vai, but Ia just puts her glass back on the table. She don't even look at it. "What exactly is going on?"

"The young man here is Jek," he says, plunging in. "He's your half-brother."

For a long silence I'm frighted that she's gonna tell him all. My heart's hammering so loud that every person in the room must hear it, an I lower my head so no one can read guilt on me.

Leather wheezes as she stands all stiff an proper. "You're lying. Or mocking me – is this a joke? How can you expect me to believe that this –" She jerks one hand towards my face. "– is related to me."

Never you mind, lass, 'cause it's just as big a shock to me. Never thought I'd end up mucking about with my own sister, to be sure. An sure as shit I never thought I'd fall for her. I keep my head down an take another gulp of my drink. Shite burns all the way down my throat.

My da switches from fumbly an lost to angry as a spitting bat in seconds. "This is not about you, Iliana! Sit down," he roars.

Ia drops back into her chair, eyes fixed on him.

"You're as bad as your bloody mother," he says. "This is how it is, and how it will be. Jek's mother is dead, and that means he belongs to me, he's mine, half-Hob or not. You don't have to like it, but you will bloody accept it." He slams his hand flat on his desk, making the glasses shiver in place. "I've had to deal with stupidity and incompetence for the last three weeks at the Court; I don't want to have to deal with it at home. Now get out, and I'll discuss this with you when you've had time to calm down."

Personal-like, I'm thinking he needs to calm down hisself, but Ia stands an dips her head. "As you wish, Father."

When she's gone, he turns to me, pours a little more vai in my near-empty glass, an then sits down.

"So?" He spreads his hands. "How do you find it here so far?"

I will my fingers to stop shaking as I take the glass. "Well enough. Wish you weren't so uptight about me learning my letters though." My head's still reeling over Ia, an the last thing I want to be doing is making small-talk with my da, in this itchy suit an my head all sticky with vai.

He laughs, throws back his drink in one slug then pours his self another. "You Hobs. You've no respect for anyone. It's part of your attraction, I suppose."

"First as I heard it." The no respect, an the attraction. Leastwise I see it, we're just kicking-dogs for Lams. Labour an whores. I don't say it out loud, though, no need to rile the man.

"Trone wrote to me about your progress. He says you're bright enough when you apply yourself."

"Never told me that." The vai is making my tongue all loose. "He just says that it's a wonder Hobs have managed to live this long, seeing as how they apparently don't have brains."

"Trone has a chip on his shoulder," my da says. "I wouldn't pay too much attention to what he says, but rather to what he does." He stands with his drink in hand an paces behind his desk. "We'll have to talk about what's to be done with you, see if you have any talents that can be put to use." He pauses before he drinks deep again. "Now, I believe that this is your half-day, so I won't waste it for you. We'll have a chat later on in the week, after I've had some time to think."

"Thank you, sir." Trone drummed that into me – sir – sounds so daft.

"Not at all. And never mind my family, they'll come around, and you'll get to know them better," he says, like he's certain of it.

Of course, he might not like just how well I know his oldest. My sister, I think. My half-sister, like that makes it better. The vai sits in my stomach, cold an heavy. I want to sick up, but I bow, an leave, heading to my rooms as fast as I can, hoping that I don't bump into no one.

Somehow, I make it to my room an collapse on my cot, my heart going like a spindle.

I'm all quiet an shaky. Saints, what if my da finds out? Ia must be hiding from me, which makes sense, as I'm in my room. Also hiding.

The door slams open, making me jump like a spooked nilly.

"It's all right, it's just me." Sharpshins sticks his head around the door. "You look like you saw your mam's ghost. Everything right with you?"

"All good, just . . . just feeling like there's too many people in the house all sudden-like."

He sits down on his bunk, across from me. "Iliana's a self-righteous little bitch, but I can promise you won't see much of her. She thinks the sun shines out of her arse, but she keeps away from the servants."

"I'll just bet she does." Did Sharps have an inkling of who that black-haired girl in the pub was? He saw her from behind, that's all.

Sweat makes me cold, makes my face slick. "Did you know?" I choke out.

"Know what?"

I shake my head. "Nothing."

"You got that little package I asked you to collect?"

He's talking about the stolen scriv. I nod an dip my hand into pocket to pull it out. That sweet glee that I got from lifting it is gone. Pissed away like a night's first sip of bitter.

"Come on, mate. Cheer up. It's half-day, you can go see that girl of yours."

"We've split," I mutter.

Sharp gives me a look, like ah well, you just met an all, an then he shrugs. "Too bad. Well, come with us for a drink then?"

The thought of going down the Sphynx, well, it's too much, so I shake my head. "It's – I'll stay here, save a bit of dosh."

"This girl's got you right miserable. You know, if it's cunny you're after, well, there's always the whore houses down the Old Way." He grins. "Or you could try something a bit different."

"Different how?"

He tilts his head, in a sort of shrug. "Well...don't really want to say. It's a flavour not to everyone's liking, if you get my drift."

"Something to tickle the sharif?" I don't need trouble now.

"Nothing the sharif will cop you for, but . . . ."

I'm interested despite myself. "Yeah, all right, I'll try anything once for a laugh."

"Good then," he says as he splits the little pile of scriven, an snorts his from his thumb. I take my half an do the same. Truth is, this is more scriv than I ever done at any one time, but I don't want Sharp showing me up, an another part of me doesn't really care. I just want to drown myself in a high.

Ah Jek, I thinks to myself. You're fucking pathetic, you are.

"C'mon." Sharpshins stands, running his hand under his nose to wipe away the last traces of dust, an sniffs loudly. "Not a word to no one, right?"

"Yeah," I echo, an follow him down the back stairs.

Twelve

A Game of Wasps

ILIANA'S PACING MY floor like an enraged sphynx, but I know my sister better than she realises, and I can see the fear prickling about her. I've taken more of Mother's scriven, and it sharpens my abilities. She's got a shifting aura, and I read fear, guilt, anger.

Jek. I smile tightly and clamp down on the rising satisfaction. *I want you to hurt, I want you to know how I feel.* "Are you going to tramp up and down my room all day?"

She whirls, the colours dancing around her. "Why didn't you write?"

Ah, attack. She learnt this from Mother, but I have my own weapons. "About?"

"About this – this – half-brother we supposedly have."

"Not supposedly, you've seen him." I sit up a little; her aura has gone a sickly sort of colour, disgust clouding out everything else. "Anyway, I was going to tell you, and then I thought it would be better as a surprise."

"Surprise! What kind of possible joy do you think I was going to get from finding out that we're somehow related to –

to a bloody Hob?" She hugs herself. "Father must have gone insane," she whispers. "Who would bed a Hob?" She holds my gaze clear and steady, but around her guilt rises in sick yellow flames.

"Well, I've spoken a little to Trone. It sounds like Jek's mother was considered quite the beauty."

"For a Hob."

"Just so." I nod. "You're taking this rather hard. It's no worse a scandal than any other House has had to deal with. We'll live through it."

"Oh, will we now?" she snarls, and her aura flashes crimson. "Father has set up a contract between Ives and Mata – how's he ever going to keep that with this kind of blot on his name?"

"Oh, you'll still get your prince," I say and swing my legs, idly kicking the air. "He bedded the girl when he was studying at the Chalice – everyone knows that scholars have to get their wildness out of their system."

Her cheeks have turned a dull red colour, almost matching her aura. "Is that so?"

I shrug. "It's what I've heard. You'd know better than me, I'm sure."

"And that's supposed to mean what, exactly?" Her tone is icy, and the guilt is back, wavering, yellow.

I narrow my eyes, wondering how I can use her, and for what. "I meant nothing by it, Iliana, save that you're at the Chalice, so you'd see this sort of thing going on all the time."

Iliana's still hugging herself then there's a sudden stillness in her aura, it goes cool and silver, then dissolves. Ah, a trick she's learnt at the Chalice, no doubt. She stares at me with a blank face. "Were you Reading me?" she says, her voice calm and slow as the Casabi River.

"Reading you? What –"

"Don't play the fool, Calissa, it doesn't become you. Besides, this room stinks of scriven." She drops her hands. "I'll see you at dinner," she says, and walks out, slamming the door behind her.

I stare at the closed door for a while, putting my thoughts in order. I've Sharpshins in my hand; and now my dearest sister. Perhaps I'll go find out from Sharpshins if he's still playing Jek along, that at least something today is going right. Unfortunately, my mother hasn't noticed her stolen scriv yet.

I want Jek gone, I want it to be just me and Iliana, and I wish that my father wasn't sotted by the thought of some dead lover's child.

If only that Hob had run when he first came. My fists close and I slip toward the servants' back stairs, hoping to catch a glimpse of Sharpshins.

Two shadows move on the landing below, and I just know, I can feel that one of them is Jek.

"You!" I call, and both figures turn. Now their faces are clear. Sharpshins gives me a slow wink. Jek just looks . . . out of his head. There's a faint tang of scriven.

I nod, a gesture that Jek will not understand, letting Sharpshins know that he's free to carry on with whatever he has with Dray, the cook, and I'll not breathe a word to my mother.

My own magic is still fluttering, picking up the last shimmering auras around the two servants. Sharp's is full of wicked glee, laughter roiling under the surface. Jek's, on the other hand, is strange. I'm used to him being cocky, arrogant, full of fire. Now he is lost, and his aura is likewise shrunken, muddy with guilt, with despair.

Then it fades, and the last of my ability to Read with it. The loss is physical, makes me want to curl up and scream. I've so little left, and all I do have is the knowledge that there will be no more – House Mata has seen to it.

"Miss?" says Sharpshins.

"Nothing." My voice sounds distant and snappy. "It was nothing. Get on your way."

The burn of the loss is so bad that it has me on my knees. The thought of having no scriven for the rest of my life swarms around me, pricking my skin with a pain so real that I open my clenched fists expecting to see puffy stings lining my palms as if I've been playing at a childish game of Wasps.

I close my eyes, doubled over the cramp that's starting in my belly. Without scriven, I will be less than nothing.

Thirteen

Singing for the Dead

I'M TRYING TO clean Lammer off me, the stink and sweat. Riam's got me working on my off day. Too many Lams, and not enough of us wrays to go 'round, but she says sweet-sweet that I can take two days off from day-after.

There's no point dressing even though the afternoon's just darkening. I'm more awake, the slowness fading.

A feyn raps on the door, and I open quickly for her.

"There's two, are you up to it?"

I go deeper inside myself, make everything empty. Mother taught me this trick first, then Mal taught me again. It is the only way I know how to not be scared, not be sad, not think at all.

Minutes later, she's back, two Lammers behind her.

"This way," she says.

Their voices are so loud, but I am used to it now, to the noise.

"Come on, Jek. Don't act like a nilly, it's just a bat."

"You're going to do what to a bat? That's – shit, you might as well go catch a street lurcher an do that."

A hard laugh, and the tall Lammer comes in. I recognise his face, he's been here before. I have learned to hate him before, but now I have forgotten, and have to learn again. With him is a shorter Lammer, or something like it. It stinks of Hob. Skin crawling, I don't want it touching me, the filthy Hob. Both of them shine with scriven, so much that I want to vomit. They will touch me with their burning magic.

"Look at it, it's hardly going to hurt you. It's tame; the Splinterfist bats don't bite, they know who's boss."

"Saints. You can have it. There ain't no way I'm touching it."

"Coward," the tall one says as he moves closer; he's already loosening buttons. My legs won't run. Mal told me – you run; they burn you. Dae's face in the fire.

"It's not even a girl."

My voice sounds in the room, small as a wasp. "Sullied."

"What did it just say?" The Hob-stinking one watches me. I can smell its scriven-sharp sweat, the spike of its fear.

I try again, but it has been too long, and I forget what I mean. "Sully the feyns. No Hobs, no Lammers. Don't touch the feyns."

"Jek, you're getting the damn thing worked up. Anyway, there's a kick to it, you'll see."

"What's the kick – it's going to kill me? I'll pass, thanks." The Hob leans back against the wall, crosses his arms, doesn't stop watching me.

"Idiot," says the Lammer. It's already pulled off its necktie, so I turn my head away. Its skin burns me.

Fourteen

The Grinningtommy

I FEEL ODD watching Sharpshins with the skinny little bat. It's not like I've never done the like before; I've plenty of times to my name both with girls an boys – but just not with a Gris-damned bat. I keep seeing flames, remembering the smell of burning skin.

Some of my high has worn down, but there're colours still dance-flickering around the bat even so. Never taken this much scriv, an I'm freaked, just on the edges of a real scriv-high like the Lammers get; perhaps if there was enough of my da's blood in me I'd be just like my half-sisters, all stuck up an mard like them.

I shake my head, an the colours on the bat's skin shiver. I want to reach out an touch them. Candyswirls, sweet as the striped lollies the hawkers sell on the streets.

It's over quickly, an Sharp is pulling away, a wet slap of sound. The bat twists, turns over onto its back, lying there, long strands of pitch hair stuck to its cheeks. It's silent, not sweating, its eyes just slits. Something in that look makes me shiver. I'm all awkward-like now.

Most my experience with boys comes from training under Marlon. It's all prices you gotta pay to learn to run a pack. Under Marlon's wing, I learned every hidey-hole an fencer an all those people that don't ask questions. Course, I also learnt to kneel an everything, but at least it was worth something. I suppose.

"Go on, Jek. You have to feel what it's like," says Sharpshins.

The bat flicks its eyes open, an stares at me proper. There's another lid still over the ball of its eyes – a milky scrap of wet skin. It lifts one hand and wipes the hair back from its face.

I don't want to stare it in the eye, so I find something else to look at. Its skinny feet, white like winter-frost. I shrug, don't uncross my arms. I ain't touching the bat, that's right certain. "Nothing I ain't tried before. Don't see no point in bats." I don't want Sharp to know 'bout the weird colours I'm seeing, but even so, something in me is wanting to touch them, run my fingers through the swirls. May be that he sees them too, but if I say something then I'm going to look like a girl that's just gone an had too much scriv-water and can't hold her drink.

"You don't have to do anything," Sharp says. "Just touch it once, you'll see."

One touch, an then I'm going, then Sharp an I can head on to the Sphynx or summat. I take a step up to the bat an put my hand on its calf. The skin don't feel chalky as it looks, just cool an dry. The colours though, I swear I can feel them. It's like putting your hands in a stream an letting fishlings nibble themselves sated. "Well, fuck me," I say, low.

"You feel that?" Sharps grins. "It gets a hundred times better."

"How come no one don't ever mention it then?" I don't want to take my hand off the bat's leg, just rest my fingers, an watch the colours skitter all over my skin, up my arm.

Sharp looks embarrassed, shrugs. "Not exactly a polite society thing."

Meaning, no Lammer would be caught dead admitting he would even touch a bat, let alone fuck the damned thing.

"Look," Sharps says. "I promised the lads I'd meet them down the Sphynx. I've shown you the whys, so you can make up your own mind, if you want it, but I'm going." He steps into his trousers, pulls on his socks an shoes. I just watch him, deciding. Down to the Sphynx for a pint, or stay here, an see what those candy-colours can do.

"I'll stay," I says an I grin back at him. "First time for everything, I always says."

As soon as he's out the door, I turn back to the bat. It watches me, all expressionless, so I'm kind-of goosed when it speaks again.

"First time?" It's got a raspy voice, like it's been chewing on gravel. Around it, the colours coil an jump. Now that it's talking again I notice its teeth, a row of little white daggers, sharp an shiny.

"With a bat, anyway." I'm not moving. Shite, I paid for this. If I don't do something, then that's more money wasted than I can afford.

It sits up an leans over to me, its fingers flicking my buttons free, an I'm too damn scared to move. I wonder if it can smell the fear like a dog would.

"Shite." I step back, knocking its hand away. "I can undress myself, you damned bugger. I'm not a Hobling." It reminds me too much of being not in control, of belonging to someone else.

It sits back, patient, an don't blink. Finally, when I'm shucked out of my clothes, I step back up to it. The colours shimmy over its skin. I don't even care that Sharps has just done what he's done or nothing; there's this burn in me to feel that dance of colours over my own skin.

There's no way to describe it, it makes a scriv-high seem dirty an sticky, this wash of shivers. My whole world is centred on this, an I forget about Ia for a while.

THE NEXT DAY everything is sunshine an spring, even though winter's biting deep. The world seems brighter.

Sharpshins grins when he sees me in the kitchens, my sleeves rolled up to my elbows, whistling as I scrub dishes an pans. "You have a good time then?"

"May be that I did." I'm about to say more when that fat cunt that runs the kitchen comes storming in like he's never been laid in his life. Now, I know it ain't true, 'cause I ain't stupid, an I see the looks an touches that Sharpshins thinks he's hiding. An you'd have to be an idiot not to notice the other little things, like easy jobs an better food, that old Sharps always seems to get.

"Look here, Hob," Dray shouts, loud enough that the pots rattle on the wooden shelves. "Why are these potatoes not peeled yet?" He clouts me across the head, an I say nothing even though for a moment I'm dizzy an the light's too bright.

The potatoes are waiting an so are the dishes. I've learned not to argue with him; there's no point – it just makes things worse. Anyway, half the time I don't even know what's going on because my head is crammed too full of letters an learning.

"I'll get on them now," I says, an scrub the last gunked-up crap off the bottom of a pan someone, probably Sharps – since it was his work – didn't bother to clean last night.

"That you will," Dray says, but my answer seems to have knocked all the air out of him, so he goes off to shout at some other poor Hob.

Today I'm worse than normal, cause there's more than just letters in my head. I'm thinking about that bat, the magic under his skin. His name is Sel. I asked the bat at the front an she told me, although she was kinda suspicious about the whole deal.

"Jek!" Dray roars, an I peel a good chunk of skin off my finger. Fuck's sake, what's the old bastard decided I've done now?

He doesn't knock me about the head this time though, just looks at me all nervous-like, sweat slick on his brow an staining his shirt. "Your father wants to see you." He's close to civil. That has me worried.

"Now?" I drop the peeler-blade an pull the loose skin off my finger. The way things are going with me an peeling, there's probably more me than potatoes in the mash these days.

The politeness don't last long, too against Dray's nature. "Yes, now, you goat-spawned Hob. Get up there and find out what it is he wants right sharp and then get back down here. These things won't peel them-fucking-selves!"

I'm walking out the black wood kitchen doors when a rag hits the back of my head.

"And clean your damn self, boy! You want to go talk to your father looking you've just been dug out of a potato heap?"

I wipe the worst of the grit off my hands an face, an toss the rag to where Sharps is standing, his cleaver poised over a split goose.

He catches it with his free hand an gives me a salute with the filthy thing. "Come back alive, you hear. You still owe me a pint."

The door to my da's study is closed. The wood is polished an waxed by years of servants. It strikes me, Prue could have stood here, right where I am now, with a duster in her hand, an wiped away fingerprints. Made the wood gleam. Caught my da's eye and fancied herself sweet enough to catch the House heir.

Or maybe it was love – I sure as shite don't know what that's supposed to look like.

The door swings back, an I jump like a spooked nilly.

"What are you waiting out here for, boy? Why didn't you knock?" My da's face looms down at me. May be that this is how they met, between rooms.

Inside the study the whole little family is waiting, an I'm not quite ready for that yet. My heart is just about up in my throat when I see Ia's neck, the side of her cheek. I make myself think about yesterday with the bat instead. Candy-colours. Magic-shivers. I can just about do it – focus all my thoughts on the way the bat looked at me afterwards, like I weren't really there.

Ia keeps her face turned so that she don't have to see me, her eyes focused on nothing at all.

It strikes me hard then, that they're two of a kind. Caught up in whatever games their families had planned for them an both of them wishing they was someplace else. Maybe that the bat – Sel – was born to his trade, same way Iliana was born to hers. It makes me feel all sudden-sad. Ia's head drops lower, like she can feel the weight of my thoughts in the room. Her mother – that old cat – has one hand on her shoulder, the nails digging through Ia's heavy winter dress.

That sneaking little brat Calissa is sitting in one of the leather chairs, leaning back an watching me with that hooded look she has an smiling all wicked-like.

"Right," says my father, as he takes his place behind his desk. There are reams of papers waiting, an he slaps one hand on the pile. "Trone tells me you're not bad with the basics, that you can at the very least sign your own name."

I can do a fair bit more than that these days, but I nod. Ives Jek. Trone's drummed it into me. There's to be no more Grinningtommys in this house. Stupid Lams. Grinningtommy is as good an strong a name as ever passed down through the Wend. Older even than Pelim, if you believe the way old women prattle.

"What's this all about?" the wife snaps. She don't like asking this. It comes out of her snarled as the iron wire they use to keep the nillies out of the Irthe groves.

"I've made a decision." My father doesn't look at her as he speaks, but catches my eyes instead. "As my only son, I'm making Jek the official Ives heir."

All thoughts of Sel and Ia an names are knocked clean out of my head.

Ia presses one hand over her mouth to stop the choking sound she's making.

"You can't do that," says her mother, all high an breathy, like she's been punched in the gut. Course, he can, an all 'cause Lams have this daft idea that it's the sires who are stronger, an that the women are all too feeble-minded to run a House. Which just goes to show that they ain't never set foot in the Low-Walk spinningjenny compound – those girls scare even me.

In her chair, calm an sly, Calissa says nothing.

"Of course I can." My father pushes a bottle of ink across the table, an holds out a fine cut pen. He slaps the papers again. "I've marked all the places where you need to sign. Mirian –" He stares across at his wife, who's thin-lipped an white as a bat. "You will witness."

An Ia finally looks at me as I scratch my name across those papers an take away everything that was once hers.

Fifteen

A Game of Wasps

THE LOOK ON Illy's face speaks for all of us. I'm shocked, of course. And it means I'll have to rethink my plans about pinning that scriven theft on Jek. If I do something that harms him and my father finds out – well, he's quick to temper and slow to forgiveness.

Mother jabs her name on the parchment, next to where Jek has signed. There's only the scratch of the nib on paper, the crackle of pages. It's so quiet. Outside, the whispering dry branches are hushed, expectant.

"There." Mother slams down the quill. "Now, if I have your leave?" She doesn't wait for his response, merely marches to the door, dragging Illy behind her like she is nothing more than a recalcitrant child.

Father pushes one hand through the thinning hair at his temples. "You understand all of this?"

Jek half-nods, then shakes his head. "You've made me heir?" And his tone is: What exactly do I get out of this, and why? He has a right to be suspicious, for my father does nothing without reason.

"You're my son, the only one who can carry on the Ives name," Father says. "We were once one of the greatest Houses in the city, and I won't have our name fade."

There must be more to it, and I wonder what it is he's heard in the Mata palace that I haven't.

"So you're desperate enough to have a bastard carry your name?"

I smother my grin. Jek has no trouble asking the questions that most people are too afraid to voice.

Father must catch my look because he frowns at me then unexpectedly, he laughs. "Well. You certainly have a way with your words." He sobers. "Your mother was like that too – not one to hide what she thought."

And we're back to his long-lost love. I roll my eyes and slip down from the chair. I don't need to be here anyway, to see just how easily the women in our family are cast aside. Even for a bastard.

"Calla."

I pause, because my father never calls me that these days. He stopped when I turned eight, almost half a lifetime ago. It's a painful name, a name redolent with evenings sitting on his lap, reading together about the nillies, while he told me of the sires and dams, explaining breeding programmes. He smelled of vai and scriv and pipe tobacco, sweet and sharp and musty and smoky.

It's all he needs to say to let me know how much he loves me. There's so much packed into that one name – his apologies, his respect for me, his knowledge that for all her magical power, I'm stronger than my sister. Strong enough to choose my own path instead of letting myself be yoked to the Visions of Saints.

With one hand on the doorknob, I look at that office properly – see Jek hiding confusion, resentment and relief. My father smiling sadly. He wished I'd been born a boy, I know that. His smile is full of *if only*.

"Goodnight, Father." I turn the knob, cold brass sticking to my skin. "Jek, congratulations." *You've won*, I don't say, because I don't even think he knew there was a battle.

For one painful moment, I lean my back to the closed door and tilt my head up. The ceiling is yellowed with shadow, and I feel like any moment now I could just sink into the house, become part of the walls and floors.

I need a high. Something to tie me closer to reality. My own stores are thin, but I don't want to risk taking from my mother so soon after Jek's little theft – the way my luck is turning I'd be caught and blamed for both. I stamp down the halls, my toes scudding against the patterns of leaves. It's always possible that Illy has some left.

The house changes in tone as I near her room, my fingers trembling against the walls. Mother's voice shrills down the passage, and distantly as the sea, Illy murmurs back.

Like a statue in one of the palace gardens, I stand at my sister's door listening to the ebb and flow of their voices as they argue, as they blame each other for my father's stupidity.

"You knew," Illy says.

"Not about this – not that he'd take it so far."

"You should have tried for more children – for a son –"

"Don't you dare tell me how I should have conducted my marriage!"

"What did you think to gain, by not having sons?"

"I thought that – I'd hoped,} my mother's voice rolls, dips and drops, "I hoped he would have bucked Lammic tradition and named you heir. That Calissa would have –"

Iliana's voice rises, a wave against the cliff. "You should have done what you were supposed to do – breed good little Ives brats – that's all you are, a brood-doe. You've no Visions worth –"

A slap. Such a sharp and ugly sound, skin on skin.

In the silence that follows, I raise my hand and rap softly on the old wood. When no one answers, I push the door enough to peer into the room. "May I?"

"Oh do come in," Illy spits. There's a red mark like a brand across her right cheek. "At least this way we know exactly what it is you're over-hearing."

There's no point in acknowledging the little dig, so I merely slip into the room.

Illy turns her back and goes to sit at her wide dressing table. She pulls the clips from her hair, laying them in neat rows on the white polished wood. Her hand doesn't shake, and she takes an ivory-backed brush and begins to brush out her hair so that it flows like a pale sunlight stream across her shoulder. She's wearing a dress of sap-green silk, and the wide sleeves crinkle and shimmer as her hand moves.

In her reflection, the red mark is slowly fading. "What do we do now?" she says, her voice dull.

My mother, who is still standing with one hand held out, looks down at her out-stretched palm in confusion, as if it were something she has never before seen, some strange appendage sewn onto her body, one over which she has no control. "We have plenty to do." Her voice is very false and bright. I am reminded of a caged bird that sings for other people's pleasure. "We have a wedding to prepare for, your father told me. He's making the last arrangements with the Mata." She clasps her hands together. For the first time, I notice pale spots on her hands, how haggard the ridges of tendons and bones make her look. My mother is getting old.

Illy says nothing as she watches herself smoothing the brush through her hair.

"Come, Calissa, perhaps you have some ideas?" My mother turns to me.

"Oh, yes. Ask Calissa." Illy drops the brush and twists in her seat so she can stare at me. "I'm certain she would love some input into my marriage to Trey."

"Illy –" I don't want to talk about this now, not with Mother standing witness, but I am open now to her attack, vulnerable as a windle moth in the first claws of frost. And my sister knows it.

She presses in. "Hmm, Calissa, dearest? What do you think – a traditional wedding, yellows? Or perhaps something more modern? After all, yellow would clash dreadfully with that Mata red hair."

"Girls!"

And so we are reminded of our place.

"Get out of my room," Iliana says to me, although there's no spite in it, just a bone-weariness as if she were sick of the very sight of me.

"Why are you angry with me?" I pause with my hand at the doorknob. "It isn't me who made Father decide that the Hob is worth more than you."

Illy lunges towards me, and it's such a moment of honest hatred that I wish with all my heart that I was high now, to see all the things she has been trying to hide from me. She spins as my mother catches at her arm, and collapses against my mother's chest, her face hidden by her golden hair.

"Get out," says my mother over Iliana's head. She has one hand in my sister's hair, stroking her.

A gasping sob shudders through Illy as I shut the door.

Reckless anger folds me in its embrace, and I march to my mother's rooms. I don't care if she finds me out. If I can't have my mother's love, I'll take what I need.

Her scriven supply is low. I tear a sheet of expensive hand-pressed paper in half, making no attempt at subtlety, and scoop several powder-spoons' worth of the scriven into the centre of the torn paper, before folding it away and shoving my bounty deep into a jacket pocket. Let Mother go beg more from my father if she wishes.

Let her sell Illy into marriage with my Trey in exchange for some magic.

With my stolen scriven like a lit coal in my silk jacket, I storm down the back stairs and burst into the kitchen yard.

There's no laundry up. The servants have already bundled up the starched dry sheets, taken them in. Overhead the sky is the cold clear blue of winter. Iliana's wedding will come in the months before Long Night. Inauspicious indeed.

There's a little wooden stool by the back entrance of the kitchen where I sit and breathe in the sharp bitter smell of the last herbs still thriving in the stone herb spiral. Fingers shaking, I draw the paper from my pocket and carefully unfold it on my knees. A brief gust tugs at the ragged edges of the paper, making it flutter. A few grains of scriven spiral up, and I lean forward, hand curling around my magic, protecting it.

A pinch of scriv will have to do, I sniff it, indelicately, and fold the paper closed. Out here in the sunshine I will wait for the magic to hit me; I close my eyes and try to let everything go.

Sixteen

The Grinningtommy

MY DA WAITS 'til Calissa leaves then turns back to me, the lines on his face all deep an serious-like.

"There are stipulations, of course," he says. "You'll only have full access to Ives's funds on your twentieth birthday, and the title relies on you providing an heir." His face is sweaty, eyes shining.

Sad thing is, he wants this so damn much, an I've never even given a thought to Hoblings. That were always just something that you expected the girls to take care of, with their jenny-herbs an seeds. I wonder if my da's already picked out some Lammer girl for me, a girl to carry an Ives in her belly. From what I've seen, he's trying to strengthen his ties to the other High Houses. I don't know nothing about nothing when it comes to that. The little rat Calissa might; she's the type who can spout useless shit about numbers an Houses an who owns what. Sad way to spend a life, if you ask me.

"Yeah," says I. "I understand all that." I lean back 'gainst the wall, arms crossed. There's more, I can see by the set of his face, an I raise one eyebrow.

"As my heir, you'll no longer be working and living as a servant." He tries for an easy grin, but it comes out all strained an tight. "There's a suite of rooms being made ready for you, in the east wing. On Monday we'll have a tailor come around and measure you." He looks at my current set of hand-me-downs. "Can't have you walking around in those old rags. Haven't seen them in many years – didn't even know that Trone kept them." His mood changes, an he pushes that sappy look from his eyes as he stands. "Well." He thumps a clear crystal container of vai onto the table, and two square cut glasses. "A drink to seal it then, my boy."

I'm not your boy, I thinks, but I'm far from dumb enough to say so out loud. Instead, I take my glass an raise it like a toast, like the scrivvers do when an old friend walks into the Hole. The vai goes down all choky, full of sour scriv, an burns my stomach.

I'm supposed to go back to the kitchens, if this had been a normal day an all. Somehow, I don't think nothing's going to stay that way now that my da's gone and made me his official bloody buggery heir. No one's told me where I'm supposed to be, or what I should be doing now, so I take the chance to run.

I'm out down Ives Hill and through the posh roads, almost to the Casabi before I think about what it is I'm running from.

Ia. My da. Fucking Ives. I'm no more fit to be taking over that House than a goat is to be a Saint. An my da should know it. Those House women are going to tear me apart in their little cat ways, an before I know it I'm going to be as good as a mouse-pet, crippled and blinded.

Shit. I stop running. From here, I can just make out the largest of the Seven Widows. Saint Aster – the first bell you see if you're coming up-river from Pelimburg. Just past that, the Wend and Digs.

Oncle.

I din't cry when Prue went, an I'm not gonna go soft now, even though thinking about Oncle makes my whole insides go frost-sharp an splintery . There's no chance the old bugger thought this would happen to me, 'course, but I know why he sold me on to House Ives. How was a Hob like him supposed to go 'gainst Lammer Law? With Prue dead, there was nowt he could do or say. Even if I was a Grinningtommy. Besides, there's only Hobs who care or remember about Grinningtommys now, an about how we're once the ones who were meant to keep the Well and all the magic that came from it. Lammers went an fucked that up too, of course. Can't trust them with nothing.

So, for sure, I'm not angry no more. Truth be told, I miss Oncle something fierce, an with things going the way they were when I left,

Saints only know if he's still right as rain.

It's a full day's walk out to the Lam heaps, but I hitch myself a ride on a passing cart, an I'm there before the sun is at full peak.

I don't quite make it past the first heaps, though. I'm walking a little dirt track that winds twixt the stinking mountains of midden and refuse, when I turn a corner and three Hobs with sharpened sticks just about walk right into me.

"Fucking Lam," says the first, an lowers his reed-spear. He's no one I recognise, an that ain't good news. Means if he's pack, he ain't one of mine.

I raise my hands, an take a backward step, all mild-like. "Hey to you too," I says. "An just might who you be calling a Lammer, you chancing wanker?"

"Well now," says the darkest one, an smiles in a way I don't right like. "Would you look here. It's Jek Grinningtommy, all tarted up an lost as a nilly, seems."

"That's never Jek," says the first. He peers. "Well shit me, so it is." He grins like the other. "I know someone who'd be dying to have a word with you, master Jek."

Arse an buggery. Marlon.

An if they get me to Marlon, I am one fucking dead Hob. There's no chance of my old pack coming to get me free from him, not when as far as they know, I upped an left them stranded as fish.

If I run, they'll have me down with those spears before I get ten paces. An if they don't, they'll holler for the rest of their pack to chase me down. I won't make it back to MallenIve proper, that much I'm sure of.

There's coin in my pocket. Enough to bribe them.

Of course, the little buggers will most likely take the bribe, let me go, an then when I'm not looking, they'll slit my throat an have the rest off me. No word will get back to Marlon. You can't push pack loyalty that far. I grin, an drop one hand to my pocket. The other I loosen, relaxed, ready. No point making them suspicious now.

"Look here," I says. "Seems I've no desire to chat with my old chum, so how about we come to a working solution." I pull out a handful of brass, an the Hobs lower their spears an step closer.

Fucking idiots.

I LEAVE THE three of them in the heaps. One with enough cracked ribs to have him walking double for weeks, an the other with very little chance of siring Hoblings. The third one might be dead. Still an all, he caught me a right nasty blow with a brass knife before I kicked his head in. With my shirt torn an wrapped round the cut, I hold my arm close to my chest an limp back towards MallenIve. There's also going to be a bruise on my shank, an no doubting that. Bastard feels like he cracked bone. Din't help none that he was wearing solid leather boots – a rare enough luxury here. My guess is he was Marlon's new second. Makes me feel close to sorry for the poor bastard.

So there's no way for me to get a message to Oncle, or to find out what's happened to him. An there ain't no way I'm limping back to the Ives House an facing that pack of she-goats.

There's the Sphynx, I suppose. I could go drown my sorrows there.

But then I'll think about Ia.

Same with the Greenfinch. Shite. It's not like I know any other places. 'Cepting for the bat rookery out in Splinterfist ward.

I jangle the brass in my pocket an think while the cart I've taken thumps and rattles closer to MallenIve.

My thinking leads me down a wide white road, in a place all quiet an still, right to the steps of the Splinterfist whorehouse. Or rookery, whatever they call the damn place.

The girl-bat inside looks at me all funny when I ask for the bat from last time.

"You're quite certain you want Sel?" she says in a way that makes me seem like I'm full of pervery.

"There summat wrong with him?" I ask back.

"Well, no." She goes all flustered an saves her face by taking my coin an sending me on my way.

Outside the door, I suddenly wonder if this is the best idea I've had. I'm feeling like shit, my arm an leg are both aching something vicious, an really, all I'm still trying to do is drown my thoughts of Ia in anything I can. Then I remember the way that bat magic made me feel – clean an right for the first time in my life, an I push open the door.

I'm pretty sure it's the same bat – he's smaller than some of the others I seen in the streets, an he looks at me in a blank still way that makes me think he doesn't even actually see me proper-like.

"Sel?" I say, an he squints, extra eyelids flickering shut.

He nods, slow, confused. "I remember you. Came here with the tall Lammer."

"Yeah, that's right."

"You were scared."

"Was not."

The bat flicks its eyes open and stares at me. Indigo eyes. They remind me of the colour of the sky before twilight takes full hold. "You're scared now," it points out.

"An you're not a very good whore. Insulting a customer's gotta be pretty low on the list of things you should be doing." I take off my jacket, all careful-like to not scrape the strip of cloth off my cut arm. "Is this why that girl downstairs tried to talk me out of seeing you?"

He sits up, interested for the first time. "Did she? You smell like blood."

Real fear grabs me tight, not this silly nilly-nervousness that's been rattling about my bones. "Hey now," I say, an back up to the door, my coat-sleeves still half on my arms. "There's laws against that kinda thing – I know – saw one of your kind burned at a stake for feeding off Hobs."

The indigo eyes go white as he drops the lids again an pulls back, face all twisted an sad an scared.

Summat about it strikes hard – I've felt like that – felt like that most of my Gris-damned life, just I always knew to cover it up. It don't do to show people your weaknesses.

Then his face changes an goes all blank an smooth again. "You're wasting time," he says, very soft.

I can't see the colours on his skin this time, but when I strip off the last of my clothes an lay down next to him, there's no mistaking the spinning feel of his magic shivering bright against me. I want to taste it, lick it off his skin like water. The whole world stops mattering, an I lose myself in bat-magic.

There's nothing in my life good as this, this silvery chalk smell of bat, like ash an dust, an the thrum of magic all round us, shrouding us tighter together.

In a way it's better like this, without the distraction of scriv. Something about it feels more in place, like I'm closer to touching his magic an pulling it right deep into me, making it mine. I stroke my fingers down the white skin an feel like I'm where I'm meant to be for the first time in my life.

Being with Sel is like waking in a dream an waiting for your mind to catch up with your body. It's an inbetween realness, too good to last.

Afterwards, he tells me that he likes the way I don't smell of scriv today.

"Really?" I button up my shirt. There's blood staining the binding on my shoulder, an he keeps flicking his gaze all nervous an quick towards it. I cover it up fast, now that the high is fading. All my fear is coming back, making me feel a little sick. Only – already I'm planning on getting more money from Trone, an coming here again. "You don't like the smell of scriv?"

Sel shakes his head, an looks at his hands, spreading thin fingers on the sheets.

"Don't worry," I say to him, feeling lost an stupid. "Next time, I won't drink vai or nothing."

He looks up an half-smiles. "What do I call you?" he says.

"Jek," I say, an I find myself laughing, wanting to stretch out my hand, an shake his like we was two Houses sealing a deal. "That'll do."

I walk out with the last of the high singing through me an making everything clearer and colder an brighter.

Oncle will be all right. An so will I. We're Hobs, an we don't stay down when we fall – we get up an fight again, fight until we're dead.

I gear myself up to face the House women an know right as rain that I'll have no problems taking them on. Let them play their little House games. I've no time for backstabbing an dancing.

I'm going to play too, but on my own fucking terms.

Jek's rules, not theirs.

Seventeen

Singing for the Dead

HE'S JEK. NOT a Lammer, nor a Hob. Some creature between the two. I have a name now, and it rolls strange on my tongue.

"Jek," I say to the room.

It doesn't answer.

I stand up. Wash. Dress. Remember to walk. To do everything expected. The feyn at the door stops me, so I look at the floor.

"Got yourself a little an admirer," she says. "Takes all sorts, I suppose."

I don't understand, and I wait to see what she wants me to say.

"Alerion's tits, you really are a lost cause. The Hob," she says, "it asked for you – by name and all." She steps closer. I shuffle back, keep watching the golden wood floor. I am blurred in the shine of polish.

"Just watch yourself," she says and sighs loudly. "You can use them, but you can't trust them, you know."

She doesn't make sense, talking about using – what would I want a Hob for? I shake my head.

"Damned wray. Don't know why I bother. Go ask Mal to tell you what happens to wrays here, and how they get free." She walks away back to her desk empire, and I think I am released. I turn and run out a side door, through the streets back to Mal.

He's not here, so I wait for a long time, I try be a shadow and fade into his walls, sit still and shrink in among the dark corners until his door opens.

"Shit!"

I raise my palms. Somehow show him that I am safe.

"You gave me a turn there, Sel. What are you doing lurking in my room anyway?" He's tired; I can hear edges of pain too. He throws his jacket down next to me, doesn't sit.

"Sel?"

I shake my head. "Sit. Please?"

He stretches out next to me on the bed, moving slow as old men. Can smell the hurt now, this close. It tastes like ash on my tongue. We say nothing, until he sighs and rises. He lights lamps so that the grey room goes golden.

"This is getting tiring," he says. "If you're not going to tell me what it you want, and you insist on hanging around here, then you can lend me a hand." He pulls his shirt over his head and turns his back to me. "I can get to the stuff on my arms, but the back's the worst. Cream's in the top drawer." He nods at the little wooden desk.

Vai-rash. I know how it itches. Burrows deep under skin. Stupid Lammers stinking of it, burning with it. My own skin echo-itches, just from seeing the weals.

When I take the cream, and my face is hidden, I ask, "You're to tell me." Fingers in cold cream, spreading cold across the burn. He flinches.

"Tell you what?"

"What happens to us."

"Oh." He leans back, knots unravelling. "You work, and if you're lucky you earn enough money to leave before you're demoted to nothing more than toilet scrubbing. Once you get to that point, you're lost. There's no way to earn enough then."

I smooth my hands down his skin, shift closer.

He makes a sound like a laugh. "Of course, freedom's a relative term. Free wrays are free to work. And all that means is they're free to starve. No one in this fucking Lammer hole will take one of us on."

I run my thumbs down the sides of the backbone and watch the way flesh dents, comes back.

"Sel," he says, after the silence has spun cocoons around us. He takes my hand and pulls it forward, wrapping my arm around his chest. "Don't listen to anyone who tells you that the vampires can be free. It's a lie Riam tells to keep you working, to keep you from slitting your own throat on bad days."

"Someone knows my name." I rush the words out, scared if I take too long I'll lose them. "Asks for me."

"Really?" He has to push the words past his teeth, and his hand goes tighter on my arm. "And you think you're going to get out that way?"

I don't understand why he's angry. Relax, put my other arm around him, hold on and wait.

"I don't think snagging yourself a Lammer-ticket out of here is in your future –"

"Tell me."

"It's supposed to be a quick way to get out." He lets go, slides his hand down, fingers stroking my wrist. "You find a rich Lammer, and you bond to him. Use MallenIve law to your own ends."

Senseless. I make a sound, but it is not the right one.

"Not many have gone that path, though. Last one from Splinterfist was a wray called Isidro, years ago. Prettiest fucking wray ever, and cocky enough that he set himself a line for some high House Lammer and reeled him in like a fish."

"What happened?"

I feel him shrug, feel his fingers' slow crawl up my arm. "He left. He got his Lammer, and he left."

"Would you?"

"Now, Sel, why would I sell myself out like that?" Mal turns. Gold light makes his grey eyes amber. He pulls me closer, kisses the side of my mouth. "I need freedom on my own terms."

So I close my eyes, listen to my breathing, a hitch. Is this what the feyn meant?

"Don't get tricked," he says. "It's about as much freedom as this is, a prettier cage, maybe, and you won't starve, but there's fuck-all dignity to a choice like that. Don't think about it."

Mal's kisses taste scared.

Eighteen

The Grinningtommy

THE PROBLEM WITH my new rooms is that now I'm right in the thick of the wyrm's nest.

Ia is half a hallway away from me, an it's awkward as anything trying to avoid her. I've become worse than a Hob with a pack-hunt on his head, always sneaking about an peering this way an that. It don't help none that my da's gone an got this fool idea that I should join the rest of the family at their evening meal. After the first one – Ia shooting looks at me across the silverware like this whole damn fuck-up was my fault, I was ready to go an hide in my old room I shared with Sharps.

After four days of this, I'm steeled to do just that, an I don't care what old Sharps has to say about it. Hopefully, none of them will think to go looking for me in a servant's quarter.

"And where, exactly, were you off to?"

Trone. I don't know how he does it, the sneaky bastard.

"Weren't going nowhere."

"Dinner is in only a few minutes, and you were planning to attend dressed like you'd just been picked out of the Lam-heaps?"

Idiot Lammers. My clothes aren't half bad now, an still they want me to get tarted up every single night just to eat that fancy crap they call food – it's just not right.

Mostly, I miss flat bread filled with fried onion an peaches an tomatoes an scallions. Instead they serve asparagus an tasteless crap like that. An I get to swallow it all down with Ia staring at me like I just rolled out of a gutter. Not the most fun a body can have in MallenIve. I've better things to do than waste time with them.

"Really, Jek." Trone sighs. "Just go down and eat. You have to get used to this at some point. None of it is going away."

It's pretty sad when Trone's become my closest chum in House Ives. Not that that's saying much. Between Ia an Calissa an the Ives head-bitch, well, even Trone's snotty manner seems friendly.

"Yeah," I says, an turn around on the stairs an tramp down to where the rest of them are waiting, turned out in all their flash clothes.

"And please refrain from using the back stairs," Trone calls after me.

I pass the kitchens, catch a glimpse of Dray sweating in his greasy grey apron, an hurry through to the dining room doors.

"Oh the servants' entrance," Ia says as I step in. "How very appropriate." She's bright an brittle, smiling at me so that her eye-teeth show.

"Illy," warns my da through gritted teeth, an then nods at me to sit.

I'm opposite Ia, thanks to this whole weird ranking thing they've got going here. It's a House thing, Trone says; where you sit shows how important you are. An the chair I'm in now used to be Ia's.

We settle into our places, no one saying a word as low-Lams come in an dish up boiled meat an vegetables an thankfully, boats of sauce to cover it all up. Except for the chink of knives on the dishes, there's no sound – everyone chewing as an excuse not to talk.

My da clears his throat, puts his knife an fork down. "I'm afraid I've been called back to the palace."

"Oh." Lady Mirian goes still. "So soon?" Her eyes are wide-like, an I don't need no Lammer magic to see she's frightened.

"Word from Pelimburg is they've definitely seen Mekekana ships. They're coming up along the Beren coast, heading for MallenIve."

"Please," she says. "Pelimburg." She makes the name sound like a spat-out fish bone. "They've not a Saint or Reader worth even half of ours. I don't even know why we still trade them scriven." She cuts into her thin pink meat, jabs at it with her fork.

98

"I shouldn't worry about that these days," my da says. "The Mata have put an embargo on all scriven trade. The announcement will go out tomorrow morning." He chews a mouthful of food. "And Blaine seems to share your opinion. He's sent some of his own Readers down to Pelimburg to see if they can pick anything up. Of course, I'm inclined to believe Pelimburg."

"Why?" For a moment Ia looks a little like the chit I met down the Sphynx, not like this cold, masked Ives princess she plays here on her home turf. She's got fire in her, hidden deep under the layers of House polish.

My chest goes hot an cold, an I look away from her.

"They've no reason to lie to us." My da crosses his cutlery over his unfinished food an leans back in his chair. "Blaine's worried, and that makes me worried. I've spoken to Trone – he's ready to move the family through to the palace grounds should I give the word –"

"Oh that's hardly necessary, is it," the lady says. "A few ships make it past Pelimburg, past the desert, so what? We've dealt with these little excursions of theirs before." Her cutlery is chinking as her hands shake.

"Not without scriven, we haven't. There's only one of the Deeps still producing. And a bare trickle at that."

Everyone's quiet-like, shocked. It's still enough that I can hear the servers breathing. They're watching from the wall, taking all the gossip in to spread through the back stairs warrens.

Lammers an their damn obsession with scriv. It makes sense now. I wasn't more than a Hobling the last time the Mekekana came to Oreyn, an I remember nothing more about it 'cepting that everyone got drunk, an they burnt the Lam-heaps early that year instead of waiting for Long Night. Don't even think their ships got nowhere close to MallenIve that time.

"We must be prepared," says my da. "I didn't tell you to frighten you, but so that you would understand. I've no idea how long those veins will keep us supplied with scriven."

Ia shoves up from the table an slams out the room without a by-your-leave, an I can't stop myself from watching her go. Sometimes I wish there was away for me to go back to the start an do everything proper-like. Or that she was never my sister. Half-sister.

Calissa pushes her plate away with one finger. "No scriven. How are you and the other War-singers planning to hold MallenIve?"

"There's scriven allotted for any upcoming military needs."

"And for the rest of us?" Her voice is flat, like she already knows that answer.

He don't want to say it, it's clear. "Nothing. There's nothing."

I don't need to sit around here listening to the Lammers feeling all sorry for themselves, so I shove my chair back an stand. "I'm going out," I says, to the room at large an no body in particular.

"Again?" snarls Calissa. "Already ploughing through the family vaults, are we?"

Best to ignore the little cow, but I can't help slip her a sly wink an a grin. "May be," I says to her, real low, before I walk out the door an into the night, leaving all my thoughts about Ia behind me. I've got something to bury them under, right enough.

I HAVE TO run to make it before Sel's shift ends. I flip the feyn at the whorehouse desk a few bits of brass, an she nods me upstairs. What's scriv to me, when I got Sel an the magic under his skin?

Sel's sitting on the edge of his bed, knees close together, shoulders hunched over. He doesn't look up when I come in, just says "Jek." His voice is all raspy an thick, an for a moment I think he's been crying or something daft like that. Then he coughs.

The sound make me freeze, makes my heart beat out of rhythm. "You dying of the lung?"

He looks up then, an I can just 'bout read his expression well enough to know he's thinking I'm an idiot Hob.

"No," he says. "Think I caught cold."

"Oh." I stand all awkward an wrap my arms tight about my chest. I don't like sickness much. "My mam, Prue, she used to make me mint-tea an lemon when I caught cold." I stare at Sel; it's kinda hard to tell if the bat is real sick, he don't flush like a Hob does, but his skin does look all sweaty-like. Truth is, I din't even know bats could catch cold like us. I stare at him. He's looking all sorry for hisself, just like any sick person would.

If you don't pay no mind to the skin that's just about the same colour as the chalk sticks that come from Pelimburg, or the extra eye-lid, you could pretend he was just a low-Lammer or a half-breed. Even the slant-eyes aren't that bad; most Hobs got eyes close to that shape.

"May be you should head on home," I says. "Get someone to make you some tea."

He nods so that his black hair falls 'fore his face, hiding one cheek. "With honey."

"Well ain't you the lucky bastard," I jokes. "Honey in your tea, I din't even taste honey 'fore I came to MallenIve – liquid scriv."

He stands up, frowning. "No scriv in honey," he whispers as he crosses the room to pull a robe from the behind the little carved room divider.

"It's a saying, you daft bat. Means it's costly." I can't help watching him pull the robe on over his shoulders. There's a mole in the small of his back, just a little to the left, an it's the only mark on his skin. I know that mole so well now, an now that it's covered away, it's like I know a secret about Sel.

'Course, I ain't the only one.

The robe he's wearing is raw, undyed silk, an the faint musk smell of it makes me think of sitting by the irthe groves, watching the windle-workers pull the cocoons from the trees under the flapping tents.

"You've already paid," says Sel.

True, but it seems pretty meaningless right now. "I'll let you make it up to me some other day," I says, grinning. Sel don't smile back, but he makes a sound like a choked-up laugh as he sits back down on the bed.

"You're sure?" His knees are too knobbly, too big, an I wonder if one day the bat's going to grow into them. He's twisting his hands in his lap, then coughs again, the sound dry an rough.

Before I know what I'm doing I grab his one hand free an pull it close, just long enough to kiss the palm, the way Hobs do.

"Get better right-quick," I says, as I run for the door, my face flaming.

WEEKS PASS, AND mostly I spend my free time, what little they let me, at the Splinterfist. I don't want to go to any of the bars around MallenIve, don't want to see people who might know my face, know my secrets.

At night I dream about Sel, about magic and the taste of his skin. It's like being caught up in a word that's not real, a world that don't really exist outside of my own head. It's going to fuck me over, sooner or later. I know it, but I don't right care. There's little enough good in my life right now, and being with self is better than thinking on all the shite.

Now that I'm no servant, mt time is all taken up with lessons on how to be a little Lammer lordling. No more working in the kitchens or sharing that stinking little room with Sharps; instead I spend most of my day shut away in Trone's little office. He's on a drive, drumming all kinds of nonsense into my skull.

"You need to know this," he says, when I push away another long list of breeding programmes an nilly-fucking-strains an birth-deformities.

"What I need is a break before my Gris-damned head explodes." I shove the book away, magical formulas blurring into just so much rubbish on the page. "I don't give a shite which nillies produce the strongest-horned kids. It's not like I can use magic anyway."

"Your family's fortune rests on those." Trone taps the breeding programmes with one gnarled finger. "Jek," he says, an closes the book careful-like, slipping a pied feather in place as a bookmark. "You're right. You need a break." He pinches the bridge of his nose, all quiet for a moment, like he's got a bad head starting. I wait until he looks up again. "More importantly, I need a break." He fishes in his pockets for a few coins and hands them to me. "Your father has given me some more money for you to use. Go out, get out of this house for a bit, clear your head. We'll carry on with this tomorrow."

The day is clear, not even midday, and I feel right weird about slipping into the kitchens to grab a bite of bread or cheese, seeing Sharps an the others looking at me like a traitor or something, so I head out into the streets, my hand tight around the money in my pocket.

The Ives house doesn't get a second look from me, as I turn down streets I've come to know as well as I know the dirt tracks down the Low-Walk.

One thing I do know for sure, is exactly where I'm heading now.

Ever since that day that I first met Sel, it's just about all I think about. An it's been a good way of making me not think about Ia, or about anything like what we did. Sel is... Sel's a distraction. He's my scriv-high, my cold bitter at the end of the day, my easy fuck.

The doors to the Splinterfist Rookery are shut, like always, but I push them an they swing open, easy an quiet. The inside is warm from fires in the grates. There's a feyn behind the counter, an I actually recognise her. I'm learning the right words: feyn means a girl bat, an wray a boy, there's some kind of power balance, where the feyns have more freedom than the others, but Sel won't tell me much, says he don't right know hisself.

I always thought bats all look the same – all I ever see is that white skin an dark hair, deep blue eyes, but I'm getting to tell them apart now. This one's name is Vira, an she kinda smiles when she sees me, though she's still frowning. I hope Sel's not gone an caught sick again.

"Oh," she says, an glances down at her book. "Sel's with someone now..." That nervous smile spreads wider. "You could always go with Mal. He's very good."

"I'll wait."

Vira drops her smile right quick at that. "Are you quite certain another wray won't suffice?" She doesn't want me hanging around, I can tell, but it's not really like I give a shite about that. I want to see Sel.

My skin itches. I've never thought about how many other people Sel touches in a day. I mean, 'course I know he does, an it's probably just been Hob-luck that every time I come here he's been free. But now, right now, someone else is touching my bat, an the thought makes me irritable, nervous, my throat an chest too tight.

Fuck me, Jek, you're jealous.

Fifteen minutes of standing in the entrance hall, an I want out. All this time, I'm thinking what some other fucking Lam is doing with Sel. Do they feel the same shiver of magic? Or is it different for everybody else? There's no way for me to sit still with all this shite rattling in my head, an I'm pacing that front room, too warm now, my new coat left crumpled up on a seat. Vira keeps giving me sour looks.

Voices on the stairs, an when I look up, I see a Lammer stopping to thank the rookery's other feyn for her help. He's no one I know – oldish, a little shabby at the edges, but his clothes are cut from heavy fancy material, an it's obvious he's old money, old House. His face is full of wide-open bliss an tainted with magic. I can smell the scriv on him, I realise. It's so sharp an strange. Haven't touched the stuff myself in weeks, not even a sip of Hob-bitter. Not since that day when I shared a vai with my da after he made me Ives in more than just name.

He looks at me as he leaves, like we share a secret, an I hate him a little. This nameless Lammer, who only sees me cause I'm dressed in Ives finery, who pretends not to notice how dark my hair is, how ragged I am underneath all this surface shite. He fucked my Sel. An I hate him.

"You can go up now," Vira says, her voice all clipped. She knows I don't need no one showing me the way. I nod at her, make my way up the miles of staircase.

Before I knock on his door, I tug at my collar an loosen the top buttons. Can't believe I'm wearing this anyway. Guess I've become a proper little Ives brat. Sweat is itching down my spine an under my arms, even though the passage here is chill. I look right an left. Empty.

For what Gris-damned reason is it so hard to push those images out of my head? That Lammer, does he ask for Sel too? Am I turning into them, full of dirty secrets tarted-up pretty by money? In the Digs I'd never do something like this, waste my money on a bat-whore. 'Course, I'd never seen a bat before that burning.

Sure as every Saint has visions, I'd never be paying to touch one.

Time's wasting, I says to myself, but I don't want to knock on that door. I'm about to turn away, go back home, when Sel, like he's a Gris-damned Reader, goes an opens the door an stares out at me with those strange tilted eyes.

He don't say nothing, only opens the door wider for me to come in.

Well, no point going back home now. I stamp into the room an cross my arms over my chest. I can still smell scriv, an I wonder how much that must have hurt Sel.

He comes up to me an touches my arm, head cocked. Which in Sel-speak probably means something, but I'm too riled to try work out what exactly. I shrug him off an go sit at the end of the new-made bed, my head in my hands.

A few years, an I'd have more than just this pittance my da's seen fit to give me. I'd have my own key to the Ives dosh. With that kind of clout, may be that I could, I dunno, buy Sel.

Fuck.

I'm as bad as Oncle an my da, thinking about Sel like he was a nilly to be traded. Even if I could, I'd hate myself for doing that to someone else. An Sel'd hate me too. I know the feeling. For all I know, he doesn't even want to go; may be that he likes it here. Who am I to go around an change people's lives?

Nineteen

Singing for the Dead

JEK'S AT THE door. Uncomfortable, in a new suit.

I come up to him and am pushed away.

"Just sit down, Sel. I'm not in the mood."

I don't understand why he's here then, but I'm tired anyway, so don't complain, Sel, don't complain. I watch him. Wait. He will choose what he wants, and I will still get paid.

My palm burns with memorykisses. I clutch my hand closed. Breathe in and out.

He sits down. "Are you happy here?"

There is no answer to that. "Not unhappy," I say, after I list all the things in my head that I could say instead. It takes a long time. Jek is laughing at me. Bitter laughs.

"Well that's a right glowing statement of your life."

I sit down next to him. Jek's clean, not stinking of scriv. Even so, I don't open my hand.

"You ever think of leaving?"

I haven't. Nowhere to go, no one to know. How to explain this? Perhaps it's better if I think of Mal, think of his ribs and mine. Bones that are like bridges. Think of all the things I have to stay for. "Not enough money."

"Yeah?" Jek leans in close now, strokes my arm. If I close my eyes, maybe this could be Mal. "It costs a lot to leave?"

"Three silver bits," I whisper.

Jek whistles. "That's a fair stash all right." He drops his hand just as I'm settling in to this again-again.

"Lie down."

So I do and keep my eyes shut. There is heat against my side. Jek's still stroking my chest. I don't understand what he wants from me. I never understand Hobs and Lams. Their heads are more broken than mine. No sense in them at all.

"What would you do if you were free?"

Stop talking. Stop asking questions that make me look for answers. "Don't know," I whisper. "Not going to happen." I open my eyes. The light is soft through the square little windows, through a chink in the curtain. The room stinks of Lammer. I want to be clean again.

Warm brush on my neck, unexpected. A kiss. A shiver.

Yes. If I close my eyes, this could be Mal.

WHEN HE IS gone, I lie a long time, trying to put Jek's words straight in my head. It is time for me to go.

I need comfort. I flex my fingers, look at my palm, think of where I should be now.

With Mal, and his sad face, the broken pools of his eyes. He's falling away from me, leaving me behind the way Mother did, and Dae.

I slip down an empty street. I am a small fish in a white river until I reach the doors of my home. I find myself back in the house where we sleep, outside Mal's room. Near him, my heart goes still still still. Every breath will make your heart still, says Mother's memory words.

"You look upset." Mal beckons me in, closes the door behind me.

The room is warm because of Mal, the room is bright because of Mal. How do I say this to him?

"Sit down, Sel."

Next to him? Before him? The choices are too much, too many things to do wrong. I shake my head. So hard to explain what I want.

"What's eating you?" His smile wavers; perhaps it is not real, and I am only imagining it. "You can tell me, you know that. Please, sit. You're giving me a crick in my neck."

Quickly sit. Next to him then, on the bed, close enough that I can time my breaths to his. If we breathe in together, perhaps he will understand me. "Want to be out of here." It comes out whispery, not the way I mean it to sound.

"Yeah, don't we all." He leans back against the wall, and I lose the timing. Even so, he pulls me close and I know that if our ribs are touching, bone between bone, then it is like being the same person, and he will know what I mean to say.

"How long?" I know there is always a price. "How long before we can leave?"

"We?" His laugh is small and sad and pulls him farther away. "I'm not going anywhere." He sighs. "However long it takes you to save three silver pieces." His arms tighten, and there is nothing between the stone of our bodies but thin skin, thin meat.

I turn, put my back against his side, let him breathe me in. Take me, run away with me, be with me.

"Oh, Sel. I can't do this anymore."

There are no words I can say back, they all sound like stones thrown into water, and I do not want to sink this time. His one hand slides down my side, like the first time. This is nothing like the Lammers, like Jek.

I think I've been thrown away, by fear, by weakness, by not being real enough to matter. Inside I am shattered, the glass spilled through my blood. I cannot stay here and let Mal's face destroy me. There needs to be a place I can run to.

"Isidro," I say. The name floats through my head like a leaf.

"You're still thinking you can do what he did?" Mal tilts my head around a little, fingers soft-bruising my jaw. "Your client still asking for you?" He snorts. "And you think they're going to drag you out of this? Don't be an idiot."

"Was he happy?"

"Who – Isidro? How the fuck should I know? Do you see me rushing off to tea-parties at House Guyin –" His anger is breaking over me, hard as storm rain. "Shit, Sel, do you even know what House this Lammer is from?"

I shake my head, just a little. Inside, I want him to hurt. I want him to be happy. I want him to hurt even when it hurts me.

He goes calm and lets go of my face. When he talks again, it's into my hair, so that I think he will choke. "You have no idea. You can only force it by starting a bond, and if your Lammer doesn't take well to that little game, and refuses to buy you, then you've doomed yourself."

"How?"

"The MallenIve sharif will put you down. You ever seen a burning? It's not...pretty."

I smell smoke, smell it from far away. "No."

"I can't change your mind, perhaps. If you're resolved. At least think about what you'll be doing. To him, as well as yourself. It's not like you can change your mind afterwards."

There was never any thought inside me about Jek's choice. Would it matter? Would it hurt him? *Mal, tell me to stay, and I will.*

Everything inside me clouds, blurs, and all I can smell now is smoke smoke smoke. Parts of me are slipping away, and the only thing keeping me together is Mal. I lean back so that his mouth is against my neck.

"Sel." He pulls his hand away from mine, crawls apart from me. We split in two pieces again, and I am only half a person. "I can't do this, Sel."

No bond between us, no ties to bind. I cannot stay in a room where I am only half-real.

"You don't have to go," he says.

But I do.

Twenty

A Game of Wasps

FATHER IS BACK after another week at the palace, more grey and lined than ever. Mother flutters through the house, one hand pressed to her head, the skin around her eyes yellow-white.

"Calissa." She stops in the middle of the passage, her voice ringing clear.

I step out of the shadows behind a towering bookcase. No point trying to pretend that perhaps she didn't see me.

"Your father is going to officially announce the betrothal soon. He wants everyone in the front parlour."

"Now?"

"Naturally." She drops her hand, fiddling with the silver thistle brooch that pins her gossamer-thin scarf about her neck. She turns and her sharp heels leave deep imprints in the carpet. I pad after her, watching as the grooves marked into the plush red wool slowly fade.

Downstairs, Father is standing grim-faced, watching us gather before him. Iliana is already at his side; she's fidgeting with her hair. Since she came back from the Chalice, I've hardly seen her – she's taken to hiding in her rooms – but I don't remember Illy ever being so worried about her appearance before. She seems to spend all her time before her mirror, rearranging her hair in cascading styles, then brushing it all out and starting over, pinning the braids into a new form. It's meditative the way she sinks into the blank look and the mindless rearrangement. She looks like a clone of our mother these days, down to the immaculate dresses, the sheaf of golden hair, the emotionless mask.

Only our father doesn't seem to notice.

It's when Jek steps into the room to join us that Iliana's expression changes, just once, and it's quickly sublimated. For a brief moment, something dark and ugly twists across her face. It occurs to me that Ia actually liked Jek. I didn't expect for that to happen. My head begins to ache – I wanted Ia to feel like I had felt, but now the only pleasure it brings me is dull, tainted by a sour taste between my teeth.

I want to ask her if she loved him, but I'm scared she'll answer me.

Jek doesn't pay my sister any attention, as if he barely sees her. Then again, he acts like he's been in a scriven fog for the past few weeks, always wandering around in that dreamy lethargic way of the scriv-smitten. Only . . . he never smells of scriv. I file the thought away. Perhaps I need to have a word with my dear little Sharpshins again. Even that brief thought is quickly deflated. I can't make any open move against Jek, not when the ground now is so shaky. Damn my father for setting him above us.

When we're all standing patiently before him, Father clears his throat and begins with an awkward smile.

"The Mata have officially accepted Iliana as Trey's future wife," he says.

Iliana glances at me then looks down.

"Aren't you pleased?"

"I'm very pleased, Father." She raises her head, and stares straight at Jek, as if she is answering him, and not our father.

Jek leans against the mantel, his movements slow, graceful. The Hob, while he is still a gangly and thin half-caste, seems to have grown comfortable in his skin, and in the suits the tailors have made for him. "So you're going all high and mighty on us? Don't that make a sweet change." He grins, his smile vicious and pointed.

Iliana opens her mouth, anger painting two deep flushes of red across her cheeks, but before she can speak her mind, the outside bell jangles on its chain. Father sighs and nods at Trone, who is hovering at the entrance arch that leads to the front hall.

In the uncomfortable silence that follows, I can just make out the sound of Trone talking with the visitor then the shivery rattle of the glass in the windows as he closes the door. He returns to the room, two figures trailing behind him. They're short, barely reaching his waist. Twin girls, no more than five years old, alike as if they were poured into the same clay mould. Their white faces have been made up so that their lips shine sweet as cherries; their cheeks have a healthy blush. Even so, there's no mistaking the eerie white tone of their skin.

Bats.

I inch backwards. Around me, everyone does the same, except for Jek, who watches them with an idle curiosity.

Trone hands my father an embossed letter, the borders of which glint in the light of the chandeliers. Gold flake – only the Mata are such show-offs. Blaine seems to think we still live in the age of House Mallen.

Father reads for a moment, frowns, then tucks the letter into his vest pocket. "A gift. An engagement gift from the Mata."

"Bats?" My mother's voice is edged with disbelief. "Are they trying to insult us?"

It is most likely an insult of sorts, or a barbed compliment. When it comes to the Mata, one can never truly tell. "The females are rare," I say. "It's fashionable in some of the Houses now to use them as ladies' servants." I don't need to mention the other interpretation – how gifting slave-servants is considered an act of charity. The fact that they've given our House a matched pair, I do not know. It's near-impossible for me to read Mata motives. However, beyond the implied insult, it's a present of no small monetary value.

"And you know this how?" Iliana says. "You've finally left off sneaking about the library for an excursion into the real world?"

Jek glances between us, grinning wider. Mocking. I feel myself flush and carry on. "They're harmless anyway. The practice is to remove their teeth –"

"What?"

I turn my head. Jek has stopped leaning on the marble mantel. He's pushed himself upright, and he's staring at the bats with something close to distress.

Already, my father has knelt down to the nearest bat's head and tugged up one lip. The gums are slick, pink. There's no sign of the pearly sharp fangs. "So I see," he says. "Well, they should be safe then, at least." He nods at Trone, who hurries forward to lead the bats off to their new home.

Fingers clutched on the edge of the mantel, almost as white as the marble itself, Jek is watching them go. His face is sallow, ill, and he swallows once like a man trying not to be sick. He realises I'm watching, and the moment is gone. Instead, he flicks me a mocking little salute. "Fount of knowledge, are we?" But it's too late. There's something there, and I've seen it.

I smile sweetly back at him. "Oh yes. I remember everything."

He frowns, the smile fading from his face.

The sharp clap of my father's hands brings us all back. I stare at him, waiting. Next to him, Iliana fidgets. "The wedding date has been set." He looks at each of us. "One month from now, Ives will join with Mata."

Mother covers a gasp with one gloved hand. "A month? Are they mad? I can't organise a wedding in four weeks." Her mouth thins. "And a winter wedding is a bad omen, Vance. You know that. To have it before Long Night –"

"I pushed for the date," Father says, and the grim tone under his words makes my mother start. "We have no scriven left."

"The unis –"

He cuts her off with a jerk of his hand. "There's nothing. The last scriv-vein is worked out. We've got Saints trying to find more but so far – nothing. And the nillies, well..." He turns, clasps his hands behind his back as he paces. "The strain is getting weaker. We think it's down to breeding straight from nillies rather than unis."

Despite the shudder in my father's voice and my own rising fear, my interest is piqued. "The loss of the horn is changing their magic?"

"Just so," he says and looks at me clearly. "We've organised a hunting party to try and capture a horned buck. But they're getting wily now."

"Vance," my mother interrupts. Her face is ashen. "No scriven. What are you saying?"

He rubs one broad hand across his face. "I'm saying we have nothing. The little that's left in the vault, but I was waiting for a consignment. Obviously that's not going to come through now." He sounds tired, so very tired.

"But the dealers –"

"Nothing."

Her eyes are round, fear leaking from her. I don't even need the high to imagine it staining the air in an oily fug.

"The Mata saw it coming. Their Saints have known for months, I'm guessing. Maybe even years. They've bought up every dust mote in MallenIve."

"Clever." Jek doesn't sound alarmed, only somewhat contemplative. "What happens to the miners?"

"I really wouldn't know. That's the Mata's problem, dealing with the unemployed."

"There'll be deaths." Jek's eyes are half-closed. "All the little Hobs starving," he drawls, then snaps his eyes open. "Not your problem at all. Not 'til they sneak into your rooms an break your necks quick as sticks."

If I didn't know better, I'd think Jek was in a Saint-trance, but that's impossible, no Hob has ever had visions. Besides, one doesn't need to be blessed to know the poor will turn on us when they starve.

"We'll have access to more scriven once Iliana is married," Father says.

Iliana, hearing her name, raises her head again, staring blankly about her as if she's just woken from a dream. "They'll need us," she whispers. "War-singers. If we're to keep the Mekekana at bay. They'll have to give us scriven."

"Just so." Father nods grimly. "All the court War-singers will be getting an allotted amount to be used in defence of the city. With that in mind, I've arranged for you to begin your apprenticeship next week, instead of a new term at the University."

"Well," I say softly. "At least you'll get something out of Trey."

For the first time since she returned from the Chalice, I see a little of Iliana's old spark. She cocks her head with a casual arrogance, her blue eyes glinting. If there's one thing my sister has confidence in, it's her own abilities. When it comes to using magic, she is far stronger than me, and sometimes I wonder if she will not one day out-rank Father as a War-singer. As much as that is possible, for a daughter.

Twenty-One

The Grinningtommy

"YOU'RE BACK," SAYS Sel. "Early."

It's been less'n a week since I was last here, an it ain't often that I'm able to come back so soon-like.

There's this image I can't shake free out of my head, of those two little bats with their mouths puckered up like old ladies', their teeth ripped out their heads. For some bloody reason they're everywhere I go, reminding me. The lady refuses them as maids-in-waiting, so they flit through the house with dusters an pails, cleaning like they was no more than Hob-slaves. I hate looking at them.

Sel is sitting cross-legged, white thin legs like long bones; his brow furrows for a moment, an then the look is gone. "Something wrong?"

"Yeah." But I can't move. He's just looking at me, indigo eyes wide, face all blank an empty. I wonder what he thinks, deep in that fucked-up head of his. My heart is working over-time, trying to pump blood gone slow an cold all sudden-like through my body.

He shifts.

I move. Dunno what it is that makes my legs an arms work, that makes me stop him, my hands on his arms, an push him back down against the hard mattress. Dunno what makes me press my face to his. If I close my eyes, maybe this could be some Dig's Hob, or Iliana.

I've sucked Marlon off enough times even when I didn't want it; I fucked Iliana in that back alley, face to face, why is it so hard to do this with Sel? To do something I want to do.

My tongue is against his closed mouth, an for a second I think he's not going to respond, just push me off an call in one of the other wrays to get rid of this client gone all mental-like an thinking there's more to this than what he's paid for. Instead, his mouth opens, an his tongue pushes against mine. The slice of his teeth makes me pull back like I've been drunk an someone's gone an thrown a pail of ice-water in my face.

"It's all right," he says.

I lift my head so I can look down at him. His eyes are wide, the indigo almost normal-looking in the dark room. Magic thrums against me, makes me shiver. So deep an dangerous. More addictive than scriv, maybe.

Somehow, we're stretched out on that bed, my body covering his. My starched cottons against his bare skin. An I'm the one that feels lost an naked. I'm about to crawl up, to run away, out of this too-small room an race back to the Ives house like a dog running back to its chain. I'm as bad as my fucking da, not able to do the things I want because of what others would think.

Before I can move, Sel's hand is 'gainst the back of my head, pulling me back down to him. This time when I feel those teeth against me, I close my eyes an shut out his face. All I need to do is trust the shimmer that's working through my clothing to brush up 'gainst my skin. Make this thing I'm feeling for him easier to deal with.

Fingers of magic dig into me, an every time those teeth make me jerk in fear, Sel just pulls me closer, with hands, with magic. He slips one hand down to work blindly at my buckle, an I push up for a moment so I can help him.

We're face to face. Something I've never done with Sel. He's stopped kissing me, but he feels hot an the magic wilder, drumming all around me so I expect to see bruises on my skin when we're done. Just as I'm about to feel the lash of magic, he lunges up an bites my neck. It's the same place Ia bit when we were in that alley so's to muffle the sound. There's wet heat against my stomach, as he bites deeper an breaks the skin. I want to scream, to pull away. But I'm tied there by magic, feeling myself pushed over the edge, an the pain is sweet, in time with everything. I don't even realise he's sucking at my neck until the shuddery fever of magic an lust has passed.

He holds me in place with a strength I don't expect from those skinny arms, an laps at the blood running down along my throat. His tongue rasps at my skin.

When he finally lets me go, his face is red, dark hair sweat-limp. There's blood at his mouth – my blood – but instead of feeling shaky or disgusted or anything I would have expected, I feel alive, my skin stinging.

I can breathe in the taste of colours; the red sheet sweet an rich, the bunched-up cotton of my black shirt an trousers rough as irthe bark, natural. I lick at Sel's throat, tasting salt an ivory an stone dust. There's the faint smell of scrub-an-sand on his skin, the way the air tastes in the low rocky hills that border Lander's Common. His blood pulses in his throat, a cool blue vein, loud as a whole damn Lammer orchestra. "The fuck?" is all I can say, my head too busy pounding with the aftershock of sharing magic an blood with Sel.

He pushes me off him an struggles up, curling his knees close to his face. He brings his hands up, covering his face like a child. He's mumbling something quick an low.

I shake his shoulder, make him look at me. "What's going on?" My own voice sounds like strings, my breath could be butterflies. No scriv-high, no bat-fucking-high ever reached this.

"Started a bond," he mumbles. "Didn't mean to, didn't mean to." An he pulls his wrist out of my hand so he can cover his face again.

"What the fuck does that mean? Sel – Sel?" But he uncurls quick-like, grabs my rumpled coat, thrusting it at me, just about shoving me out the door. "What the fuck – Sel?" I drop the coat back to the floor an try to twist his hands down from my shirt collar.

"Please," he says, while he pulls my collar high so that it covers the bite on my neck. "Not a word, not a word. Don't tell anyone." He's frantic, an I swear I can feel his fear prickle up my own spine.

"Why not?" I say, even as he pushes me through the doorway.

He stops, pulls himself up so that he's looking at me. Really looking at me proper. Normally, Sel's all hunched-like, an he just comes up to my mouth, but then I realise he's hiding hisself all the time, trying to skulk when in actual fact, the bat is almost as tall as I am. I don't think he was that first time.

I look at him. There are red stripes on his hips where the skin stretched over bone an muscle. The bat had a damn growth spurt an

I didn't even notice. That makes me feel worse than anything else – that I never noticed.

Neither of us expect what I do next; I lean in an kiss him, mouth closed against his. He makes a muffled sound then shakes his head. "Don't." There's a strength to his voice that I ain't never heard.

"Why not?"

But he don't answer me. He shoves me away with one hand then shuts the door in my face.

PIEBALD CROWS ARE stabbing the brown grass on the verge outside the bat-rookery. With the sun high an the winter light streaking through the bare trees, I see everything as I should. My neck aches something wicked, but for all I'm confused an wandering around in a daze, I feel cleaner, like I been washed in well-water. Shivers set in, an all sudden-like I realise I left my coat in Sel's little room.

Don't think I should be heading back in there though, not with that look that was on his face. So I pull my collar higher an dawdle down the quiet streets. Sunlight bursts off windows, making them blink an wink, an I take a turn I haven't been down in a most long time.

The pavements are crowded with hawkers, selling food an tat. The smell of roasting goat, oil-fried flat breads spiced an salted, an crunchy greenstick wyrms makes my head sing. My stomach grumbles, but I'm not really hungry. Don't think I could eat at all. I'm on overload – every sound an smell batting about my head, drowning me.

A street-vendor in a long bulging coat is holding one hand out; a windle-moth with a wingspan like a wren's sits on his palm. All over his coat, lazy moths crawl, so that it looks like he's wearing a shifting velvet tapestry. They'll be dead in a week, but I want to buy one anyway. Moppets, Prue called then, and she would call me out when I was but a Hobling to watch them flit this way an that under the summer moon.

The low-Lam spins patter like silk as I dig for a copper bit, an take the fat girl from his hand. She's tame as a cat, an I can almost hear her purring against my face. Her wings flutter copper an brown an pink an gold, leaving fine dust on my cheeks, on the faint stubble I haven't bothered to scrape away.

With the moth perched on my shoulder, I take the twists an turns that lead to The Sphynx's Laugh. No chance that I'll bump into

Ia here now; instead, her an her jumped-up Saint of a mother are running themselves stupid over this wedding. A wedding which my da says I best be at – first formal public appearance of the new Ives heir and all that shite.

Faint an far away the bells of Saint Bale call out the hour. In a few moments the High Bell of Saint Gris chimes once, low an ear-aching loud. Then the other Saints around the city answer, an for a moment the air is solid with sound as MallenIve marks midday.

The clamour is enough to make my head ache, an I push open the Sphynx's dark an stained door.

The keep nods at me as I trot inside. It's quieter here, as the last chimes fade. No one pays me no mind, there's only a few small groups scattered about, talking low. No laughing or noise, no music. The small stage is empty. Place don't feel as it should, even though the same brass taps an edges glint in the light of the fires an lamps. Rows of drinks an strange bottles shine on the shelves behind the keep.

All the fires are lit, so I don't need my jacket in here anyway. I find an empty table, easy enough now that the price of a bitter has gone to the moon an back, an sit with a half-pint, letting the windle-moth crawl over my fingers, her whiskery feelers fluttering, fat velvet belly dragging soft against my skin.

I've no idea what I want to do, where to go. I think I want Sel, an that makes me nervous-sick, like I'm about to throw up. My damn bitter sits on the table, still full, reeking of scriv even though I know it's been cut an cut again.

A bell jangles, voices laugh as a bunch of students come in, bringing the cold with them.

"Hey, Jek. Haven't seen you here in a while."

Sharpshins. I look up.

The tall low-Lam is grinning at me like we're still best friends in the world, though I've been shunted out from the kitchens an dropped into the middle of all the Ives scheming.

"What's this then?" he says, an at first I think he means the moth, but then I feel his fingers flick 'gainst my neck. Quick-like, I put up my hand to cover the bite, but Sharps is already looking at me, his face gone yellow an sweaty. "Sweet Gris," he hisses as slips down onto the chair next to me. He drops his voice. "What the fuck, Jek? Is that what I think it is?"

I shrug, hunching my shoulders up an keeping them there,

better to hide the mark. "Don't know. Why don't you tell me what you're thinking?"

"It's a bite. Fuck me." He leans back an whistles low. "You are so deep in it now. Do you even have enough money to finish this? I mean, it's not like your father is going to start handing out your inheritance for shite like this."

"Shite like what?" I drop my shoulders so I can twist in my seat an stare him straight. "Stop mucking about an tell me what the fuck I've done here."

"You don't know?"

"Something about a bond," I mumble.

"Yeah mate, something about a fucking bond all right." He laughs. "Didn't think you were into that kind of thing, but yeah." He pauses, looks down at the windle-moth crawling on my fingers, an nudges her so that she'll crawl to him. "You've started a bond, which means you have to buy him, your bat. Hardly no one ever starts it. Well, House Guyin did, but that fucker's insane anyway –"

"Buy him." I take the moth back. For some reason, I don't like the idea of Sharps touching her, like I don't trust him not to just crush her so he can see my reaction.

"That's what I said. Three silver bits, last I heard. High-Lammer money."

"An what if I don't?"

He lifts one shoulder. "Like I say, this ain't a usual thing. You let it bite you; unless you can prove in court that it attacked you, then you're law-bound to buy it. And we're not all lax about bat-law here, not like in Pelimburg –"

"And if the courts say it was him?"

"Was it?"

I ignore him an press on. "What happens to the bat?"

Sharpshins leans back an stares at me all level, an calculating. "They burn it, Jek. What the fuck do you think, that they give it a medal and a pass?"

Of course they fucking burn it. Memory-smoke, the smell of burning skin, that little bat's eyes weeping blood as it cried for its dam. Not a fuck is that happening to my Sel.

I know where I can get a third bit from. In my da's office, there's a wooden safe-box. I could pick it. Marlon taught me. Might not have been good enough for his liking, but with enough time an enough copper wire, I can get it open. An that's good enough for me.

'Cept I do this, an my da will string me up like so much winter meat for drying. There's got to be a way I can make him see things my way.

Think, Jek. There's no time now to be plunging head first into this shit. Gris knows how the Lammers would twist it, an if we're going to be honest, my da's been almost all right to me, trying to make up for being such a coward over Prue. If I go an steal from him, then I'm doing what I said I wouldn't – turning on family an all that shite.

An if I don't? I think of Sel, burned up just like that bat was on Lander's Common. I couldn't do that neither – let Sel get chewed up by the court machines.

Shite, my head hurts; I've no brain for scheming the way the House girls do. Taking everything plain as faces is the way I work best, but there's no room for that here. If I do this, if I do right by Sel, I have to find a way to make it up to my da too. It's hard building up broken trust, an there's no way I know how to do that – less I could make him see why I did it in the first place.

An I can.

Things go clear, the way it must be for Saints, the way they know what paths they need to take to make things come out right in the end. I can make my da see why I'm betraying him. But first I'm going to have to steal summat back from him – summat that means more than a handful of silver ever could. That's if he even kept them, 'course. He did. I know he did, sure as I know the sun rises every day. All I have to do is think of the way Prue was over those letters, how they kept coming even if she wouldn't write back to him.

He had to have kept them.

"Here." I shove my drink across the table to Sharpshins.

Back outside, the cold is worse after the shelter of the Sphynx, an I tuck my moth deep into my shirt pocket so she won't feel the frost-wind.

Twenty-Two

A Game of Wasps

I'M SICK OF this wedding.

"What do you think of this?" Mother holds another sheaf of glittering silk up next to Illy, who's rolling her eyes and sighing in irritation.

"I don't know. It looks like every other one you've gone through in the last hour." I flick through the book of swatches that some spinningjenny eager for Ives patronage dropped off.

"Calissa, don't. I'm at my wit's end. We have so little time left, and the dress is still not done."

"It would have been done if you'd picked a fabric. Why don't you see if you have Visions over which pattern will ensure a happier marriage, complete with a litter of little Mata princes?" I drop the swatch book back onto the round side table, where it makes a satisfying thump.

Illy snickers, then swallows the sound down when Mother gives her a look that could send a sphynx running for the deep desert.

"You're no help," my mother snaps. An entourage of seamstresses and designers comes crowding into the room with armfuls of rolled satins, the colours muted, understated class. "Go send a message to the calligrapher. I want to know what's happened with those invitations. He said they'd be here today."

"Mother . . . the invitations arrived two days ago; they've all been sent."

Illy and I share a look. Mother has obviously, finally gone insane.

"Well, find something to do," she says as she grabs a pale golden silk that floats like a moth's wing. "This is nice, I suppose." She turns her attention back to me. "If you can't do any good here, then go see that the kitchen orders have come through."

I don't argue, even though I know Trone has already overseen everything pertaining to the food and dining side of the arrangements. Anything to get out of this dull room, watching my sister pinned into wedding robes so that she can be bound to Trey.

Instead of going to the kitchens, I wander the house. Father is back at the Mata palace, presumably to work out the defences should the Mekekana actually attack. Without scriven, there's a palpable fear that someone will bring up the Well as a viable alternative.

More than six hundred years have passed since Mallen Erina opened the Well to stop the first Mekekana attack. No one will ever be foolish enough to do that again. Wild magic is so unpredictable; it moves under the skin of the land as a huge dark river with a thousand tributaries that network the world, flooding the mantle above it with life, flushing the seeds and the skies alive. And only once has anyone dared to drill down and tap straight into the turbulence and trickery of the wild magic.

I don't know much, because the histories are shrouded by the two hundred years that followed. Two hundred years of magical chaos – the sphynxes, the unicorns, the wyrms, the vampires. Gris only knows how many other things were born of that time.

Opening the Well is a last resort, and not a choice to be made as long as we have another route left to us. While we still have even a grain of scriven, and the Saints keep searching for more deposits.

The front door slams, the glass panes rattling in their settings. I peer over the edge of the banister and catch a glimpse of Jek's dark hair.

He's out of breath, skin flushed. He looks up at me and frowns. "Aren't you lot meant to be putting the big to-do together?"

I almost smile, because Jek sounds as bored and annoyed by the whole thing as I am. Naturally, I say nothing to him, merely flick my rose skirt as I turn away and head to my rooms. No matter what my father has done, I can't quite bring myself to grovel at Jek's feet for whatever scraps the bastard will throw me.

Instead, I end up lying on my day bed, wondering whether to waste the last few motes of scriven that are hidden in the knot-hole of my desk.

The ceiling creaks, spilling fine dust down on me, making me sneeze. My father's office is on the floor above my rooms, and no one should be there. I sit up, moving slowly so as not to make a noise. Yes, definitely the sound of footsteps, someone trying to sneak; someone some place they shouldn't be.

Jek.

I don't bother putting on shoes, and I fly up the worn steps silent and unnoticed, my feet barely making the wood shudder.

A door clicks shut just as I turn the last corner of the corridor that leads to the study.

"What are you doing here?" My voice is a low whisper, almost a growl.

Jek is standing outside the door, hands shoved in his pockets. "Nothing. Got lost is all."

"Really?" I pad closer. "What's in there?" I point to the lump where his right hand is thrust inside a bulging pocket.

He pulls his hand out, and smiles. The thing he's holding is huge; a windle-moth with all the colours of spring and autumn quilted across the open wings. The moth flutters its wings. They vibrate, making the colours run together. "I think I'll call her Calissa. Here, Calissa," Jek croons to the moth, which bobs its feathery feelers in return.

A dull flush creeps across my cheeks, but I don't move.

"Turn out your pockets."

He frowns but does what I ask. Empty.

"An why would I need to steal from myself?" he says.

I say nothing, just wait for Jek to leave. He sighs and puts the moth up on his shoulder before loping down the passage. The moth crawls from his shoulder down across the back of his jacket like an arcane House symbol.

When Jek has disappeared from sight, I try the doorknob. The door stands firm; the room is locked. Perhaps I was just imagining the worst, and my half-brother really had managed to get himself lost in the winding passages of our house.

Unlikely. I shan't forget that for all the polished veneer he's been given, Jek grew up in the Digs, and he's as crafty a cur as the ghettos have spawned.

Twenty-Three

The Grinningtommy

MY HEAD'S POUNDING by the time I reach the rooms my da's turned over to me. A knot of a headache is growing at the back of my skullbone. That was too damned close. I swear that girl follows me about like I'm a mouse an she's the kitchen mog. It's unnatural. There's something wrong with her – girl needs to get a hobby. Take up embroidery or something the like.

She almost had me there. A moment earlier an she would have caught me in the doorway; no way I'd be playing the lost fool then. Good thing the moth was in my pocket too – I just kept that silver bit careful-like in my palm, an got away with it too. Sleight of hand, Marlon called it.

Darkness is falling outside, an Trone will soon be ringing the dinner bells. I still ain't worked a way out of the dinners, even with my da away at the moment. It's a mighty chore, sitting there watching all these women glaring at each other while they make small talk about this wretched wedding that's hanging over everyone's head like a woodsman's axe.

I lock the door then go sit on the neat-made bed. The sheets are straightened an tucked, covers shook out every morning by the girls I worked with just a few weeks ago. I drop the stolen silver bit. The covers are stretched so tight that the coin gives a little bounce. Some dead bastard's head is on the coin. Not hundreds sure who he is; Trone's been avoiding ancient history with me. Says it's bad enough he has to suffer through me trying to memorise the basics of reading an writing. I snort. He thinks he has to suffer. Should come see what it's like on my side.

Careful as can be, I pull the writing paper from the sneak's pocket I sewed into this Ives jacket. There were so many of them in his safebox, all yellowed an crackling, an covered in Prue's hand. I didn't have time to do more'n than grab the top one an hope for the best. I figured that it would be the one he read most often.

The paper shivers in a sudden wind, the leaves shushing in my fingers. I could read it now, know everything that was between them.

May be that I'd know Prue better, understand why she hated me so much.

I sit for a long time, longer than I mean to, not really looking at the letters, just staring at the spidery writing 'til it blurs into stains an nothings. Then I fold it up tight an shove it back in my pocket. Get on with it, I tell my self. Not time to sit here soppy as a Lammer poem.

The jacket I was wearing when they brought me here is folded up an shoved deep at the bottom of the wardrobe. I fetch it, smelling must an pig shit an stone dust an scriv an sweat. It's rank. This is what I reeked of when I got here. No wonder Trone an Dray made me scrub down.

Prue's two bits are still in the pocket, shoved under a scrunched-up kerchief that has seen better days. If someone tried to clean this jacket now the whole damn thing would most likely fall apart. I trace the seam where Prue patched a tear. The material of the tacked-on patch is heavy an faded blue; I think it came from one of her own coats that was gone to wear. It was a real nice coat an all, I guess it could have been a gift, could have been something my da gave her. Without thinking, I tear the patch from the jacket sleeve an tuck it into my shirt pocket. The old Dig's coat I throw on the floor. They can burn it for all I care.

Three bits. Enough to buy Sel's freedom. I feel shite-awkward about taking that last piece from my da, though. In the Low-walk there's rules about this sort of thing, about favours an who owes who what. It's complicated, but he's earned hisself at least a bit of leeway. Still, there's no way I can ask him for it, not for that kind of money without him asking questions. I'm hoping that he don't notice it's gone, or if he does, that he thinks he just miscounted or something like that.

He's been trying to do right by me, after all. In his own stupid Lammer way.

Well, there's no getting out of this dinner, so I'll have to head on down to Sel tonight after. At least now there's no one worried that I'm going to run. What Hob'd be stupid enough to give up the kind of money an name that's been handed to me, is what they think anyway. I stroke the windle-moth an put her in a sweet-wood box with a hinged lid that I leave propped open a little for air, out of a draft an the worst of the cold. Could swear she waggles those feelers at me like she was saying goodbye.

"'S all right," I say to her, all soft. "I'd never really name you after that snitty Lam. Moppet's a good name though." Prue would've liked it well enough.

They're all seated an waiting for me by the time I get downstairs.

"Well," sniffs that old cat, "I suppose we should thank you for deigning to come down."

My da told me to call her Lady Mirian, but I like seeing how far I can push her before that stiff face cracks. "Ah, Mirian, you all know better than to wait on me." I wink at her, an she scowls as I take my seat.

The food's tasting better these days than the slop I was getting in the kitchen, although it's still a mite bland. Guess that's the upside of eating here. Downside is the company, natural-enough.

"Trone tells me you went on a little excursion today." She tries again, even though it pulls her face all sour an skew with the effort.

"Went for a pint," I say. Which is true enough.

"Ah." She keeps silent while a gaggle of serving girls in House uniforms dish up our meals. When they're gone, she frowns at me. "There will be a suit fitting for you tomorrow, so I do hope you have no further plans to go splash your money about."

"Another one?" I don't rise to her little bait about the money, she's just pissed that I'll be getting access to the Ives coin – what's left of it after this whole business with the scriv – in a year. Gives her plenty of time to spend it like water if she's determined. I don't give a shite. Money wasn't enough to keep Prue; my da threw her away to keep his name on the will. Trone told me.

My da wants an heir. Like fuck that's gonna happen now. Shite. I close my eyes an wonder if there're ways past this – if I can buy Sel, an still get tied to some House chit. Knowing Lammers, there's probably some way 'round. House sires seem to bed as they please, as long as they know their wives are keeping the bloodlines clean.

I can hardly taste the tack. Knives tap, glasses clink, people chew, an above it all, a clock ticks, scraping time.

When does Sel leave the Splinterfist rookery? I know he don't live there, but I've no idea where the little bastard actually goes when he's not working. I scratch at my neck, careful to keep my collar high. The scabbed skin is itchy an red; the high I got from the half-bond long since gone.

Soon as it's polite for me to leave, I'm up an out from that room. No one even asks where I'm going.

At the front door is a letter tray, an I stop when I see the stack of envelopes piled there. Looks like this wedding will be a big thing. I turn over the top letter – the seal is not one Trone's taught me yet – a round, four-petalled flower. The next is easy – the irthe tree with its knotted roots: Rendal. New House, big money. They've made their fortune in silk. I toss the envelope back down onto the pile and wrap my arms about my body as I stamp out into the winter night.

"HE'S NOT HERE."

"So can you tell me where 'bouts I can find him?"

The feyn snaps her ledger shut. "Not supposed to. He's off-duty. If you're that desperate, there's plenty other wrays working t'night."

"I don't want another fucking wray. I'm looking for Sel."

"And I told you, he's not working tonight."

"Listen here, you daft bat, did I say I was looking for a fuck?" It's useless. The feyn just stares at me down her nose, like I'm a weevil she's found in her stir-pudding. If bats even eat oatporridge, which I've no idea. I need to try another tack, so I take one deep breath, let it out, an talk all soft an charming-like. "Please, if you'll just tell me where I can find him..." I slip my hand into my pocket and take a few of the coins I've left over from Trone. I slip them across the counter at her, an smile. "Please?"

She pockets them right quick an practised, with a look this way an that to see that no one's watching. "He's in the last building on Whitur. Big white thing. Turn right, and go down to the end, you can't miss it."

That's probably as much as I'm going to get out of her.

"Thanks, love," I say.

It's not far, the building she means. I've passed it so many times, never knowing that Sel lived there.

By the time I reach the tall white house the glass doors are already closed, locked. I hammer on them for a while, but the place might as well be empty for all the reaction I get.

I take a few backwards steps until I'm standing in the middle of the cobbled street, craning my neck so I can look up, see if I can spot anyone behind the empty windows. Nothing, not even the flick of a curtain.

A figure is walking up the road, moving with that quick, slippy quality that bats have.

"Oi!"

The wray stops, looks over at me. I wave it over, an it comes to me with a face all cloudy an suspicious.

"You know Sel?"

The wray nods.

"Well, can you get him to come down here an talk to me?" I spread my hands. "Just talk, I swear."

"No," says the wray, as he turns to walk up the stairs to the front doors.

"Fuck." I lurch after him an grab hold of his shoulder. "Listen chum, serious now, Sel knows me, right. Look." I scrabble through my pockets for the last of Trone's money. "Here." I shove the coins at him. "C'mon, for your trouble."

He stares at my hand, at the small pile of copper pieces, then reaches out an swipes them. The bat don't say nothing as he unlocks the door an slips inside. He's just a shadow through the dark glass as he disappears up a curving staircase.

Now all I can do is hope he actually goes an fetches our Sel. I slide down the glass an sit my arse on the cold stone stairs. I can wait here all fucking night if need be. Even if it is freezing.

I swear he leaves me there over an hour, an I'm cursing that damn bat from here to Pelimburg when the door swings open an I fall backwards, bashing the back of my head against the stone tiles.

From where I'm lying I can see Sel. Leastwise, I think it's Sel. I've just never seen him dressed proper. He's wearing neat trousers an a clean black shirt, although I can see where someone's darned the fraying cuffs. I wonder if he did it hisself.

"What are you doing here?" he says in that fucked-up weird

voice of his.

"I-I forgot my coat."

He frowns. "I don't have it."

Quick as I can, I scramble up to my feet. It's freezing out, an my bollocks are gonna shrivel away if I stay on these steps any longer. "Can I talk to you?" I nod into the darkness of the white building. "Inside?"

"Not allowed."

"Sel."

The silence beats in our faces. Now that we're both standing an I can look straight at him. Out of the rookery, he don't slouch. There's something there in his eyes, a flickering, like he don't know what to do or say, but he's not quite ready to slam this glass door into my beak.

My breath puffs, little boggert wisps. "I have three pieces of silver," I blurt, worse than any boy with a girl for the first time: look, I got you flowers, look, I bought you this stupid ring, look, I can buy you.

It's not like that.

A third eyelid flicks over his pupils from the side, making his eyes look milky an veined, raw as undyed silk. Bats only do that if the light's too bright, or they're ill, or they don't like what you're saying, or a million other things. That's all I know.

"What for?" an he speaks so slowly, so soft, that I have to strain to hear him. With those eyelids down, I can't read nothing from his eyes, no emotion nor giving way.

I dig my hands deep into my pockets, 'cause they're starting to shake now an I really don't want Sel to see. "For the bond." It sounds so stupid now that I say it, that I'm ready to turn tail an just run back to that Ives house and settle in like the heir my da wants.

Give up everything I want for myself.

Good little Jek, sit down, lie down, roll over an die.

Twenty-Four

Singing for the Dead

IDIOT JEK. STANDING there in the cold full of shivers. I did this to him.

"Fine." I hold the door open.

He slips in, grateful. "Do you want this?" Jek says.

Want what? Don't know. Here is a home, a place where I know myself. With Jek...what will I be? No more Lammers high and low, all different all through the day. Just the same one every day. I look at him, try to be clear. To see him without all the shifting. I wish Dae were with me, so I could think again.

If Dae were alive, where would we be?

Jek shakes his head. "What do you say?" He holds out his hand. It is full of silver, three blinking silver eyes.

I think this is what I wanted. It's so hard to remember. I think I wanted to prove something. Whatever it was is gone. "Come." There is only one place to go. Riam will know what we must do.

Footsteps behind me on the stairs, so very loud, so very Hob. Soon soon we reach Riam's door. Black door to a white cave.

I knock.

"Come in."

So we go.

"What's this, Sel?" Riam frowns, angry. Confused. I don't know.

Not knowing makes me lose myself. I put the three coins on her desk, one by one, careful to make sure they are real. Not something I made up.

"Well, I won't lie, I didn't expect this from you." She looks across at Jek. "Who are you? You're no House I recognise."

"Ives."

"Is that so? Do you know what you're getting yourself into, young Ives?"

"Don't care," says Jek. Stubborn stubborn Jek.

"Hmm. You say that now." Riam turns to me as she takes a small bundle from a chest. Oh. Mother's seed-pearls. "These belong to you."

Don't want them. Don't want more memories. The ones I have are bad enough. I shake my head, trying to shake Dae from me, shake mother, shake death away.

"Are you certain?"

"Yes."

She sighs, flips one silver coin back at me. "I'll not give you more than that for the pearls, understand?"

Tuck the coin away in my empty pocket. It's Jek's; I will give it back to him later. Pay him back for making him do this.

I remember now. I did this. I wanted it enough to make him believe he wanted it. My head hurts. Glass splinters inside. And I wrap my thoughts up in soft wool so that they stop cutting me. What was it I meant to do? I feel faded out, not really here.

"And as for you," Riam speaks to Jek. Perhaps I am a ghost. "You've no idea what you're doing, do you? This is as much slavery as what he had before. I can't think why or what you want to get out of this, but if I hear you're hurting him, I will find a way to reach you –"

"It's not like that –"

"Here." Riam throws a flat thing on the table in front of Jek. "You make sure that it gets sewn to his left lapel. It's proof of ownership."

Jek puts it deep in his pocket. Says nothing.

"Well? What are you two waiting for? Get out of here."

I didn't mean to make her cry.

"Sorry," I say before the door closes.

We go downstairs.

"Don't you have stuff to pack?"

Shake my head. If I go back up, I might see Mal.

"Oh."

Outside it is very cold. Stars wink down on us. Jek is looking at the thing in his hand, the thing that Riam gave him. "I don't fucking own you, Sel." He throws it on the ground.

I have seen something like it before. A bird. Like an eagle, all on fire. Mother had a pin like that. Once. Once. Dae and I would play with it, in the dirt, play games. Look I can fly, Dae said, and he dropped the pin over the cliffs. I have forgotten Dae's voice. My eyes are wet.

Mother cried that night too.

It is a bird that makes people cry.

Twenty-Five

The Grinningtommy

THE SUNLIGHT IS already hitting the rooftops by the time Sel an me reach my street. Took so damn long cause you'd swear Sel's never seen nothing in his life. He keeps stopping to look at shite.

"It's a fucking tree, Sel, leave it already."

"What kind?"

"I have no idea. Do I look like I grew up in the royal park?"

We walk a bit further on, an I see something I don't expect – rounding the lane ahead is my da's carriage. He's back from the Mata a day early, an there'll be no hiding from this whole shite-storm. Hang my blasted luck.

Well, best get this over soon as possible. Don't think it's going to be a load of fun when my da realises what I've done. "Sel," I say. "You ever seen a windle-moth up close-like?"

He shakes his head.

"I got one. A big thing, big as this," I spread both my hands wide like wings. "I'll show you her. She's real friendly. Smart too."

"Moths are not smart."

"Just you wait. You'll see."

Sel rolls his eyes at me. At least he's lifted that damned membrane. It makes him look too strange, too different.

The steps up to the door feel steeper than normal. May be just that I'm tired. May even be that I'm scared. I shake my head. I won't be my da, won't pretend for the sake of a name. I grab Sel's hand, an he jumps. I let it go, feeling stupid then unlock the door with the new key my da had carved for me.

I've just made it into the house, an I'm shoving Sel ahead of me up the stairs when the rattle of the glass tells me my da is already here. Damn but the old man can move right sharp when he wants too. "Shite," I hiss under my breath.

Light spills in from the door, an all I can make out of my da is a black shape all crowned on the edges like he's someone's nightmare Vision come to life.

"Shite," I say again.

"What is that?" my da asks, an I know he already knows the answer, can see Sel clear as day on the stairs behind me. There's no mistaking a bat for a Hob or a Lam.

"Fuck." In my head I'm scrabbling for excuses, trying to think of a way to get out from under that anger I can feel brewing.

"Why is there a Gris-damned bat in my house?" he says, but his voice is quiet. "Don't bother to answer." He holds up one hand, palm out to me.

"Sir?" Best to play my cards as slick as I can.

"A servant came to me, told me that he thought you'd been going to the bat-houses. Said he thought you'd gone as far as to let one of them bite you."

Fucking Sharps. I swear I'll kill the glass-backed wanker. There's nowt for me to do now 'cept suck it up. I nod once. "I did at that."

He stalks in, the long winter coat flapping about his boot heels with a whip-crack sound loud enough that I almost jump. "What," he says as he walks closer, "did you think you were doing?" He stops right close to me, on the first stair.

"It's too late now to change it," I say, feeling the words tumble up out of me.

"Change what?"

"I – I bought him."

Roaring silence fills the house, like a wind rushing about my ears. I squint an hunker down, waiting for him to leather me.

He don't do nothing though, just stands there still as an old bone.

I open my eyes an look up at him all wary-like. I've fucked up big here; won't be long before he packs me an Sel off, an it'll be back to the Digs with me, an I've no idea what the two of us'll do there. Starve. Get burned before the sun is even halfway to the ground again.

"Why?" my da says finally, his voice all wheezy an choked like he's trying to keep all this anger back in him, holding it on a tight leash.

Feels like it takes me forever to dig that letter out of my coat pocket, like it's jammed itself in tight an doesn't want come out an see the light. Finally, I pry it out an hold it out to him. It's shaking a little, fluttering like moppet wings.

He takes it from me without saying nothing, but I can see in his eyes he recognises it.

"He's to me like Prue was to you," I say finally, though it's hard as can be to make myself say the words. I want him to remember everything he felt for Prue, so I don't have to spell it out loud.

The memory of Prue hangs twixt us. He don't look down to the letter in his hands, an I'm sure as I'll ever be that he knows everything on it by heart, an the thought makes me feel sick in my throat, that I done this to him.

"Get downstairs," he says. "Wait in the small book room. And don't leave from there before I've spoken with my wife." His voice is cold, tight.

So I nod, let him know I understand, an I beckon Sel to follow me off to the small room that leads off from the front parlour. My da don't move, so we have to squeeze past him on the steps. He's looking at his hand, at the yellow paper, an not at me. "I'm sorry," I say, very soft, but I don't think he hears.

"C'mon, Sel." I grab his sleeve an draw him after me, an I don't look back until we're in the small room, smelling of musty paper an candles an gas-lamps.

It could have been worse. Could have been better too.

"Where's the moth?"

"In my rooms. I'll show you it in a moment."

"Everyone will hate you now."

"Don't talk rubbish, chum. Everything's going to be just peaches, you'll see." I slump down onto the couch. "Come, sit down here, stop hovering like a – like a –"

"Bat?"

I snort. "All right. I'll stop saying it. Look. I promise."

Sel curls up tight as a cat next to me an puts his head 'gainst my shoulder. In a moment, I realise he's gone to sleep, breath tickling my neck. I'm tired too, but from upstairs I can hear shouting, an I know that it's all about me.

I try block them out, but the sound only rises an rises. Even Sel opens one eye in a thin slit. That damned third lid is back, half-covering his eye. I reach out an cup one hand against his face an run my thumb against his lip. Sel doesn't move, but he closes his eyes. The veins are tiny, blue, the eyelids so thin.

"Everything will be just fine," I promise him. "I'm not my da."

Twenty-Six

A Game of Wasps

DOORS SLAM, AND I wake, the last vestiges of my dream shattering.

I pull my dressing gown on and slip downstairs.

Jek's voice drifts up from one of the rooms below. I know he left yesterday evening, but that he's only back now this morning... He must have arrived after my father, who is stamping down the stairs, away from my mother's chambers. Something has happened.

When he's gone from sight, I rap at my mother's door.

She opens it, and her lips are bloodless and thin, her eyes ice storms. "What do you want?" she snarls.

"I heard shouting."

"Did you now?" She looks so utterly vicious, and at the same time so wild and frightened that I take a step back. "Your brother has ruined us," she spits. "As I knew he would. I Saw it, but would anyone listen to me –"

I smile. Finally, it seems he's fallen, and I can't be held to blame.

By the time I get away from my mother's rage and down to the last section of stairs, Jek is nowhere to be seen. My father stands below me in the entrance hall. He is tired, sad, the lines on his face made deeper. Without noticing me, he turns and walks towards the little alcove that leads to the small book room where I sometimes like to curl up to read. Quiet as a ghost, I follow him.

Once he's inside I put my ear to the door. Jek's voice comes through clearly. "It's done," he says. "There no backing out-like."

"Do you realise what this means?" My father's voice is low, threatening. "The Mata can still end Iliana's engagement. And how are you supposed to marry – with this –" He spits in disgust. "I've arranged for the daughters of prominent Houses to be at Iliana's wedding, so that they could meet you."

"I din't know all that," Jek says. "But I do know there's others what's done this – the Guyin –"

"And look what happened there. The heir to House Guyin is an outcast. He's not invited to any events, the courts are closed against him." A sudden thought strikes him. "Where did you get the money?"

"It was Prue's," Jek says. "You gave it her, when she left." His voice is very soft, and I press closer against the door to hear him better.

"She kept that? All this time?" Father is silent for a while, and I draw back, nervous that any minute he will come hurtling from the room, and I will be caught out. "And what are we to do with it, Jek?"

"Him."

My father sighs. "Wait here. I need to make arrangements. You're not to go anywhere, is that clear?"

I dart away, back up the stairs before they can see me eavesdropping.

IT'S A BAT. A Gris-damned bat.

Mother and Father have been screaming at each other for most of the morning; now she's locked herself in her rooms, in a snit. Father is stalking the halls, and Jek, grinning like he won, is sitting in the front parlour, lounging on one of the vintage couches, his feet on a Felini table, scuffing the polished wood. Next to him, the bat sits, watching the commotion with slitted eyes. It has long dark hair that falls in its face, and the clothes it wears don't fit it properly, showing too much of his long white wrists. It's thin, hunched like a dog beaten one too many times.

"Father's mad," I say.

Jek glances up at me then dismisses the thought with a wave of his hand. "He'll get over it." He doesn't sound as sure as he looks.

I take the opportunity to get a closer look at the bat that's caused all this trouble. "Bat," I say, and it looks up at my voice. The slanted indigo eyes are startling in the bone-pale face, and it doesn't blink often enough. A membranous third eyelid partly obscures its iris, and the bat looks frail and tired.

As I stare, the bat looks right at me, and then ever so slowly, bares its teeth.

"It hasn't been defanged."

"Of course not." Jek stands, even as I take a step back. "This is Sel. We're bonded."

I can't believe he actually said it, made it real. He let it bite him. My flesh feels cold and sticky at the same time, and I step farther back. A fanged bat, loose in the house, and worse – bonded to my half-brother. Father's right, the Mata are going to stop Iliana's marriage. A more foul blot on the name of Ives, well, I couldn't imagine it. "You're joking."

In answer, Jek pulls at his collar. His neck is bruised, but I can see the clear mark of fangs. The bites are deep, slow-healing, and around it the bruises are a sickly yellow. Bile rises in my throat, and I press my hand to my mouth, willing the sickness away. "How could you let it touch you?" I whisper. "Do you bed goats and dogs too?"

"Fuck." He stands, nods at the bat. "I'm getting out of here. Not sitting around to listen to this shite."

"Be the same outside." The bat's voice is too deep for its slight frame, and sharp and painful as the sound of gravel underfoot. It slumps further into the couch. "You'll see."

Warring emotions cross Jek's face then he returns to his seat. His boots hit the hand-polished table with an audible thud, and he crosses his arms.

A perverse fascination keeps drawing me back to the bat. Sel, Jek called it. I've become used to the two little bat girls, but they're children, and they've been made safe. This – this ranks with having a desert sphynx loose in the house, roaming the hallways.

There are rumours about Guyin and his bat, that they met in a teahouse. I never believed it, thought it was just petty talk, and now here comes my half-brother with this bonded animal, flaunting it. He doesn't understand that you can't trust them. They're damaged by wild magic – products of the Well.

Behind us comes the sharp clack of my mother's heels on the stairs. She stops, and I glance back at her. Her face is drained, and she descends no farther. Her hands are clasped on the banister. She looks ready to fall over. "So it's done," she says then turns to me.

"Your father has decided to put them on the third floor of the right wing. I'm to inform you that you're not to go there, under any circumstances."

"Why isn't he telling us this himself?"

She sniffs. "He's gone to the Mata. Damage control." She takes a cautious step down to the next stair, her attention focused now on Jek. She doesn't even look at the bat, as if it doesn't exist. "You're to move your things. Trone will show you what rooms are yours. Stay there until your father," she spits the word, "sends word otherwise."

Twenty-Seven

The Grinningtommy

SEL HELPS ME move to the new rooms, 'cause no one else bloody will. They're right at the end of the third floor, far from the family rooms, with no quick way to get from here to the second floor. There's also a door at the end of the corridor that can be locked to shut off the whole section. Locked from the outside, I note. There's even an iron bolt. Guess my da's not leaving nothing to chance. Seems they all think that Sel's gonna go creeping through the house at night, munching up the Ives family like they're mice.

"Here," I say, when I carry the sweet-wood box into the new room. "Have a look." I open it up.

Inside the windle-moth is pressed into one corner, stiff as a fairy caught in frost. She's dead.

Sel picks her up all careful-like, an balances the corpse on his open palm. He looks at it for a long time. "They don't live so long," he says, an I'm not sure if he's saying it to comfort me or what.

"Yeah." I lift it from his hand. She's beautiful, even dead an still. I wipe my face with the back of my hand, find it wet. Crying like a Hobling over a damned moth. I must be tired, my eyes watering.

Still an all, I can't throw her away just like that, so I put her on the mantle over the fireplace.

"You can have more," says Sel.

"I don't want more."

"Doesn't matter what you want." He tilts the box to me so I can see the underside of the lid. It's covered with little black specks, like seeds.

He puts the box down an shuts the lid. Quiet, he strips off his darned black clothes an his shined, button-up shoes, packs them away neat an careful. Folded an edges all straight. I've forgotten what it's like to have only one set of tat. Sel reminds me.

The crows are croaking below, sun shines through the dusty curtains. It might be the middle of the day, but I crack a yawn an get undressed. This is all so fucking weird, to crawl into bed between cold sheets that haven't been aired out an feel cool skin against me. I throw one arm over Sel an pull him close so we fit together. I can feel the pulse of his body beating next to my ribs, an I trail my hand down his side, along the smooth line of his shank. Run my fingers back up to play 'gainst his hip, pressing hard into the hollow there, to pull him closer to me. Quick as a cat, I press a dry kiss to his shoulder blade.

I've not shared a bed like this since my days learning pack law. An even then, when all was done, Marlon wouldn't want me over at his shack, so I'd slip on back home to where Prue would be waiting with her face crinkled with worry.

No, I've never just slept next to someone.

We sleep through the afternoon an night, an only the sparrers singing from the dead trees wakes me the next morning.

No one comes this way, an it's almost like we're been left alone on purpose. Right enough I know that it's 'cause the only person in this house who might just take it in his head to talk to me is off wooing the Mata an telling them that this latest shift in the Ives House ain't nothing to worry about.

I wonder how well that little play is going down.

Sel's fast asleep, curled up on his side. His back is hot against my belly, an all that skin so close puts me in mind of what we could be doing if Sel was awake.

He's snoring, the way little Hobs do, dead out to the rest of the world, so instead I just kiss his neck an wriggle free from the blankets.

I have to shift it across the cold room, jumping into my clothes about as fast as I can. No servants came in last night to bank the fires, an the room is cold as a grave pit. Well I'm no high-Lammer with lily-hands, so I take it on myself to start a fire in the grate. Soon the logs are burning merry as sprites. There's a mirror in this room an I stare at it, then dampen a flannel in the cold wash-basin an dab the crusted blood from my neck, pressing careful on the bruised skin.

I look at Sel one last time to make sure he's still asleep, then head from the room to go an see if I can scrounge us a bite to eat. Or me a bite anyway. I still have to wrap my head about the thought that from now on, I'm Sel's breakfast an dinner.

I'm whistling as I half-slide down the banister, heading towards the kitchens when I almost run straight into my sister on the landing. Gris be a shitting goat – I forgot she was back from the palace – on a break from her apprenticeship.

It's cold as a slap to the face with a wet flannel.

"Ia," I says.

"Don't call me that."

We stand facing each other. For a moment I remember the feel of her raining magic down around us. From the sharp look in her eyes an the flush of her cheeks I can tell she remembers it likewise. My gut twists.

We stood outside the Greenfinch an she cried. I remember that too. If anything, that makes it all worse.

"Get out of my way." Her hands are shaking, an she pulls them behind her back, but it's too late. I've already seen, an she knows.

"Come now," I says. "That's no way to talk. We can start this fresh, right now." I hold out my hand, like we were two high-Lammers at some society shindig, just met. "Past is past." I think about kissing her, compare it to kissing Sel, an everything inside me feels black an rotten an confused. *Take my hand*, I think. *Take my hand, make this easier for all of us.*

"Why ever would I do that?" She arches a brow, a tic she's learned from her cat of a dam.

The warm feeling I got from sleeping next to Sel is fading, an instead all I get is this cold an iron smile. I drop my hand. "Don't get pissed with me," I says. My head is all shivery inside. "You're the one who was all dressed down an looking for a Hob to f –"

"Will you hush!" Her eyes fly wide. "Do you want every person in this house to know?"

"Look, Ia."

"Don't –"

"Yeah, yeah." I wave her quiet. "Look. There's no good come out of us clawing at each other. You're for the palace, anywise. There's no one has to ever know." I drop my voice soft an take a step closer. She backs away, an I stop. "I ain't never going to tell no one about it, trust me."

"Fine."

We stand, not looking at each other. The floor on the landing here is carpeted in a dark red wool, an the space between her slippers an my boots is too small. I look up. "I thought you were pretty shiny for a Lammer, truth told, when I saw you at the Sphynx." I fix her with a grin I don't right feel. "It could have been different . . . ." I stop, don't know why I'm telling her this, all my regrets. Next thing I'll be in some tea shop jotting down love-struck poetries.

"Gris." She sidesteps. "Please, just let me go." That blank mask is gone, an instead she looks like a kitten someone's about to drown. All terrified an broken.

I move out her way. "I was never stopping you," I says, but she's already gone past me, up to where the family rooms are all shrouded with wedding plans.

Twenty-Eight

A Game of Wasps

THIS IS THE last of my scriven. I hold my index finger up to the light; it's hardly more than a faint smear, and the grey dust takes on a silver luminescence. I've been saving it – for what, I don't know, but the ache is so bad that I need it. I need it now. Today.

I should have taken it to get through Iliana's wedding.

The best we can say of that particular day is that the Mata did their duty, and we did ours. So now Iliana is gone – swept off to the glass palace. She's with Trey –

Ah. That's it. Not another second without this. There's not even enough to justify getting a glass pipette to take it with, and I sniff it from my fingernail, common as a Hob.

The bell is ringing. Breakfast. I suppose I should go.

I brush my hands together and wipe the creases from my skirt. In the mirror I look wan and tired. There are shadows under my eyes. With no time to fix that, all I do is dust some colour to my cheeks so that I don't look washed out and draw my mother's attention.

It will have to do.

Downstairs, everyone is already at their place, waiting for me. The bat is next to Jek, although he never looks up, and he always seems on the verge of crawling under the table or something equally uncouth. Father, in his infinite fucking wisdom has decreed that we will do our best to make the bat feel part of our family. It is a bitter joke, how Father is so easily reined and ruled by the traces of his failed love for a dead Hob.

Winter has set her claws in deep now, and there is always a fire in the hearth. The glow from the flames gives the bat a less sickly appearance, casting its marble skin gold. Around it I can read faint nervous flickers; the bat feels panicky here, like it's scared that we'll all somehow turn on it and tear it apart. I want to feel no pity for it, so I jerk my gaze away.

"Forgive my tardiness," I say as I take my seat opposite them. Next to me, Illy's chair is empty.

My father just grunts in response. He looks almost as bad as I do, and it strikes me that even with the Mata-supplied scriven, he's still far short his usual intake. His aura slumps, tired and grey.

If the Mekekana hear of this, how weak we've become . . . I shake the thought away and help myself to porridge with cream and butter and sugar.

It's taken a few weeks, but somehow, the presence of Jek's bat has become less disturbing. We hardly ever see it, only at breakfast, which Father insists all family members must attend.

Family. The thought makes me shiver. I'm actually family to this animal, thanks to the bat law that MallenIve implemented to keep civil ties with the city of Urlin.

The sound of a knife on toast. Father asks Jek to pass the butter dish.

Breakfast has become less strained recently, I'll admit. Where at first Mother would sit stone-faced, not touching her food, while Father ate as if nothing was wrong, too heartily, too tense, now I can go whole minutes without thinking about that damned bat. At least it never actually eats at the table. It drinks nilly milk, making one glass last through the entire excruciating mealtime. I think it feeds off Jek at night.

I push my half-eaten porridge away, feeling ill.

The bat looks up from its glass. At the same moment, Sharpshins comes in and begins to unobtrusively clear away excess dishes. He makes a wide berth around the bat, scowling as he does. It's the only time his expression changes. He schools his face as he comes around, but even so, the bat watches him, frowning.

Sharpshins has always been easy to Read, perhaps because he's my creature. All around him the air churns, black, venomous green. Anger, hatred, lust.

Lust?

It is so quickly sublimated that I lean forward, as if I could catch it again. There. When he looks at Sel. It's a deep colour, bruised and rotted – the heart of a red peach, full of worms.

Next to him, Jek starts, jerking his head towards Sharpshins. He narrows his eyes and frowns, sensing something that he shouldn't. Wariness flares, stained with silver.

Without the scriven, I'm next to useless; today's last pinch of dust is the only reason I picked up what I did. The lack of any scriv-trained abilities does not seem to matter to Jek, though. Perhaps we will become like Hobs one day, relying on intuition and facial expressions instead of the secrets scriven can whisper to us.

I wonder.

It's not as if we have any other options left to us, not unless some Saint comes through with a vision of scriv-deposits, and like we did before with Mallen Gris, our society follows them like goats to new pastures.

Twenty-Nine

The Grinningtommy

"JEK."

Some damn fool is whispering at the door then knocking, soft-like.

"Jek." Louder this time. Sel is sleeping next to me. He's deep out of it. The high from feeding has faded, an I can only just see the magic under his skin.

Another knock, an I throw the bedcovers off an stamp to the door.

It's Sharpshins.

"What the fuck d'you want?" The bastard hasn't spoken to me since I bought Sel free. Dunno what he thinks to talk to me now. An I got a pretty good idea it was him that sent word to my da at the palace telling him about my thing with Sel.

"Your father sent me to get you." He looks through the cracked-open door, sneers.

"That right?"

"Yeah, seems his lady's been complaining about missing scriv."

"An that's got what to do with me?" But I shiver. Least wise, if Sharpshins is talking truth, I'm in for a bollocking. I just have to hope that Sharp din't tell them about sending me off with a key to the lady's chambers. Bastard's as like to twist the tale to his own ends as a cat is to play with string.

Plus I'm in no one's good graces in this Gris-damned house. It won't be long before my da notices more than just some missing scriv.

Sel gave me that silver bit of his – the one what Riam gave him. I been meaning to put it back in my da's safebox, but there just never seems to be time-enough. An now it's too damned late.

"What did you go an tell him, Sharp?"

"Nothing," Sharpshins says, an shrugs. He's got an evil smile, the prancing bastard, an he turns it on me now. "But it's best you don't keep him waiting."

I look back at Sel, still sleeping fast, an wonder if I should wake him. Nah, no need. If there's shite, he'll know 'bout it soon enough. I dress quickly in the grey light while Sharpshins waits, still grinning like a mog what's caught one of those locusts that sweep into MallenIve every year, an he's just playing a bit until he tears its legs off.

"He's waiting for you downstairs," Sharpshins says, looking back at me over his shoulder.

"Not in his office?"

"No. He said to bring you to Trone's room."

Well, might be that my da really has noticed my little pilfering. Well, not so little, but hardly noticeable next to the scriv-crash. His office is too close to the private rooms, may be that he's gonna dress me down proper an don't want to go waking the Ives ladies with his shouting. Well, I've dealt with worse, thinks I. So best to get it over with. Too late now for him to change what has been gone an done.

Sharp's flitted on down the stairs; he's standing in the lee, lurking worse than any vamp, but I shove my hands in my pockets an set off after him, down towards the little room Trone's used as an office, where he taught me my letters.

"In here." Sharp opens the door, waves me in.

The room is dark, no one's bothered lighting the lamps yet, an it takes me only a flick of a nilly-tail to realise the room's empty.

"Hey." I turn. "There's –"

The door shuts in my face an the key rattles, making the old unused lock groan.

"Bat-fucker," says Sharp, the wood muffling his voice. "Filth-tracker. If I'd known what you were going to do, I never would have showed you the Splinterfist."

I'm not worried. Sharp's trying to prove himself the big Lammer. I've seen plenty bluff an brags on the Digs. There's no spouting from this yellow-spleened pot-scrubber that's going to scare me. I lean my back against the door, fold my arms an turn my head. The wood is cold against my face. "Well, you did," says I. "And what's done is spilt, as they say. So why don't you just get on with your social climbing an catamiting, an I'll get on with mine."

"You know," says Sharp, chummy-like an soft. He must be leaning in close to the keyhole. "I thought I'd done you in with taking you to Ia's little haunt. I near pissed myself laughing when you went and chatted her up."

I jerk away from the door. "You knew that was her?" Shite, so the Sphynx was a set-up. Played by Sharp – Ia an me on little strings, skin-puppets to make the Hoblings laugh. I grit my teeth.

"But," he carries on, "that didn't last long. Even getting you hooked on the bats didn't work. There you were, high as a Hob-kite all the time, and you still somehow managed to turn it to your advantage."

"What advantage?" I says. "Locked up like a Mata-whore? You've a strange sense of good, Sharp-my-lad." A thought hits me solid between the eyes. "You wanted me caught with that scriv too?"

No answer's as good as a yes, but I'm getting an inkling now of Sharpshins's flaky head. He's not right, like a scrivver that's been down a mine too long. "Sharp?"

He's gone. That or he's sitting outside the door giggling quiet-like to himself. Maniac.

"Right, chum. What do you want then? It's not like I've done nothing to you." I ponder. "'Cept maybe pass some of my dishes off on you once or twice."

Still quiet. Gone for sure.

"Actually," I says to the silence. "Was more than twice." I take a step back an have a squizz at the lock. It's something I could pick, given tools an time. I kick the door. The wood's so thick an solid that it makes only a dull sound. There might be summat in Trone's desk I could use, so I go rummage about there, but the bastard is as neat an whistle-clean as he can be. Paper ain't gonna help me.

Outside the window a sleepy dove coos, then goes back to sleeping. It'll be time enough before anyone comes down here, leastwise, not this early. I slump down an sit on the floor with my back to the door. I tilt my head an look up at the shadows. It's only a few hours 'til dawn, an I've waited in worse places. Not gonna give that scriv-head the jollies by screaming to be let out. I'll sit it out 'til Trone starts work.

An then the fear hits.

The force of it makes me stand, double over, holding my stomach. I'm sweating like a slaughter-hog an I can barely breathe.

It's not mine. I never feel like this, this broken an panicked.

Gris. Fuck. I'm gonna choke on someone else's fear an I din't even know that could happen. Just what the fuck kind of game is Sharp pulling, an how? I wonder if he's roped some Lammer into making me feel this – if there's a way they can even do that, and then I'm screaming so hard I can't even swallow, and my spit runs out my mouth. I wanna vomit, but my stomach is empty.

There's an image burned into my head, the only place I've ever seen terror the way I'm feeling it now. That little vamp, the one the sharif caught on the Wend, the way it cried on the stakes. The blood in its eyes.

There's blood in my eyes.

An I can hear voices.

Booming in my head. "Hold it still."

"Gris, Sharp, the fucking thing just bit me."

"I said hold it."

My mouth is filled. I cannot scream.

"That'll stop that."

Hands on my wrists. Only they're not my wrists. Pain, pain across my face where something's cut me. Hands. Hands all over.

Someone is screaming in my head, over an over. Calling my name. I focus on that, grab it like a line in a scriv-mine, an pull back into myself. I can taste Sel's magic, the shivering high under my skin, in my blood. On my tongue. The blood in my eyes cools, stops running. Power under my skin, like nothing I've ever felt. Everything with Sel, what came before, was nothing. Compared to this. I feel like I could eat the world.

Sel. They have Sel.

I break that door like it's nothing more than a board shelter on the edge of the Wend heaps. The door flies apart under my hands, an I race up the stairs to where Sel is calling for me, deep in my head.

There's five of them, an I have just time enough to count that, see their faces all white an black with shadow when Sel's magic tears up my bones like hot needles. My breath comes in wheezy-screams, an I feel like I got caught in one of the spinningjenny's machines, mangled an shredded, before the magic spills out of me an rips those fuckers apart. One of them is still bollocks deep in Sel when the magic pulls him back an rips off his face. It makes a sound like tearing wet pulp-boxes on the lam-heaps. He screams all thick and choked as his eyes burst.

I stand in the storm-centre an watch.

Blood in every direction, on the walls, the skin, an over it all the low Lams scream like pigs on killing day.

Thirty

A Game of Wasps

I'M LYING IN bed pondering on how to make my father strike Jek as his heir, mostly using the argument that his bat is unlikely to provide our House with a litter of Ives brats, when Mother's voice, shrill and wordless, comes ululating from above. A servant is already at my door.

"Miss, your Father says to stay –"

I push past her, not even bothering to cover my nightdress or put slippers on my bare feet. The screams are coming from Jek's quarters.

My mother is standing in the entrance to the passage, hanging onto the doorframe for support. She's ashen, her hair a bedraggled mess that hangs in her face. I've never seen her like this. There's a shadow of blood on her hands, emptiness in the hollows of her eyes, and then it's gone, like an after-image. The spatters on her cream nightdress don't disappear though. Her knees are stained.

She barely notices as I step past her, her eyes are vacant, and she mumbles, croons softly. I can just hear her say, "There's magic in the veins, I know where it lies," and then she's behind me, and I'm inside the darkened passage of Jek's wing of the house.

Even in the short time he's been here it has changed. There's dust on the rail, cobwebs already knitted into the corners. No lamps have been lit, and the faint light that pools from the bedroom only makes the shadows and webs look bigger, darker. I tip-toe, the carpet soft under my feet. Every now and then, something dampens the thick wool, and it's no stretch of the imagination to work out what it is. The copper smell of blood furs my throat, and under it, the reek of faeces, vomit. Am I entering a charnel house? Did Jek's bat finally reveal its true nature and tear my half-brother apart? I need to know.

There are no voices raised now, just a cloaking silence that is heavy and unnatural. I peer through the open door.

Bodies. The bodies are what I see first. They're hard to miss, spread open like gutted pigs, their ribs sharp and white through the gore. The walls are covered with blood. Entrails are looped over the unlit chandelier, making it rock. Someone here has just lit the reading lamps, and the oil sputters. In the flare of light the blood is almost black, and I stare.

There's Sharpshins, my little gossip from the kitchen. His head is twisted almost off his body, and his limbs look as if they have been filleted. Worse still is the yawning cavern of his belly and ribcage. The missing organs must be somewhere among this litter of pulp and bloody meat, but there's no telling which they could be.

Magic drips along the walls, black and bitter-strange. It mingles with the blood and meat, and everything takes on a close feeling, like the magic is sentient, watching my reaction. I shake my head to clear it, but the magic stays: an oily sludge that slowly seeps into the room. It is already growing fainter, and I tell myself that there is nothing there, that it is a trick of the light, that my senses are disturbed by violence and dreams.

My father stands with his back to me. His shoulders tremble, but without the scriven, I have no idea whether it's fear or rage that moves him. Finally, I look to the bed. Jek's bat is curled up, white and naked, his knees drawn to his chest. He lies on his side, head buried under the mound of slicked pillows while Jek sits on the edge of the bed, one hand on the bat's shoulder. Blood streaks the bat's thighs, but I don't know who it belongs to.

Jek is as white as his pet. I don't need a scriv-high to see the fear on his face.

"I don't know how I did it," he says.

A hand clutches my arm, and I shriek. The sound makes my father and Jek look to me, just as my mother drags me back from the room.

"Sweet Gris, you weren't supposed to see that," she says, as she hauls me back down the passage, away from the carnage. "Why can't you ever do what you're told?" She sounds herself again. "Why can't you do what I See?"

Five. I counted five people dead. Their bodies were slick with alien magic. "What happened?" I wait for her to tell me what the magic was – what power was unleashed and used in that room.

She lets go of my arm. "The kitchen. We could all do with some tea."

Privately, I think my mother must have lost her mind, but I follow her anyway, somewhat amazed that she even knows where to go. The kitchen is brightly lit, filled with the anxious faces of the staff. The sight brings my mother back to herself. "Tea," she commands.

By unspoken agreement, we drink it at the staff table. Neither of us wants to return to our part of the house, and the staff are looking disgruntled by our presence, now that they've gotten over their initial shock.

The tea is hot and over-honeyed. A maid brings me my slippers and gown. Already, the image of the corpses in Jek's room seems unreal. "What happened?" I ask.

"Jek," she says. "He killed them all. We don't know why, or how."

But I think I do know why, because I understand something of Sharpshins, and I remember reading his intent once with the last of the scriven. I say nothing. I'm not here to stand up for Jek; he can clear his name himself, save his own skinny self from the iron death sentence. Honestly, I never thought Sharpshins would act on his feelings. How strange for me to have misjudged him. It's the lack of magic; it's making me sloppy. Scared.

And there's a new problem. I understand why Jek would have killed Sharpshins, but the *how* of it escapes me. That room, it burned with magic, dark and oily. And most definitely not scriven. No one has mentioned it, even though the pall of it is leaking down through the ceiling even now.

Did Jek do that?

If he did, why has my mother not said anything? Why did my father stand in the midst of it and not breathe a word?

It occurs to me that I may be the only one who noticed it, attuned as I am to Reading. A shiver courses under my skin, rippling gooseflesh in its wake. A new magic – and one that only I can see. A magic that Jek can use. How else did he tear our servants apart as if they were no more than paper dolls? Greed flushes up my arms, sending the chill from my body.

Scrivless magic. Where did it come from, and why did it choose to manifest through my magicless half-brother?

More importantly. Can I learn to use it?

Thirty-One

Singing for the Dead

FOR THE FIRST time since mother and Dae died, I can think clearly. Even string the words into a shape that pleases. Jek sees the world like this. I wince, and shake my head, willing the sting from my skin, the ache from my back and body.

"I don't know how I did it," Jek says, speaking to his father. Fear makes him choke on his words.

I open my eyes. The Ives sire watches. He shifts his look from me to Jek. I curl tighter; wait the magic out. It's dying soft as rain falling. I feel it land on my skin, like ash and sorrow.

"Get on some clean clothes, get the bat dressed, and get downstairs."

"What?"

"Don't argue. Not if you want me to get you out of this." The door slams.

A soft touch on my shoulder, down my back. Jek's hand shakes.

"Sel?"

"I heard." I make myself sit up and face the dead and all the pain I brought them. I dress for the dead. There are songs to sing for the newborn and the dying, but I've lost them long time ago. I know I used to know them.

"What just happened?"

There are no words. I try pull them from Jek's head, but the fade is coming, and I'm losing the pleasing shapes, the understanding. "I don't know. I don't know." Gone. "Jek?"

I dress fast. Jek wipes the blood away. I make sure to follow, set one foot in place, one step in the space where Jek stepped. Down the stairs, outside, stamp in the cold, mist from my mouth. My breath is smokeless smoke. I spin between the falling white ash. Pain is all through me, to my core. I'm broken. Worse than anything that came before.

"Stop it from doing that," the Lammer says.

Jek's hand is on my shoulder. "Come now, Sel-love. Still."

"The coach will take you straight to House Guyin. Here." A letter in the sire's hand, held out to us. Paper shivers like an old leaf.

Jek takes it. "Guyin?"

"I'm going to try clear this up, and it's the safest place for the two of you to be right now. And he owes me this much."

The nillies snort. I reach out and touch them. Their noses sniff. The blood smell of me and the dead makes them quiet and wide eyed.

"Leave the nillies alone, Sel." Jek pushes me away from their noses. "Hop in there."

The coach is dark; it smells like straw and must. A clicking tongue makes the nillies move on, and we are away. Behind me, the magic eats the deaths, like it should. I curl up into my pain and hold myself together before I fly apart.

Thirty-Two

The Grinningtommy

I'VE NEVER GONE this way through MallenIve, but I'm barely taking any of this in. My head hurts. Fuck – my pores hurt – my skin burning like the magic poured straight out through every pinprick hole in my body. And it's not just my pain, 'cause I'm still feeling... I look at him, even though I don't want to none.

Sel is quiet now, curled up tight, watching through the windows, his face pressed up to the glass, his breath making a fuzzy halo. For a moment, he'd seemed normal-like, but that's gone now. I caught a glimpse inside his head; it's like a broken bottle, sharp glass an leaking thoughts.

Guyin. The House Shamed. The last Lord of Guyin bonded with a bat, so goes the rumours, an I guess they're truth because I can't think of a reason otherwise that my da would be sending me there. I know there's no friendship twixt them. An for all Trone's got me talking as poncy as any Lammer, I don't think that Guyin is going to go an help me 'cause he thinks I'm some House heir to court.

The coach bounces along the cobbles, an outside the grey dawn is turning chill an light. Somewhere behind the clouds the sun is rising. If I was in the Digs now, Oncle would be up, boiling dandelion root an binding his hands. Or Prue, when she was still able to walk, before she coughed herself to death, she'd make us a hot drink. All sudden-like, I miss the bitter grit taste of dandelion tea. The layers of jackets. The rags in the windows. The hate in me is quiet an faded now. Instead I'm worried, about Oncle, about what he's doing now the mines are closed.

This must be the first snowy winter in ten years. We've never had a winter so bad. I don't want to picture the old bugger cold an hungry. I close my eyes an press the thought away, think about Sel instead. Not that that's any better. He's cold too, in a different way, all shut up an not making sense an hurting. I can feel the hurt: raw pain, second hand. There's no way to put out my mind exactly what they did to him, an I've no words that will make it right. Can't even touch him.

The coach crawls slow through the streets before bouncing to a halt. The nillies stamp while I climb out the coach. Steam's rising off their backs; Trone's pushed them hard to get us from House Ives before the damn sharif show up.

We've stopped before a house with a plain redbrick face, though it's bigger even than the Ives house. It's newer too, with wide blank windows an a fresh-painted door, blue as the smoke that comes off the winter fires in the Digs.

"They're expecting us?" I glance up at Trone, still wearing his nightclothes under his thick wool coat. He shrugs, tightens his hands on the reins an flicks the leather across the nillies' backs. The coach pulls away.

We stand on the wide clean pavement before the Guyin house, while the wind blows dirty snow around us. Well, no point waiting out here to freeze to death, so I take the steps up, the letter fast in my hand. The Saints only know what my da has written that's going to save us now.

The knock hurts my knuckles, an I wince.

"Are we safe now?" Sel's voice is all boggert-soft.

"Not bloody likely," I says as I turn to him. He's stopped on the third step so he can sit on the stone edge of an urn pedestal. For the first time, I notice he's barefoot. Fucking vamp can irritate me no end; sometimes it's like Hobling-watching, a job I did my best to get out of when I still lived in the Digs. His feet have turned blue. A spatter of dried blood crosses the top of his left foot. I swallow down my vomit an shake my head, like that will kill the pain-echo twixt us. As I turn to knock again a light has come on, the wick sputtering an dancing, making the shadows jump across the curtains.

The door opens, an a tired-looking Lam looks out with hooded eyes. He's already dressed, in a full suit with a waistcoat an pocket watch chain glinting gold. It's obvious he's the lord of the house; I guess not even poverty an shame can kill a Lammer's natural attitude. I was expecting a servant, so it takes me a moment to pull my thoughts straight an thrust the letter out at him.

He takes the letter with a slow curl of his fingers, his eyes not on it, or me, but on Sel, sitting in the snow with his cold feet an his new clothes.

"I'd heard rumours. Didn't think it was more than that." He looks down at me, pointed. He's older than me by a good many years, but still younger than my da. There's a touch of grey at his temples an shadows in his eyes. "You'll be the Ives boy, Vance's little bastard."

I shrug. "There's a letter." I nod at the paper he's holding. "Explains it all."

"Really?" He still doesn't look at it or invite us in.

From the house comes a deep an gravelly voice, like Sel's a little, if he were older. "What is it now? Some half-grown urchin knocking for a dare? I told you, you should let me answer –" A bone-white face peers around the Guyin. "Harun?" He looks at me, at Sel. "Well fuck me. Get in out of the cold, you idiot children."

The Guyin smirks, crumples the letter into his pocket then swings the door open. "Far be it for me to even pretend to be master of my own home."

I go haul Sel up, an shove him into the house. Leastwise I'm glad to be out of the cold.

The house might look rich from the outside, but it's all a different tale in here. I've seen better furniture on the Lam-heaps down the Wend. The Guyin's vampire sits down in one ratty chair an leans an arm on the rest, watching us both with that slow look they have, the blinks too far apart. The Guyin – Harun – just stares at us, like he expects us to start entertaining him. I've given up trying to get the daft bastard to read the letter, so I just climb into the story. "We've killed someone. Someones."

Harun lifts one eyebrow, says nothing.

"I can smell it," says his vamp. "When did you start using his magic?" He tilts his head to where Sel is standing at the door, like he's scared to come in.

"Dunno what you mean. I feel it all the time, but I don't use it.

Don't even know how to answer you straight." 'Course, after what's happened with Sharp I got a pretty good idea what he's talking about, an it makes sense that somehow I pulled that shivery magic straight out of Sel an used it like the War-singers do. 'Cept they use scriv, an the magic is already inside them. My head hurts. I have no fucking clue what's going on anymore.

The vamp leans forward. "Of course you know what I mean. You've tapped the magic. And you'll only have needed to do that if the bond made you. Is this the first time?"

I nod.

He slumps back, glances at Harun, who's standing like a graveyard statue.

It's like they're talking without words, because Harun sighs as he pulls the crumpled letter from his pocket, an smooths it out so he can read.

The vamp gets up to light more lamps, an the room goes warm an cosy-like. "Stop hovering," he says to Sel, an puts a hand on his shoulder, steering him to the chair. I grab at Sel as he passes, catching his wrist.

The shriek that comes out of him makes everyone jump. I pull back. Oh Gris. How did I forget the feel of Sharpshins pushing that wrist back 'til it just about snapped the bones – I stand there dumb an useless. It's Harun's bat that pulls Sel close, shushes him.

Harun jerks his head. "Isidro, get him calmed down, and then we'll have to drag Jannik and Felicita down here; try and get these children out of this."

Still holding Sel, Isidro closes his eyes. There's magic in the room, flowing between the bonded pair, an I wonder that I never noticed it when I first came in.

Harun's crushed that letter up tight again, so tight his knuckles have gone yellow an shiny. "You did what you had to. The bond made sure of that," he says to me. He passes a hand over his face and looks a decade older. "It also means that everything we've been trying to keep from the other Lammers is going to come out into the open. There's no way to get around that."

"Meaning?"

"You've given them another reason to fear us, Ives Jek. And if we try to save you, what happens to us?"

Thirty-Three

A Game of Wasps

MIDDAY, AND THE servants have cleaned the blood from the walls and floor of Jek's room. The bodies are pieced together and covered under shrouds while we wait for the sharif to inspect them. Mother has barely left my side all day, and her whole body trembles constantly. She keeps looking around, wide eyed, and her movements are jerky and out of time.

I've seen Father only briefly, his face harried and pale, the strain white around his eyes. He's been rushing from place to place, trying to hold together what's left of the Ives dignity. Since Jek arrived, we've been dragged down by association, and still it seems that our father doesn't see it. Guilt is a scourge that drives him, and I wonder if he sees Jek as anything more than a way to make up to his lost love. He's talking now to a Mata sharif. I can't hear them, but his hands gesticulate wildly, like he's conducting a Lera opera.

Illy has come home in a rush of powder and silk. She's taken on that scriv-smell so typical of the Mata. If it wasn't for her presence here today, I would be sure we'd already lost her to them. Even so, I'm not certain we haven't. She comes alone. For the best, I suppose, although it does indicate that the Mata are washing their hands of this little affair. If Iliana isn't careful, they'll wash their hands of her too.

"What did that bastard Hob do?" Illy's voice has a splintered quality to it.

I narrow my eyes, watch her face for minute changes. Without scriv, it's almost impossible to read what she really feels. "He killed five servants, using magic." I tell her of the bodies, adding in details with relish so I can watch her mouth curl in disgust. I wait for her reaction, for any slip she gives.

"Not possible," Illy says. "He has no magic. He's nothing." She darts her gaze about the small side parlour where we've cloistered ourselves. Mother is sitting on the edge of a hard chaise, her knees primly together, her hands folded in her lap. She's staring at the fire, and her face is bathed in orange light. The fire dims a little bit before Iliana looks back to me, and licks her lip, her tongue just darting out once before she takes a little gasping breath. "It was the bat. The bat must have killed them, and now Jek's protecting it, like the lying fool he is –"

"If he is," I say, "then the sharif will find out."

"He is."

"And if he isn't, then we'll have questions answered. Either way –" I pause to sip at my sweetened tea. "You'll have a chance to get your inheritance back." And I, perhaps I will find a way to get Jek's magic.

Iliana's eyes fly open. "Is that what you think this is about?" She stands, knocking the little glass table as she does. Tea spills, cold and reddish. Illy never takes milk. "This has nothing to do with Ives. I'm Mata now, as if you've forgotten." She looks at me with a sly smile. "Hardly likely, is it?"

"Iliana." I don't have the patience for her spite. Trey isn't mine anymore, and bitter as that is, I've swallowed it. I've had to. My father has drummed into us all that we must accept what happens, and to use it as best we can, to whatever advantage we can. Deep down I always knew that I would never have Trey, not when I was the second daughter. I'll be sold off to some aspiring House that Father wants to curry favour with. But, Iliana does have him, and so we will use that in whatever way we can.

I close my eyes for a moment to gather myself. I can be brave; I can look at her and accept my lot. "Sit down. I need you here. Damage control."

"What?" Illy sits, despite her anger. "You need me? I'm here for Mother and Father." Two high spots of colour are on her cheeks, but her eyes are shining with a fevered brightness. She doesn't blink.

"And Father has apparently lost his mind, sending Jek off to House Guyin." We both look at Mother. She still hasn't moved. The less said there, the better.

"It's all about that stupid Hob-girl – Jek's mother," Iliana says. Her voice crumbles and she leans closer to me. "Do you know that Father wrote to her?" She pulls back a little, frowning, a faint moue of disgust twisting her mouth. "Love poems. I found them when I was four, gave them to Mother because I thought they were hers."

I remember this, faintly. Screaming and fire and tears. Still, the thought of Father sitting in his office love struck as a nilly in spring, penning odes to some serving girl – well, I find it hard to believe. How little we understand of our parents. They are a species so alien, it's hard to believe that they felt like we felt, once.

"Damage control?" Illy repeats our father's words back at me.

I snap out of my thoughts. "Yes." I twist my cup in its saucer. "Illy, do you have any scriven on you?"

That takes her by surprise, but at the look on my face, she nods and unclasps the bag at her side. She taps out a little silver case no bigger than a compact mirror and hands it to me. The Mata's centred sun and its halo of bramble-roses is engraved faintly on the lid. I skid my fingertips over the design.

"Not too much," she says. "It's all I have."

"I'm sure Trey will give you more if you ask." There. I said the name, and the world didn't break open.

"No. Everyone's rationed, even Trey." She says the name very softly, as if she might anger me. "They're worried."

The Mekekana, of course. I've seen the headlines, the word from Pelimburg – the city's Lookfars have seen the Mekekana take Lamb's Island. The first time in many years since the trading stopped. These are no trade ships.

Soon. It will be soon.

The war is limping up to us like a silver-jackal.

"What do you need it for?" Illy asks as I dip the tip of my index finger into the ash-like powder and rub it against my gums. "Are you trying to Read what happened? The sharif will work it out for themselves."

"No." I close my eyes and feel the slow giddy twirl of the scriv settle in my stomach. Gris – how I've missed this. I feel complete, the ache in me filled and healed. Slowly, I raise my head.

Above us, the heavy alien magic is dripping through the ceiling, spreading like a black stain. "There's something very strange in this house," I say. "I've never seen the like." The unnatural magic is fading. With every sense enhanced, I can see the edges slowly dissolving.

The firelight is too bright when I open my eyes, and I realise Iliana has forgotten to raise her shields while I've been in a scriven trance. She's churning with a grey-green colour, so thick that I can almost taste it in the back of my throat, acrid and chalky. She's so sad. I suck in a breath. I've never seen my sister like this, never. I pull my gaze from that dreadful, lonely misery and glance up at the stained magic. "Iliana," I say. "The house is soaked in magic. Soaked."

"Can you see it?" She perks up. "Is it something we can use? Like scriven?"

I shake my head. "I don't know, but if we could, if we could harness the kind of power that ripped those men apart –" I stare at her face. "Illy, the Mekekana wouldn't know what hit them."

"But we can't – we don't know how."

"No, but Jek – or the bat, I'm not totally sure – one of them can. We need to know how. And they're the only ones who know what really happened in that room."

"J – Our brother is as good as dead." She looks at me, the sadness that is shrouding her tempered now with resignation, with quiet hurt. "You know that. Not even Father will be able to pretend otherwise."

"You're right." I sigh and lean back in my chair. Iliana forgets though, she forgets that we have one more person on our side. Someone who is not of our House. Someone with far more power in the palace than we could ever hope to have. "He will die. Unless someone speaks for them at their trial . . . ." I wait. "We need that information. It's House Ives's chance to gain face." I wonder if she'll see what I'm seeing, put together the puzzle pieces to build the same picture. She's not stupid, but she doesn't think like me – about how we can use people. I want it to feel like her idea, getting Trey to say what we need him to say so that I can study this magic. Use it, perhaps.

Illy puts a finger to her mouth to chew at a nail, a habit I thought Mother had long ago discouraged. "You want me to save them? Save Jek?" Her voice rises in a muted shriek on his name, before she clams her mouth shut.

"I want you to save the magic. And that means Jek and his bat. You can talk to Trey; you can make sure there's a voice in the Mata that will speak for them."

Her expression doesn't change, but her aura wavers, rippling with a milky uncertainty. "No," she whispers. "I won't do it. I don't care. . . ." Her voice is far away, and I don't think she even sees me anymore.

I press my palms together and bow my head. I know what I can do. "Illy," I say softly. "You will." I look up at her, hold her gaze. "You will, or I'll tell Trey about what happened with you and Jek. And I will tell them both who you still –"

"No!" She stands, her face white. Her aura disappears as she brings down her shields. "You –" She covers her mouth with one hand and glances at Mother.

"I know," I say.

"Shut up." Her words are muffled still. She drops her hand and stares at me like it's the very first time she has truly seen me.

"I will do it," I tell her, and I keep my face hard as glass, even though with every word I feel my inners crumbling to dust and nothing. I never thought it would destroy me so utterly, to use her love against her. I thought it would be a victory. My mouth tastes of ash. "Unless you agree."

Illy crumples, sitting down on the chair with a solid thump. There is still no colour in her face. She tilts her head and looks up at the ceiling, at the slow drip of magic that only I can see.

"If I'm right, it will make the Ives name good again."

"And if you're wrong?" she whispers.

"Really, if I am, what does it matter? Ives is a tangled mess. It certainly can't get worse."

She covers her fear by carefully placing the scriven box back in her bag and fiddling with the clasp. With a whisper of silk she stands and holds her hand stiffly out to me as if we were strangers. "I'll see what I can do."

Thirty-Four

Singing for the Dead

THE DARK'S GONE, and I sit far from the fire. The Guyin Lammer has called his friends. He says they will be ours. We are meant to believe him.

They are adult, stern and quiet. Anger storms around them, the room is thick with it. I hide behind Jek, smell the power. They have come because the Guyin said they had to.

"We've a problem," the Guyin says.

The two new people turn, smooth and slow.

Next to the Guyin, Isidro watches them, with power all around him, dark like a nightcloak.

"Yes. It's all over the Courant," the woman says. "The Ives boy tore some servants apart with magic. Hob magic, the gossip rags are calling it."

"Shows what they know, damn tabloids." I like this wray, the younger one, his fast fingers dance as he talks twitchy as a fox. He has a face like Mother's, with wide eyes, a sharp nose. "Still, it might be best to let them think that." He shrugs. "Saves us the scrutiny. Felicita has enough to deal with at the moment."

Isidro stands. "If we stand by and do nothing, they'll both be put to death. Do you think House Pelim so far above us that you can happily allow a wray to be put down, exterminated like a street cat?

Is that what you'd want, Jannik?"

The Guyin taps taps taps his fingers, spiderwalking them on the wooden arm rests, watching watching the wrays fighting with words. Jannik says nothing in answer and looks to the woman, perhaps for support.

"I understand yours and Felicita's position, Jannik – we all do – but the wray is barely more than a child. I don't even think he knows what's going on half the time." Isidro is speaking for me, so strange.

"He's brain-damaged?"

Next to me, Jek bristles; I can feel his flickering anger burning my skin. "There's nowt wrong with Sel's brain, he's just a little . . . ."

"Confused?" Jannik arches a brow.

"Broken," says Jek.

I shiver, trying to hold the brokenness inside, so it doesn't show.

Isidro glares at Jek. "Broken how? The wray barely makes sense. Frankly, I'm amazed that my mother even allowed him to work."

"I've seen inside his head." Jek is soft. "He does know, he understands, but it's like everything comes to him in little pieces, an he has to try an stick them all back together-like before it makes sense. Like a Hobling's puzzle."

Jek says the words that I can't find; I stop shaking and let him talk for me.

"Trauma? What do you think?" Isidro asks Jannik.

"Hmm, possibly. I've heard of similar breakdowns when one of a bonded pair has died." He pulls his hair back from his face, agitated, brow wrinkled. "But then death has always followed within a few hours, and that's hardly happened here."

"So we can rule out a bonding." Isidro looks at me. I want to hide from his cutting eyes. "What about a twin?"

"Same result. I've never heard of a twin surviving longer than a week or so once the other is dead. Whatever has happened to him, it's neither of those scenarios. I can look through Felicita's library, see if we have something there I've overlooked." Then his face clears, and the anger is back. "Speculating as to the wray's sanity isn't what I'm here for." He curls his hand on his Lammer woman's shoulder. "Felicita shouldn't be travelling in her condition. Isidro, you're well aware of it, and yet you've called us out here. Either tell us what you want us to do, or allow us to depart."

"I'm not telling anyone what to do. I'm asking if you'll help. If you'll be willing to stand up in a Mata court and explain the bond and its . . . limitations."

"Are you insane? We are hated enough as it is –"

The Lammer woman next to him stands and laces her fingers over her belly. "I will speak, if they will accept the testimony of a bonded Lammer such as myself. House Pelim is still a name to be reckoned with, even here."

Isidro bows his head. "Thank you, Lady Pelim. You have our gratitude." Pretty, mocking words.

"It's not just for the wray. The Hob will die too. Two deaths – I do not think our secrets are worth that."

The need to leave, need to get out, rises inside. Oh death, I can face you. Dae faced you. But I cannot let Jek take your hand. The wrays will help. Or they won't, but I must go, must leave, there is too much fire in the room – I can't remember how to be calm the way mother taught me.

Dart, quick as a swimming fish. And I'm gone.

Thirty-Five

The Grinningtommy

THE DOOR SLAMS behind Sel, an I stare at it for a split second before I lurch forward. A hand on my shoulder pulls me back.

"Don't worry about him. There's nowhere in the house for him to go." Harun's grip is tight, making my magic-licked skin crawl. Don't want some strange fucking Lam touching me right now, not after what I can feel what happened to Sel. He lets me go, nods to the chair. "He'll be fine," he says. "Sit."

I slump into the couch an watch the door. Nothing. Best pay attention to what these fancy Lams an vamps have hidden up their coat-sleeves.

Isidro turns back to the others. "Are we in agreement then?"

It's a long time before Jannik nods, but Felicita puts her hand on his an sighs all angry-like, an they both turn an bow their heads.

"Done," says Isidro. His long dark hair is pulled back from his face, an in the firelight his white skin looks gold. He looks high-born as any House Lammer. I never knew vamps could look like that.

The flames are too warm an bright. My head is going all blurry, like I spent the day drinking bitter in the Scrivver's Hole an then stepped out into hot sun. I feel myself falling, but it's not-real. Like it's happening to some other Hob.

"Took a while for it to hit," says a voice, all conversational. I can't open my eyes, but I recognise Isidro. Bat talks like he bloody owns the place.

"Hmm," Harun says. "Hobs – he's a half-breed – perhaps that's all it takes. A bit of mongrel blood to counter the energy drain."

"Interesting." Footsteps, an then the whish of a silk jacket as someone kneels next to me. Fingers pry open my eyes an I can see Jannik's sharp white face. "Can you sit up?"

I can't move my head, but I manage to make some gurgling noise that the stuck-up shite takes as a yes, so he pulls me up an drags me to my seat.

The lady is fussing with a tray on a side table, looking sidelong at me. She's short and curved, no hard angles to her, except maybe in the way she stares at me. Those eyes are sharp and clever, and even the way her hair is all curled and soft like any lady who spends all her days being pampered ain't enough to hide that hardness about her. Here is someone who'll do anything and smile sweet-as while she does it.

"Here, drink this," the lady says, an her voice is cool an low. The Casabi sounds like that – river-dark, there's a hint of something else there – something dangerous. Her face is close, she's almost smiling, holding out a glass of what looks like nilly-milk.

I open my mouth to ask for something with a bit more bite to it, that I'm no Hobling still drinking milk from my mam's brass, an she practically pours the shite down my throat. I choke, swallow, an feel the burn as the laced milk settles in my belly.

"Ta," I says, an she laughs.

She puts down the half-empty glass. "There are too few of us that we can afford to let them die." She gets all serious-like then, an frowns. "Can you guarantee us our safety?"

Harun looks at his vamp, shrugs. Isidro is the one that answers her. "We'll be safe, Felicita," he says. "They might hate what we are, but we've done nothing that they can use against us. We've covered our tracks in the past."

Felicita sighs. "And we're supposed to trust to luck that nothing buried will be uncovered, I suppose." She looks back at me. "Come now. Let's go find your partner. I'm certain that in the meantime, Lord Harun will deign to provide his guests with some repast." She turns her head to glare at him, then laughs.

It's the first time someone's called Sel my partner, an it sounds weird to me, even if I guess it's truth. I get up on shaky legs to follow her out of the fire-lit rooms, into the hallway an up a flight of creaking stairs that puff dust round my feet.

If I put my head to it, I can feel the binding between me an Sel. Whatever happened in that room, it's tied us tighter together. I don't think I like it over much, but at least it's good for something, cause I can tell that the daft little shite has gone an sat hisself in an empty room, an I follow the traces of him to the closed door at the end of the passage.

"Here?"

I nod, an she pushes the door open. There's Sel. Sitting on the floor of a music chamber in front of a large piano. There's dust everywhere.

"I didn't touch it," says Sel slow as a dream. "It played itself. Singing for the dead to come and gone."

There's no music, not a drop of sound, an Felicita gives me a look – the kind that says a whole lot; that says, *are you quite sure that your little friend is all there*? I ignore her an go crouch down next to him. He's calm an quiet, like nothing at all has happened today.

"C'mon Sel-love," I say soft-like, so she won't hear. "Let's go lie down or something. Them what's downstairs says they'll sort us out; they'll talk to the Mata. Everything will be fine, you'll see."

Sel gives me a withering look but stands up anyway.

"I'll ask Harun where you can sleep," says Felicita. "And your Sel needs to feed, so don't bring him down, you'll upset the others."

I've no idea how she knows that, but I guess her an that stuck-up vamp of hers been together long enough that she's reading the signs or something. At any road, it explains the tight feeling in my belly an the squeeze in my throat.

She's back not long later, an I pull my hand away from Sel's shoulder.

"Follow me. Harun says you can use the Blue Room, provided you try not to touch anything." She laughs then, a sharp sound vicious like jackal's teeth. "Don't mind him. He's always been a prickly sort, even before his House practically disowned him. Unlike some of us, he's not used to losing face."

With Sel holding my arm, we follow her down dusty passages an dustier rooms. The only room that isn't coated in grime looks like an apothecary's workshop, all gleaming glass an bone an ivory gadgetry.

We go past that to a small chamber.

It's easy enough to see why it's called the Blue Room. The walls

are white, true enough, but the sheets an curtains are made from
some stiff fabric printed with these twirly designs in a dark blue dye.
The room smells like must an dust, an the candles have all been
chewed at by mice. The water pitcher an basin have the same
pattern. If I were still in a habit of nicking Lammer-gear, I could fetch
a decent brass bit or two for them.

"Get what sleep you can," she says. "It won't be long before
your father has to tell the sharif where you've gone."

"Or you lot turn me in."

She shakes her head. "No one here will do that to you, rest
assured. Personally, I think it would be best if you turned yourself in
– a show of good faith – but Harun has spoken with your father, he
says, and it seems that they have their own plans."

"Bully for them."

"Yes. Still, there's no point trying to explain anything to lords
when they get ideas in their heads."

Sel is walking around the room, picking up the little bric-a-brac
that give the dust in the room shape. "Put that down," I say, when I
see he's twisting a pricey-looking nilly statue around in his hands.
"Before you go on an break it."

Felicita laughs cold. "If you want us to believe that there's more
than a child's mind in your partner's head, then you'd do best to
believe it yourself."

"What do you mean?"

"You've started a bond – the Saints only know why you decided
to something so utterly foolish – and that makes you equals. Treat
him like it."

"I do."

Sel puts down the nilly; he's looking at me with his head cocked.
"No you don't. Sometimes you forget."

It takes just that to put me in my place.

Felicita narrows her eyes. "It's not love that binds you, anyone
can see that. So I have to wonder what the two of you thought you'd
get out of this. I'm going to guess it wasn't a political alliance," she
says, dry as anything.

There's no answer I can give her straight. I want to tell she's all
wrong-like, that she don't know nothing about me an Sel, but she's
got old eyes, like she's seen way more than Saints. She shakes her
head. "You poor fools – you've really no idea what you're going to
do to each other."

"So why don't you go an tell us, instead of talking round in circles, Lammer?"

"Felicita." She drops a fake-curtsey at me. "House Pelim to you."

"Fuck me, they must have loved you running off with a vamp," I says. "Is that why you're in this shite hole?"

"Something like that." She dusts off a chair, an takes a seat. "I'm going to assume that neither of you knows the first thing about how to keep your secrets safe in your head. And I can't imagine that Jannik is going to have the energy to try and train you. If he even had the time. So here's what's going to happen to you now. You'll start to feel everything he does, and he'll do the same for you. If you're close together, you won't be able to tell his thoughts from yours, and you'll never know if you're doing something because you want it, or he does. Sound fun?" Her voice catches.

I stare at her. "You taking the piss? So we'll stay apart."

"Good luck with that." Her smile is thin. "It will hurt."

"So?" I shrug. I've hurt before, I can take it. In my head, Sel shivers, leaf-thin.

That smile don't fade, though she shakes her head. "Make it easier on yourselves, find some way of loving each other. Choose it, instead of being bound into it."

An I hate this talk of love an that shite. I look down at my boots, an wait for her to leave.

Her skirts rustle, an I feel her pass by me, for a moment, she rests her fingers on my shoulder. "Hobs – you never do want to see what's right before you."

When her footsteps are long faded, I sit down next to Sel.

"She's right," he says, all bleak-like.

I still don't have words; don't want to talk about what she's just said.

"I do need to feed," he says,

"Oh. Right." This is awkward as all, an I've no idea what to do or say. I mean, normal-like, there'd be no problems, but I can't see us rutting now, not after everything that's happened, an that's the usual way we go about this whole feeding thing. It's Sel who reaches out for my arm an solves the problem by biting down into my wrist. The pain is sharp an sudden; the high that hits me all messed up. Dark, twisted – I think it's because of that fucking magic-tap.

He drinks until I'm feeling dizzy then lets me go an curls up on his side, still dressed. He goes to sleep just like that. Of course, we've been up since before the bloody sun, an I realise just how tired I am when I lie down next to him an close my eyes. It would take a pack of rabid Wend Hobs to get me up now, I thinks, just before I fall asleep.

As it turns, it's not a Hob pack that wakes me, although that would have been a bit more welcome-like.

"This the lad then?"

I open one eye to see a puffed-up uniform, a low-Lammer with a beady eye an a truncheon. Fucking sharif. You give a small man a big stick an this is how it turns out.

There's more than one. Next thing they're dragging me to my feet, an before I even have time to wake up proper-like, something burns at my wrist. First I think it's Sel's bite, the wound torn open or something, an then it hits me when I smell the hair on my arm burning. Iron.

They've put me in fucking iron.

Next to me Sel screams, an I know they've done likewise to him. Only now, I can't tell my pain from his. Gris-damned bond is fucking with my head an Sel's panic is only making it worse. It's just enough iron to hurt, to stop me from making the tap, but not enough to stop me from feeling Sel across the bond.

"Jek," says a voice by my ear, an I twist to see Harun. He grabs my shoulders an keeps me upright, calms me like a good hand will a frightened scrounger fore they lead it off to die. "Go with them easily," he says. "Your father and I will see you in the court. Trust us," he whispers, an then the iron jerks me forward.

It's hard to think when all your mind is focused on pain. I've seen people in iron before, seen Oncle's burnt black palms after a day hacking scriv from the deep. But the miners always wear gloves, and I've never seen up-close what a pure iron burn is like. That thin little collar Trone snapped on me when he took me from the Digs was nothing compared to this.

If I could, I'd chew off my own fucking arms. My head is pounding, an Sel won't let it go – the panic, the pain. "Sel! Shut the fuck up!"

He goes quiet, except for these raspy uneven breaths. There's sweat in my eyes, blinding me, an I can't lift my hands to wipe it away so I just stumble forward, letting the sharif take me wherever they Gris-damned please.

Thirty-Six

A Game of Wasps

ONLY A DAY has passed since our father sent Jek into hiding. Father came home yesterday looking old and worn, and locked himself in his study without telling us anything.

There's been news, of course. The MallenIve presses have been working double time to spread this latest scandal through every House and hole in the city. Mother left the MallenIve Courant on the breakfast room table, open to the article about Jek and the killings. Our name is splattered all over the paper. We will never wash these stains clean.

There's Jek's name, linked with ours, and the scandal of his bat. The story talks of manacled Great House heirs, forbidden bonds, murders, sharif-arrests. They make it sound so tawdry.

I close the journal, and turn it face down. That doesn't help. The back-page opinion piece has a headline that reads "Is this the end for House Ives?" and promises an exposé of all our most notorious failings. I scan down to the sub-heading: "The last of the Old Houses falls".

I've heard nothing from Iliana, and I wonder if she even bothered to speak to Trey. I could have gone myself, perhaps, in my messenger's uniform, but there is a gaggle of reporters at the back and front doors, waiting to capture us as we fall, so that they will have their stories. Even if they weren't there, Trey made it clear. We shouldn't see each other again.

All I can do is wait and trust that Trey will speak in court. Hopefully Iliana will convince him. If he says nothing in Jek's defence I suppose it will fall to me.

At the very least, I should tell Father what I think. After all, he still holds some small measure of respect in the Mata court, being as powerful a War-singer as he is. And when we find a substitute for scriv, and the nillies start foaling live unis, we'll be high again. Jek could bring us back to our peak. I roll that thought in my head and grimace.

Upstairs the house is silent. The bodies have all been removed. Father's study door is closed.

I take a deep breath before knocking softly. "Father, it's Calissa. If I could speak with you?"

He throws open the door unexpectedly, and I start back. His skin is sallow in the oil lamp light. Behind him his usually neat desk is littered with paper. On the floor, several crumpled balls of paper have taken up residence, and the study looks like nothing so much as a trash heap in the Hob quarters.

"Calissa," he says, but he's unfocused, as if he doesn't really see me. I can smell vai on his breath, sour. His thinning hair is standing on end where he has run his hands through it countless times this evening. All this worry, and it's not for us or our name, it's for Jek.

Even so, there are worse things than my brother, and the Mekekana are one of them. We can use Jek, and when we're done, we can find a way to dispose of him. I clear my throat.

"We have a weapon against the Mekekana." And I have a chance to get my magic back. It has been a long time since we faced the Meke without magic. It's the kind of horror story that we tell children, but now the nightmare is on the verge of turning real. If they reach us, they will destroy us the way they do all things of magic, crush us beneath their iron wheels. If we do not have something to fall back on, someone will raise the idea of opening the Well again.

My father stills, but I catch the slight tension in his fingers, the way his fingertips against the wood have whitened. "Go on."

"Jek, and the bat. If we can find a way to harness what they did –
"

"And what makes you think it was either of them? It could be something Sharpshins did. And if it was because of the bat – for all we know harnessing that kind of magic could be as bad as opening the Well."

I shiver. In this moment I could almost believe my father was a Reader, the way he so accurately nails down my fears.

There is no person on this continent, in this world, who would truly want to open the Well, I tell myself – not after what happened the last time. Two hundred years later, and we still find the ruins of what came before, the twisted, mummified bodies deep under the sand. The things in the deep desert – sphynxes, manticores – even the bats wouldn't exist if the Well had not been opened. We unleashed our nightmares when we tried to use wild magic.

"Please," I say. "Just listen to me." I do not think that Jek's magic is on the same scale as the Well. It can't be.

Father immediately sighs and rubs one hand across his face. "So you think it was Jek, and that we can use this magic." He opens the door wide, admitting me into his sanctum. "Anything to support your theory?"

Inside the gas is hissing, running low in the lamps. The light is failing. I brush twists of paper off a leather seat, and sit down, my arms flat on the high arm rests. "There's definitely a strange magic in the house. It's not scriv-based. I can Read that much of it."

Father has taken his seat behind his desk, and he looks intently at me over his steepled index fingers. He doesn't ask me where I got the scriv. "Yes?"

"It's centred on Jek's rooms, and it began fading after the two of them left. I'm almost certain that it's a direct result of – of what happened. That it's some kind of bat or Hob magic."

"And you think we could turn that kind of destructive force against the Mekekana? Interesting."

I play my trump. "If we could at least convince the Mata court to look into the possibility, we will save Jek's life – for a while at least. Perhaps long enough for you to think of a way to have him freed."

"Delaying the inevitable," he says, his face grim. He looks up from his hands and stares at me. "But it's something." He stands. "Thank you, Calissa, for bringing this to my attention." The door swings open under his hand – my invitation to leave. "Especially since I understand that your relationship with your brother has been somewhat strained."

There's none so blind... "There are more important things than sibling rivalry," I say. "I would put aside this foolish enmity to save our face."

He smiles at me, with something like genuine affection.

I've barely had time to treasure his silent praise when the twilit silence is lost in the clanging of the Seven Widows.

Coaches stall in the streets as the Seven Widows peal out their song of war. The pavements are flooded with onlookers, and still the great bells chime. Nillies with cloaked messengers riding low on their backs gallop through the twisting alleys, dodging pedestrians with a supernatural ease.

We are all standing on the House steps, looking down the slope of the hill to where beacon fires light the city perimeters. The crowd surges with sound, and there will be no sleeping tonight.

The Mekekana are crossing the red sands. They will soon be at the city gates. Father has gone to the palace, where all the War-singers will be gathered now, counting the grains of scriv and wondering how and when to use them.

Of course, we can't see the Mekekana's ships from here, but scouts have ridden out into the deep desert and taken flashes. An emergency three-leaf paper – quickly and shoddily printed – is already making the rounds. The metal ships with their thousands of reticulated legs are reproduced in grainy black and white, fuzzy and indistinct.

The ink leaves smudges on my fingers and thumb.

Now more than ever, with the vast iron armies clawing their way across the desert, we need whatever magic we can use. My whole chest aches, constricting around my organs until each breath feels impossible, each heartbeat a slow dull thud. The things they will do to us if we cannot fight them. I remember those nightmare stories, *The Books of Blackness* that Illy and I read to each other by fatcandle light. A shiver races under my skin, and I gasp involuntarily. No. We have Jek. We have something to clutch at.

Never will we fall to the Meke.

SOMETHING HAS CHANGED inside me.

Fear. I suppose. I've gone numb, thoughts chasing each other through my brain, a million what-ifs. I try and ignore them, all these little snares that say *we will fail we will fall we will suffer oh Gris we will suffer*. No. I've set Jek in place as best I can, but that doesn't mean I have to stand here waiting for things to work out. There are things I can still do if I can find the courage to make my move.

Courage. I don't even know what that is. All I know is sneaking and twisting and keeping in the shadows while others take the fall.

The streets are full, busy, and no one notices me walking through the crowds. At home they will not realise that I am not somewhere within the grounds. The paper is still in my hands, and I drop it into the gutter. The ink is all over my palms, leaving them grey and filthy. I stop and look all around me, and for the first time I realise where I'm going. Or at least stop lying to myself about it.

It's supposed to be hate that drives me, not fear. I will myself to lose the terror, to focus all my energy back on hating my brother, to stop being so damn afraid, but my arms are shaking. In the middle of a crowded street, with the Saints singing war, and commoners shoving this way and that as if this was Long Night, and all my chance of getting scriv finally gone, I start to cry.

And it hurts. If Iliana does as I ask, and if Jek comes through, then I'll still have lost – lost Illy's trust, lost to Jek. And if I don't lose then there'll be no magic for me, and the best thing that could happen is to die under iron when we fall to the Mekekana.

Coward. A spineless little mess, without any real grit to it. That's what I am.

Or I can be something else. So easy. I laugh – there's nothing easy about going against a lifetime's pattern. But for all my cowardice, for all my fear, at least that's something to use. Fear is a goad that makes us shed our skins and reinvent our lives.

So all that's left is to do what no one expects, to take a chance, a Vision unSeen. I put my grimy palms to my eyes and try to stop the sobs, but they run through my whole body, wracking me. In the end, I stop gasping them down and just let myself cry for the first time that I remember. When everything inside me has emptied, I feel tired, but cleaner.

Is this how people are supposed to feel – heavy and light at the same time?

I walked to the rookeries while I sobbed. Something drew Jek here, and I want to know what it was. What magics he found with Sel.

The buildings are white-washed, stern. The first of the Widow's fires has been lit in the centre tower – Saint Mallen. Soon the others will catch flame too. My city turns to a nightmare. People scrabble through the streets, taking their families and meagre belongings closer to the centre of the city, where they will be afforded some small manner of protection under the War-singers.

No bats are fleeing through the streets. I stop someone, pulling them to a halt by hanging on their jacket sleeve. "The bat whorehouse," I snap, "Where is it?"

The low-Lammer shrugs out of my grasp. "How the fuck should I know? Ask him."

I look in the direction he's pointing, to where a slender bat is leaning against a wall, watching the flight of the city with something that looks like bored disinterest. I rub my palms down my coat, and march towards him across the wide street, though it feels like I'm fording a river.

A cold wind is blowing through the streets, raining looseleaf papers warning MallenIve of war. They are trampled underfoot, turning to tattered ruins.

The bat watches as I cross the street, pushing through the crowd, making my way steadily closer to him. When I am only a few feet away, I stop. Stare. He's older than me, perhaps in his twenties. He's looking at me with a bitter scowl that almost masks the amusement in his eyes.

"Why aren't you running?" I finally say to him.

He grins back, mirthlessly. "Why aren't you?"

"I – answer the question, bat."

"Where exactly would you like me to run to?" He pulls his hands from his pockets and spreads them in question. "To the protection of the Mata Palace, perhaps?"

"You will die." I don't know why I'm warning him. "Don't you understand that?"

He looks at me properly, and I edge backwards, before being jostled closer to him by a passing crowd of Hobs.

"I know my place, thanks." The grin is back, teeth glinting, humourless. "That lot just lifted your purse."

"What?" I spin, but the Hob pack is gone, mingling with the hundreds of people around us. I feel for my sphynx-leather purse to find my pocket empty. "Gris be damned!" I don't even know why I had the money with me – it's not like I was really going to buy a bat.

I just came to see.

See what?

When I turn back to face him, I find him studying my face in a way that makes me distinctly uncomfortable. "House Lammer?" he says. "Perhaps you should head home before someone does worse than rob you."

"I don't need a damn bat looking out for me," I say, drawing myself up. I grit my teeth and force myself to ask the question – the reason I came to him. "Where would I find the bat whorehouse."

He laughs in surprise. "And what in the Alerion's name would you want to go there for?"

"I hardly think that's any of your business."

"Of course it is, seeing as I bloody-well work there."

I jerk back. Somehow, I thought that all the whores would be like Sel, damaged and disturbed. I didn't expect someone who would talk back to me, and treat me like I was just some little stupid girl lost. This throws me – my semi-formed plan of finding a bat to see what magics they might have is dashed.

He squints at me. "Do I know you?"

"I sincerely doubt it." Now I wonder if Jek has been with this one too, and it sees some similarity in our features. The thought makes me ill.

"I have to go," I say, stepping backwards, away from him. I don't even know why I'm explaining anything to the bat-whore.

"So I take it you're not looking for a rush then," he says, then shrugs loosely. "Pity. You looked like money."

I pause. Perhaps this is the thing that drew Jek here. "A rush?"

Before I realise what is happening, he darts forward and touches my face. Magic slaps me, cold and sweet.

Then it's gone, and so is he.

I stare through the crowds, pressing my fingers to my cheek. Then I lower my hand. The bat has given me something to ponder, and perhaps the hopes that I've pinned on Jek are not as foolish as they might at first appear. With my thoughts spinning, I retrace my steps back to my home, and pretend to be a good little House daughter, while a new path coalesces in my future.

Thirty-Seven

The Grinningtommy

THEY LEAVE US in two cells in the Sharif quarters. Sel is in the opposite one, kneeling on the floor, his head down.

"Sel?"

He looks up for a moment; there's a cut just under his eye, bruising now. My face aches in the exact same place. I remember feeling the blow, Sharpshins's ring cutting the flesh.

Worse than that now is the iron.

"Won't be long," I says. "Someone will get us out soon-like, you'll see." I can't even go up to the bars to get closer. The heat of the iron roars across my face.

Sel is rocking on his knees, muttering something, something about his mother an counting. He might be talking about his dam, or Riam, I don't even know. It's true what Lady Felicita says: I don't really see him as a person, more like a wild thing that's mostly tamed. A pet. It makes me feel sick inside, that I've been stupid an thoughtless as any Lam.

Even though the heat is something wicked, I scoot a little closer so I can talk to him.

"Where's your mam?" I ask. "Do you think she'll come?"

"No." He crawls into a corner of the cell an presses his back to the wall. His eyes are covered with that white lid. "She can't walk now. All turned to dust."

"She's dead?" I need to keep talking, take his mind an mine off the pain, the searing. "Mine too. She caught the lung. Coughed herself to death."

He quiets at this. "She died to save me." Sel shakes his head like he's trying to shake the thoughts into place. "Me or her, me or her. She chose me."

I don't quite follow, so I carry on. "You know your da?"

Nothing.

"All alone then?"

"No, have you."

I guess he's right. The bond is stronger, so I can feel it, like it's almost real as rope. Makes us family, I suppose. Family are meant to look out for each other, the way Oncle looked out for Prue when she came back an had me. If my da hadn't decided he owned me, I'd most like still be there with Oncle, the two of us looking out for each other.

My chest feels tight. With the mines closed, Oncle could have starved to death, anything. When I get out of here, I'm going to find him. Marlon's pack be damned. I need to let him know he did as he had to, make sure he's okay.

I think I fall sleep for a while, through the pain, but I wake when I hear all the bells in MallenIve clanging. I yell a bit to see if anyone can tell me what's going on. No answer.

The bells ring through the night, an my head pounds in time. My stomach is empty an hollow as a Long Night drum. I'm so hungry I'm sick, an now on top of everything else, I have a headache from the noise. Right now, if they turned around an told me I'd be dead without even a trial, I'd probably welcome them like a cheap whore. Fuck me, I'm tired.

"Wakey-wakey, lads. There's others better than you waiting, and them as don't like to wait long."

The fat grinning face of a sharif comes into view. He's pulling on thick leather gloves so that he can unlock the cells, touch the chains. There's another sharif just behind him, although this one has a worried look.

My da must be here. I pull my sleeve over my burnt wrists with my teeth so it don't look so bad. Don't want to distract anyone right now, just wanna get the fuck out of here, even if it means I'm going straight to court. I'm putting all my trust in those vampires an lords, an really, I'm hoping that it'll be enough because there ain't nowt else. I'm a Hob, an I've killed five low-Lammers. There's no way those Lams up in the palace are going to look kindly on me.

It's not my da waiting outside, but palace sharif in gold-an-rose uniforms. They take us without speaking, an we're led through the streets like we're old nillies good only for the butcher's block.

The palace is glittering in the early light. The sky is still black even though it's gone early morning. Black smoke. It pours from seven big fires lit at the Widows' towers. The Saints are all still ringing.

"What's going on?" I says, but the sharif don't answer me.

After a minute or so, one of the younger ones speaks. "Mekekana. They've been spotted in the desert."

"Close?" Shite. It must be bad if all the Widows are burning warning fires.

We climb up the hill side, to the huge bone-an-ivory gates that circle Mata Palace.

The guards at the palace don't say nothing when we're led in; they're too busy running around under the pealing of the glass bells.

A fat secretary with a sweaty, pasty face takes my name. He listens when Sel speaks then marks him off as property on the form. Sometimes I wish Trone hadn't taught me my letters. Prue was right. They're more trouble than they're worth.

I'm still wearing Ives's good clothes, even if they're manky from the cell, an I draw myself up as much as those fucking iron bands will let me. "He's not property," I says. "He's a free vamp."

The secretary stops scratching at his papers. "What do you say?" He squints so his eyes almost disappear into the puffy folds of his face. "I see no badge."

"I threw the fucking thing away."

Now he's looking at me proper, like he's really seeing me. "Excuse me?"

I shift my hands so the iron chain moves across his desk. The low-Lammer squeaks back, away from the heat. "Put it down – he's Ives. Not fucking property." I'm too hurt an tired to think straight, so when the secretary fumbles for his dropped nib, I almost don't believe it. I don't even know right what Sel is; putting him down as an Ives seems good a plan as any.

"Fine," says the secretary, as he scratches it out an marks Sel's name next to mine. "Now. Ives. If you'll just be so kind as to follow these nice gentleman here, I am sure they can show you and your blushing bride to your suite."

There's no point saying nothing to that fat cunt, laughing at me as he watches the sharif prod at us 'til we stand. I just keep my head up an my eye on Sel, an hope that as much as I'm feeling his terror, he's feeling my hope that Ives will be good for something after all an that my da an his High House chums will come through for us.

The sharif puts us in a small room, windowless an with nothing in it but a single bench. They lock the door an leave.

"Here," I says to Sel. "Come sit next to me."

He does, an when he's quiet an still, I take the iron around his wrists an hold it so that the metal don't touch his skin, resting my elbows on my knees so my arms don't shake too much.

My hands burn, but it's somehow better than before.

"I'm hungry," says Sel, after a little while.

"Hush, I know." Now I understand what Felicita was talking about, 'cause his hunger an mine are all twined up together, making me itch until it's almost bad enough to drown out the pain from the iron. Almost.

Just as I'm wondering how would be the best way to let Sel feed, the door rattles an a new sharif is there, looking down on us.

"They're ready for you," he says. "Up."

A chill takes me, the way it did back when I was out nights with Marlon, stealing an sneaking. It's part fear, part rush, an I have to breathe deep before I can stand without my knees giving me way, before I can follow the sharif out to whatever punishment is waiting for me.

For us.

Thirty-Eight

A Game of Wasps

"IT'S FROM YOUR father, miss."

I take the letter that Trone is holding out to me. Outside the window a messenger is waiting for my reply, and his face is impassive. There are no clues to be found there. Trone shrugs at my raised eyebrow.

As usual, Father jumps straight to the meat with no time wasted on salutations. He wants me at the Mata palace to view the trial, he says. That doesn't explain why he insists that Mother and Trone accompany me. It takes a moment before I realise – he's trying to get us out of the House and into the sanctuary of the Mata, without raising any panic. Interestingly, underneath his signature is penned a hasty addendum. *Roses have thorns.* He's talking about the Mata, with their briar rose and sun standard, telling me not to trust them. He should know better than to write it down. The letter was sealed, that much is true, but the Mata could have seen a way round that.

"Read it," I say, and hand the letter back to Trone. "Did one come for my mother?"

"I just handed it to her, a few minutes before I found you," he says. His mouth moves silently as he reads, a habit I don't remember from him. Nerves. Disbelief, perhaps. "All of us?" he says when he's finished reading. "I suppose it's safer..."

"By how much, I wonder." I take the letter from him, and let it catch flame on a nearby lamp, before dropping it into the fireplace to blaze into nothingness.

"I'll have the maids pack you bags for several nights." He snaps back into his persona of industrious problem-solver.

In less than a half-hour, Trone has us packed and ready to leave in the main coach. It's normally used for official visits, for when we want to impress, but right now it's the only one available – Father has the other. I suppose in our way, we need to impress the Mata if we are begging them for protection. The nillies are ready to go, stamping in their traces.

The weak sunlight has turned the cobbles in the road to shadowed humps and pits. The snow-clouds have been swept away, and the wind is cold and sharp. Black smoke still pours across the sky, and the wind blows it across the sun's face, so that for an instant, it looks like a storm is gathering over the city. The light is a dull grey-yellow through the coach panes.

Trone clicks at the nillies and we lurch forward.

"This is ridiculous." It's the first thing Mother's said to me all day. "Dragging us off to the Mata. There's no need."

"Did you See something?"

My mother flushes and pulls her fur-trimmed coat closer about her. "One doesn't need a Vision to know that our actions put us further in the Mata's debt. Already, we are too reliant upon their good will."

Actually, my mother is right, and that must mean that Father is terrified. What have they seen up in the palace that the rest of us haven't?

We draw up at the ivory-carved gates, and a palace guard waves us through after one look at the thistle and smoke painted on the coach door. Mother sniffs. "We could have been anyone," she says.

I look back at the dwindling figure of the guard – he has the wide-eyed look of a scriven-high. "He's a Reader," I say, and feel a pang deep inside me, in my very marrow, at how much I miss that sharp, clear feeling. That knowledge, that way behind people's lies.

Servants take our bags and lead us to our quarters. They've set up a suite of rooms for our House. It's beautifully decorated, with subtle touches that nod at our status. A meal is set ready for us, and a serving of hot red wine, heavy with spices, breathes exotic steam into the cool air. Fires have been lit in both fireplaces. They take the worst of the edge off the draughty palace atmosphere.

"Miss Ives?"

I hand my coat – soft rust leather, trimmed with the reddish gold fur of a desert sphynx – to the waiting servant, who bustles off to hang it on a coat stand. He returns and lowers his eyes, giving me a deferential bow. "Your father has instructed that I bring you to him as soon as you have eaten, and refreshed yourself."

I don't bother wasting time. "I'm not hungry. Lead on."

The court is being held in a round room near the heart of the palace. In here, I cannot hear the Saints' bells calling from the Seven Widows.

There are no windows, and the walls are lined with chairs. Most of these are empty. Across the hall my father is deep in conversation with a lord in an expensively cut coat, albeit somewhat out of the current fashion. He has golden brown hair, long and slightly curly that hangs loose to his shoulders. The lord flicks me a glance from hooded eyes, then dismisses me without a thought.

There's a dais at one end of the room, with a lectern set up and a plush, comfortable-looking chair behind it. At the moment it's empty, but soon the Mata judge will preside. In the centre of the room are two chairs. They wait for my brother and his bat.

I thank the servant then cross the cold marble floor to stand at my father's side.

He inclines his head sharply as I approach, acknowledging me, but he doesn't stop his conversation.

"You've how many?" he asks.

"All of us," says the lord. He laughs grimly. "All four." He has a cravat of crimson at his throat. That and the silver unicorns embossed on his cuff links means he can only be Guyin, and I suspect, the estranged lord. The last heir of the main line of that family. The next thing he says confirms it. "Yew and his...Lark are nowhere to be found. The last we heard they were run off by his family and went into the desert. We suspect that they died."

My father's lips thin. "This is my daughter, Calissa." He beckons me closer, lays a hand on my shoulder. "And this," he says to me, "is Lord Guyin Harun."

"Just Harun will do." He holds out his hand before I can curtsey.

His fingers and palms are warm and dry, and he seems remarkably calm. Jek is no relative of his, so I don't suppose he worries over-much whether he lives or dies. We have something in common then.

"A pleasure to meet you," I say.

"Really?" He raises one eyebrow. "I doubt it." Before I can respond, he drops my hand, and nods at someone across the room.

Three people have just entered. Two of them are bats, and the few people who are talking in the judgement room go silent. The group draws up to us, and I feel suddenly flustered. The only bats I've ever seen are the two little girls, and Sel.

And the whore in the street.

The girls are silent and young. Sel has never said a word to me or any other family members, he speaks only to Jek, and even then he hardly ever makes sense. The whore was different, but I don't want to think about him, not now. I don't want anything showing on my face.

It's strange to see these bats in their fine clothes, the one walking arm in arm with a lady of obvious wealth and social standing, and how they seem so very like us. They are pale and dark haired, it's true, but until they get close, and I can see the third eyelid and the sharp teeth in their smiles, they could be low-Lammers indulging in some outlandish fashion of dyed hair and heavy makeup.

"Harun, Lord Ives." The lady speaks first, her accent tainted with the dark coastal drawl of Pelimburg. "How long before court is in session?"

"Not long to wait, I should think, Lady Pelim," says my father. "The Mata are here."

He's right. Illy and Trey enter the room and walk straight to the small line of seats behind the judge's lectern. Two other red-haired Mata and their demure wives follow them. None of them speak to us, or even look too long in our direction. The court settles into place, just as the heralds announce the entrance of the High Mata, the lord of all MallenIve.

High Lord Mata Blaine is a sturdily built man in his early fifties, the grey streaking through his golden-red hair. Clean shaven, and the deep lines on his face are clearly visible. Dominating them all is a deep scar – a strike from a day when duels were still the easiest way to settle a disagreement. The only man I have ever seen who wears a weapon in public, he carries his sabre at his side. It is the same lacquered blade that cleaved the man who gave him that scar. Beyond his proficiency with a weapon, he's a Saint of considerable power, and my father says it's more than likely that he predicted the fall of the Scriven mines long before the last vein ran dry.

He settles behind the lectern, glances around the room then clears his throat into the silence. A servant opens a side door. Two figures are led through in chains. The smell of iron and burnt flesh, sweat and exhaustion enters with them. Jek and Sel are taken to their seats, and the silence thickens as we wait for them to be bound in place.

"Let us make this quick," says Lord Blaine. "We have far more important matters to attend to." He shuffles through the papers on his desk. "Certainly, it seems direct enough." He looks over the papers, straight at Jek. "You, presumably with the help of your...partner...here, eviscerated five servants of the House of Ives. Murdered them."

"Self-defence," spits Jek.

"Ah. They were attacking you?"

"No. Attacking Sel."

"I fail to see how that qualifies as self-defence."

"My lord." Harun stands. "If I may?"

Thirty-Nine

The Grinningtommy

IA DOESN'T EVEN look at me when she enters, not that I worry about that once that Mata Lammer comes in, all pomp an swagger. He's a big man, red-headed, an with a look like a mean-tempered sphynx. Before I even realise the court's begun, he's barking questions at me.

Lucky for us we got Harun at our back, 'cause he stands up smooth an talks for me. Good thing too because I can barely think through the pain, an with Sel so close, his terror fluttering over me like a moth in the dark, well, I don't know if I'll be making much sense.

"There's something I need to explain – a demonstration, if you will," says Harun.

The old Mata nods. "Go on then."

Harun looks back at the others, an Isidro stands, walks slow over to join him.

"What's all this about?" the Mata says.

Harun is shrugging out of his coat.

Next to him, Isidro is clasping his hands together so that the tendons on the backs stand out all sharp. He takes a deep breath, then looks up before walking closer to the lectern, straight toward the Mata lord.

"My lord, if you would demonstrate your ability with the sabre on my friend there," says Harun. A muscle tics in his cheek, an the cords of his neck are thick. "I'm sure all will be explained."

The Mata steps out, stopping a few paces from the vamp. He looks to Isidro, who is waiting with his head down, staring at the floor, then back to Harun. He raises an eyebrow. "You want me to kill your bat?" He laughs.

"I want you to try, my lord," says Harun.

"Well, Guyin, since you've given me permission, I'll do more than try." The blade rattles as he pulls it free, an just as the lacquered blade flashes towards the waiting vamp, magic boils up, that same magic that poured through Sel an me an tore Sharp an his goons apart. Only it ain't coming from us.

Harun is at the middle of it all, an if I forget the pain long enough to focus, I can just about see it as it spits from him to tear at the Mata.

Lord Blaine pulls back, his coat sleeve all scratched into ribbons, the blood already staining his shirt cuffs. The sabre is across the room. Isidro ain't got a nick on him. The vamp ain't even moved.

"What just happened?" Blaine says, his voice a growl.

"Self-defence."

"You're mocking me?"

"No." Harun pulls his coat back on an walks over to Isidro. A look passes between them, an again I get that feeling that they're talking without saying nothing out loud. "It's a side-effect of the bond. The vampires can't do any magic of their own, although they are magical creatures. When one of us is bonded to a vampire, we become able to tap that magic."

"At will?" The Mata wraps a strip of cloth that some servant has brought him, an ties it tight around his wrist, pulling it with his teeth.

"Not entirely. We can direct it most of the time, but if the vampire feels under threat, then we have little control over actions taken to defend them."

"How little?" The Mata nods at the servant who brings him his sword, an he slides it back home through the sash of his coat.

"Hardly any, to be perfectly honest. I have some measure because I understand the bond, and Isidro and I have been together for fifteen years. The Ives boy –" He looks across at me. "Would doubtless have no control at all."

"And you think this is what happened?"

"I'm almost certain of it. Jek did say that the five had attacked his partner, which would have triggered the magic."

"His word only," scoffs the Mata.

"Sel's too."

I take a breath; there's no way the Mata will get any sense out of anything Sel says, an Harun knows it.

"The word of a bat." Blaine laughs. "I think not." He settles back behind his lectern. "Let's say that I believe this story. And you say all of you –" He waves one hand. "– are capable of this?"

"Yes," says Harun.

In their chairs, waiting, Felicita and Jannik nod.

"So what is to stop me from putting you all in iron – as you've just admitted that you tap wild magic and you're a danger to every citizen of MallenIve?"

"Because, Father," says a man in a soft clear voice, an like everyone else in the whole damned court, I turn to see the youngest Mata standing straight up, Ia sitting quiet-like at his side. She doesn't look at him, just straight at me, her head high, her cold blue eyes shiny as marbles. "We can use them to take down the Mekekana."

Everyone starts talking. Calissa, next to our da, smiles a tight little smile, an stares at me an Sel.

Ia catches my eye, an nods once.

Forty

Singing for the Dead

PAIN PAIN PAIN. The red man grins. More Lams come to me, arms out. I try to step back, to get away, and the iron holds me down.

"Set the bat free first, I don't want this accidental magic tearing anyone to pieces," says the red man.

Iron on iron, then the pain drops away and crashes to the ground.

My head is mostly my own again.

"There, little wray, you'll be fine now." Isidro is talking to me. I know what I must do. Go still, get my thoughts neat. He touches me, makes me stand, I must be obedient, do what the wrays say. Yes.

In my belly, there is a hunger waiting

"Saints, those burns are deep."

"We'll treat them at the House. If Ives agrees to let them return with us, that is," Harun says.

The red man booms, "And what about the Mekekana? When do you think you'll be able to go up against them?"

"Harun and I could do it now. Jek will need some training to be able to tap at will."

"Why not Pelim? Too weak, I suppose. Bloody women."

The sounds all stop, the voices stop. If I close my eyes, I can hear the sun shining. Not the sun – Jek breathing, his iron is gone, and I can feel him right again, here in this room. He is here, not gone into the iron.

"Because it's not safe for me to do so, Lord Mata," the Lady Pelim says. "Perhaps in a few months' time –"

"Useless. You and your bat – that's all you can offer me?"

"Give us a few nights with Jek and Sel, and we'll have that number up."

"And what good are the four of you going to be?"

"When the last of your scriv stores runs out, it'll be four more than nothing, Lord Mata."

Jek laughs. It booms in my head, and I try to hold my head still, to stop the sound from being inside me.

"You've got one day, Harun. And then I want to see a demonstration against the Mekekana. Understood?"

Harun bows. Everything will be sunshine, I can feel it.

"Come now." Isidro steps close, pulls me and Jek in his wake.

I touch Jek, let him know that I'm happy, because death has walked a little farther away from us. Make him understand, and maybe he does, because he gives me a smile.

Death turns his back on us. We are free.

"Hey now, Sel-love, why did you go an shove those irons up an down your wrists like that?" He pulls at my sleeve, clicks his tongue "You daft bugger, there's burns everywhere."

The hunger is in my throat now, the smell of skin, blood beneath.

Jek pulls away, squints. "Fuck."

Around us, the wrays are breathing fast, hunger-light making their eyes sharp. They're feeling my need. "Idiots," says Harun. "Isidro, we'd best hire them a separate carriage."

"I will arrange transportation," says the red man, but all the voices are falling away now. Gone like that. The flutter is calling louder, the boom-rush of blood and heart.

Forty-One

A Game of Wasps

THE CROWD FLOWS out to where Mata Blaine's servants are bringing a small dog-carriage around to the bone gates. The air is prickly and uncomfortable, and despite the cold, I'm sweating, feeling damp and sticky under the layers of heavy fabrics, my ribs pinched in by my corset. The other two bats are keeping a wide berth around Jek and Sel. The hunger is thick, palpable, and I'm not the only one in the crowd who can feel it. There is much muttering, a nervous stamping of feet. Sel is staring at Jek's throat with an intensity that's hair-raising.

Harun steps forward and takes the little bat by his upper arms, forcibly pulls him back and holds him still. He does it calmly, his face impassive. Jek looks up, and shock makes him look lost and child-like.

"Get in." Harun nods at the little dog carriage; it's a Mata toy, the shining sun on the door out of place among the black bare trees that line the avenue.

He's still holding the bat fast, and its teeth are showing now. The crowd edges away as Jek snaps back to himself and scrambles into the little domed carriage. Harun shoves the bat in after him and closes the door.

The little carriage trots off, the Mata servant flicking the reins across the backs of the two black nillies. As soon as they've left, Harun turns to Lord Blaine.

"We will bring them back here by sundown tomorrow, if that suits?"

Blaine nods. "I'll have my Readers find you a suitable target for your demonstration." He bares his teeth, mocking Harun with a smile. House Mata and House Guyin have never been close, always jockeying through history for a place at the top.

They make formal goodbyes, and Harun leaves in an ornate carriage; he's apparently made a point of using the finest his family owns – a display of wealth and power to remind people that no matter what choices he may have made, he's still the official heir of a powerful line.

Another carriage follows his, even more splendid perhaps, and so rarely seen – the white sleek transport of House Pelim. I can just barely make out the insignia of leaping dolphins picked out in silver lines along the carriage's sides. She's even made sure that it's drawn by four ghost-pale nillies, their fur tipped with black, which turns them eerily silver in the weak winter sun.

When all the carriages have disappeared under the black boughs of the avenue, Father turns to Blaine. "I thank you for your leniency," he says. It's probably not a conversation I should be overhearing, but as always, the men seem to forget that I am around.

Blaine cuts my father short with a jerk of his hand. "Don't thank me yet, Ives. If the boy proves useless, I've no trouble having them executed. We can't have wild magic like that uncontrolled, it's far too dangerous." The thought of Jek failing and dying at the Mata's command would once have filled me with happiness. Or at the very least, some kind of relief. It doesn't.

How unexpected: I don't want Jek to fail – not if it means I lose the only chance at magic that I have left. The memory of the bat-whore in the street still clings to me, and I dust my hands together as if that will brush it from my skin.

"I understand, of course," Father says stiffly. He stares down the empty expanse of the avenue. "Regardless, the others seem to have no problems with self-control. I believe your son is right, that we have in our grasp another weapon against the Mekekana."

"A woman, a fallen Saint, and a half-breed child? The only one I've any faith in is Harun."

"There could be others."

"There are none."

"I meant," my father says, "that we could make others."

Blaine scoffs as he turns to stare at my father. "And how would we convince people to willingly bond with a bat? There are few who would turn to such perversions without a second thought."

He's right. I try to imagine what it would be like, to touch a bat's pale flesh. Would it be cold, clammy, like some cave-beast's? I shudder. The one in the street touched me so briefly I can barely recall the feel of it.

"True, but it may be something we will have to consider, if we are to survive a full-out war against the Mekekana with no scriven."

"You find me an army of willing Lammers, Ives, and I'll probably give you a medal for it. And even if you could, the bat population is less than fifty. It will be a very small army you offer me."

My father is silent, lost in thought. The lines of his brow are gathered in a worried pucker. "We need to do something before –"

"You forget that your House only stands on my sufferance, Ives. When the scriv finally falls, what use will I have for you? Think on that, and don't press your luck with me."

The threat is implicit. My father goes silent then inclines his head. "Lord," he says and draws me away.

As we leave, I try to catch Iliana's eye, but she keeps to the far side of Trey and doesn't look in my direction. I want to thank her, but I know it would kill her for me to acknowledge what she did. I know how it tore me up to give Trey to her, but at least I had him for a while. What did she ever have?

Trey himself only nods once, carefully, then steers my sister off to some suite of rooms deep in the crystal honeycomb of the Mata Palace.

"Iliana seems well," Father says. "Marriage agrees with her."

Does it? I hadn't noticed. She looked wan, lost. She is no match for Trey, but she's also not a fool. It wouldn't have taken her long to realise that her marriage is a sentence, a lifetime of sharing the bed of someone who sees her as no more than a silver chain – fine, perhaps, and beautiful, but still a chain. My mother was wrong, there can be only misery in Iliana's future.

"Yes," I say. "She seems happy."

I want to vomit.

Forty-Two

The Grinningtommy

SOON AS THE carriage door shuts, Sel slams down next to me on the hard leather seat, his hands on the lapels of my jacket.

There's no point going for my wrists, the skin is burnt an blistered. He's already scrabbling at the buttons at my throat, almost tearing them straight off their threads.

His teeth sink in hard an fast, an for the first time, I don't feel magic, just need. Terrible hunger.

I've been hungry before, growing up in the Digs, so I'm more'n able to deal with going without for a day. All they gave me in that damn cell was some porridge an water, most of which I couldn't eat 'cause it hurt too much to move my hands, but fuck, nothing, not even a few days without food feels like what I'm getting off Sel. He's bitten deep too, an he's not catching all of it. Blood is running hot down my neck, making my shirt an jacket sticky.

He still won't let go, even though now it's gone beyond pain, an my head's dizzy. Panic hits me, 'cause I can't breathe, can't think, can't even push him off. I feel like one of those daft little lindwyrms you sometimes turn up in soil, what just lie there with their eyes closed, playing dead an hoping that whoever found them will just fuck off.

Sounds like a good idea – makes sense to me – play dead, an

wait for Sel to stop this. It's not like I can move him anyways. Can't even open my eyes now. Terror hits me hard in the chest, knocking all my air out of my lungs, makes my heart feel fit to burst.

The teeth pull away, tearing my skin. Blood is pouring down now, hot, smelling like metal an death. The little carriage jerks an rattles down the twisting streets an I wonder how long before we get there, an will it be soon enough.

"Shit."

I want to laugh, 'cause I ain't never heard Sel actually curse, an then something is pressed to my neck, stopping the worst of the blood.

"Jek," he says, an he sounds sane an straight. Worried as fuck, too. I can't say nothing, tell him not to worry, that I'll be fine. "Jek? Look at me."

The heat of his body leaves. He's still keeping that cloth pressed at my neck, even though I dunno why he's bothering, 'cause it feels soaked through already. Then he shoves something against my lips. Salt taste of skin, an then blood.

"Open your mouth," he says, tired an frightened. I dunno why he's frightened. He's stopped feeding an I'll be fine, once I've slept an rested a bit. He keeps pushing his arm or hand against me until the blood is smeared across my chin. I get a small taste, heavy and thick an metallic as scriv. There's magic in the blood. Before I know it, I'm drinking it in deep, the slight burn of it against my tongue.

It's his wrist, I see, when I open my eyes. Somehow, I've held him in place. My fingernails are dug deep in the burnt an weeping skin. He's looking at me funny, but he's not pulling his hand away.

Then it hits. Pain doubled on pain, laying over my own. My body feels different – all scrawny, the weight of my arms an the tension across my back ain't mine. My throat burns, my wrists. His wrists. I can feel my teeth an tongue, hard an soft – filled with the taste of Hob blood. My hands curled around the soaked cloth that he's holding pressed to my neck. I see myself, pupils wide an black, the dirt an blood on my chin. The guilt isn't mine, the worry. The fear that he's done summat he can't fix. Again.

In his head. It's like a mirror all in pieces, reflecting back on itself over an over. I see faces I don't know, smiling a thousand times with sharp teeth – a female vamp, older, tired an thin, another vamp that looks like Sel, only this one is laughing like I've never seen Sel laugh. The faces warp, are blown away in thick black smoke.

I remember the smoke, but is it my memory or Sel's? There's a field filled with Hobs, an in the middle of it a pyramid of old dried wood. There's a figure burning.

It's Lander's Common, seen from high up.

He pulls his wrist out of my grasp an drops the cloth. "Don't look inside my head, you fool Hob."

I'm back in myself again. "Fuck. You saw the burning?" The wound on my neck is crusted a bit now, but when I move, the blood starts again, though not as bad as before. Sel picks the bloody kerchief from the seat an hands it back, careful-like not to touch me. Then he nods, just once, without taking his eyes from me.

"You knew him?"

"Dae." He lifts his hands, covers his face.

The coach stills, an we both lurch on our seats. Sel drops his hands. The bite on his wrist has left a red streak down the right side of his face. He looks like he's just come off the worse in a fight, his eyes all dark, an the bruise on his face purple under the blood.

Neither of us moves even though I can hear the stomp of boots as the servant climbs down to open the coach door.

Sunlight comes in, too bright, making me blink. My stomach is heavy, an I want to vomit, but then I think of what will come up, an I push the blood down. "Who's Dae?"

But Sel's already out, hopped down onto the cold cobbles, his breath steaming in front of him. More coaches are pulling in behind us. The bare face of the Guyin house glares down on us all.

Guyin an Isidro step down from their carriage. Isidro gives us both a quick look, an I realise right smart that I'm soaked with blood, an magic is booming in my head. The air around him is rippled. I feel like if I could just concentrate, I could read auras like that stuck-up half-sister of mine. But those kind of Lammer-magics are out of my reach, I guess, because it don't matter how much I squint, there's nothing else.

"I take it your friend has fed," Harun says to me, snapping me right back. He says it all dry-like, with a half-smile, even though there's nothing funny about almost being killed by – well, by someone you spend most of your time with.

The damn cloth is still in my hand, an right now I'd like to throw it into that grinning Lammer's face. Guess I must have learnt some self-control, because I just drop it to the ground instead. Sel's keeping as far from me as possible, like if he got too close he'd do something he would regret.

It gut-punches me that this ain't my self-control at all, but his. I wonder how long it will be before it dies.

What part of me is running in his veins, I wonder. Maybe that's why he seems a little saner than normal.

"We'd best get you inside," says Harun. "I need to get started on training now if you're to have any sort of control by the time Blaine sees you."

"What?" All I want to do this moment is crawl into a bed an sleep for a year. Maybe two. But that damn vamp Isidro is already behind me, ushering me up the wide steps.

"Don't worry," he says. "We'll see to those wounds first, get you something to eat. But Harun's right. There's no time we can waste. Although –" He swipes his thumb across my chin, and stares at the tacky blood. "This will help. The bond is sealed."

Those kind of words are heavy, but Isidro says them so light, like they barely matter. I'm cold inside, an no hearth-side fire is going to warm me now. I climb the steps an go in to the Guyin house, into the darkness where Sel's already disappeared. "Oh yeah, How so?"

"You'll have consummated the bond, blood to blood. It'll make directing the magic easier. Sit."

He shoves me down onto an old red couch, next to Sel, who's still not looking at me. Instead, the damn vamp's staring at where he's clamped one hand around his mucked-up wrist, stopping the bleeding with his palm. The blisters have broken, an the skin is weeping fluid an yellow muck. Shit, my own wrists don't look no better, an it all seems too much, to concentrate on anything but this awful prickling screaming pain. There's no way Harun an Isidro are going to make us learn to control the tap, not when I can't think right, an my thoughts are all broken because of Sel.

My teeth are chattering in my head, I'm shaking. Even though someone's lit a fire, an the room is warm, warmer than outside for sure. The cold has burrowed into my bones.

"Here." Harun puts something in my hands, a glass of bitter, and I drink it all in a single swallow, spilling some. Beer runs down my chin and washes a clear path through the drying blood.

"Felicita," says Harun. "There's a salve that will help with those burns. Isidro knows where it is, if you'll be so kind as to find something that we can use for washing and binding."

"Oh, I get to lead the doe around, do I?" says Isidro all arch-like, but there's teasing under the bite, and Felicita just sighs, like she's grown used to a lifetime of snide little jabs.

"We can both play at being servants," she says. "I always find it so amusing." She leaves, taking Isidro with her, an Harun pours me more bitter. The buzz of the pain is fading a bit, an I drink this one slower, letting it heat my belly an calm my head. He's given Sel a glass of milk, except that Sel is sipping at his, making it last.

Jannik watches us from across the room, eyes narrowed.

"Who was Dae?" I ask Sel again, an he can't hide from me, can't run away. Then I remember the image, the bat laughing, the one I thought was Sel. An I know it wasn't; it was the little bat we watched burn on Lander's, after they caught it in the Wend. "Sel?"

"My brother," he says in a voice that's so small an lost, that I think maybe I've broken him more. I want to take the question back, but I guess it's too late. For that – for everything.

Jannik said something though, something about how twinlings don't live long if the other is dead. So I guess Dae was younger than him, maybe by a year or two. Maybe that's why his head is so messed.

It's like he knows what I'm thinking, 'cause he shakes his head. "Born together, supposed to die together. I was supposed to die. Mother took my death on herself. She died so I wouldn't." He lifts his head, looks around the room. Felicita an Isidro are back, an she's holding a bundle of torn linens and an ivory bowl.

"Isidro," says Harun as he stands to take the salve an wrappings. "We may have a small problem here."

"So I heard."

"I don't like this," Jannik says. "He's wrong."

Felicita comes to kneel between us. The bowl sloshes water as she wets one of the linen strips to clean away the worst of the burnt meat an dirt an the pus that's under the cracked skin. As she dabs, silent, Harun asks Sel questions.

"Are you sure your mother took on your death? Maybe you misunderstood what was happening."

"She turned to dust. For me. After Dae burned." He shrugs his hands loose from Felicita, an the pain shoots up my arm, makes me grit my teeth. Gris be damned, if this bond is going to make me feel every little thing that Sel does, it's going to make me madder than a spring nilly. I'll be wrapped up tight an put away in that stone prison underground, an never heard from again.

Sel's sorry. He's sorry that his mam died. An he's angry with her too, for choosing wrong. It's not that I know what he's thinking clear-like – more that I can feel these little fluttering moth thoughts that crawl through his head, one over the other, never still.

Forty-Three

Singing for the Dead

IT STINGS. WASHING away the burning just makes it hurt more. I don't want to look at Jek and see Dae in his head, the way he saw him. On fire. He was so close, he could see the blood in his eyes.

The woman keeps cleaning. I try not to wince, try not to think of Jek's memories of my twin.

"Dust? I don't understand." Harun looks over at Isidro, asking for answers I don't know myself.

"It's simple enough. At least the concept is – that a feyn could take on her wray's death. So few would do it, though; it's something only one of the powerful lineages could pull off. And, even then, perhaps for another feyn, but not a wray." Isidro turns to Jannik. "Anything in your family histories ever turn up a story like this?"

"Well certainly I've heard it mentioned, but always as a fable or children's story, not as something that would really happen."

Isidro comes to me, kneels down and makes me look at him. "Are you telling the truth, little wray?"

I've got no answer, because they do not want to listen. I saw my mother's face crumble, saw her drying up like a twist of burnt paper as she took my death deep into her. They do not want to hear this, none of these wrays do, because they know just how awful it is that a feyn died for me.

The woman dries the burns, dabbing carefully at my raw skin.

"That's the best I can do." She smears cold gel on her fingers, touches the burn. Like ice on flame. I shiver, forget my thoughts.

"If, and it's a large if, the wray is telling the truth as far as he understands it, it might go some way to explaining the mental problems he appears to have."

"Not appears." Jek is growly, and I almost smile because of it. "It's all broken in there. We need to fix it."

The wrays and Lammers look at each other. Meaningful glances whose meaning I cannot see. The clarity is going, fogging up like breath on a cold glass.

"How do you think this is going to affect the tap?" Harun says

"Well, we do know that they can do it. It's a matter of how much control they'll have," Isidro answers.

"And how much is that going to damage him further?" says Jannik, the wray who looks like Mother – the nervous one who only cares what happens to his Lammer and the little mongrel in her belly.

"I hadn't considered that." Harun paces. Pours himself a drink.

Jannik shrugs. "I truly have no idea. I'll go through our library. Perhaps there's something I've missed. In the meantime, I'd suggest proceeding with caution and keeping an eye on his mental state. On both of theirs, the bond being what it is. If there's a significant change, then it might be best not to train them and to keep the tapping to a minimum. If you would excuse us, I'll go and see what I can dig up in the stacks."

Then he's gone.

"I don't think we should push them tonight," Isidro says.

"And if they fail Blaine's trial? We need all the time we have."

I'm falling apart, hold myself close, hold myself together. I want to be alone with Jek, blood to blood, and hold onto myself.

"Look at them, Harun. If you're expecting any great results tonight, then you're delusional. They're tired, and I'm worried about this stolen death. I want to hear what Jannik comes up with before I push these two into something that could permanently wound either of them."

"And if we don't take that chance, they might die." Harun is full of guilt and hurt, and I think of Mal.

"I know that!"

"Well," says Jek. "Personal-like, I'm happy to have a kip an a bite to eat before I start dealing with magic-tapping an all this other shite."

Harun looks straight past me, through me, looks at Jek. "Perhaps it would be best to tackle this with refreshed minds and bodies. I'll have someone bring you food in the Blue Room, and we can begin your training early in the morning."

Relief.

I follow them, ghost quiet up to the room, with my bandages like trailing broken wings.

"Here," Jek says after the doors are closed behind us, closing us in blue. "Sit. Let me fix that."

He winds the bandages up again, putting me together. We sit on the bed, and outside the house is still, not breathing. Jek smells of blood.

"Sorry," I tell him. A pain flowers inside my throat, and I know I did not want to do this to him. I wanted something real, and I couldn't have it. So I dragged Jek into this instead. "Sorry," I say again. I want him to know I mean it.

"Come now, don't move your hand. I'm not done yet."

I make myself hold still for him. Breathe.

Sel, he doesn't say.

When I open my eyes, the bandage is tight, warm. It will hold me closed. My skin will grow again. "Yes," I say. "I will always be broken."

"Stop reading my fucking mind." The words are tired, not biting. "Come on, let's get some sleep before those bastard Lams decide it's time to put us through our paces. Might as well be fucking trick-nillies the way they act."

The fires are lit, and the room is warm, warm enough to sleep in. I lie down but the fire makes me hurt inside. I miss Dae.

"Stop thinking, you daft bugger." He slips one arm around me and pulls me close, makes the hurt run away. Under the blood, I smell Jek.

I relax a little, skin and muscle turning softer, and I want to kiss him lick him taste him, but I don't know how to tell him that.

He holds me tighter, his breath in my hair.

It is time to let go of regret.

Forty-Four

The Grinningtommy

NEXT TO SEL, I sleep like the dead. Or maybe that ain't such a good way to put it, considering. It's early morning now, the sky outside all dark an starry. I've pushed open the curtains a little, an the city is twinkling all pretty as a Hob's glass ollie. The lights an the ice sparkle. The factory towers are spitting fire an smoke into the stars, an the seven watch-fires are burning still.

The bells are quiet for now, tongues stoppered until further news. I turn an let the curtains drop closed. Sel's breathing slow an quiet, deep under.

On the mantel a clock ticks quietly, but even that makes too much noise. Four in the morning, an outside the first birds are shifting in the naked trees, cooing an cheeping at each other.

I don't know how Harun thinks he's going to train us to tap the magic in less than half a day, but there's no other way out that I can see. Can't run, can't disappear. Much as it raises my hackles, for now, I have to trust Harun an his cronies.

Someone knocks at the closed door. My heart does a double thump, an for a moment I think it's Sharpshins waiting on the landing, like a ghost.

It's not – just that stony-faced bat Isidro.

"Harun asks that the two of you join him in the downstairs

reading room," he says. "We'll get started straight away."

"Yeah, all right," I says, but he just stays there, looking at me over his thin nose.

"Now," he says. "Wake your wray."

"Sel, move your lazy arse," I says, not taking my eyes off Isidro.

Sel wakes, groggy-like, an manages to dress himself in the almost darkness, although I hear him smack his shin against a bed leg, an curse. The sound of it makes me grin – Sel swearing an behaving pretty close to normal. Maybe this bond thing, an using the magic, will be good for him an not bad like Jannik thinks. I hope so. I'm getting right attached to him, even if it would take a herd of wild nillies an the threat of my arms an legs being torn off to get me to admit it to anyone.

The last person I loved – the only person I loved – was Prue, an look what that got her.

I shake the thought out of my head, an me an Sel follow Isidro downstairs to a part of the house I ain't seen before. Harun is waiting for us in a room lined with bookshelves. He's pushed the chairs an table to the side so that there's a decent bit of open space in the middle.

"Good," he says when we come in. "If you'll stand there with Isidro, and Sel next to me."

We take our places on opposite sides of the room. Sel is still sleep-headed, an he peers across at me with his eyes all gunky an half-open.

"I want you to close your eyes," Harun says to me.

Even closed, the light flickers shadows on my eyelids, an there are colours in the darkness.

"Concentrate, and tell me what you see," he says.

"I can't see nothing with my eyes shut, chum." But no one answers me, an I feel stupid, standing here with my eyes tight, waiting for something to happen. "What exactly am I looking for, anyway?"

The silence grows. For a minute, I think they've gone an slipped out, quiet as can be. Left me here like an idiot, blind-alone in a room. Then I hear the breathing next to me, ever so quiet, an I realise that not only that, I can feel Isidro off to my right, warm, heat radiating at my side. I go still inside; just listen an wait. Breathing, heat, an slow as honey, I start to see him, the heat taking shape, growing limbs an features. I can see Isidro. He's all still one colour, a kind of crimson, like he's been drawn with chalk on the side of a building. Slowly the lines fill in an I can see him clear as day.

"What the fuck." I open my eyes. Sel is staring, but not at me, he's looking at Isidro.

"Did you see anything?" Harun asks.

"Yeah." I nod towards his vamp. "This one here. Pretty clear, only he was all in one colour."

"Well, it's a good sign, at least," says Harun, after his bat shrugs. "You can see what Sel wants you to see. The colour discrepancy is somewhat worrying, however."

"So that's it? That's tapping?"

He laughs. "No, that's an exercise in the depth of your bond. It's strong enough that you should be able to control the tap, and it didn't take you too long to focus. All good signs." He beckons me over. "We'll do it again. This time try and sense Sel instead."

"What? How can he see his self?" These damn Lammers got me more confused than ever; nothing they say ever makes sense.

"No. But you should be able to see the magic."

"Nope," I says. "I ain't got no talents. I could take a bucket of scriv an not see nothing." 'Cept candy colours moving under Sel's skin, like eddies in a river.

"Jek. This is not scriven. Forget everything you know about scriv and talents, because if you're bonded, you can't touch the stuff again anyway."

"How's that?"

A hand rests on my shoulder, and Isidro leans close to my ear. "Because it hurts us. Now, do as he says. Already the sun is rising, and time is slipping."

He's right. Daylight shines in from the long narrow windows between the bookcases, an the oil lamps are dull. The streets are quiet, except for now an then there's a far-way sound of wheels an hooves on stone. I take a deep breath to push down the sudden fear that when the sun falls, I need to be able to tap Sel's magic like I've been doing it all my life. It feels like a fist in my chest, squeezing everything out.

It's not so much me dying, although that's pretty shite. It's knowing that Sel will too, an it'll be because I weren't good enough. I close my eyes an slip back into the quiet, like I did when I "saw" Isidro.

I know where Sel is. Standing across from me, not more than a

few steps away but I just can't get a fix on him. There's too many
people in this room, the sound of all their breathing is irritating the
shite out of me. I snap my eyes open. "I can't do it."

"Give it some time, and try to relax," says Harun. "You're
standing with your shoulders hunched."

So I roll my shoulders back an down, stretch my neck, an when I
close my eyes again, I try to keep that slack feeling in my body.
Sounds rush over me, an I let them. It's not sounds I'm after.

Slowly, so slowly that I wonder that I'm not imagining it, a black
cloud appears in front of me. I mean, I can't see it, but it feels black,
dark an not-solid.

I've seen this, or something like it. I've seen it wild an tearing
those cunts from House Ives apart like paper dollies, an I've seen it
sweet an sharp as a sword, slicing through the cloth of Lord Mata
Blaine's fine overcoat.

Sel. Or rather, his magic. It's the flutter against skin, the trick that
brought us into this whole mess.

"Yeah," I say into the still room, my eyes shut all tight-like. "I see
it."

"Good." Harun's voice has moved. "What I want you to do now,
is pull it into you."

Now, I've no clue how I'm supposed to get that right, but I know
I sound like enough of a fool already, so I just concentrate on
imagining that it's flowing towards me, like smoke.

Nothing happens. A clock ticks through the closed door, that's
how quiet it's all gone.

The minutes pass, an still that smoky shape don't budge. Sweat
is trickling down the side of my face, my shoulders have hunched up
again. Just as I take a deep breath an try harder, I hear the sting-slap
of skin against skin. The pain hits me, second-hand, an my eyes are
open even as I pull the magic straight into my belly an throw it at
Harun, whose hand is only now dropping from where he has
slapped Sel across the face like he was a disobedient Hobling.

The magic goes straight for Harun, an I'm sure it's going to tear
that bastard in two. Part of me is sick with fear. Another says, *all
right you bastard, you'll get as you deserve*. But the magic stops. Harun
holds it at bay, blocking me.

"What the fuck did you do that for?" I scream at him, after the
shock is gone.

"You needed a trigger. I provided one."

"You cock-sucking piece of Lam-filth."

But he just smiles, like I'm a big joke an all. "Look. It worked. Now, all I need you to do is remember that feeling."

"I'll remember it all right."

"Good. I've no particular desire to spend the rest of the day slapping your little wray here."

"Fuck you." But now I've calmed down some, I can feel Sel's magic running through my blood an body. That Lammer might be a complete bastard, but he has a point. Anything to make sure Sel an me aren't back in iron by the end of the day, waiting to burn.

BY THE TIME the shadows are long, I've got it down. Mostly.

"You need to take a break," says Harun. "It's the best we'll get in such a short time, and the come-down is bound to hit you sooner or later. Eat something." He looks at a small timepiece chained to his coat, frowns, an then snaps it shut. "We've perhaps three hours before sundown, so rest, and be ready."

He's right, I'm feeling shaky already, an I remember the come-down from killing those low-Lam bastards. I need to be together for this trial of the Mata's. Won't do us no good if I'm barely able to crawl by the time the clock strikes four.

They come for us after a few hours, all in their pomp an finery, like the whole world needs to know that the Mata are out. This is the first time I seen their by-the-wind up close, an it's a dead-odd thing, like a giant balloon with tentacles. Through the thin, crimson skin of its floater I can see the sky; below that the tentacles are dissolving some poor bastard animal. I've no idea how the damn thing stays in the air, although there's vents inside it, an a fin on its back like a sail. The tentacles are hooked all over. It's an ugly fucker all right. Dangerous too. Those hanging spirals that look so pretty, well, they can poison a Hob or a Lam, make him die over a few days. An so, natural-like, the Mata have a hanging carriage strapped under its belly, between all those death-dealing streamers like they're having a party. Show-offs, the lot of them.

"The blaas only sting if they taste skin," Harun says to me, as he hands me a glass full of pale cream. "Put that on every piece of exposed skin, if you'd like to stay alive."

"What's this then?"

"Something the Mata developed so that non-War-singers could use the blaas. Just put it on." He's tired too, an angry-nervous.

The cream is cold, but it feels nice enough, even making my few burns sting less. I put the cream on Sel's face an hands, careful to cover him so that those tentacles an stingers don't get any shot at him. "Close your eyes," I says, an he lets me cover his eyelids. His eyes feel like something alive, quivering under my fingers. "There. Done."

He blinks. Cocks his head an looks at me all serious, like he's trying to make up his mind about me.

When we walk through the hanging tentacles, an climb up the small rope ladder to the cabin, the tentacles just slip over me. Where they touch it feels a little burny, but not enough to do more'n annoy me.

Only Harun an Isidro come with us. Jannik's still beak-deep in his books, an besides that, there's no point in making the lady waste her time gadding about when there ain't nowt she can do.

Inside the carriage is plush as fur, lit with hanging lamps. The windows take up the two longest sides.

MallenIve is falling away below us, 'til it looks like a model city someone's glued together from wood an paint. I don't want to look out on that small city, it makes my stomach turn, but Sel has gone an pressed hisself against one window, an he's grinning like he hasn't noticed we're about to have our fate decided all sharp-like.

"Look," he says. "I can see everything."

Mata Blaine clears his throat. "We've got a Vision. A spy pod, only small, coming up from Pelimburg. It will do. And if this succeeds, then we'll have taken out one eye of the Mekekana." He seems all cheery, like this is just a good time out, a hunting party. Guess for him, it is.

We've only this one chance to prove ourselves a weapon.

The by-the-wind bobs higher, an the city gives way to the patchwork farmlands that spread from the river banks. The soil is silt-rich, but this deep into winter only a few crops with dark green leaves grow near the banks. The rest of the fields are black. The desert scrub comes into view. From up here, the red sands look brown, an the few scrubby bushes can hardly be seen at all. Behind us, the sun is setting, an the shadows are slipping Hob-quick over the sand.

My da has come along, although he hasn't spoken none to me. Not a single word. He watches me even as the Mata makes bluff jokes, an he laughs at them, like the good little Ives dog that he is. He looks worried as fuck though, an he keeps glancing over at the Mata, like he's waiting for the blow.

A door clicks an a servant comes through from an aft cabin, bringing steaming wine 'gainst the cold, an trays of hot food. I can't eat nothing, cause my stomach is lurching in time with the Gris-damned by-the-wind, but I take some wine.

"Do try not to drink it like water," says Harun, but he don't stop me from taking a second glass when that one's done gone down my gullet. In fact, it's a good thing, 'cause I'm feeling all strung out, an the wine is making me settle, taking off some of the edge.

Harun an Isidro also drink, although they sip it slow. The spiced steam makes the swinging carriage full of the smell of cloves an winter. Sel only has one sip an pulls a face.

After an hour or maybe more, I'm feeling fidgety. Sel's settled into a corner seat, his cheek against the glass, as he watches the black below us.

"So where's this pod, then?"

The Mata looks up. "We should see it soon. The nav will give us word when he senses it."

Even Harun is interested now. "Your navigator is a Reader?"

"He'll bring us down when we're close. Don't want the bastards seeing us." Even as he says that, the by-the-wind gives a little lurch, an then banks down.

The fore cabin door opens, an a thin Lammer looks out. It takes me a moment to place him, an then I remember where I seen this red-headed lad before. It's Ia's Mata prince – Trey. A Reader to guide us to the mouth of the Mekekana.

"I've picked up a strange aura," he says. "Too big for a sphynx and moving straight towards MallenIve."

"The pod?"

"More than likely. I'm bringing her down, and we should land about five furlongs from her in around twenty minutes, give or take. If we could close all curtains?"

The Mata Lord nods, an the little servant rushes to pull the heavy black curtains together, so no trace or drop of light will give us away to the Mekekana pod.

Forty-Five

A Game of Wasps

FATHER'S BEEN GONE now for three hours. Watching the hands move across the clock isn't making this easier on me.

I need to know.

If Jek can use the bats for magic, if any Hob or Lammer can do it. I'm holding all my hopes and my new Path on this night. I need proof that Guyin and Pelim are not just random flukes. I need to know. I've no magic without the scriven, and while the Saints have been searching out new veins, they've found nothing yet. Certainly nothing of any use. Without magic, I'm nothing.

The same goes for everyone else, so I suppose that makes this shortage of scriven the ultimate equaliser. Without scriv to bring out the latent magic, we Lammers are no better than Hobs or low-Lams. It's not something I ever thought would happen in my lifetime.

Could I even touch a bat, let its magic inside me? The thought makes my skin cold. Instead of thinking about the bat, I imagine what the magic felt like. Alien, nothing like scriv, but honey-sweet all the same. Perhaps just the taste of it will be enough to blind me to its source.

Or perhaps, if I were to drink vai, or something rawer, stronger, so that I barely knew what I was doing, perhaps then. But the idea of having to first touch the bat in order to access the magic makes my skin crawl and my heart beast faster with a sort of sick fascination.

I've always been good at justification. Gris knows, I've done many things I knew were not right, and I've always managed to talk myself into them. I'll find a reason to make sure I do not regret my choices.

The clock ticks. Barely a minute has passed since I last looked. If I sit here any longer I'll drive myself insane. There must be something I can do to pass the time.

One thing about being confined to the palace is that they have a vast library. Even the MallenIve library doesn't compare with the Mata's. The MallenIve library is open only to Chalice students and alumni, but who needs bother with that when the Mata collection is at my fingertips?

A page takes me to the shelves that stock what little there is on the bats, and I scan the titles through the thin film of dust. I gather an armful of books – here a treatise, here a handful of the few articles devoted to them in the scientific journals, and a fat squat book – purportedly a history of the bats, although it reads like nothing so much as a set of children's tales or horror stories. The page helps me carry them back, making a note of the titles as he does.

In my new set of rooms, a servant has left me a covered tray of food. It's doubtful that my mother even noticed that I skipped dinner. That is if she even took any herself. I eat as I read, stopping only to make the occasional note, but by the time I've scanned through the paltry information, I realise I still know next to nothing about the bats. If anything, I'm more confused than before.

Technically they're magical beings, like sphynxes or dragons, but they are self-aware; they have a language that has similar roots to Lammic, and according to the blurred histories, they have a royal family of sorts, scholars, singers. A system of power-based hierarchies.

Something nags at me, at how neatly their history dovetails with the opening of the Well. Two hundred years ago, pure magic was unleashed, and poured out of the open rent destroying the world of Oreyn as we knew it. We learned that as children, that it was Mallen Erina's disastrous choice that birthed the magical beasts, that brought all our dreams and nightmares to life.

But I never learned the names of the bats; that wasn't considered important.

Or maybe it was too important.

There on the page before me, is the name of the first ruler of the bats – a Lira Sandwalker.

Erina may have died in that first flood of wild magic, but her daughter Lira didn't, and House Mallen was spurned, made to walk out into the land their matriarch had destroyed, deep into the shifting red desert.

It was assumed that House Mallen died. The books say little about them, after they fell – they are nothing more than a footnote, a date, a name.

I don't think they died.

But I don't want to think on that, on what it might mean. Did the destroyed House of Mallen change under the magical fall-out, just as the lions turned sphynx, the snake wyrm, the deep-sea fish into sea-drakes?

Did the Lammers give birth to the bats?

It can't be. We are better than them; I've known that all my life.

I slam the book shut, and dust rises in a smoky cloud, making me cough. Most of the information I've been able to find is about the males – wrays they call them. Information on the feyn is brief and scattered. Mostly it agrees that the females are rarer, and possibly far more powerful than the males.

We have two feyn. The betrothal gift. I ring a hand pull and wait. A few minutes later a puffing servant knocks timidly at my door.

"There are two bats – two little girls – that were brought with us from House Ives. Bring them here."

She's gone as soon as she's curtseyed, and I have to wait only a short while before I hear her footsteps on the carpeted landing. At first I think she's come back alone, but when I fling the door open, the two bat girls are behind her, silent and staring at me. Their indigo eyes are dark in the shadowed hall, and they look decidedly alien with their upward-slanting eyes, blank pale faces, and sunken mouths.

"That will be all," I say, and the servant bobs another curtsey and slips away, leaving me alone with these two little creatures.

We stand for a while, staring at each other. I've never spoken to them before. "Sit down." I wave my hand to a low divan opposite my desk. The two obediently climb on and sit, watching me, their fingers intertwined.

"I need to know about your magic," I say. "How it works, and how it's possible for Lammers to access it."

They look at each other, little brows wrinkled. Finally the one, slightly taller than the other, speaks to me. Her voice is very low and her words malformed, so I have to strain to hear her. "We cannot help you," she says.

"You know nothing?"

"We were brought up in a Lam-house, miss," she says, and I notice she barely moves her lips when she talks, so as to hide her bare gums. "We know nothing of other bats."

Gris. That means I'll have to try speak with the others, the ones Father went to for help, and there I will have no power. They have the protection of powerful Houses, and that gives them a status that I'm unsure of. I dismiss the two feyn, and they leave without looking back, fingers still curled together.

A third option remains, I suppose, were I to find it in me to make a dash back to the bat whorehouse and question the other. Without realising it, I find my hand brushing my cheek, trying to recall the sweet wildness of the magic he touched me with. The rush. I stay that way for a while, just thinking.

The clock hand seems to have barely scraped past twenty minutes when I push open the curtains, as if by some miracle I will be able to see the blaas from here. Outside, the night is a flickering mass of fire and streetlamps and veiled stars. The darkness presses in from the desert, filled with the shadowy threat of the Mekekana and their iron machines.

My thoughts are a tumult of fear and confusions – everything hinges on what my brother does now.

I look down at the closed book on my desk and wait. There's nothing else for me to do.

Forty-Six

The Grinningtommy

THE BY-THE-WIND COMES down, an the carriage hits sand, skidding an bumping an making a shirring noise that aches in my teeth.

The lights have all been blown out, an we step out into the winter desert. Under a fat moon, smoke puffs from our mouths. I pull Sel a little closer to me, because no one will really notice that in the dark, an he's warm an solid. Soon as I touch him, the magic jumps, pulsing between us like it's alive. May be that it is. We can do this. We'd sure as fuck better be able to, at any road.

"I couldn't take the risk of bringing her in closer, so we've a fair walk ahead," says Trey. "But it's moving pretty slowly." He starts walking away into the night. Everyone follows, all quiet-like except for the *shh* an crunch of the gritty sand under our boots.

It's about fifteen, maybe twenty minutes of walking in that black cold night with the stars shining down on us like there ain't no problem in the world, before we see the shadow of the pod. It's smaller than I thought it'd be, hunched an rounded as a dung-beetle, moving across the sand on skittering pointed feet.

It's a black hole cut into the side of the low dune and the star-mapped sky. Sel shivers, an the magic pulses twixt us.

"It will probably have about five Mekekana in," says the skinny, red-head boy.

The older Mata turns to his son, then looks back at where me an Sel are standing an waiting to do this – whatever they expect of us.

The thing is made of iron, I can feel it from here, dark an full of hurt.

"Well," says that bastard Lammer king. "What are you waiting for? Prove that you're worth more to me alive."

So I do, I close my eyes an concentrate on Sel's magic, tap it like Harun has drummed into me, an aim. We spent hours doing this – teaching me to direct the magic. I'm pretty lousy, but the pod's a big enough target.

It sits in my head, a raw shape – anti-magic, a burn in a silk cloth. Magic pushes out of me, streaming black fire, an it hits. I know it does, because the backlash slams into me hard, instant. I ain't never felt so much magic tear through me. When I open my eyes, I'm staring at Sel's face, his hair hanging down, all the stars whirling around him.

"Are you –" He holds out his hand, an I manage to sit up. There, where the pod was crawling not a few moments back, is a smoking, twisted shape, like I pulled the heart out of it with my hands.

Thin screams on the air. The Meke dying, caught in their own iron beast, hot metal to their skins.

"Impressive," says the Mata, an he crosses his arms over his chest as he watches the smoking wreck. "No finesse. You're more of a hammer than a blade, but the end results are the same." He looks down at me, where I'm still half-sitting on the ground, my brain pounding an hot.

I feel like I'm going to sick up right here on the sand. But I'm not, I won't. Not while this bastard is watching me, looking for weakness. So I pull myself straight an manage to stand, although really, it's more like I'm using Sel as a leaning post.

"Now," the Mata says. "Can you stop the screaming?"

"Kill them, you mean?"

"What else?"

This is the finicky part, 'cause my control is pretty shite at best, plus I'm feeling like someone just swapped out all my bone marrow an replaced it with scriv-dust. Lucky for me, Harun steps up.

He don't say nothing. I only realise what he's done when the screams cut short.

"Are you satisfied with your demonstration, Lord Blaine?"" he says in that silk-stone voice. "Or is there anyone else we should kill?"

Now, Blaine knows that Harun's stepped in to save my face, but he also knows he has new weapons against the Mekekana, so instead of tearing Harun a new one, he grins, like it's his birthday an someone gave him a new fucking palace or something. "I'm most pleased," he says. "Satisfied? Perhaps not."

"The boy will be drained by destroying such a large target," Harun says. "If we have your permission to head back?"

While I'm not looking forward to going back in that bobbing gas bag, 'cause I'm sure to be sick all over the damn thing, I'm still glad when the Mata nods an starts walking back the way we came.

We walk behind the others, leaning in against each other. Sel's got his arms around me, an normally I'd be all pissy about that, but it's just to keep me standing. Right. I grin; may be that I feel like a I've been flattened by a nilly cart an then trampled for good measure, but Sel an I have bought ourselves more time. "I guess we're a good team then, Sel-my-love," I says, quiet-like.

"We've turned back the death," he says, and his breath is warm against my chin.

Right sudden, I don't care who's watching. Everyone is walking a ways ahead of us, so I stop, an pull Sel close an tight.

"Huh," he says, 'cause I think I kinda squeezed the breath out of him. The magic is all around us, not black an oily like before, but the way it was when we first touched, stroking an rippling down our skins an knitting us together. He's so happy. I can feel it like a bubble coming up my chest.

Which is a weird feeling when you're already sick. Next thing, I'm doubled up an puking up what little bit I drank in that stupid carriage. The wine leaves a taste all acid in my throat, making my eyes burn an water.

"Jek," says Sel, and he shakes his head. "You're a strange-strange Hob."

I start laughing. On my knees, hard grit beneath me, an feeling like shite, an Sel makes me laugh.

WE GET TO sleep in late the next morning. Most of what I remember of getting back to MallenIve is rocking about under that gasbag, an everything is half-dreamy an unreal. The only thing that makes it worth remembering is Sel curled up next to me on the cushioned seats, his heart beating me back home, like a drummer's song to keep a miner swinging his pick even when he's just about ready to lie down an die.

But all that feels like it happened to some other Hob, an I stretch slow, easing the ache out of my muscles an bones. Sunlight is making dusty patterns through the curtains. The room comes into focus. Blue on white, stuffed full of Lammer-ornaments, ugly things that cost more than they should.

"Awake." Sel is lying flat on his back, staring up at the ceiling, an at first I'm not hundreds certain if he's talking to me or the ceiling. It's like that with Sel.

"Yeah, alive an awake," I says.

He turns his head so that he's looking straight at me. "Oh good."

He sounds, well, almost normal, so I push up on one elbow an squint at him. "You're feeling . . . all right-like?"

"Might be." He closes his eyes. His eyelids are very thin an papery, flickery. "You're in my head, Jek."

I'm not. I've been there, yes, like when he bit me that last time, an the thought makes the bite burn, itchy with scabs. But I'm not now.

"Yes, you are." His throat bobs. "Putting my head back together, putting it straight." He's still not looking at me, lost in his own ideas. It's not good, to be falling like this, falling this deep. Although from what the bonded Lammers have been saying, may be that I don't have no choice in it, that every time I tap, I'm going to get all sappy like this, turn into some love-struck Kial, like in the story.

Only problem is, in that story, everyone dies.

"You're hungry."

He's right. "Are you going to be able to do this all the time now? Know every damn thing I think an feel? 'Cause, I don't think that's all wonderful-like – a Hob needs to have some privacy, you know."

"I know."

"Sel."

"I'm pissing you off." But he's grinning, an I don't know, may be that I could put up with Sel knowing every damn thing there is to know about me, as long as he's happy an sane. I drop my head an pull a pillow over it. Pathetic. I've turned into a sappy bastard. Might as well go out with a little flower pinned to my sleeve an skip down the streets singing love songs. I groan, an the down muffles the sound.

Sel is shaking next to me so I pull the pillow away, worried that

I've gone an done something. He's laughing, not making a sound.

"You're an odd little bugger, Sel-love, you know that?" I stop him by kissing him quick, sliding my tongue over those needle fangs, mainly 'cause I know he likes that.

He shoves me off him. "Not just me. Listen, the sun is singing. People will want us to wake, to dress, to nod our heads for yes."

Fuck it. I've lost him again.

We go downstairs to where the others are waiting for us. My da is there, dressed in a clean new suit. I'm still in the sweat-stained baggy set of clothes I've borrowed off Harun, the sleeves rolled up past my wrists.

"Jek," my da says as he steps forward. There's something in his right hand – a rolled-up scroll of thick paper – an he holds it out to me.

I look at it, then at him, one brow raised.

"It's your pardon," he says, an shoves it towards me again.

"So that's it then, one piece of paper an it's all over with?"

"Take it. And read." He's tired, but I can hear something in his voice, like the kind of laughter you have when you just don't understand someone, the way I feel about Sel sometimes, so I take the scroll an roll it open.

It's a piece of work all right. Official hand-painted insignia at the top, in crimson an gold ink, the sun fierce as a sphynx. Of course, the writing is all looping an fancy, which makes it extra hard to read. Seeing as how my letters aren't the best in the world, it takes me a while to get through all the fancy talk an show-off long words, but I do.

I look up. "I'm free, if I fight for him?"

"Essentially."

"Well." I twist the paper up tight an pass it back to my da. "Guess it's better than the other option."

"It's yours. An official document." He's definitely smiling now, relief plastering that silly look on his face. "Lord Blaine wants you and Sel." He glances over his shoulder to Harun. "And you, to meet him first thing tomorrow to discuss the use of your magic against the Meke."

"He holds no iron axe over our necks," says Harun, in that false mild way he has.

"It's your city too, Harun. If this place falls, you'll die like every other Lammer in MallenIve. Are you going to hold a grudge for all your life?"

"A grudge?" He unfolds his arms an walks up right close to my da. "Is that what you call it? Turned out of the ancestral home? Insulted in the streets –" He jerks back, an presses his palms together, like he's asking a Saint for Visions. "Did you know," he says, all conversational again, "that children make dares with each other over who is brave enough to come and strike my door? That this city has turned Isidro and myself into boggerts, closed its doors to us, and spat on us. And now," he grins, an his teeth flash white. "They want our help."

"Please, Lord Harun –"

"I went back into your city, Ives, not for you, or for any other of the Great Houses. I had no intention of making of myself and Isidro a weapon to be toyed with by that fool Mata. I did what I did so that two of our kind wouldn't have to die."

There's a long silence, an my da an Harun watch each other, like two desert jackals circling before a fight. My da sighs. "I can't force you," he says. "But I would appreciate if you would go."

"I might go," he says. "If it was worth it to me."

"Worth it," my da says flatly, an narrows his eyes. "In what way? I have little to give –"

"You have two girls – gifts," Harun sneers, "you were given by that puffed-up Mata. The feyn – I want them."

Next to him, Isidro bares his teeth. Even though it's midday out, with the afternoon sun high, an there's a fire burning in the hearth, the room feels cold an all unwelcome.

Sel shuffles back, picks a teacup off the table. The tiny click of bone porcelain is almost too loud. He doesn't do anything with it, just holds it out like he's never seen the like before. "The ones without their teeth," Sel says to the cup. "All ripped out one by one." He looks up at my da, eyes wide. "With iron pliers."

My father swallows noisily; I think he feels that same thickening air that I do, an he realises that those bats, an all that magic, could just as easy be turned on him. True, we'd all be executed. But he'd still be dead.

He nods. "It will be done."

Forty-Seven

A Game of Wasps

TREY WANTS TO see me.

The words on the letter blur, and I crunch the thin paper up tight in my fist. His handwriting is obliterated.

We'd agreed. I'd agreed, because it was what he wanted, that we would not see each other again. And here in my hands are words that could pull us together, and his marriage to my sister apart. He wants me to meet him by the theatre. Before noon. It's not safe for us to be seen meeting in the palace, and I should not go.

Of course I will.

The clock on the old white-washed pub across from the theatre is just at eleven, and the sun is a distant coin, old and cold. I shade the light with one hand, scanning the crowds. There are few people out; the warning fires and bells have made everyone nervous. The War-singers are holding the air around MallenIve tight as stone, and only their word will allow anyone to leave or enter, but the city also knows there's hardly any scriven. We're all just waiting for the inevitable, for the barriers to finally drop and for the distant Meke ships to plough through our homes.

I sigh and lean back on the stone bench, my fingers chilled despite the fine leather gloves.

"Calissa?"

He's behind me, come around from one of the narrow alleys that border the theatre. I tilt my head. Trey is frowning, pale. There are shadows under his eyes, making him look years older.

"You look –" I say, when I swallow past my love and despair.

"Tired." He waves my sympathy away. "Come." He holds out one hand. "We need to talk."

I don't take his hand, though I do follow him through to the old pub, The Fountain of Mallen. Trey's not dressed in his usual finely tailored suits, but in a sweat-stained, travel-rumpled coat that would better suit a common Hob. There is no disguising that shock of red hair, but somehow, no one pays him mind as he passes. Readers have this invisibility inherent to them. We are the ghosts of MallenIve.

Inside the Fountain the air is still and cool, for they've lit only one small hearth, and there's almost no one inside. An elderly keep with a shock of white hair that curls over his shoulders is polishing a glass as we enter, and he nods at us once.

"Two vai," Trey says.

I take my drink, although I've gone off the taste of vai completely. We go to a little cosy table tucked into a far nook. We are out of sight of the wide stained-glass windows. Cool grey shadows curl around us with a silken whisper.

We stare at each other across the polished wood with its faint scars of drinks, half-moons of old beer glasses.

"How does it go with my sister?" I say.

Trey shakes his head, snapping out of his silence. "We've no time for this." He stretches one hand across to touch my fingers then pulls back again. "Your brother and his bat wiped out the Mekekana pod."

"I know this. My father told me."

"Well, now my father will be sending the bats to Urlin, to try gather more bats to MallenIve's defence."

The thought is startling. Urlin is to the north, the citadel of the free bats. There is no love lost between our two kingdoms. "Are you sure?"

He nods. "I'll be going with them. The blaas will leave in a few hours."

"Why are you telling me?"

He sighs, rubs his hands through his hair, and it leaves the red tresses mussed, making him appear fragile and too young. "I think," he stops, tries again. "I think my father is only sending us away because he has other plans."

"What do you mean?"

"I mean, he's setting us off after fancies, because he wants Guyin and your brother out of the city. He wants me out of the city."

"You? What – I don't understand." I curl my hands into fists. Even without scriv, I can feel Trey's nervousness.

He looks about then speaks so softly I need to lean closer to him to hear. "I – I saw something. My father has opened the room of shattered bones, the room of the Well," he whispers.

It takes a few moments for the news to sink in. I press a hand to my mouth, even as I feel the blood drain from my face. "He can't mean to –"

Trey cuts me off. "No. He says it was merely to give him time to think upon his options." The look on his face is enough to let me know that he doesn't quite trust his father's word.

"He cannot open the Well. We almost destroyed the world the last time."

"I know that." He leans back. "My father is no fool. He wouldn't open the Well without good cause." He takes a sip from his vai and pulls a sour face. "That much pure magic at our fingertips, though...it is a temptation."

"No one can control it." I think on my reading, on the realisation I've made that the bats are nothing more than Lammers twisted by the magic from the Well. That Mallen as a house still stands – and even under its own symbol. Indeed, the Eagle of Mallen may have fallen, but it rose in fire and magic as the Alerion of the vampires.

I keep my mouth shut about that – Trey will think I've gone mad – spouting such filth.

"If you don't believe that he will use the Well, why have you come to tell me this?" I keep my voice light, just a hint of confusion to flavour the playful tone.

"Because, if – should –" He shakes his head and sighs. "Never mind. You are right. No one would be so foolish." But the look on his eyes says differently, and I wonder just how worried Mata Blaine has become, and what he would do to keep his kingdom.

"You're worried." I can read him, even without scriv. "Then do something to stop him."

"What?" He sighs in exasperation. "You want me to confront him. He'll never listen to me, you know that."

"He'll never listen to you because you don't stand up to him." I clench my fingers into tight curls, the nails cutting at my palms. "And you never will," I say with an acid tongue.

"Calissa –" He stops, his face too pale, mouth twisted.

I never want to see him again, see how weak he is.

"I wanted to see you."

His voice brings me back. I look up from the cold silver surface of the vai, into eyes that are a perfect summer blue. "You were the one who said that we shouldn't."

He shrugs, leans back and tips his glass from side to side, watching the vai flood back and forth like a tiny trapped sea. "There will be a war. I'm leaving soon – I'm going to Urlin as navigator for the blaas. Who knows what I'll come back to." His smile is weak, soured with fear. "People will die. That's always the way of war."

I stand and pull my coat tight across my chest. I hurt. I hurt. "I need to go." I hear each word as if it were a bell – clear and distant.

"You haven't touched your drink."

"Vai makes me sick." It makes me think of my father, of his study, of how I lost him to Jek. I turn away, leaving my beautiful Trey sitting alone at the table, with nothing but the echoes of his face in my head. I even make it all the way to the pub door and out into the too-bright sun without turning back to look at him.

Forty-Eight

The Grinningtommy

WE LEAVE THE Guyin House before the birds are even awake,
Sel still rubbing sleep from his eyes.

"There a reason that bastard wants us there so damn early?" I
ask.

Harun grunts. "It's a power play. He doesn't like not having the
upper hand."

"You pissed him off right proper killing those Meke for me," I
says, an that makes him laugh.

"Yes, I did at that."

Isidro's staying at the House because those little feyn arrived late
last night. Isidro took one look at them an didn't say nothing for the
rest of the night. He's got it in his head that he can make them teeth,
Harun says.

"You think he'll get them teeth right? I mean . . . ." I've no idea
how he's planning on tackling that problem, but I don't want to
think about what old Blaine's got waiting for us. Another trial, a trip
into the desert to blow up Meke ships – who knows.

"If Isidro wants something badly enough, he'll get it," Harun
says, an there's a far-way look on his face, like he's remembering
something.

We spend the rest of the ride quiet-like, the wheels of the Guyin coach clitter-clattering over the round stones. The coach is open, an the city sweeps past around us. They've doused the warning fires, probably scared the winter-dry irthe trees in their silk tents would catch flame, but the air still smells of smoke, thick enough to make my lungs hurt.

Sel's leaning over the edge of the coach to stare at the vendors come early to set up their road-side stalls. Bright-coloured material flaps as they pin their stands together – shade cloths an drapes to cover cheap wood trestles. Some have got their fires going under kettles an grills, selling breakfast an Pelimburg tea to the low-Lams rushing to work.

The sun is just rising over the palace, making the whole thing look like a wedding cake some Lam-mother spent too much brass on. I pull Sel back onto the seat next to me, grabbing his coat before he can go tumbling right into the gutter.

"Wasn't going to fall," he says, but he stays next to me anyway. That cut on his cheek is closed up, the skin around it grazed. I can still feel Sharpshins's fist smashing into my own face, even though it happened to Sel, Sharp's stone-set ring splitting the flesh. I can feel other things too. How do I bring it up – yeah, so I felt you, I felt what happened – that was a bit of bad luck, what? Fuck no. There's no pretending it didn't, an that damn cut across his face is like a warning-fire, reminding me that there's more an worse.

"Does it still hurt?" I say, an nod at the cut.

Sel answers the question I didn't ask. "I'll heal." He hunches up his shoulders, an he looks more like he did the first time I saw him, round-backed, like he's trying to hide behind his own body. He says it the same way someone would say "Nice weather we're having," like it's something he's used to.

I can't breathe.

Sel must guess what I'm thinking, or he's reading some of it through the bond, I don't know right anymore. "Don't," he says, an grabs my hand. It's awkward, both of us are wearing gloves an he grips too hard, like he's scared I'm going to let go. I feel my cheeks going hot an red.

Harun can see us an the whole stupid hand-holding thing, but he pretends not to notice. I flip the edge of my thick coat over our hands, an squeeze Sel's fingers with my own.

I only let him go when the coach stops before the palace gates. Men in crimson uniforms are lined up two deep by the door, an they part as Harun storms up the wide staircase with its long steps. My boots slip on a film of thin ice that glitters under the rising sun an just about fucking blinds me.

One of the guards sniggers when I stumble. Sel glares at him as he catches my arm.

"Never mind him," says I, but Sel's looking at the guard like someone slapped him through the face. He hurries through the doors, half-dragging me along behind him.

"What?" I say, out of breath as the doors close behind us, cutting the morning light off with a snap.

"Customer," says Sel.

Jealousy comes roaring back, an a part of me wonders how often Sel's past is going to come tear at us with its old sharp claws.

TURNS OUT MY da has had this jumped-up idea that Urlin will send us vamps to fight in our war. An the Mata agrees.

Harun is scowling like he just bit into a peach an found a worm. Or half of one anyway. Him an the Mata have been arguing back an forth for most of the morning, an he's still shaking his head.

"I don't want to deal with her," he says. "You have no idea of what it is you're asking."

"I know exactly what I'm asking – no, telling – you to do, Guyin." The Mata rests one hand on his sabre hilt, all casual-like, but no one in the room misses it. "I spoke with my archivist. He says there are always more, what do you call it, wray than feyn. With that kind of imbalance, she'll be practically salivating to dump some of the excess on us."

"They're not extra –" Harun waves one hand in the air. "Rolls of silk, to be shunted around. They're people. You're asking for them to leave their families, their friends, all so that they can come here to be third-rate citizens. Weapons in your Gris-damned arsenal."

"I am well aware of what I'm asking." The Mata leans back in his chair. The room is pretty bare, but it's obvious who's boss, what with his chair carved out of a black irthe tree – a whole one, with no seam or join. He stretches his legs out an eyes Harun. "We'll offer something to sweeten the deal."

"What, exactly?" Harun looks far from convinced. The spice-reek of winter jinberries fills the room. He waves a serving-girl away as she comes in with cups of steaming wine. His glass is still full, long turned cold.

"Citizenship. Lodging – decent lodgings – and the deed to said."

Harun says nothing, but his eyes say, "carry on." If the Mata is telling the truth, that's a fair bit of sugar. Houses in MallenIve don't come cheap.

"A title equivalent to War-singer."

"That will mean nothing to the vampires."

"Ah, but it will mean something to the bonded Lammers."

Finally, Harun leans back an sips at his cooled drink. "Will you get rid of this damn foolishness with papers?" Harun's explained to me about the whole alerion-bird crest – it means a vamp has papers allowing him to be out past sundown. Isdiro wears one. Turns out Jannik is from some kind of free vamp family from Pelimburg; he's three generations free, an back in the coastal city his family are too wealthy an powerful for even the Mata to push. House Sandwalker, whatever that means.

"It's something we could look into, provided the bats were properly tied to a House," the Mata says, slow, considering.

That's the biggest bribe yet – taking away the pass laws for bonded vamps. The Mata must really want us to go.

Now the bargaining begins, an I'm bored already, even though I expect to be sitting through this shite for the next few hours. It seems the Mata is more worried than ever, or he wants rid of us right quick, 'cause he agrees to a fair few of Harun's requests.

A court scribe is recording the deals, an finally, when everyone is as happy as they're ever going to get in this lifetime, Harun an Blaine sign. My da stands witness, an I'm called to sign too.

Soon as all is done, Mata Blaine is clapping his hands an calling for the by-the-wind to be made ready. Turns out we'll be arriving at Urlin in full Lammer-style.

Urlin is deep in the mountains where the Casabi springs, cold an young. We'll follow the river until we reach a city that no Lammer has set foot in – a place that's used to threaten Hoblings. It is the sanctuary of the vamps.

Isdiro hands over the two feyn girls to Jannik an Felicita. Her face is white when she gathers them to her skirts, an she strokes their cheeks as she bends down to kiss them both. I've never seen her so soft, so mother-like.

"I should be going with you." Jannik's twisting a fine silver band on his little finger, so thin that it's only now that I spot it, 'cause he's plucking at it all full of nerves.

"I understand why you cannot."

Jannik glances back at Felicita; this look passes across his thin face. I think he'd do anything for her. He turns back at Harun. "I have family ties," he says, an hands him a sealed letter. The red wax is cut deep with a symbol I've come to recognise – the flaming eagle of the Alerion. "If you should run into trouble, then use this."

Harun takes it hesitantly. "Would it be better if I did not?"

Jannik smiles for the first time since I've met him. He has crooked teeth, but it's not ugly-like, just his self. "My marriage to Felicita was not . . . an event that attracted much happiness." He grins. Even Felicita gives a quick mocking laugh. "I have relatives of power in Urlin, and they will help me for name alone. But they will not like to be reminded of what I did."

The paper crackles in the crisp air, an Harun nods an tucks it deep into his breast pocket. "Stay well." He kisses Jannik's mouth the way two old equal Houses will when they meet or leave, an out-of-date custom that Trone told me about when he was still trying to drum shite into my head. Never actually seen no one do it before.

"Go well," says Jannik.

Harun turns to Felicita an does the same. "Take care of them," he says, looking down at the little twin feyn. "Isidro says the new teeth will hurt, and that if it gets really bad, to give them some bark-water and lady's gown."

She smiles thin. "I know. He's written me pages of instructions. I know what to keep an eye open for."

Isdidro looks like his stomach hurts. "Frankly, I should be there to watch for any reactions – no one knows exactly what the horn is going to do –"

"Isidro, hush." Harun is grim. "Felicita will do what she can."

"I'll keep notes," she says. "Promise."

"And I'll be able to read this illegible scrawl that passes for your handwriting?" he snaps.

"I'll dictate it to Jannik," she says back, baring her teeth. "He can put it in verse."

HALF AN HOUR later we're being herded into that rocking carriage cradled under the belly of the by-the-wind. I swear that thing looks at me with its tentacle clusters of tiny eyes, jellied an insane, like I am a morsel of something sweet.

It's just barely still daylight when we heave up into the cloudless sky. The ground drops away, an we speed through the air, wind whipping the poison streamers 'gainst the glass windows. They leave marks that dry like snail tracks, thin an silver.

The sun is setting to my right, an it turns the red sands redder still, like someone spilled a bucket of pig's blood after they hung the poor sod up to drip clean. The Casabi is a girl's red ribbon, an far away, so far that they're nothing more than purple mist, are the Wyvernsback, where Urlin is hidden.

Isidro spends most of the time pacing the little carriage, weaving his way in-between the tables an our legs.

"Will you sit down?" Harun growls, an Isidro, well, I can actually feel his temper flare up around him, like wings.

"Do you lot ever actually turn into bats?" I says, all casual-like.

Isidro glares at me, an then I hear Sel laughing. Although at first I think he's choking.

"No," Isidro snaps, but the tension is gone.

Harun's laughing too. "You do a good impression of one," he says, an Isidro scowls an slumps down next to him, arms crossed on his chest.

"I don't want to go," he says. Then softer, "And I do."

"An you're all worried about what? That you'll like it so much that you'll want to stay?" I lean forward, an snag a pastry from the tray left on the low table. The benches are against the walls an covered with hard cushions, but the tables have been set into the floor, screwed in place with bone.

"No." Isidro shakes his head. "That I'll feel like I don't belong."

"But you don't," says Sel, clear as day. "None of us do."

"What would you know?" It's a cruel jab, an Isidro must be feeling real shite if he's taking it out on Sel, something he never does, though I've heard him be sharp enough to just about everyone else.

But Sel don't seem to to worry, or take no offence. "Mother was from the citadel."

Isidro stares, says nothing.

There's nilly blood put out for the vamps, but neither of them have touched the thick drinks. I guess cold blood gone thick as stir-porridge is about as appetising to them as it would be to me. Now that I've been around the other vamps for a while, I can feel the hunger making Isidro cranky. I glance across at Harun, who catches my look an sighs.

"Eat," he says. "If this thing flies as fast as Blaine claims we'll be there by daybreak. You don't want to be like this when we meet the

Lady."

Isidro reaches out one hand to take a glass, an says nothing. He cradles it in his lap a long time before he actually takes a sip. "They never say her name in the rookeries," he says. "She's like a distant goddess, the Alerion."

Harun snorts. "She's the same as anyone else in a palace. More breeding than sense."

"Not true," Sel says, an we all turn to look at him, so he pulls his knees up an kinda half hides behind my arm. "She made Mother run."

Natural-like, after that little titbit he says nothing else, just keeps his head down an his fur-lined coat close about him, like he's hiding from more than just the cold.

Later, it turns out that the wide benches fold out again, an so do the flat cushions. They make narrow beds, wide enough for one person to sleep comfortable, or two squashed up close if they don't mind hair in their face, an heat covering them.

Sel an I actually manage to sleep, although for once it's him scooted up behind me, with his arm tight around my chest, instead of the other way round.

I wake up when a gust of wind buffets the carriage so hard the traces make snapping sounds an the carriage swings like an acrobat. Around me is darkness, just the slow sucking noise of the by-the-wind as it eats the air, an the creak an crack of leather.

When I shift, trying to tuck myself deeper under the layers of thin blankets an mine an Sel's coats, I see the figures of Harun an Isidro like a shadow play. Harun's on his back, Isidro curled over him, kissing at his throat. Or biting maybe. There's the smell of blood in the air, an behind me Sel murmurs in his sleep an holds me closer, until I can feel his hot breath right by the pulse on my neck.

I think he can smell that blood too, because he shifts an I hear his breathing change. He's awake. His body tensed all sudden-like. I keep watching the two others, not wanting to move. Isidro is kissing Harun now, an the slow movement makes me hard, makes me want, an I don't have a clue how Sel would deal with that.

In the end, I lie still long enough, keeping my breathing even an slow, that Sel goes back to sleep.

Instead of feeling relieved though, I feel like my throat is too tight, an my chest is a solid ache.

Someone wakes me by shoving my shoulder. There's nothing

comfortable about sleeping on a little hard bench in a swinging carriage hundreds of feet up in the air. My neck feels like someone rode over it with a cart. Twice. It makes a loud click as I stretch out the worst of the pain an stiffness.

"Mata Trey says we're approaching," Harun says as he flicks open one velvet curtain.

"Gris." Light hits my eyes with a cold bright slap. Behind me Sel is curled up tight, drowsy-drunk with nilly blood an too little sleep.

Neither of the vamps seem keen on enjoying the view, so it's just me an Harun that are standing by the windows as the by-the-wind sweeps low along the plains. Gold light turns the sky pale at the edges, an the red sand glitters. Here an there rocks break out from the hard-packed sand, in odd wind-sculptures. We're flying low – low enough that I can see brush tangled around an between the huge rocks. Uni land for sure. It's good ground for the herds; place to hide from sphynxes, there's grazing, an with the Casabi running narrow an cold, plenty of water. The river is all different-like here, straighter, deeper, an blacker. Up ahead, the Wyvernsback rises raw an rough. The sand meets her feet in a red wave, an then I see them, turning like a river of fur an horns. Wild unicorns, a herd of them moving like one animal, galloping across the desert.

"Fuck me," I says. I've never seen so much money in one place; even my da, who owns the biggest breeding farm in MallenIve, would be struck dumb at the sight of all those horns, white an cold with magic. The horns rake backward, in huge spirals. They look almost too heavy for the unis' necks, an I wonder just how much money is in all that twisted horn.

"Look there." Harun points to three white shapes trailing the unis. It takes a moment for me to see what they are. One stops, raises his cloak from his head to look up at our by-the-wind. Black hair an a face like bone. Three mounted vamps. The first raises his arm an flicks his hand, an the three are off, steering the wild unis away from us, bringing them round to the foothills of the Wyvernsback.

Then they're gone, hidden in the crumpled foothills.

I turn to Harun as he drops the curtain. "So many," I say, shaking my head. "Do they own them?"

"So it appears." His face is grim. If the vamps have that kind of wealth, the trinkets an baubles that the Mata sent with us will be worthless.

Half an hour or so later an everyone is awake, mostly dressed an ready. Both vamps are in shitty moods now, like someone's gone an pissed all over them. Even Sel is all snappy.

"What's your problem, chum?" I say. "You're not the only one who doesn't want to be here."

He cocks his head an squints at me. "Don't you feel it?"

"Feel what?"

Quick as a wyrm, Sel grabs my shoulders with both hands, almost shaking me. That contact is all I need, 'cause it's like been hit with pure energy. So deep an strong an wild that I can feel it buzzing in my teeth.

"Sweet Gris," I say, even though my jaw is clicking, ivory clattering against ivory. "What the fuck is that?"

"That," Isidro says as he pulls on his gloves, "is the Alerion. The Lady of Urlin."

Forty-Nine

A Game of Wasps

I WANT TO question the two feyn again to see what else I can discover about their people's heritage, but I'm unable find them. Eventually, a servant tells me that they were handed over to Harun – his price for going to the distant city of Urlin.

I stalk my father down in the main hall. It's crowded with War-singers, heads bowed, their faces creased in concentration. Father will have to take a break at some point, so I slip into a chair to wait. Illy's here too, somewhere, but I don't want to look for her, don't want to see her.

Naturally, she finds me.

"What are you doing here?" she snaps. She's holding a glass of water in one hand and a small ornate bowl in the other. A grey smattering of scriven fills the bottom of the bowl, fragile and ash-like. She smells of old sweat, of a body slowly collapsing in on itself.

"I need to speak to Father." I can't help but be drawn to the fine silver band on her smallest right finger. Trey has one on the left, echoing hers. I make myself look at her face.

"He's busy."

An impatient sigh is rising in my chest, but I manage to throttle it. "I know that, Illy. That's why I'm waiting."

We shouldn't be doing this, slicing at each other. One deep

breath, and I force all my resentment down, so deep no one will ever find it. There, a smile, I can even make it warm, sisterly. "How are you faring?" I wave one hand about the room. "It looks as if every War-singer in MallenIve is working at holding the barriers."

"They are." But the bite has gone, she just sounds tired, confused. "We're working in shifts." Iliana sits in a second chair opposite to me, carefully balancing her precious scriven as she does. "The Mekekana are stronger than before – and there are more of them." She leans in close. "No one is to know anything, anything at all, but Trey told me that Pelimburg is gone –"

"What?"

"Hush." She glances about. "Keep your voice down." Then she nods. "The last word was three days ago. Since then – nothing."

Pelimburg. Gone. The very fount of our Houses, destroyed. It cannot be real.

The shock must show on my face.

"Remember, Calissa, not a word." She stands, sips at her water. "I have to go back." Illy tips her head to the silent War-singers in their ivory chairs, little tables holding the scriven bowls at their left knees. "Keep well."

"You too," I say, but she's already slipping between the others, and I don't think she hears me.

She pauses to brush Father's shoulder, and he rises from his trance, head shaking. A few minutes later, he's joined me. "Iliana said you were waiting to see me?" The lines on his face are so deep and sharp that shadows pool in them, making him look haggard. "I need to eat." He holds out one arm for me to take. "We can talk in the dining room."

He leads me through to a room set with wide windows, giving a view down to the royal parks. This time of year, with not even the summer rains to help, the grass is dead and brown – a fine, yellowish stubble. The trees are mostly naked to the winds that sweep in from the desert, but a few evergreens imported from Pelimburg still cling to their needles.

I've been to Pelimburg once, when I was very young, and I remember little of it, but there are a few memories, like a faded lace cloth – the smell of salt spray on the stone promenade, the curving grey and blue cliffs that fall into the churning water.

Cold air tinged with salt and the faint tang of rotting seaweed. The gulls. Father gave me a piece of bread to throw up in the air, and it never even hit the ground. The black-backed gulls caught it in mid-air and flew off squabbling. It's impossible that all of this is gone now. I refuse to believe it.

We take our seats in a little alcove with white curtains drawn back to look down a rolling hill to where Mallen's Folly nestles in a copse of withered trees. In the stark light the Folly looks older, the walls collapsing in tumbled skirts of stone and rubble. Inside that neglected building lies the way to the Well, the room of shattered bones. Looking at it now I know that whatever Trey said about keeping this to myself, I need to let my father know.

A waiter brings a platter of food out for my father, and he offers me a choice of the meals they have prepared for the War-singers. I wave him away. "Just a glass of wine, please."

Father raises one brow but says nothing at my request. "Two," he tells the waiter, who bobs and leaves us.

A few minutes later, I'm fortified with my first sip of the strong red – wine from vineyards that are most likely burning as we speak. If Pelimburg fell, then the small villages around her in the wine country will have gone down with her. The wine tastes so bitter and black I almost put it down again.

"I spoke to –" How can I explain this tangled thing to my father? I start again. "Someone came to me," I say, carefully. My father's face doesn't change. "He said that the Mata Blaine has entered the room of shattered bones." My voice is pitched low; no one must hear this but him.

Father swallows his lump of gravied meat and chokes down a sip of wine. "Is that –" He coughs, eyes watering. "No," he says when he recovers. "Impossible. I would have heard of it." But he can't help the sidelong look as his gaze slides to the folly, then back to me. "Perhaps if you could tell me who it was that came to you with this snippet, I might be inclined to consider it."

"I cannot say."

The silence between us is not empty or comfortable; it is filled with regrets, with ghosts and shadows and secrets.

Father stands with a sigh, pushing his chair away in a loud scrape. "I must get back."

"Will you at least think about it –" I don't want to say "watch the Mata," not here and now when the sound of our chairs has made the few other diners turn to stare at us. "Perhaps it may even be that the bats and the Lammers were sent to Urlin with another plan in mind.

After all, Harun has never trusted. . . him."

"Calla." He smiles. "Do not worry yourself. We will hold the shield, and soon your brother will be back with more bats – more vamps." His smile broadens. "Already we have a few candidates come from the rookeries; even now, Lady Pelim is training up the first bonded recruits."

I start. I didn't know that. I'd heard that a bare handful of Lammers had shown up willing to bond with the bats. Of course, Father could be exaggerating, trying to ease my fear. "And what of them? A smattering of weakling Lammers bound to whores. Father . . ." I think of those lower-Houses, finally handed power even as my own is taken away. "We need more than that."

I need more than that.

Fifty

The Grinningtommy

TREY BRINGS THE by-the-wind down in an open plaza, an we step out to get our first good look at Urlin, or the Citadel as Sel keeps calling it.

It's a black fortress city, not sprawling an stretched out like a dog before a fire, the way MallenIve is. Instead Urlin rises higher an higher to a point. I have to crane my neck to see the highest towers, an even then I have this feeling like there's more still that's just out of sight. The stone is dark, glittery as scriv.

Harun says that's because the Wyvernsback is old volcano territory. It got its name from all that slow smoke pouring off it hundreds of years ago. That, an the ragged curve of the mountain, like it has folded its wings down an is just biding its time.

The plaza where we've landed is red dust swept clean an empty, although every now an then something rough an bright winks up between the sand. Harun stoops to pick up a chip of amber rock, an when the sun strikes it, it burns in his fingers like a piece of star.

"Diamonds," he hisses an drops it.

The sun has crept over the last of the Wyvernsback crags an it hits the plaza, making it light up like the night sky just fell at our feet. I shield my eyes. The others have done the same.

Out of the light, a figure is coming up to us. The glare fades, as if the diamonds suddenly remembered they're just rocks with history, an I can make out the figure clear as well water.

He's a tall vamp, like Isidro, although he's not half as pretty. He has wide cheekbones an the slight tilt to his eyes like some Hobs an bats have, only it's more noticeable on him.

He spreads his arms wide an dips in a little bow. The wide sleeves of his white robe fall back from his hands. "Greetings," he says. "And welcome to the Citadel." It's the same way that Sel says it, as if it's the only city worth mentioning in the world, an MallenIve ain't nothing more than a collection of huts an holes that doesn't deserve the name of city.

Harun steps forward with Isidro moving next to him in that spooky unison that the couple sometimes slips into. They both bow low. "Greetings. We come from the Mata Blaine, on his wishes and under his protection," says Harun, his head still lowered, though he looks up at the waiting vamp. "We wish to speak with the Lady of Urlin."

With a flick of his hands, the vamp lets them know they can stand straight. "We shall see that she gets your message, Lammer." He stares straight up at the by-the-wind, to where that red-haired bugger Trey is standing in the carriage door, wind-blown hair across his face. "He may not enter," says the vamp. "He stinks of scriven."

"As you wish." Harun's being the most polite I ever seen him. He ain't a man who cares much what people think. Felicita says it's 'cause he's the only scion of a powerful House – he's never had to temper his self for no one.

The vamp seems satisfied, an he turns his back on us, the white cloak flaring about his shoulders. His robes beneath that are loose. I've never seen anyone in get-up like that – no trousers or waistcoats an long jackets, just these swinging clothes. "This way," he says, an we follow. Sel an I stumble along at the back as we're led through narrow doors into a room cool an dark as a cave.

The windows are slits, letting in hardly any sun. The light that does come in stripes the grey floor like a tabby cat. The walls are thick, twice as thick as any wall in MallenIve.

"I will take you to our guest suites," he says, as if visitors from MallenIve drop out of the sky all the time. Nothing flusters this one. He's a vamp Trone, used to running everything.

The passages in Urlin twist this way an that, an I'm lost as a Lam in the Wend by the time he stops before a set of bolted doors. Harun an I both look at each other at the same time, an I can see what he's thinking – it locks from the outside. We're not really guests, looks like.

We're inside when the door snicks shut, an there's the rough sound of wood splintering against wood as the bar is slid into place.

Between the four of us we could easily split the door open. But there's bound to be more vamps outside, standing guard.

"Shit," says Harun, an he takes a seat on a low couch covered with a white cloth.

Everything in this stone room is touched with white.

Isidro stalks the length of the room, stopping to peer through the slit windows. He's walked that damn room maybe a hundred times when we hear the wood sliding back at the door. Isidro stops still like he's turned to a statue, an Harun looks up through his hair. Next to me I can hear how Sel's breathing has gone fast an ragged-like.

"Sorry to have kept you." It's that Trone vamp. "My name is Jael. I am the Lady's aide." He pauses an looks at us each in turn. "You must be tired from your journey, and hungry too." He waits, like he's expecting an answer.

Isidro glances at Harun, who just sinks down deeper into his seat, like he's saying, "your people, you deal with this".

Finally, Isidro shrugs. ""We are." ." He says it careful an slow, an I get the idea that everything we say could be a weapon against us. Isidro an Sel are afraid, an that fear gets under my skin, an itch I can't scratch.

Jael bows. "Please, thn kindloin us. We will be eating in a few minutes."

There's something about the way he says eating that I don't right like, but food sounds like a decent enough plan.

The vamp waits for us as we wash hands an faces in bowls he has servants bring in. They're wearing those same loose robes in shades of cream an grey an tan. The material has a coarse look an texture that is familiar. It's not windle-silk, but it's something I've seen before. It's bugging me until Sel speaks.

"Nillies," he says. Then I see it. Shining strands of magic. But he's wrong, it ain't nilly mane. This is hair taken from live unicorns. Maybe a strand at a time. If they've clothed a whole city of vamps in living hair, with the magic trapped still inside, then I don't even want to think about how many unis are out there running through the desert, property of the Alerion. We're out of our depth.

"This way," says Jael. We follow him out, the servants crowded silent behind us, watching us with those slow-blinking eyes. The weight of their stare is heavy on my back. It's something I ain't felt since the early days of taking over the Digs pack, when it seemed everyone was an enemy, an I was just waiting for someone to try to kill me for the claim.

We walk without speaking, though I'm pretty sure Isidro an Harun are talking in each other's heads. Sel an I have slipped into that silent conversation once or twice before, but it's hard to keep at it long with Sel the way he is. A bit like walking through a field of glass. It ain't something you do for fun.

The stone walls are bare, but as we wind our way deeper an higher into Urlin, tapestries an paintings slowly start covering the grey rock. They get thicker an thicker, until it feels like we're walking between crowds of unicorns, burning suns, robed an bitter vamps scowling down at us from the walls.

Not that I end up looking at much. I have a headache starting at my temple, the kind you get from staring too long at a bright light. I squint, an Sel makes a sighing noise. "You're feeling her," he says. "The sun in your head."

Now's no time for Sel to start going all loopy, but I can't even say nothing back, because my head feels like it's going to explode.

With the next turn the passage walls drop away, an we're left standing in the entrance to a huge hall, lit bright with lamps an sunshine. Normal-like, vamps aren't too keen on bright light 'cause it hurts their eyes, that's what Sel tells me. They can cut the worst of it with that third eyelid, but it also means they can't see proper.

The room is full, an all I see is dark hair an bone-white faces, eyes all milky-white. I mean, I know now that vamps don't all look the same, but when there's a hundred of them all packed together tight as spinningjennies in the factories, well, they kinda blur together.

That headache's worse now, an when I look up over all those massed vamps, I see why.

She's beautiful. Not in a way that makes you go, *look a shiny knockout girl*, but she's a flicker of power, colours – like those candy-cane colours I felt on Sel the first time we touched.

The Alerion smiles down at us, an I realise that I'm standing there with my mouth open like a Hob who's just seen a girl's brass for the first time.

She walks toward us, an the crowd of vamps parts for her. Her skin is so white it that it seems like I should be feeling snow-coldness sweeping off her. Her black hair is coiled about her head, an she has eyes like Sel's, a little too wide to be Lammer or Hob. They're the same shape, an that's what I'm drawn to – Sel's eyes in this unfamiliar face. She's the only one I can see who hasn't slicked that third white eyelid across.

When she smiles, a pressure lifts, an I sag. I'm not the only one. All around us are sighs as the vamps breathe normal-like again, as if this Alerion just gave them permission to live.

My Gris-damned head feels like it's going to explode.

"MallenIve rookery trash," she says, looking at Isidro and Sel. Her voice is rough, but somehow it slides over my skin anyway, snagging on me like a cat's claw on a lady's silk hose. "And Lammers. How very . . . interesting."

Harun clears his throat, maybe because Isidro is looking too much like a mouse to say nothing. "We're here as ambassadors of The High Lord Mata Blaine."

"Yes?"

The room is still again, everyone waiting to hear what comes next.

"As a token of our cities' friendship, Mata Blaine has sent you gifts, gifts that he hopes will please."

Her grin widens. "What could he possibly send me that I would want?"

Harun pales, stammers. "P-perhaps nothing," he finally says. "For certainly, there is nothing in MallenIve that would do you justice."

She sighs, an it's like a wind rippling through leaves. When she speaks again, I'm not ready for the snap; I've been lulled like a babe in a cradle. "Get to the point, Lammer. What is it that the Mata needs from me, that he sends you crawling and begging?"

Harun's throat bobs, an then he decides to just get it out-like, no more wasting time in a pissing contest with the Alerion. Truth told, he's out-powered. We all are. "The Mata is sending an open invitation to vampires to move to MallenIve. Reports say that you have too many wrays, and he's offering to help the balance."

"Really?" Her eyelids flicker, an one corner of her mouth curls up all slow an secretive. "How very thoughtful of him, but I do have to wonder at this sudden philanthropy, this hand of friendship extended to my people, when before the Mata has made it quite clear what he thinks of us."

"The Mekekana," says Harun. "It's because of the Mekekana." He jerks one hand palm up an raises his head. "He's offering property and status to any vampire who will bond with a Lammer."

She frowns. "And why would he want that?"

"Because of the tap. Only Lammers can tap and direct the magic..." His voice trails off, because that scary feyn is frowning.

"What of the scriven?" she says, after the silence grows long an dangerous. "Do you not have your little powdered rock to draw out your magic?"

An here it comes, because we're basically telling her we're defenceless. "The scriven has run out."

The Alerion tips back her head an laughs. The sound echoes off stone, an only the tight-packed bodies muffle it enough that my head don't explode. Sel is crouched down, his hands over his ears.

"Your pardon," she says, when the laughter fades. "I will think on this." She gestures with one hand, an a wave of vamps fall back, making the room seem less crowded. "For now, we invite you to join us in our midday meal."

Three vamps come forward, each leading a uni on a woven halter. The animals stand still an tame as if they really were nothing more than big goats, only with that one deathly-sharp horn pointed back like a dagger.

The Alerion darts forward. A fountain of blood shoots out from a severed vein. Another bat is already catching the spray in a wide ceramic bowl.

She does the same to the other two, then heals the unis with a word an a touch.

Isidro gasps.

Even Sel takes a step back, hovering behind me like he's trying to hide. "What?" I hiss at him.

"She's a healer," he says, low an quick. "No one, no one, very few." He shakes his head like he's shaking all his thoughts back into place. "Power."

It's Isidro who explains to me in a hurried whisper. "We can't direct our power. That's why the bond with the Lammers is needed."

"Yeah, I know that."

"Well, she just did. And she healed. That's not something that even the bonded pairs can do."

So she's fuck-off powerful. Like we didn't know that.

Fifty-One

A Game of Wasps

HOUSE IVES ENDS on a knife-blade.

They come for us in the small hours, between morning and night, servants rushing in, raising us from our beds. Their faces are white; they talk too fast.

Mother and I race like ghosts through the Mata Palace to arrive at the shrouded corpse.

Illy is already there, waiting for us.

All I can do is stare at the shape laid out on the table, and try to find something I recognise, some hint that this wrapped slab of meat was once my father. Illy can't talk – every time she opens her mouth to say something, all that she manages to cough out are choked sounds, meaningless. I cling to her, and we are sisters again, both lost and frightened and knowing that we are powerless children in a world of adult betrayal.

In this, it is my mother who suddenly gains strength, who draws her calmness about her and stands straighter, surer. Being a widow gives her a kind of dignity she never had as his wife. "How did it happen?" she asks the faces.

There is mumbling, uncertainty, conjecture. Finally, the War-singers and servants around him seem to agree on a plausible story. He was robbed – a knife wound. The blood spreads on his chest, a long line. A knife wound they say again.

A sabre wound. It will not do to voice this thought.

"What did they take?" my mother asks, and her voice rings clear as Saints.

A scriv-pouch. His purse is missing.

On his fingers, the house rings are untouched.

A very picky thief then.

And I know my father must have confronted the Mata, must have asked about the Well. If I had kept Trey's doubts and fears to myself, my father would be alive, wouldn't have died this ignoble death, this lie. I hold tighter to my sister, and sob into her neck, as her tears burn mine.

Servants come to take Illy away, back to her place in the War-singers' chambers. A war does not wait on one family's grief.

Mother steers me back to our rooms, and it is only her hand at my back that keeps me forcing myself forward, that makes me walk upright. The Mata is going to use the Well, and my father knew. And now my father is dead.

"Sleep," says my mother. She has the servants pour me tea with lady's gown in it, which I sit and hold in numb fingers but do not drink. Then she dresses and is gone again, in a whirl of silver and grey and with her face kept blank as glass.

I set the tea down and dismiss the servants from our rooms. "I want to be alone," I tell them, and they are quick to leave, gratefulness evident in the speed of their departure.

When I am finally alone, I fish my thin neck chain out from under my clothes and hold up the key to my father's heart, loosen it. I feel like a Mekekana ship, walking with an ugly clacking, all disjointed and unnatural as I make my way to my father's chest, to unlock the little safe-box he brought with him from our family home. Inside it is money, silver pieces enough to see us through the next few months – I grab a handful of these, drop them in my lap. There are deeds to properties, court-approved wills and documents. I care for none of them, rifling through the crackling sheets until I find what I was looking for – a slim collection of letters, older even than me, bound together with a girl's hair ribbon, faded silk. I know what these are. This is my father's love, spent on some girl, some girl who lived her life on her knees, sleeves rolled up to her elbows while she scrubbed floors, or washed glass. Spent.

By the time Illy and I were born, he'd burned up what was left of his love in grief and regret. Illy and I never stood a real chance, being flesh and blood, and a reminder of his own guilt.

I hear a noise, an awful choking sound like a cat with a hairball, and it seems so distant and vulgar that I only realise it is me when I have pulled the letters to my stomach and curled myself up around them. Harder and harder I press the edges of the letters into my belly, crushing them, making myself ache. I cry for myself and for my father. For Illy and for my mother. All the people who could never match up to my father's own failures. And when I am done, I let my last tears fall for Jek, who will never match up to my father's hopes.

The letters are ruined, the thin paper torn now under my violence, the ink smudged from the sweat on my palms. There's no point in putting them back; the only people they meant anything to are both dead. And why leave them as a reminder for my mother? Slowly, my body aching, I uncurl myself and make my way to the hearth. The papers flicker, burn merrily, and are soon gone.

Outside the first of the crows are cawing miserably in the cold. It's too late now to go back to sleep. I fetch my stolen money, tuck it into the pocket of my favourite jacket, then call for a servant to come bathe and dress me.

The Mata will not make us crawl.

I SPEND THE day in the eating chambers, making notes about the bats, drawing routes, wishing I was a Saint and knew what paths there were to take, and all the while I watch the Folly. If the Mata is even thinking of going there, to the Well, then he has to be stopped. How, I'm not sure, but a possible answer is unfolding beneath my hands.

I've taken up residence in that little nook in the War-singers' eating chambers. No one seems to care. I sit at my table and watch through the sun-struck glass, hardly daring to drop my gaze in case I should miss something.

"The servants said I'd find you here."

I don't turn my head, not even for my mother. She sighs and slides into the seat opposite me. The faint perfume of summer jasmine folds around us.

"Before he was...killed, your father told me what you think."

That snaps my head back. He wasn't supposed to mention it to anyone; not even my mother. I don't trust her.

She frowns. "I cannot try for a Vision." Her voice trembles. "And even if I had scriven, I'll admit that my power would never be enough to see the Mata's futures, or even to read the destiny of an entire city. It should have been," she says, more to herself than me, a panicked whisper. She splays her hands on the table, palm up like a beggar. "But there's something in the air that's black and hungry, and after your father... I don't need a Vision to know that the future is grim."

I swallow. "You think he will open – do it?"

She leans back. "He was ever a man prone to rash decisions. I believe he will."

"How well do you know him?" My mother's history was never important to me, but there is something in her voice, something scabbed over. She never talks about herself, only Illy, and Ives, and honour.

"We were meant to be wed, until it became apparent that my powers were no match for his." She pulls a face that makes her look older and more bitter than ever. "His father believed that I would taint the magic-line of the Mata and so my own father had to scrabble about for a suitable alternative. He married me off to your father, who had just caused a scandal with his Hob-servant, and so couldn't point fingers at anyone else's failings." She clenches her hands then flexes them again. Her palms are white, leached. Finally, she looks up and stares at me. Her eyes are red-rimmed, sunken. "Yes. I know the Mata well." She smiles tiredly. "As well as you knew your dearest Trey, and I believe that Blaine will turn to the Well. He is a man with an unshakable faith in his own power. Men like him cannot believe that they will ever fail."

I'm shaken by her reference to Trey, and she must see it in my face.

"Yes," she says. "I'm not half as blind as you believe. Always, Calissa, I've watched you, watched to see what path your choices would lead you down. I know what you're meant to do – I've Seen at least that much." She shakes her head, and a carefully pinned lock of hair slides free to curl against her cheek. "I will not let you become like me, a vessel holding only regret. While men will tell you to sit quietly and do what they have decided is best for you. I'm telling you this now: with your father's death, you are freed. Do what you want and damn the rest." She takes a deep breath and stands. "Remember that, and it will be worth it."

When she's gone, leaving behind only the faint talc and perfume memory of herself, I sit with my hands folded on the table, and stare at the Folly without really seeing it.

I'm thinking of something else instead. A way to stop the Mata, and perhaps a way to revenge my father's death.

What is it that I truly want? What path has my mother seen in my future that she would never tell me. And do I have the courage to take it?

There is a way for me to have magic again, but the cost is too great. I shake the hair from my eyes, and take another sip of wine from a city that no longer exists.

Fifty-Two

The Grinningtommy

THE UNI BLOOD is tipped into small bowls – more like flattened cups – an handed out. I guess 'cause we're supposed to be guests, they hand to us first. The Alerion passes the cup to Isidro, an she's just barely covering a smirk. Him an Harun drink without a waver, an she comes to Sel next.

Sel, who right now is trying to hide behind me.

She frowns. "Look at me, wray."

Her voice is a command; it's so strong that even though I'm no wray I feel like I need to stare up at her, do whatever she says.

Her frown deepens, an there's a flicker of something in her eyes, like she's almost worried. "What's your name?"

"Sel."

"Your full name, wray."

Sel just looks at her like he don't understand. Finally, he says, very slow an soft, "Ansel," an then he drags his gaze from her an looks down at the floor. "I forgot the rest. The words don't come anymore."

She pulls back, lips curled. "What's wrong with him?" she hisses.

It's Isidro who comes up calm an explains. "We believe he lost a twin, and that his mother took his death upon herself."

The Alerion takes a step away, like Sel's a piece of shite in her path. "She died for a wray? Unlikely. She would never –" Then she clams up tight.

"And yet it appears to be truth." Isidro puts a hand on Sel's shoulder, an Sel stops shivering an mumbling about forgetting. I didn't even know Sel's real name was Ansel. I'm wondering how much else about him I don't know, never thought of asking.

"He has a familiar look," she says. An then she does something strange-like, stalks close to Sel an takes his face in her fingers so she can tilt it up. "What was your mother's name?" She asks it all gentle.

He stills, an his eyes are wide – deep blue like the twilight sky after a blister-hot day. For a moment, he looks at her – really looks at her – an I see Sel like he should be, what he really is under all that broken mess. He's sharp an clear an beautiful as the Alerion.

Then that damned third lid snicks into place, an it's gone.

There's fear writ on the Alerion's face then she covers it up right-quick, makes her face a mask. She drops her hand as she turns to me. A servant next to her hands over a fresh cup of blood, an she holds it out.

Now, I might have drunk Sel's blood, but that was a need – this, I look at the blood, red an bright, too thick an hot – this I don't want.

"Drink," she says.

Since I'm of no mind to start a war or get us killed all because I don't want to do this, I take a gulp of air an reach out for that blood-full bowl.

It tastes like iron, stings my throat. How Harun managed to swallow this down, I don't right know. I had no idea how iron-rich uni blood was; this is like choking down fire. No one else coughed or threw up, so I'm guessing it would be bad form.

There. It's down, stay down, an for the love of all magic, don't make me speak any time soon.

"Good," she says after I've drunk from the bowl. "Now, you are our people too." She says it in a way that makes me wonder what she means, but Harun an Isidro don't seem upset by it. I wish those two bastards would warn me about things before they bloody happen.

"We've shared blood, as good as any bond-word the Mata could offer." She spreads her hands an raises her voice so all the wray an feyn can hear her. "You have all heard the Mata's request. Those who wish to take the offer may come to me and petition a right to leave."

There's a silence that's not, like the vamps are all about to break out in whispers but are waiting for her to leave, for that powerful feel to fade away so that they all have room to breathe again.

"By tomorrow," she says an smiles wide enough that her fangs are clear as day, "You will have your answer. If none come to me, then you shall know the Mata's offer does not suit."

Harun blinks. "And if they do?"

"If." She laughs. "Then perhaps I will let you leave."

"Perhaps?"

The room is too dark all sudden-like. A cloud blown across the sun.

"Now," says the Alerion, "Jael will see that you are made comfortable while you wait."

WE'RE FUCKED. THE look on Harun's face is clue enough.

Jael minces about like he's a fucking Lammer his self, showing us which rooms we will sleep in, where we will find extra blankets should we need them.

"Servants will bring you water to wash with," he says. "And some refreshment." I'm hoping he means food, because while the unicorn blood might have fed the two vamps, my stomach is still a churning mess. I don't right know how they keep that shite down. It's worse'n vai.

When Jael's gone, Harun sighs an slumps down into a chair covered with white cloth.

Isidro asks the question we're all thinking. "What are we going to do?" He walks over to Harun to stand behind him, rests his hands on the Lammer's shoulders an kneads them with slow movements that grind deep into tired muscle. Harun winces then shrugs his shoulders back. "We wait. Everyone there heard our offer. We can only hope that it was good enough to tempt some into speaking against their Alerion."

"She's a bit of a bitch, that one," I says.

Harun laughs all hollow-like. "She's damn powerful, Jek, and I don't think the Mata's offer is going to swing enough vamps to speak out." He cricks his neck to the left then leans forward out of Isidro's grip. "I need to be able to offer them something more," he whispers. "And I don't have that power." He rests his head in his hands an stares at the floor.

"Look in her eyes," says Sel, an we all turn to him. He steps back at the attention, nilly-nervous, his eyes wide. "She hurts people," he says, after a few swallows. "Can see that – offer kindness."

"What? The kindness of being a third-rate citizen in MallenIve?" Harun raises a brow, sighs. "I should have pressed Blaine harder."

"Actually," Isidro says slowly, "the wray might be right. In every city there are those who live on the edges, the burdens, the unwanted, the Hobs," he says an nods at me. "Sorry."

I lift one shoulder. It's nothing to me. He's right. The Hobs are the filth on the fringes; we know what the Lammers think of us. Moaning about it won't change nothing.

"So." Harun isn't staring at the floor now. "We look for those – those who probably weren't in that hall today."

Isidro nods.

Someone raps at the door, an all of us go quiet, staring at it.

It must be the servants that Jael promised. I grin. "You wanna know where the down-trodden are," says I. "You speak to them what's at the door right now."

"Enter," says Harun, an he has a sly grin that would do a hunting sphynx proud. He nods at me, an I have to push away the strange feeling of knowing I said something that Harun an his crew thought was worthwhile. Pride. Fuck me. Pride at getting some Lammer's approval. I've stepped too far from the Digs to ever go back.

The latch grates back, wood scraping wood, an a small vamp trundles in, followed by two others. They bring with them bowls an pitchers of water an folded cloth for drying. There's another tray, with more little pitchers and mugs balanced on it. The smell of sweet tea – mint an honey, like we sometimes drink in summer, fills the room.

The servants shuffle around, silent, heads down, an I think – this was me – only I hope I never had that look to me, that scared silent look, like you might as well ask for permission to breathe. "What's she all got over you," I says, loud into the room, "that you're quiet an scared like nillies knowing the butcher's here?"

They say nothing, but one of them fidgets then slowly puts down the tray. "Is it true?" he asks, but he's speaking to me, not the others. Maybe somewhere in me, despite all the learning and language an fancy manners that are filling me up, I'm still a Hob.

"What – the offers? For sure." I glance at Harun, who nods at me. If anyone's gonna be the one these boys trust, it'll be me. "You interested?"

The vamps are silent, looking across at each other, talking with their eyes. The first one speaks again. "Not us," he says, an bangs the ceramic around, loud enough that his words are just about lost under the noise.

"Who then?"

The vamp steps up closer to our little group, his voice still low. The others are setting up the tea, moving bowls an filling them with steaming water from the pitchers. "The ones who have displeased her." He swallows. "She pulls their teeth –"

Sel makes a choking noise, but Harun an Isidro are quiet an grave, not a flicker of nothing on their faces.

"Tell them this," says Harun, an he steps up real close to the vamp. "Tell them that we can heal them."

Isidro scowls, turns his back an leaves the room, although Harun carries on like he don't notice. "Tell them to petition her, but to say nothing about this offer, and we will uphold it."

The servant nods, then quick as smoke in a wind, they're gone, an it's just the three of us left.

When their footsteps have faded away, Isidro comes back out into the room, an he's shaking. It takes me a moment to realise he's angry. I've never seen Isidro lose it like this, but even so, he's quiet when he speaks, the kind of quiet that's heavy with rage, as if each word would drop like a stone in a well. "How could you offer them that?" He's looking only at Harun. Me an Sel may as well be boggerts.

"Because I know you can do it." Harun is calm. He looks up. "You will do right by our feyn, and you will do right by the vamps we bring from Urlin."

"So sure of yourself, are you?" Isidro snarls. "I've looked at what I can do for those two girls." His eyes are bright, glazed. "I've fitted teeth for them; between us we screwed those damn ivory pegs into their jaws, but they will never be normal, and it will hurt them every single fucking day of their lives." He's shouting now. Never thought I'd see him do that.

Sel creeps behind me, his breath too quick an scared.

"But they will have lives. More than they have now." Harun's face doesn't even flicker.

Isidro is silent for a second. "Fuck you," he says. "I will do it, and you know I will. But you'll be the one that explains the pain."

An then he's gone again, back into their private bed chamber.

The steam on the bowls is thinning. I want to wash before the water turns cold. An I don't want to stay here looking at Harun, feeling the weird painful bond gone ragged between the two of them. Never thought I'd have to spend the rest of my life tugged by other people's feelings. I hate it, an now thanks to my bond with Sel, I'm feeling more an more of it. Reading them like they read me.

Is this what makes people family – this wounds and hurt? Why the fuck did I ever think I wanted it. It's too much to pay.

On the good side, we have something to offer to someone who will take it. On the bad side, it'll be the dregs, the weakest people in the Alerion's city. At least it means we've got a hope that she'll let us leave.

Later, the servants are back with a message. The vamp speaks like he's worried the walls will hear him. He tells us that the defanged vamps have considered the offer, an they've agreed to petition the Alerion.

After they leave, Sel goes to our room, and it's just me an Harun left.

He sighs, leans his head back an looks up at the vaulted ceiling.

"Sleep," says Harun to me.

But I don't want to. I don't want to be alone with Sel.

An that Gris-damned bond lets out too much, 'cause Harun cocks his head at me an says "You have to face the life that you have, Jek."

"I din't choose this."

"Few of us do." He smiles, all tired so it don't reach his eyes. "We just make the best of what we're given."

"SEL?" TRUTH BE told, I hope he's sleeping.

Nothing ever goes the way I want, I think I'm coming to realise. Sel's wide awake; even if I hadn't seen the flicker of his eyes, I'd have known from the catch in his breathing when I pushed the door shut behind me.

I want to turn an run, to not face this shite that's between us. The longer I leave it, the worse it gets, like a small cut that's left open to pick up all the filth from the Wend an gotten sick.

Even though he's as dead as can be, I give a little of my hate over to Sharps; all this is down to him. First bringing me to Sel, an then fucking up the only vaguely good thing that came out of that mess.

A waste of hate, I suppose. There's nowt left of him but other people's memories, an when we've turned to clay an red dead sand, then there won't even be that.

It's four paces to the bed.

This – this must be the hardest thing I've ever done, because I'm always the one who turns my back, who walks away. With the pigs, I just went as far as I could away from them, so that their screams never reached me, so I din't have to deal with no one's pain but my own. With Prue, I made like it was all right that she never wanted me, din't want to call me hers. Even made a kind of peace with my da an his being a yellow-livered coward. We don't choose our family none, I finally realised, just got to take the blood twixt us for what it's worth. I just looked at all this shite the world had given me for a family an realised it was better to forget it an run, not deal with the tangle of it all. Did a good job of it too – running the Dig's pack, getting drunk on miner's bitter, an high off bats.

An here I am now with nowhere to run. Might want to avoid this like everything else, but I can't. I'm sitting with a problem I can't outrun, can't drown in a high or pretend never happened, don't matter. Harun's right. Maybe I din't choose the life I got, but Sel's the realest family I ever had, an that's something worth clinging to. He's here because of what we did, and there's my part in that to face. It was that Pelim lady who said it best – choose it, instead of being bound into it.

Sel's up, sitting on the bed with his back 'gainst the wall. His eyes are like pale stones in the dark, the third lid down. What do I say? I've no idea how to cross that small space between us. I couldn't do it with Prue, an I can't do it now.

It was clear-like she was dying, an I couldn't sit next to her an put my arms around her like a Hobling an call her mam. She couldn't do it neither, course. So guess where I get that from. But Prue died, an in the end, there were a thousand things I would have asked her; why she came back, why she never spoke about my da, or told me nothing about herself at all, or how I could have made it right twixt us.

This time no one's dying, but there is a war on, an I'd be lying to myself if I believed everything would come out right as the rain in summer. An it's the same two things scaring me now that scared me then – that one, I'll be pushed away, an two, that I wouldn't, an what would I do then?

One deep breath, that's all, an there's less than a few feet twixt us. It's not a lot. I make myself shift closer. Never close enough, an I fumble my words, try say something.

It's Sel who reaches out an pulls me close, tight 'gainst him, like he knows neither of us has ever been good with words. I bury my face against his shoulder, an my lungs are burning an I don't know how to breathe right or nothing. He holds tighter, so tight it feels like he's crushing me with those skinny arms.

All those years I've never cried, 'cause you don't cry in the Digs, not if you want to live, not if you want to get somewhere. Never cried when Prue wouldn't hold me as a Hobling, never cried when Marlon took me in an taught me, used me. Never cried when Prue died, when Oncle turned me over. Feels like a thousand years of trying to choke all that shit down, 'cept it never went nowhere, just waited there biding its time.

"Don't cry," says Sel, "I'm not a moth." Which makes the whole thing worse because I wanted to forget that moment of weakness.

Suck it up, Jek, I keep telling myself, *stop this stop this stop this.* Because there's no place in this world for someone weak.

Sel bites me, low under the burn on my neck, an that sharp pain brings me together, stops me. I pull away, so I can get a better look at him. He's just Sel, with his pointed face an hair that's too long to be short an too short to be long, so it's always in his face. I kiss him, cause that's not going to hurt no one.

His hand is a fist, gripping my shirt, pulling it free.

"Don't," I say between kisses.

This time it's Sel that pulls back. He don't say nothing, just looks at me with a question in his eyes.

"'Cause –" An then I can't say the rest. It's not like he's forgotten what Sharpshins an his mates did to him. So instead of speaking, I do the one thing I know I'm good at. When you learn under Marlon, you learn to be good. Since I took over my own pack, I've never knelt for no one, always said I'd die before I do that again, but this is different. This isn't someone shoving my head down, showing me who's boss. This is a choice.

I unbutton Sel's fly quickly even though my fingers are shaking hard.

"What –"

I don't really give Sel much of a chance though, cause one lick down the neat crease of skin down from his hip to his groin shuts him up fast. I can do this, because I chose it.

His hands go to my head, an for a moment I tense, thinking he's going to tangle his fingers in my hair an then, no matter what I'm telling myself about choice an all that shite, I will lose it. There's too much of Marlon in that, but he slides his hands lower 'til he's resting his fingers 'gainst my neck, almost like he's feeling for a pulse.

I look up at his sharp gasp, to catch his eye. "This all right?" I say. "I'm not hurting you none?" My voice sounds different, choked up like I'm scared. Probably best I don't talk tonight.

Sel shudders, nods, presses his fingers a little harder to my neck, an I realise he's stopping the blood flow from the bite. It's that one thing that makes me realise I can do this, an I close my eyes. Taste skin an salt. Feel soft curling hair under my fingers. Hear his breathing change, speed up.

His skin smells like flint – dry, nothing like the sweat-sour stink of the Wend. I taste sharp magic, biting at my tongue, citrus sweet.

Afterwards I lie next to Sel. We're both tangled up in each other, half-dressed, sweaty. My mouth has that thick taste, like I can't swallow; an it's not just the taste in my throat but memories an something I'd call love if I was given to that kind of fanciful shite. Sel's heart is thundering by my ear, where I'm lying 'gainst his chest. One arm is curled round me; we're both holding on. To what, I don't right know. I feel a little like I've been dumped into the Casabi, an that slow river is pulling me under, weeds around my ankles, an Sel's there drowning with me. There's no one to save us so we may as well go down together.

So maybe that's all there is to family; it's people willing to drown with you. I sigh an kiss the skin over his ribs, an wait 'til my head is straight again. Sel's magic is all around us, in my blood an under my skin.

The shadow of Sharpshins is fading.

But the war is still waiting for us.

Fifty-Three

A Game of Wasps

IT FEELS AS though the whole of MallenIve is standing with bated breath, waiting for Harun and Jek to come back with good news. My father's death has passed unnoticed, a brief funeral held in the chill wind, and a new tomb on the family plot. But my mother is moved, suddenly strong, as if her constant headaches died with him. She rushes through his papers, makes notes, deals. Tells Illy and me to stay strong. She has put out the word to the Splinterfist, Glassclaw, and Fallingmirror rookeries, telling them that any vamp willing to bond and train with a Lammer will get full citizenship.

There have been few takers. They don't believe us. It's hopeless.

"So this is your army, is it?" says Lord Blaine. "Impressive."

My mother smiles, holds her head higher. "I am acting on instructions my husband left me. He said it would take time."

"We don't have time, Mirian, and you play-acting at running your House isn't going to change that."

"There will be more," she says. "We just need to wait on Lord Guyin's return. They just need to be sure..."

"You doubt my word?"

My mother shakes her head once, the movement jerked out of her. "Not me. But there will always be some –"

"I have no time for games. You get the Lammers into this. I can't have a hundred bats arriving from Urlin, and barely a single Lammer to bond with them."

"Few Lammers are going to do it," I say, and they turn to me with incredulous expressions. As usual, they've forgotten that I'm here. "Extend the offer to the Hobs."

They stare at me. "We know that Jek can access the bat magic."

"He's a half-breed. It's the Lammer in him that makes him able to," says Blaine, although he doesn't look me in the eye. "No." He dismisses the idea. "We will not offer that much power to the Hobs."

So it's all down to the Lammers then. I swallow, and even though my mother is warning me, frowning, even though I know that my father is dead because of this man, I still myself and carry on. "Perhaps then if we convinced Lord Guyin and Lady Pelim to stand forth as examples, you'd have more volunteers from the Houses?"

"Examples of what?"

"High Houses that have bonded." Gris, Trey wasn't this stupid, he could think quickly. Or maybe he could just think like me. "We need to make the bonding look acceptable. If the two are feted publicly, perhaps at a ball, then that might encourage others to take the chance."

"But I don't find the bonding acceptable," Blaine says.

"I know. And it shows." He isn't pushing harder for this – because he doesn't want to. There's no way to see the Folly from here, but even so I glance instinctively in its direction.

Blaine turns to my mother. "You let your daughter speak like this, to me. You're setting a bad example."

"You have to admit she has a point."

"So what do you expect of me, that I throw a royal party while the war dogs snap at our heels, and make these bonded pairs our guests of honour?" He sneers.

I look up. "It would be a start."

The Lord Mata holds my gaze then slowly shakes his head. "I'll have to think on this," he says, and I already know he means to try for a Vision, to see if this path is one he should take. It strikes me that the Houses of the Saints are crippled by this need to test through every decision before they can make a move. It slows them, it makes them doubt.

When he's gone, I turn to my mother. "Do you think I should not have spoken?"

"No. You did well; it is an idea with merit – one we all need to think on."

"I have another idea," I say.

My mother waits for me, patient and unmoving. Something, even if it isn't grief, has aged her.

"You bond me to one of the bats. As an example."

Her face twists. "No one expects that of you. Your father wouldn't have wanted it."

My father is dead. "What about you?" I ask her very softly.

She cannot answer me. She purses her mouth to stop the trembling and turns away. "Take your own path," she says as she walks away from me. "Only your own."

A few hours later, when I'm taking tea alone in our suite, Trone walks in and sets a white card on to the table. It sits like a poisoned blade on the tablecloth, between the pots of jam and the china cups.

So. While we wait for Guyin and Jek to come back with their news, while the wet sods dry on my father's grave, and while the Mekekana sit at our doorsteps like hungry iron sphynxes, we shall have a party.

THE GRAND HALL of the Mata Palace is decorated in winter white, the long tables draped with cream cloth embroidered with cream thread. The sun emblems are a little rougher under my touch, but otherwise barely noticeable. An interesting touch, that House Mata have played down their colours. Perhaps Blaine really does want this to work.

I've taken my place next to Mother. Opposite me, Iliana sits, her face a quiet mask. I don't think she even sees us anymore, and I wonder if she is in mourning, if she worries for Trey, or if she is relieved that he's not here tonight. It doesn't take scriv to see that she's bone-tired, frightened. I turn my head away.

The palace is not as quiet as it used to be, now that the High Houses have been moved into the empty suites. Even so, we all keep to our own little patches of turf, and this is the first time we have gathered under the Mata flag, all in one room. If there was enough scriven to go around, it would be hard to breathe, with all the magic that would have pressed around us within these four walls. Instead, it is just the claustrophobia of too many people in one place, the sweat of anticipation, nervousness, disapproval.

People have heard of my father's death, and a few approach to make their mumbled condolences, before they fade back into the crowd. We take their pity in silence.

At the head of the room is the crosswise table of the Mata. Blaine is there, with his delicate wife next to him. She's from Mother's family, a distant cousin, but one with stronger ties to the Mallen magic. She has that same cool, distant look that my mother has perfected, and she gazes through her lashes at the gathered Houses, her expression bored, disdainful. I wonder if Mother hates her.

There are empty seats to her right and to her husband's left. Two on each side, bookended by the Mata sons and their wives. Iliana did not merit a seat at the Mata table, and it says more than I like about how quickly the Mata are cutting their ties to us in the wake of the murder.

Silk rustles, and by an unspoken command we rise as the Mata does. Two people are walking into the hall now, led in by a herald.

Lady Pelim and her bat. She's wearing full noble robes, an archaic gown. It is handed down through the generations and taken out only on the most formal of occasions. Pelim is a small woman, and on her the gown and its layers of silver under-robes are not flattering. They draw attention to the bulge at her waist. The heavy white outer robe is embroidered with leaping silver dolphins, and her auburn hair seems darker against all that cold glitter. How meaningless Pelim's symbols must be now; has anyone even told her of her city's fall?

Holding her arm is a bat, slightly taller than her, and slender, with a nose that is a little too big, a feature accentuated by his drawn-back hair. He is wearing a silver ribbon to tie it back, and his face is set in a frown.

They take their places at the Mata table. Lord Blaine sits, a smile sewn in place. We follow him, the noise of a hundred chairs or more scraping back on the marble floors loud and aggressive.

Everyone in this room knows what is going on. People sidle looks at their youngest sons and daughters and wonder if it would be worth the loss of family honour to sign them over, to bond them to a bat in exchange for royal favour and a scrap of magic. If I know anything about House desperation, several offers will be made after tonight, although few will ask their charge's permission. I sigh. It is the way we do things, and I shouldn't complain, but it is those same rules that took Trey from me, that bound my sister to him instead.

The idea I finally gave voice to pricks at me like the sting of a wasp trapped in my palm. There comes a time when you open your hand to see if the wasp will fly away, or whether you've made it yours, still and quiet. I have played that game. Haven't all children? But tonight I think I will play it for real.

I glance at my mother. Together, she and my father made plans for me, I'm sure. Mapped out my future in a ledger, as if I were no more than a doe to be bred to the right buck. My mother saw something of my future, something she will not tell me. Perhaps my father forbade her, I do not know. She catches my look, stares back at me, and gives me the slightest dip of her head.

Yes. I will find my own future, and not one that my father wished pressed on me.

Servants have begun bringing steaming platters to the tables, and I know I cannot leave now. I need to wait a little while, to make sure that the people around me are settled deep into this charade of a dinner.

My stomach is in knots, but I allow the servants to offer food that I ladle onto my plate. I do not even look at it, and when I eat, I do not taste it. I drink wine and feel nothing. Deep in my mind, I hold my wasp, and wait.

When the people around me begin to talk, their tongues loosened by wine, I slip away. Nothing is ever simple, but I lean close to my mother's ear and whisper to her that I need to lie down, that the wine has gone to my head. She smiles tightly, nods, and I leave.

There are bats somewhere in the Mata Palace, the handful who have come from the rookeries, but I have no idea where they are. If I had scriven, I might be able to track them down in the glittering maze of the palace, but I have nothing.

There is only one place where I am certain to find bats. The thought makes me shiver. I'll need the coins I took from my father's box.

The sound of my slippers on the cold floor is a small echo in the silence as I race through the empty passages to the suite of rooms set aside for House Ives. Inside, I slip out of my dining finery then dress in the messenger's uniform that I keep hidden beneath all my other clothes. I pause at my reflection. My face is pale, my cheeks flushed fever-bright.

Can I? And the wasp stings again, and I know I can. Must.

Three stolen coins in my pocket, tied into a lace kerchief so that they won't make a noise, and then I'm out, taking the twisted darkened passages into the night. Cold hits me with all the force of a fist or a kiss, and I take a deep breath that freezes my lungs and makes my chest ache.

It will take me the better part of an hour to make it to Splinterfist, so close to my old home, and I have no time to waste. I set off down the lamp-lit streets as the occasional fine powdery flake falls. There are clouds above, but they are too thin to be a threat.

Fifty-Four

The Grinningtommy

TIME'S UP. THE Alerion has called us into the hall to let us know her answer. We're all nervous as shite, even if none of us show it. It don't matter none, when that blasted vamp will be able to read us easy as a primer.

The hall looks different; there's a throne all carved of red wood an yellow ivory. The crowd from yesterday is quiet. Everyone is tense: backs straight an shoulders knotted tight.

The Alerion is sitting on her throne. Next to her is an empty silver cage – big enough to hold a man.

A knot of vampires stands to the right, huddled like damless pups. They have a cowering look to them, an I don't need to see their empty gums to know that this sorry lot must be our vamps. Instead of the white robes, they wear black, an while most of the Alerion's vamps have hair long as a Hob's, these have been shorn. Their stubbled scalps gleam in the weak light from the candle-lamps.

"So," she says as she rises, an sweeps one hand to where the vamps cower. "Your army." She sneers. "A worthier role for them I couldn't imagine."

Harun bows low, like she's honoured him. "We thank you for your generosity, Alerion. We will make arrangements to leave, and to provide transport for our new comrades."

"Oh, their transportation has already been arranged." The way that vamp smiles after makes the hair stand on my neck.

She waits until Harun is upright again an flicks her hand. Flash-quick, the waiting circle of vamps sweeps in around our new comrades. They're gone, hidden behind the bodies an the robes of white, but I hear them scream. There's the bitter taste of sick in my mouth, and Sel's horror beats at my head, inside my skull, making me choke.

When the others fall back, robes red, the shorn vamps are nothing more than dead things.

"They will sail Ur, in the coracles of the dead," she says. "Perhaps they will reach your city, perhaps not." She lifts one shoulder. "As for yourselves, I did not realise I'd agreed to let you leave."

We're all of us looking at those corpses, an sweat is sliding down my brow. It's not only Sel's fear in my head, it's Harun's, an Isidro's. We are fucked.

Harun clears his throat, an I'll be damned if there's not even a hint of a waver to his voice. "I thought that should we have volunteers, that it would be a moot point." Harun puts one hand to his breast pocket, like he's going for something, then thinks better of it an drops his hand back to his side. It's in a loose fist, an he seems not angry, just calm.

"Ah now, see where assumption leads you." She's smiling, like she's playing a game. One she thinks she's winning. Of course, when you think that, you better be damn sure you have all the pieces.

Harun sighs, an this time he reaches up to the pocket an draws out a folded envelope. "I did not wish to do this, but I have a letter for you." He hands her the paper, sealed with the symbol of a burning eagle.

Her eyes narrow as she takes it, an she glances once at Sel, like he's done this to her.

There's a crack of wax an it spills blood red on the stone floor. It takes her a long time to read, or perhaps she just reads it again an again, like she can't believe what's written there. Then she looks up, an her face is all cold an angry. "This," she says holding the paper out, "is a threat. You dare to pit Pelimburg's House Sandwalker against my family?"

"I have not read it," Harun says. "It was given to me should you try detain us."

She throws the crumpled paper down an stalks forward. The

vamps scatter out of her way. Sheep, the lot of them.

"You listen well," she hisses, when she's close enough to us that the other vamps won't hear her. "Tell that loathsome wyrm of a wray Jannik that I will do this not because of the weak and posturing threats he thinks he can make in his mother's name, but because of what his mother has done for me in the past. With this last, there is no more bond between the two Houses of Sandwalker."

"We're free to leave." Harun doesn't make it a question, but he's frowning. Whatever Jannik's gone an done has troubled him. Personal, I don't give a shite, as long as Jannik's name is enough to get us out of this mess.

"Yes." She whirls back, like the puppet-dancers on Long Night. "But before you do, I would like a word."

Harun pauses. "Certainly," he says, stepping up to follow her.

"Not with you. With the little wray that you dragged into my city."

Sel. She means Sel.

I grab at his wrist, making him hiss in pain. "Sorry," I says but I don't drop my hand. There's more I want to say, but all I can do is think it, hope he understands. I don't want him alone with this mad bitch, with this woman who don't think nothing of torture or murder.

"Jek." Harun shifts so that his back is to the Alerion, so that she cannot see him pleading with me. "We're on shifting sand here. Let her speak with Sel, and then we can all leave."

"I will speak," says Sel, although he's staring at the ground, not at any of us. He shakes out of my grip an walks over to her.

"Everyone will leave," she says.

None of us move. Blood makes the room smell coppery, an for a moment, I'm back on the street by the Scrivver's Hole, by the butcher's an remembering that day, an the way it changed everything. My throat is too dry to speak. All I can do is watch Sel walk away from me.

"You may go," she says to us an nods at the door. It's not an invitation for sure. There's deep hollows under her eyes, I notice now, an her skin is thin, almost blue. Something's made her weaken.

Harun takes my shoulder an steers me about, making me leave Sel alone with her. My Sel smiles at me as I go, like he wants me to know it's fine, not to worry.

I hate being lied to.

Fifty-Five

Singing for the Dead

I WATCH THEM go and wish them well.

Since we came here I've lost everything again. I could hear Jek. Could talk. Make sense. Not anymore.

"Look at me," She says.

There's something in Her voice. Stars and brilliance. Mother's death. I must do what She says. She has hard eyes. They hold me still.

"I thought you looked familiar. It just took me a while to realise the obvious." She steps back, pulling her cloak close. "I can give you back everything, do you know that?"

"Don't understand."

"Not yet, no. Your mother – my sister – took upon your death, but she was no healer, not like me."

"Sister?"

"Yes. My sister, younger sister. She met with my future mate, behind my back, and then ran when her belly was full. And what good did it do her, hmm? Two wrays, worthless. One dead, and the other barely functioning. She should have let you die and come crawling back to me." She smiles. "I can be benevolent. I too know how to forgive."

Death is in the room, stalking me.

I turn my head. There is a cage. An empty cage next to her throne.

"I kept my promised mate there. Sixteen years in a space small enough to cripple him. When he died, I knew it meant my sister had finally fallen. And now here you come, a little interloper, a reminder."

I can't think. Everything is broken. I see mother's face like a shadow over Hers. I do not know who is talking. It's safer here on the ground, my hands over my head.

"Come now, child. I've seen inside that head of yours." She leans down.

I can feel Her breath at my back. Desert wind.

"I can give everything back to you," She whispers, soft sweet, poison. "Everything. But you have to keep a promise."

"Promise?"

"You will relinquish your name, your family. I will take it, and this line will end with me."

A name is just words. Sounds and shapes. Nod.

"And," she says, "you will take my sins from me."

Sin is nothing. I have seen sin use my skin.

"Ah." She pulls back. "Good. Your people will be leaving soon. We shall not waste any further time. Step closer."

So I stand. Do as she says.

"Now. Close your eyes, little wray, and trust me."

Darkness. Then Her mouth on mine, lips closed. Press. I can feel teeth behind them.

In my head.

She's in my head.

Inside.

The pieces fall, she smashes everything. Fine mirrors, glass, everything. Rebuilds. Blood on my mouth. My own. She's bitten my lip.

And then, each piece ground fine, built again. A thought. A word.

The city in my head slowly rises, and it brings pain. I can see her weave her magic between the memories and dreams. She is rebuilding me with a curse. I can never come here again. If I enter her citadel, I'll be dead as the sand below us. The words say so. She's buried them so deep I will never be free of them.

And I'm inside her head too, and I understand. She's using me, blood to blood, to heal herself. I feel sadness, mine. I feel fear, hers. And anger, belonging to us both.

My mother's name slips from me, like a silver fish from my hands.

Images. These are not my memories. My mother – young. So very young and beautiful. This is not one of mine. A wray who looks like me, who looks a little like Dae. So very young.

I see the wray again, older, mouth collapsed around empty gums.

He dies, turn to dust in a silver cage.

These are not my memories, but they are in my head, making bridges between all the broken pieces.

There are words, and I can see them, think them use them. I am drowning under things that are not mine. I am drowning. Shaking.

"And now, little wray."

"Please, please. Take them back," I say to her. I do not want these thoughts that are not mine. Don't want to see my mother through hate and envy.

She smiles, flashing diamond teeth. "Run along, little wray, with your head sewn back together. You can carry my burdens for me now. It's a fair price to have your mind back."

I cannot stop shaking. I have all the hate and anger and fear and jealousy and distrust in the world. Can't even speak now I'm shaking so hard. A door opens, but I can't look up. Can't unbend, uncurl.

"What the fuck!" Jek's voice, always angry and scared under the bluster. "What did you do to him?" So familiar.

"Healed him."

"The fuck you did."

"Do not take a step closer, Hob, or I will end him now. It's in my power."

"What?"

"He agreed. I would heal his mind, but within these walls, I have complete control over him."

Silence. No, not silence. I can hear myself, whimpering into my hands. At least, I think it's me.

"Jek?" Harun, always the voice of reason. "Come now, we need to go." There are hands on me helping me up, and I start to scream because it hurts sweet sweet pain burning. It's her, all the bits that are her, that cannot stand to be touched.

I look up. Hear myself talk. "You can't touch anyone."

"Get out." She sounds calm, but now I know under all that she is far more broken than I have ever been. She caged my father because he could do with her sister what he never did with her. She's made me like her. I will hurt at every touch.

She reads my mind. Bound to me, closer even than Jek maybe "You will learn to live with it, wray, or you will be like me."

Dead inside, I think, and I know she hears me.

"Get him out. And you may tell your Mata that this is the last bargain between our people. No Lammer or Hob or bonded vampire will ever be welcome in the Citadel again."

"Sel, Sel. Can you stand?" Jek is kneeling next to me, a hand out to grab. I want to take it, to prove her wrong, and I do.

For a moment. Then I'm screaming, shivering, burning.

"The sooner you leave, the sooner he will be well," she says. I can only hope hope hope that she is not lying. Twisting the truth to make us believe.

My mother is speaking to me, inside my head. Only it's not to me, but to Her. My mother fighting; screaming angry words. One hand pressed to her stomach. Am I there? Curled about Dae, asleep in soft liquid darkness? I want her to hear me, to hear that I'm sorry, that I wish she hadn't died. That I'm sorry I bonded with a Hob, that all her death and Dae's bought me was slavery, of one kind or another.

Mother is screaming at her, "You wouldn't know love if it sunk its fangs into you, Ria. You don't understand anything about anyone. You're like Mother – cold and heartless. A slinker and a schemer. That's why he didn't want you. He saw what you were, and he knew he couldn't live like that!"

And her voice, cold and higher than it is now "Do whatever you want. Run, because if you don't, I will tell everyone about that bastard child in your womb, and his part in it. You stole my mate. Mother has burned feyn for less, you stupid selfish bitch."

My mother goes quiet. "I was going to leave anyway. I had no desire to disgrace you."

"Go then. There are a few hours left before daybreak. If you're so eager to save my face, then go. You could take a coracle. Go down the Ur like a corpse. Maybe the Lammers in MallenIve will take you in. You can work their whorehouse rookeries." She starts laughing, a desperate cackling crying sound, a rush of air and tears.

"I'm waiting for Meyem –"

"Who isn't coming. He told me everything, Lina. Everything. He was weeping, begging my forgiveness."

My mother says nothing, but her face falls, goes white white white, and then she turns. In my head, or maybe in Ria's head, someone is saying *no no no come back come back and it will be like it was and we can be good together we can work you'll see like when we were children*. But my mother isn't listening.

Fifty-Six

The Grinningtommy

"WHAT'S WRONG WITH him?"

We're standing in the diamond plaza, while Trey checks the last of the fastenings on the by-the-wind carriage. Sel won't come near no one, an he's just saying the same thing over an over, "Come back come back come back."

She made him worse. I don't know what the fuck that bitch said to him, but we were doing better last night, Sel was coming right, coming normal-like, an now he's back to this.

"Leave it," snaps Harun. "Get in there. We need to get back before the Mekekana do any damage. I've no idea for how much longer the War-singers can hold those shields. We'll deal with Sel when we're home." Like that's a solution.

I try an touch his magic, pull him over to me, but Sel screams like a baby burned for the first time, an I pull back.

"Come Sel, little wray," Isidro coaxes him. He might as well be holding out a sugar cube for a wild uni for all the good it does. "We'll get you home, and everything will be fine."

"Don't lie to him," I says. "You think lies will make anything better?" I want to scream, to cry, to lie down in the diamond dust an smash my fists into the ground, but all I do is jump up into the swinging carriage an hold my hand out for Sel.

"Don't touch," he says, an crawls past me to curl up in a corner with his hands over his ears.

Isidro jumps in, an Harun last, shutting the wooden door tight, sliding the bolt into place.

"We're ready," he yells to Trey, an the by-the-wind farts an lurches up, smashing the floor of the carriage into the ground.

Then we're up, Urlin is falling away. Below us is a field of white robes, as the vamps come out of their black city to watch us leave.

There on the Casabi, the little round coracles are bobbing, on their way to MallenIve.

The boats of the dead, she called them.

ISIDRO KEEPS LOOKING back as the last city lights of Urlin fade into the starlit sky.

Next to me Sel holds his hands over his ears an whispers to himself. I'm watching him unravel. He was coming right, an now all that sanity is spilling out like water. I stick my fists deep in my pockets an don't look up none at Sel. It hurts to watch.

He won't let me touch him.

Isidro finally manages to pull himself away from the view an looks over at Sel. His face twists, an he shakes his head, though he don't say nothing.

"What?" Harun asks.

"If we'd not offered them such a pretty lie, they would still be alive." Isidro looks back an forth between us, his head moving slow an deliberate as a hunting cat.

"And I was supposed to know she'd turn on them?"

"I didn't agree. You should have trusted me."

Harun snarls an slams a fist down on the table.

But Isidro carries on like he don't care none for Harun's temper. "I tell you, the Mata wanted us out of MallenIve. He knew this was worthless –"

"It was not worthless!"

"Oh yes? And what have we gained?" The vamp slides down in his seat, like his legs were boneless, an crosses his fingers over his belly. "The Lammers would never have bonded anyway. Even if we'd come back with an army of wrays, it would have been useless."

"The Lammers need magic," Harun says. "We suffer without it. You don't understand Lammers. Without magic they'll feel they're less than Hobs." He nods at me. "Your pardon."

"Then tell me why there are a mere handful of bonded Lammers in the whole of MallenIve?"

"We had the scriv."

"And you still will, as long as the Mata's stockpiles last. As long as they feed their Saints with dust and pray for Visions, pray that more deposits will be found." Isidro shakes his head and slumps lower. "No. You think we are animals."

'Course, he's right an all. "We have to change their minds," I says. "You an Harun, an Pelim an Jannik – you have to be more public. Those are big House names. People will sit up an look, will maybe start thinking a bit."

"You want us to parade ourselves among the other Houses?" Harun laughs. "And exactly what about this spectacular show will change their minds?"

"Well, they might stop thinking you're all ashamed-like of what you did."

There's no answer, Harun just stares across the cabin, his eyes like little flames in the low light.

"Point," says Isidro, an flashes his fangs at me, folding his arms across his chest before he looks back at his bond-partner.

"Don't start."

"The Hob's right. We've been telling you for years now that the more we skulk about, the more it looks like you're trying to hide us."

"I –" Harun swallows, an shakes his head before carrying on. "I don't like what happens when we make public appearances."

"I can handle a little spit and insults." Isidro stares at him, but Harun won't look him right in the eye. The by-the-wind rocks, an one of the fatcandle lamps flickers out. "They'll get bored of it soon enough."

They say nothing, an it's another one of them private conversations. If I concentrate, I can almost touch the edges of it. Angry, full of words better not spoken anyway.

The by-the-wind shudders again, an Harun looks over at the shut door leading to the fore cabin. When the by-the-wind rocks for a third time, he stands an makes his way over. "Trey?" he says to the door, an a moment later, the Mata is staring him down.

"A little trouble," he says. "Nothing to worry yourselves over."

Another lurch, an this one sends Sel flying to the floor. He lands on his hands an knees, an I slip down next to him to try help him up. He shakes me off, climbs back onto his seat an curls himself up tight, whispering into his knees.

"How little?" Harun asks, an raises one brow.

"Ah." Trey's face is white an shiny in the remaining lamp light. Sweat films his skin. "Perhaps not so little."

"What is it?"

He slumps against the door frame, one hand clenched white on the wood. "Sphynxes," he says. "A hunting pride."

Harun frowns. "I heard nothing. Are you certain?"

"Can sense them – shit –" The by-the-wind twists in the air, sending the loose papers leaf-flapping across the cabin. "They've got the blaas's scent. They're heading straight here." "How many?"

Trey shakes his head. "Not certain. The group's too big for me to read separate auras. As they get closer, I can give you a number."

"Wonderful," says Harun. "We'll sit here patiently until they're close enough to count, shall we?"

"Watch your mouth, Guyin," Trey snaps. "You forget who you're speaking to."

"We can argue hierarchy in the afterlife, Mata." Harun steps closer to him. "Can they reach the blaas?"

He swallows, nods. "They can sing it down."

"I didn't know sphynxes hunted blaas."

"They don't. They're hunting us."

Everyone goes still, an the only sound is the gas noises of the by-the-wind, the creaking of leather, an Sel's hurried whispers.

Trey leans his forehead against the frame, looks sideways at Harun. "Can you take them out? I mean – there are two bats in here."

"Aren't you the sweet-talker," says Isidro, through his teeth. "Vamps. Better?"

"Marginally, but in truth you only have one." Even as Isidro says it, we all look down at Sel, who's wrapped his arms around his head.

"We could take out . . . two, maybe three," Harun says, as he stares at Isidro, who nods in agreement. I can feel them though, an neither believe it.

"There are more than that, I'm certain."

"I can try to tap Sel," I says, an as I say it, I can feel myself aching inside, like a cramp in my gut. It's not me, it's Sel.

The by-the-wind makes a noise like a shitting nilly, an we skid into each other as it drops.

"Seven," says Trey, his voice calm, although his eyes tell a whole 'nother story. "And something else, I think. Something big." He slams one palm against the wood floor. "Fuck! There are too many things out there for me to Read."

"Tap him," says Harun to me, jerking his head.

"And that will probably destroy what's left of his mind," Isidro counters. "Haven't we been responsible for enough today?"

Around us the wind screams, an then we hit the ground with a thud an scrape that knocks all the air out of my lungs. Wood breaks, an the glass from one windows shatters, covering the floor of the carriage with splinters.

"Mad or dead," hisses Harun. "Not much of a choice."

There's a new sound, an eerie wailing that I never heard the like of before. It's not something I want to hear again neither. My eyeballs feel like they're gonna burst in their sockets.

Trey's white, his skin as bleached as any vamp's. Through the shattered wood of the side of the carriage I can just make out shapes moving in the dark. Huge, bigger than I expected, an I'm terrified. This is worse than when I went down that old dug-out scriv-mine when I was a Hobling – the one where the cave-in killed three of Marlon's pack.

They're howling at each other, sniffing the air. One sphynx turns its eyes to me, an they glow green, round as plates. Another pads closer to the wrecked carriage, lips curled back as it sniffs. Sel's up close to me, almost close enough to touch, an I can feel his heart hammering through his skin, through me, his fear inside my head. Fuck, it's so bad I can't even move, pinned by the bond.

"There's something else," says Trey. "Big, moving fast." He takes a deep gasping breath, 'cause I think he knows we're going to die.

Harun's crawled over to Isidro, an they must be tapping, because the next thing, I feel the magic build an pulse out quick as a whip. The sphynx pulls back with a yowl, blood on its face.

"One small scratch," says Trey. "Is that all?"

"Magic against magic," Isidro pants. "Never works well."

"Shit," says Trey, an we're in agreement.

They lash out with the magic again, just as something hits the carriage from the side. Those damn sphynxes are trying to knock us out. Big cats playing with mice in a box.

Sphynxes can talk, but these are playing in silence, an mind, I'm not complaining. I never heard a sphynx talk, but if that bone-crushing howl is anything like their speech, then I'm glad for it.

As another blow rocks the carriage, the wood jerks under me, there's the crack of leather stretched taut. The by-the-wind is trying to get away.

I'm hoping we'll still be with it when it does.

They've started howling again. My insides are turning to jelly at that awful sound. But there's something else under it – a thundering, a drumming on the packed sand.

"Oh Gris, no," says Trey, choking on the words. "It's a Mekekana ship." He holds tight to a seat, pulling himself into a crouch as he shakes his head. "Can't be. What are they doing out here?"

"They might have seen the blaas, wondered what was happening." Harun is watching through the ragged hole, eyes trained on the skulking shapes outside.

Trey's whispering, an I realize he's talking to the by-the-wind, talking with whatever scriv he has left, trying to calm her, coax her back into the air. With a lurch, we're rising. Sel looks up, uncovering his head, an the fear retreats a little, enough for me to ease into a better position. The carriage is hanging awkward-like, an I'm guessing that some of the leather traces were broken in the fall.

We jerk again as the floor tilts, an a handful of papers an loose objects slide down, bumping an rattling on the wood, before they fall through the torn gap an flutter out of sight.

"The sphynxes aren't coming for us anymore," says Harun in wonder. "Never thought there'd be a time when I'd be glad to see the Mekekana."

"As long as they're distracting each other," Isidro says, an laughs. It's the kind of laugh that comes after you been terrified, manic an breathless.

Something strikes the carriage again, rocking it in its leather harness. The by-the-wind is dragged back down, an I hit my shoulder on the edge of one of the chairs as I stumble. Everything moves scriv-slow, an I wonder why I don't seem able to move fast enough to grab the edge of a chair. My fingers scrape on splintered wood an glass. It's just not enough, because the next thing I'm falling through that hole, an down into the middle of the sphynx pride.

I hit the ground with a thump that knocks all the breath from my body. Try to focus, but my head is swimming, sick. Above me the by-the-wind is jerking higher, farther away. Still tied to her is the carriage, hanging on three of the four traces. An then it's gone, replaced by a huge face. A head like a lion with eyes that are not cat-like at all an a mouth that's too flat, too Lammer-like.

The green eyes blink, slowly. A paw bats me from the side, an I'm sure it cracks a rib. There's pain an the snap of breaking bone.

"Sweetmeat," says the sphynx. It smells of thunderstorms.

I lash out at it with magic, tapping Sel even as he's pulled far away by the frightened by-the-wind. All I manage is to slice across its nose. An piss it off. The sphynx growls, lowers its head to me. Its teeth are sharp, mottled yellow daggers in that Lammer mouth. The smell of old meat an rot blasts down on me, making me gag. I turn my face away so that I don't have to watch as it comes in for the kill.

Something hot hits my cheek just as my ears explode with the sound of roaring thunder. I twist my head, look up to see the sphynx's head bursting in a shower of brain an bone an blood.

"Shite!"

The noise starts up again. It's like no sound I never heard before, although if you took all the windle-spinners in the world an set them turning, it might come close. The noise tears the sphynxes apart, ripping through them like magic. There's another sound, a slicing of air an the dull thud of small heavy objects hitting sand. Dust puffs around us an the sphynxes turn tail, leaving me half-pinned under a dead paw.

Silence. Just for a moment, an then all I hear is my own lungs making ragged sounds, thick an wet. There's no sign of the by-the-wind in the starred sky. It takes everything I have to try push myself out from under that huge paw, to not slice myself up on the open talons.

Footsteps thud across the sand, an I go still as a frightened rabbit. The footfalls are heavy – boots. A voice. It's no language I've heard before. It buzzes an grates in my head, the words too fast to tell apart.

My head is at an angle when they come into view: boots, black an heavy. I twist my neck, pain shooting down to my chest, an see four men carrying strange black tubes on their arms. They're all tall – at least six feet. Even the Mata Blaine comes in an inch or so shorter.

The air buzzes an crackles as they stare down at me with spiders' eyes that glister under the stars, that reflect me back at myself. Then one jerks its hand up to pluck out its own eyes.

Not eyes. Some kind of head gear, an the face beneath looks Lammer – looks normal – if maybe a little square. He turns to talk to one of his partners, an I see the small rounded ears. Mekekana. For certain. They've destroyed at least two adult sphynxes, were ready to take on the others, an it was only these four. Alone.

I shiver. This is our enemy. We have nothing – a handful of bonded Lammers an bats to fight them with. We're fucked.

The leading one kneels down an presses his squat fingers 'gainst my chest. Another string of words an the other three snap into action. I try fight them off, but they're heavier than me, an they truss me up tight as a feast-goose.

The leader pulls a small chain from his pocket, nothing big. Looks like a necklace, something shiny for the girls, but I can feel the cold burn of it from here. He slips it over my head so it rests on my clothes, not burning me, not yet, but cutting me off from any kind of magic that I could use. With only my legs free, they march me away from the corpses an over a rising crest of rocks an dunes. A few scrubby plants are clustered about the rocks, an they catch at me with thorny branches, trying to keep me back. My ribs shoot pain through my whole body with every step, an I can hear myself gasping.

There's a Mekekana ship hiding in the lee of a tall dune – the something big that Trey was picking up, I guess. If we'd had a decent Reader, he wouldn't have been fucked over by the sphynx's auras; he would have known what was out there, waiting for us. Damn useless Mata.

I've never seen a real Meke ship up close. It squats like a giant beetle, iron shell black. The front part has thousands of legs or claws, an the back is wheeled, two flattened ovals that look slick, almost wet. The whole thing reeks. Metal an the factory smell of burning hair.

They're taking me into iron. A whole stinking ship of it, an I start yelling, struggling, because if it hurt me to be in chains, I don't want to know what being in the belly of the beast is going to do.

Fifty-Seven

A Game of Wasps

I'VE NEVER BEEN into the Splinterfist Rookery, but now I stand before the featureless building, and I know that I have to enter. I don't think I can, but there's a thing inside me, a thing that used the scriven and liked the power in knowing people's emotions, and it wants. It hungers. All I know is that there is magic to be used, and I do not understand how anyone can turn it down, no matter the route that one must take to reach it. And, I console myself, are the bats not us? Weren't they once Lammers too?

The steps fall away beneath me, before I even realise that I'm walking up to the blank white door. Lights flicker behind drawn curtains, even now at this hour, and yellow warmth spills from the chinks in the drapes to stripe the street below.

The door swings open under my fingers, and I stumble in.

"May I help you?" The voice is cool, female. A bat, a girl bat in a long black dress that buttons up to her chin, is staring at me, her eyes hooded. "Have you lost your way?" she says, and I don't need scriven to read her suspicion.

I pull myself together. "No," I say. "I'm exactly where I want to be." Then I stop because I've never done anything like this in my life, nor ever dreamed I would. Fear crawls up my throat, and I'm ready to turn and run, when the bat's face softens.

She smiles at me. "It's unusual for a woman to come here." The bat walks closer to me, one hand held out to draw me in. "Please forgive my rudeness." I look up into her face, and I realise that no matter how gentle her face, or how soft her voice, she cannot hide the hate in her eyes. It is something about her I can understand, and I snap back to myself.

"I want one older than me, but not by too many years," I say. "Something pleasant to look at." If there's such a thing, although Guyin's bat is almost striking, despite his pale skin and strange eyes.

"Is there anything else that you require?"

I don't understand the question, and I frown, because I thought I'd already told her what I needed.

She seems to take pity on me. "Some of our clients have peculiar appetites," she says. "I take it you don't."

She's wrong, of course, but in a way she doesn't understand. I don't hunger for someone else's pain, or even my own. All I want is that roiling magic I felt Harun use in the court. And I know I need a bat – to bind myself to one – and I can live with the idea no matter how distasteful it may be, to be able to have that power.

"You have something suitable for me?" I say, my voice cool. There's no more time to waste on questions. I've no idea how long this will take.

She stares at me.

"I have coin."

The bat dips her head. "If you would follow me." It's not a question, and already she's turned on the balls of her feet, her movements cat-like and graceful. I've seen Sel walk, and it's not like this, not with this ease and confidence. Here's a person who could match me at my games, I think.

We climb three flights of stairs, and she leads me down a narrow passage to stop before a closed door. She turns and waits. When I do nothing, the bat nods to the closed door. "Enter," she says. "He will be ready for you."

I doubt it, but I grit my teeth and push open the door and close it behind me.

He looks up at me and smiles, and there's something in that relaxed, slightly curious glance that makes me almost not notice the fact that he is sitting nude, waiting for me, or whatever customer would walk through the door. The room is very small. I wait for the sound of footsteps to fade until the silence falls soft as snow. He doesn't move, just watches me.

I've seen him before, spoken to him. The same recognition jolts through him, and his calm smile flickers.

Maybe because it's different here, the air spiced with intent, that I'm unable to talk to him. I'm going to back out – now that I'm here, staring into a face even slightly familiar, I can feel my resolve crumbling. I wanted this to be anonymous then it would have been easier.

He says nothing, and the silence grows more awkward.

Do this, I tell myself. *Do it, it's what you want.* He touched my face, once, and there was the sweetest sting of magic in that. I hold on to that thought, focusing on the promise of it.

I close my eyes and find the words. "How badly do you want your freedom?" When I open them again, he's no longer smiling, merely staring at me, his eyes not wide or narrowed. He's waiting, saying nothing. "Well?" I prompt.

He stands. The bat is taller than me by an inch or so. "It's not normally the first question I get asked. I'm wondering how to answer."

I pull the lace kerchief from my pocket and unknot it as quickly as my fingers will allow, though they're numb and clumsy. Three silver bits tip out onto the bed covers, and they glare up at us from the crimson folds.

A shuddering breath greets them, and I look up.

The bat is staring at me. "I take it this is not to be a regular transaction."

"I want to bond with a bat."

He laughs. It's not the reaction I expect.

"Do you know what it is you're asking?" His eyes are saying he's not interested, insulted even. Already I've failed.

No. I won't let myself give up now. "Yes. My . . . half-brother has already bonded himself to . . . ." One of you.

His face goes closed. "Is that so?" The bat walks over to an ornate wooden screen on the side of the room. "Seeing the nature of the transaction, I hope you won't mind if I dress." He doesn't wait for my response as he slips behind the screen. I sit down on the bed and stare at the screen's panels. The three coins I dropped are next to me, and I scoop them up. I hold them so tightly I can feel the head of Emperor Mallen II digging into my skin. These are old coins; they carry the weight of changing times. It's fitting then that they will be used for this transaction.

He steps out into the centre of the small room. The bat is dressed in a plain black suit, buttoned boots that are worn down low at the heels, but polished bright despite that. He wears a red shirt, and the collar and cuffs stand stark against his skin, against the unrelenting black of his jacket. It's what he was wearing when I saw him in the street. Suddenly we are no longer client and whore.

"Mal," he says.

"I'm sorry? I don't understand –"

"My name. It's the least of formalities, I think, if we are to do this."

My heart leaps into my throat. "You're willing to do it?" I wonder if I shouldn't just leave, run from this room with my messenger's coat flapping about my heels.

In answer, he stares at me, long and cool.

"I'm Ives Calissa."

"Yes. Half-sister to Jek, I'd already gathered as much. How is Sel doing these days, when hordes of your servants aren't torturing him?"

Heat flares in my cheeks. "That's not fair – I knew nothing about what was going to happen. And, besides, I suggested a way for my father to persuade the Mata to drop the sentence."

"By making him a weapon." He sits down on the bed, too close, and I feel hot and nervous. "You suggested – word was that it was the Mata's own spawn that came up with that plan."

I inch away. "Believe what you want."

"And now," he carries on as if he hasn't heard me. "You wish to bind me to yourself, and turn me into a weapon too."

I've sidled as far away from him as I can, until I'm pressed close to the headboard. In this small space, I don't want to end up accidentally touching him. "Not you. Us. I'm going to make us into a weapon."

He shifts his head, glances sidelong at me. "Interesting interpretation. And how do you propose to achieve this when you can barely stand to be in the same room as a *bat*?" He spits the word, makes it sound vile and hurtful. I suppose to him, it is.

Calling up every bit of determined strength, until I am close to myself again, I lean closer to him. "What do you need to bond? Sex? Blood?"

His eyes are grey, cooler and darker than any other bats' I've seen. I can't tell if he's angry or merely thinking. "If I wanted this, wouldn't I already be at the Mata palace, begging for my share?"

"Please," I say. It's hard to force the words out, and when they do come, it's a distant whisper. "They'll never let me otherwise. Please, I need this. I cannot be whole without my magic. I'm half a person."

He stares at me and says nothing, but there is a flicker in his gaze, as if he has heard those words before. I clear my throat, clear my weakness away and when I speak again my voice is stronger, my own again. "What do you need?"

"Bites," he says finally. "An exchange of blood."

That's all there is to it? I'm surprised. "And what about the sex?" I think of Jek, so caught up in his little sordid thing with Sel.

Quiet laughter threads through the room. "It's one way to initiate a bond, and it helps, but it's actually more a side effect. The bond is between blood alone." He nods at my look. "Yes, Ives, you can bond with me, and never share my bed." For some reason, he's still laughing at me, real laughter, as if he finds me amusing, childish. Naive.

I am wary, uncertain now. He seemed so sure that he didn't want this, and now he's changed his mind. Was it something I said? I breathe deeply, and let my worry go in a shuddering gasp. "Then it's settled." Silver glints on my palm, and I drop one coin back onto the scarlet spread. "A coin for each step of the way," I say to him.

The next movement is a blur. Something strikes my neck, making me scream. He claps a hand over my mouth, and I feel, oh Gris, I feel his teeth slide out of my flesh, the blood well up in the punctures he's left behind.

"Shh," he says, and he's so close that his breath is warm on my cheek. His hand is hard, callused, and he keeps it clamped over my mouth, grinding my lips against my teeth as he bends to lap at the spilling blood. My breath is coming fast, and all I can think of is that a bat is running his tongue along my skin, drinking my blood. He pulls away.

"How am I supposed to do this if you can't relax?"

I make a muffled noise, and he pulls his hand away slowly, as if he expects me to start screaming the walls down any minute. "You could have given me warning," I say, when I think I'll be able to talk. Even so, my voice sounds too high, strangled.

Blood is running down my neck in thin tickling rivulets, and I lift one hand, press it to the trickle and pull them away again. My fingers are stained red. Around me, sound booms into silence, and my fingers tremble even as my vision greys.

"Breathe."

I snap back. "I am breathing."

"Look here, Calissa." He presses the coin into my blood-smeared hand. "I can't do this; neither can you. Go home."

"People will die." I stare across the room, focusing on the wooden screen, not on the silver bit.

I feel his shrug then he shifts his body so that he's sitting side by side with me, both of us staring at that frame. It has scenes from Mallen Gris's great discovery of the scriven mines, while Ives Verrel holds up a lamp for him. "There's nothing new in that," he says, but his voice is soft. "It's not up to you save a whole city."

"No." I shake my head. "But I'm an Ives, and I will try. I can't do it without magic." There's the truth. "I need that more than I need to save people."

"Well, you're refreshingly honest." There's laughter in his voice again. "Come." He twists his body so that he's half-facing me. "I'll do this slowly. Tell me if I should stop."

And I don't say anything, even when that mouth comes back and closes over the wounds in my neck, and sucks at my skin. After a while, I stop thinking, concentrate only on my breathing. In. Out. In. Out. The world has dissolved away by the time he pulls back from me and says my name.

"You'll want to give me that second coin now." There's blood on his chin. Metal hits metal, and the two silver coins lie next to his thigh, looking up at us. Emperor Mallen's face is set in disapproval, but from the histories, I think that's hardly unusual.

Mal swallows, scoops up the two coins, and drops them into his jacket pocket. I pull a kerchief from my sleeve and press it against my neck, waiting for the flow to turn sluggish and for the pain to fade a little.

"I could do this myself," he says. "Tear a hole in my wrist, but tonight calls for ceremony." He hands me a little white dagger, and as I take it from him, I feel the skitter of magic. Uni ivory. He could have bought himself free with this. I stare up at him, puzzled.

"It's not mine," he says. "Riam would know if I tried to hock it." He holds out his arm, wrist under my chin.

"I – I don't know where to cut."

"Any vein will do. Just don't go and try saw my hand off, Ives."
He's joking, and when I look up from the fluttering blue lines of the
veins, I see him grinning lopsidedly at me.

"You're laughing," I say. "Why?"

"Because if I don't, then who will?" His face is serious again.
"Come on, Ives. Do it. My arm can't take the suspense."

The dagger slices the flesh, making it split and peel back around
a red line.

"Deeper, please. If you want this to work." Pain flickers through
his voice, and I can't look up, just press the tip of the dagger into that
red waiting wound, and push it in, feeling the give and burst of flesh
and vein. The blood streams down his skin, making dark patches in
the coverlet. He takes the knife from my fingers and sets it down.

"Third coin."

In my tight-closed fist, it waits. One flick, and I've sealed it, paid
the final part.

"Drink." He holds out his arm.

While I hesitate, the blood spills, and the damp mess grows.
"How much?"

"I'll tell you when to stop." His voice is mild, but he speaks
through gritted teeth, and I hesitate no longer.

Cupping my fingers under his wrist, I draw the wound up to my
mouth, and swallow down blood and disgust. Something shivers in
my belly, a tickling sensation, similar to the first stirring of a scriv-
high. I pull away. "What –"

"The bond. Magic." He smiles, and I'm acutely aware of the
sharp teeth. They are rimmed in red, and he licks at them like a cat.
He nods down at where I'm clutching his wrist so hard that I've
made the skin dent. "Carry on. It's not sealed yet."

Head bowed so that my hair falls across my cheeks, cutting Mal
off from my sight, I drink again, drink and revel in the shimmery
feeling spreading out from my core, along my skin, rippling though
every nerve and hair, so that I feel like I'm standing in a field before
the break of a lightning storm. A hand on my shoulder stops me, and
Mal pulls me away.

The whiteness of his face is more pronounced, and he has slid
that awful white eyelid down over his dark grey eyes.

"Do you also feel it?"

"Of course." His voice is raspy. "How could I not?" He takes my
fallen kerchief, crumpled and stained, and presses it to his own

wound. We sit in a silence that, while it's not comfortable, is almost comforting.

"There are a few ground rules."

His head jerks up. "You're the cool one," he says as he stands. The laughter is back in his voice. "Go on then, tell me about these rules."

"You can't feed on me the way Sel does with Jek."

He frowns. "There's no choice."

"That's rubbish. You can live on nilly milk and blood. I know you can."

"No. You don't understand. It's not so much me as you."

I stand, because it's making me feel vulnerable, being lower than him. "What are you talking about?"

"The magic calls to blood. You'll need me to –" He shuffles. "Um, how do I put this, re-enforce the bond. If not sex, then feeding, and without sex, believe me, that will be more often than young Sel and your half-brother."

Cold runs through me. "Are you saying that unless you feed often, I can't tap you?"

He stares back at me, that alien unblinking gaze. "That's exactly it."

"Fuck." I slump down.

"Oh very ladylike –"

"Shut up. You know nothing about me."

"True. May I sit?"

It seems strange that he's asking me now, but I wave my hand without looking up, and I feel the bed dip as he seats himself beside me. "Never mind, little Ives. You'll have plenty of time to work out our lists of rules and understandings." I'd think he's mocking me, but his tone is sad, almost regretful. "Before that, there's something else we must do."

"And that is?" I raise my head, and the movement pushes down the last vestiges of horror. I chose this, I wanted the wasp, and for that I needed to take the sting.

"We pay a visit to Riam."

Fifty-Eight

The Grinningtommy

THE MEKE HAVE thrown me in an iron cage with a solid floor, solid roof, an one solid side. The other three sides are barred so I can look out into their nightmare world. Iron all around me, at my back, below an above. They took my shoes an jacket, an left me here.

The burning presses against my skin. I crouch in that fucking cage, stripped to the waist. My shirt is on the floor so that I can at least stand on it an not burn my feet black. The heat comes through the material, an I keep shifting, putting more weight first on one foot, then the other.

They're gone. Left me alone, an the lights flicker an jump. My head hurts so bad I can't hardly think.

Would it be worse if they were here?

Probably.

Still an all, I'm scared shitless that they've just gone an left me here to die all slow-like. My throat is dry, an every swallow hurts more.

Not sure how much time passes me by, but I lift my head when I hear a door whoosh, loud as rushing water. Five men march in, their boots metal thuds. It makes the iron shudder. Heat licks across my skin.

They've taken off those bug-eyed helmet things, an their heads are small, too small on those bulky bodies. The front one is thinner an smaller than the others, an I realise it's cause their uniforms are armour, an this one wears none. He steps a bit closer to my cage, while lights flash behind him, an voices crackle from the thin air. He clears his throat.

"Ah, hmm. Good day. My name is Gregory. What is your name?"

The words are stiff an old-fashion, but he's definitely speaking Lammic. He turns to the man next to him an rattles off some gibberish, but the man nods an goes to the wall. Overhead light floods the room, an I cover my eyes. Everything hurts.

"That is better, yes?" He don't wait for me to answer. "You were riding in one of the puff-animals. It was attacked by . . . lions. These people rescued you."

"An stuck me in iron."

He peers over the wire-frame glasses, eyebrows raised. "Yes. Most unfortunate, but it is the only way we know to stop you using your weapons against us." He's got cold eyes, an his face is seamed an pale. Old, an he never sees the sun.

He must know how much it hurts. Or maybe he don't, but if I tell him, then I'm doing something stupid-like – worse than walking blind into a rival pack's territory armed with a spoon.

"Would you like to leave?"

The question kinda throws me. Course I do, but I ain't such a fool that I trust the Mekekana. They've no reason to help me. None at all. There's always coin to pass hands, nothing ever comes for nothing. So I nod, an wait to see what the Mekekana is going to charge me.

"Your supplies have run out," he says. "The scriven, your...magic," he spits the word out like it's a sour berry, "Should be fading. And yet, we find this." He flicks his hand, an the guard makes the light go away. Machines click. On the far wall, there's a glowing image of the spy pod that me an Sel tore apart. It's magic too, to make paintings appear from nothing. Still I say nothing, an wait.

He taps his foot, crosses his arms. When I don't move, he walks closer to the image. It's made with light; I can see that now. His shadow falls across it, an the harsh light hides his face. Grey hair stands out around his head, the light picking up each fine strand. "What did this, then?"

"We still have scriv," I says. Not giving them nothing; for all they know, I'm just some poor Hob caught in the wrong place at the wrong time.

He sighs. "Do not games play with us. You were travelling in the puff-animal. Only your royalty use it. This we know. You are important; your people will not want you harmed. Now, tell us about your new weapon."

Sweet goat-fucking Gris. The Mekekana think I'm one of the Mata. It's almost funny. "I told ya," I say. "We still got scriv."

"Not enough to do more than what you are doing now – holding the shield barriers."

"An you know that how?"

He frowns, jabbers with the broad guard next to the entrance, the one who is standing with his tube weapon held against his shoulder. They go back an forth a bit, an then old man Gregory trots all quick up to my swinging cage, careful to keep out of reach. "We have methods that we use to map scriven deposits."

I prick my ears at the thought. They have Saints too? Interesting. An have they found any other scriven – 'cause information like that could probably buy House Ives a fucking throne. "So may be that I'm not talking about the mines." I shift my feet, put my weight on my right an arch my left. The burn eases a little. Just a little, mind.

"No." Gregory shakes his head. "This is not right. I have never seen this kind of damage from a scriven attack." He stares at me, an I see his eyes are a watery grey blue, like a sky too full of rain. "Your people have a new weapon, and all you have to do is tell me what it is. Not how it works, see, nothing to jeopardise you, and then we will set you free."

'Cept of course, anything I say will come back to me, me an Sel. If I say we're tapping the bats, then all the Mekekana have to do is focus on wiping them out. So I keep my mouth shut. It's not like I trust the word of a Meke anyhow.

Old Gregory's forehead wrinkles, an his jaw twitches. "Nothing?" he says an smiles. All the anger dissolves from his face, an that makes me scared. I can deal with angry an out of control, but not the look on his face, that cold calculating stare. I've seen looks like that, last on Sharpshins's face.

If I'd known what he was planning back then, I would have watched him more careful-like. An now Gregory has the same look, like he's thinking about what could hurt me, hurt me the most. I shiver.

He holds one hand out to the side, palm up, the way the beggars do on Little Rode. Cloth rustles, an the man next to him moves forward. He's got something in his thick fingers, a small black box that ends in two points.

"You will hand me that shirt," says Gregory, an he nods at the cloth that I'm standing on.

"Fuck you."

"Please, I'm giving you a chance to hand it to me with some dignity, yes?" He smiles, a sweet smile like you'd expect on the face of someone's granny. "See? I am giving you a choice."

"Ain't you kind." I spit between the bars, but my mouth is too dry for a decent hock.

Gregory steps back, an flicks that open hand. The guard comes forward like a well-trained hunting dog, an I hear a crackle –

Fifty-Nine

Singing for the Dead

SWEET FIRE IT hurts, Jek hurts. Jek hurts.

I wrap my arms around my head, while the blaas spins in the wind. We are shaking, we are all shaking. The binds are breaking. The traces. Everything.

"Sel! Sel!" I know this voice. A voice that makes me calm, that pulls me together again, like a needle in a torn glove. I don't want to touch him, but I press through the Alerion's pain-gift and try to breathe.

There are arms around me, and I smell skin, smell Isidro. "We will find Jek." I can hear the lie; he doesn't believe the words. I pull away, the touch too much for me to take.

"If he's still alive." This, the young redhead. "I mean, he just got rolled by sphynxes, there's probably not enough of him left –"

"Shut up!" Harun says.

Isidro stays close, not quite touching me. There is silence, except for the sound I make, because I can feel Jek's hurting, and I need to speak it. Isidro presses his mouth close to my ear, so that his breath tickles. "Hush now, Sel. As long as you're alive, so is he. We will look for him. There are others who will help us. Home first, and we will take everyone we can, and we will find him." His belief in his lie grows as he speaks, until he has tricked himself into telling the truth.

All around us the carriage shakes, or I shake. I don't know.

I find the words. "Iron iron iron."

"What's it saying?"

"Something about iron."

"They're burning him in iron," I say, feeling the clean edges of the words, how they come when I want them, the right ones in the right place.

The voices all grow loud together then a blackness shoves through me. Through Jek.

I WAKE LATER, my head cold and empty. My skin is burning. I raise my hands to see the skin peel back like it has on Jek, but it is only dreams. I am whole.

"Welcome back, Sel," Isidro says. He's still next to me. I make myself reach out and touch his coat sleeve.

"This means the Hob is still alive?" the Mata asks.

"For now." Harun speaks so that the anger and worry are clear under his words. It is so real that I want to hold the emotions, study them like butterflies under glass.

Isidro presses the fingers of his free hand to my wrist, to where I'm still holding on to his sleeve. It stings, but I grit my teeth and let the small pain pass. I realise that the further away from the Alerion we draw, the more the pain fades.

"You're certain that it's the Mekekana who have him?" Harun says, not to me, but to the Mata.

"No, Guyin. I'm not, but the only aura in the area after the sphynxes left belonged to that damn ship, and if the bat is screaming about iron, well then it stands to reason."

"I know. I was just hoping that you might have picked up something else." He sighs, like a wind blows though grass. Distant. "Can the blaas go any faster?"

"I can push her, but she's ragged already. And to be honest, I don't see a point. Your Hob's bound to be dead before we can get back."

"And so we shan't even try? How will that look, I wonder, to the vamps your father is trying to court?"

"Don't put your words in my mouth, Guyin. I didn't say I wouldn't do it. I might not like the idea of bonding the bats and Lammers, but it is the only –" He pauses. "I-it's the only weapon we have left. I'm not so great a fool as to do something to destroy that."

"You hate them, and yet you see their potential. Well, at least there's that. We can all be grateful."

The redheaded Mata wipes a hand over his face. He's trying to wipe his pride clean. "Wasn't me; Ives Calissa brought the idea to my attention."

"She did? I didn't realise you had much contact with her."

"She's my wife's sister."

I can feel the last scriv in his head; he's whipping the blaas forward with his scriv-sick magic. Tired magic. Weak. It is the Lammers' time to fall. After this they will be nothing.

"Isidro, stop him from making that noise, I need to concentrate."

I can't stop the sound; it needs to come out, Jek's pain. I'm slipping.

"Whatever your lordship says," Isidro snarls. He sits down next to me and starts speaking softly. He tells me a story. There are words. I must hear them. They are important.

Sixty

A Game of Wasps

I FOLLOW MAL through the twists of the Splinterfist rookery, up to the eyrie where Riam holds court.

She sits behind a white desk smooth as a river-pearl, dressed in an old-fashioned dress of crimson silk. The waist is cinched in so that her breasts and hips are exaggerated. Against her skin and the coal-black curl of her hair the red is startling and bloody. When she stands, she's no taller than I am, but she's piled her hair atop her head in an artful fall of ringlets.

But it's not the hair that makes it seem as if she's towering over me, it's the sheer force of her. Bound now to Mal, I can feel the strength of her magic pricking at my skin.

She looks at us, frowning, but Mal doesn't need to say a word; already I see comprehension in her eyes.

"Why?" She's not talking to me.

Mal merely shrugs.

"You could have gone down to the Mata Palace with the others if you were so desperate to earn your freedom." She closes her eyes, a pained expression deepening the fine lines on her forehead. "Such as it is."

Instead of answering her, Mal steps forward and drops the three silver bits and the blood-stained white dagger on her desk. They make a dull clunk.

"Sit." Riam waves to the empty chair in front of her desk. Mal takes a second one from against the wall, dragging it next to the other, and we both sit. I fold my hands in my lap and wait in silence.

Riam barely looks at me as she rifles through a desk drawer to haul out a slender leather volume bound in a deep scarlet hide that matches her dress. Desert sphynx. Once she's found her place and dipped her pen, she fills in a series of ledgers, tallying up Mal's life in a catalogue of what he's earned and what he owes. Finally, satisfied, she gives him a handful of coins, and a badge of embroidered scarlet and gold.

It's a bird, an alerion. A strange symbol: death in life, life in death. No House will use it; it's considered an evil omen. The last House to wear an eagle was annihilated – Mallen's fallen crest.

"You will sew this to your left lapel," Riam says to Mal, "and the House crest of your new owner on the right."

I find myself starting at the word "owner". The Mata haven't done away with all the old rules then. Mal, however, just stares back at her with a blank, mild look, as if he hasn't heard the insult. He places his hand over the alerion crest and draws it across the table. "Thank you," he says, very softly, as he stands.

When we're out the cold office, I ask him about the alerion-bird crest. "Why do you need that?" I say.

"It's the symbol of a free vampire. It means we can walk the streets of MallenIve without papers." He has his hand deep in his pocket, and I think he's holding on to that little scrap of embroidery as if it were worth more than even the silver I gave.

"It's a strange symbol to use for freedom." I want to see if he knows, if he understands where he comes from.

At that, Mal turns to me and grins, a lopsided smile that holds bitterness as well as humour. "Death is a kind of freedom," he says, then the smile dies. "Actually, it stands for immortality." He won't say more on it, and we walk in silence down the empty, ice-bitten streets, our feet sliding on the slick cobbles. More than once, he catches my arm to stop me falling.

The bells are ringing the hour when the spires of the Mata Palace rise above the gabled roofs. Not long now, and my heart shudders in my chest. Perhaps Mal can hear it, because he takes my hand as we walk to the bone-carved gates. I want to shake him off – this is a transaction, an exchange of power and money, not a love-sick thing like Jek got caught in – but it's comforting, and so I leave it.

People are crowded behind the gate, bundled against the cold, holding aloft lanterns that cast jumping lights and flickering shadows. I hear my name, even from this distance.

It's only when Mal tugs at my hand that I realise I've stopped. "My mother is going to kill me," I say, thinking of the face my House will lose now. As soon as the words are out, I feel stupid, because I realise suddenly that she might not have pushed me into this, but she led me to the path then let me go, knowing what I'd do. That I'd hold the wasp.

The faces turn to me as we draw closer, and there's my mother, her features bleached out with worry, with guilt. Her relief is obvious when she sees me, when her gaze travels down to take in my hand clasped in Mal's bone-white one. There's no doubting it now, what this means.

"You knew," I say, as she slides through the crowd towards me. "Why didn't you just tell me?" The distance between us closes, and a prickle of sweat-sick fear starts at the base of my spine.

She says nothing, but there is self-hatred, churning guilt, pity. I can feel them batting at my face like strands of broken webs. Is this from the new bond? I can only assume so. Where before, with scriven, I could see the colours of emotions, know the lies from the truth, this is more like being immersed in someone else's mind. Bile rises in my throat.

More people start crowding around us, and I'm battered down with relief, resentment, fear, disgust – myriad different seething dreams. The beginning of a migraine flares through my head, burning along the paths of old thoughts, ending behind my eyes in a searing flash. I think I fall.

"Ives?" There's a voice against my ear, whispering. Breath blowing strands of hair back, tickling, but no overload of emotions. Someone else edges closer, kneels next to me and again I'm caught in the terrible rush of fear and love and anger. I scream.

"Step back! You're hurting her."

"I'm her mother." Anger tears holes in my stomach. I'm scared that if I open my eyes, I'll see my own blood on the ice.

"And surely you see what you're doing?" Mal is angry too, but it's just something I hear, not a wave that drowns. Mother stands and steps away from me, and the pain lessens a little. Only then do I realise I'm holding Mal's hand so tightly that I've dug into his skin.

He helps me sit, and I blink my eyes open. There is blood on our joined hands. Who has stung who?

"Why?" I say through dry lips. The ice beneath me has melted into my clothes, and I start shivering, unable to stop. "What's happening?"

"I have no idea," says Mal, but he doesn't let go of my hand, and there's no pain in my head, as long as everyone keeps their distance. He helps me stand, and we walk into the palace, through a widening gap as the people draw back to let us pass. Their emotions flutter distantly, beating against my head with broken moth wings, and I keep raising one hand as if I could brush them away. My feet feel like they're barely part of me, and I'm staggering. Mal's the only one who keeps me upright.

Mother stalks ahead, her heels striking the stone floors, her voice clear and ringing like one of the Widows, telling the others to keep back as she leads Mal through the warren of the palace.

She keeps well back as Mal leads me to my bed. I climb in, fully dressed, in that shivery, half-aware state that normally comes just as a fever hits.

My mother's voice.

Illy's.

Mal's.

They're arguing, voices raised and lowered like the wind that drives on a storm. I curl up and press my hands over my ears. I want them all to go away so that I can think. Perhaps Mal reads my mind, because I hear him ordering my family out of my room. Unbelievably, they listen – even my mother, although she's grumbling as she retreats. The door slams shut, and the last of the butterfly brushes fades.

"Here." Water splashes into a glass. "Sit up and drink this." He's holding out a wine glass, beaded with drops. I manage to take it, even though my hand is shaking so much I slop ice-cold water down my chin and the front of my shirt. The pain has settled into a tight ball at the base of my skull, as if I've been drinking Father's vai by the bottle-ful, and I realise quite suddenly how very thirsty I am.

"What –"" I choke on water, swallow. Try again. "Gris. What's happening?" I look up into clear grey eyes and can see nervousness etched into Mal's expression.

"What's your talent?" he asks. "On scriv, I mean."

"I'm a Reader."

He nods, still troubled. "And it looks like you still are – after a fashion. We'll have to get hold of one of the older bonded wrays and ask if he knows of any other Readers bonded to a vampire." He shakes his head, and his hair swings around his face. "Come to think of it, I've never heard of one."

Blood drains from my head; I can feel dizziness spiralling up, and I'm falling.

"Are you saying that it's always going to be like this?" I whisper. "No one can come near me?"

"Well we can," he says. By *we*, he means the bats. That's why nothing happened in Splinterfist. "Although I'm sure that's not very reassuring," he says drily, and he surprises a painful laugh out of me.

Sixty-One

The Grinningtommy

THE MEKEKANA SPLASH me awake with ice water. There are burns all down my side where I've been lying on iron, an I struggle up, tearing blistered skin.

I'm still in that Gris-damned cage, an my feet feel like blown-up pigs-bladders, like they're hardly attached proper to me. The pain's all mine though, an as my head swims right, I feel it.

I try put my weight on first one foot, then the other, an wish I had my shirt still so's I could have stood on it. The chain they put on me is gone; instead there's a heavy burn at my throat. I don't need to be able to see to know they've put a band of iron 'bout my neck. I open my eyes.

"Ah. You're awake." Light burns my eyes, an they feel red an swollen. Lift my right hand to find my one cheek is raw. Cowards, knocking me out an beating the shit out of me while I'm down. All for a fucking shirt.

That old bastard Call Me Gregory is dressed all neat in a pin-striped suit, like he's off to go see a play or take in some formal entertainment, like the House-Lammers do. "Now," he says. "As you can see, I have qualms none about letting you burn slowly, so it really is best that you tell me what you know."

My throat is so dry, an my tongue so swollen, that I couldn't talk even if I wanted to. So I just stare at him, shifting my weight, right to left, left to right, right to left. We look at each other, an the silence is heavy as the iron around me.

"I see." He turns to the two men behind him and jabbers instructions at them before he leaves without looking back. The nearest of the two guards pulls that black stunning stick out again. I know what's coming, an there's nowhere for me to go. I back up until I'm almost pressed against the iron. Their shoes squeal. It's the only noise I can hear over the blood pounding in my ears. Number One unlocks the cage an stands back, watching me with a look like a dog with a bone, wary that it's gonna get snatched. Number Two climbs in an aims that damned stick at me. I duck, an he misses, but I'm not fast enough to do that a second time. All I'm thinking as the blackness hits is that at least I won't feel the burning while I'm out.

. . . .

"– AWAKE?"

Something slaps at my face, an I open one eye. I can't really see much-like; everything's all fuzzy an grainy. The shape in front of me comes slowly clearer, an it's my old chum Gregory.

"Ah, back with us, I see. Yes." He moves around, an I try follow him, but something's pinning my head down. It's cold under my cheek. A table. Not iron or I'd be screaming my head off, but not wood neither. It's cool an smooth as an expensive pot. All I can see now is my right hand spread flat on the table. One of the guards is pinning it down at the wrist. The scabs from when Sel an I got arrested are being rubbed off, cracking, an there's blood on the white table. It hurts, but in a dull achy way, nothing like the fresh burns on my back an arms. They sting like someone's rubbed salt in a cut.

The man holding me down has hands wide an flat an hairy; he could probably snap my wrist with no more thought than he'd break a twig.

"I'm afraid I don't have time to waste on niceties," Gregory says from behind me. It's strange, not being able to look at the person talking. "Every moment I waste waiting for your cooperation is a moment stranded in the desert around your city. Not something I'm keen to prolong, you must understand." He talks as if we were chums, like he's just explaining this to me they way he would to a slightly thick Hobling. "So –" An his boots tap tap tap on the floor until he's standing in front of me again, an I can see the buttons on his grey coat an the curled black-gloved hands hanging against his thighs. "I'm giving you another chance to explain to us how the Lammers are able to attack us without relying on the scriven."

He waits, one hand tapping his thigh, playing a little drumbeat to measure out his patience.

Somewhere out of sight, a clock is keeping ticktock time. There's just those two noises an the soft sounds of breathing.

"Nothing?" he says, an crouches to peer at me. He looks saddened, but that don't last long. He straightens, an then I hear him talking in his jagged language, all hard edges an spit-sharp vowels. He walks to the end of the room, an at the last minute, his hand on the door, he looks back at me, an says. "Please understand. I would have preferred not to have to resort to this. This is unfortunate, but necessary, yes."

An then he's gone, the door shutting slowly an smoothly quiet.

Now it's just me an those other bastards. The ones with hands like meat an iron. None of them speak Lammic, I already know that. Even if they could, I wouldn't give them the kicks of asking what it is they're going to do. They're gonna do it anyway.

The one holding my head an arm moves an puts all his pressure on my wrist. Blood booms in my head as I'm waiting for him to break it, but he just holds me there, an smashes my hand flat, splaying my fingers. I try to curl them up, to pull away, but that just earns me a clout at the back of the head, hard enough that I throw up on the white table.

The guard smears my face in it. It's nowt but thin bile, sour an rancid. He gets tired of that an pries one of my fingers free, holding it straight. That's when I get a clear view of the other one. He's walking up with a handful of needles, flattened strips of iron that come to a sharp point, each one about as half as long as my little finger.

My brain makes the connection, an I start screaming through my dry throat. Struggling. The bastard holding me down can hit me as much as he wants, I figure that'll be better than what's coming.

They hammer those fucking nails in under my fingernails one by one, an it doesn't matter that by the end I'm screaming myself raw to tell them everything I know, they carry on like machines, like they're deaf an dumb an can do only one thing at a time.

My face is wet – sweat an tears, an I don't understand why I'm not passing out. Shouldn't there be a limit to what a body can take? But when they finally stop, I'm still awake, my whole body cold an shivering. I've retched again, I think, but there's nothing to come up, an all I can feel, all I can concentrate on is that terrible deep burn under my nails. They let go of me, but I'm too damned scared to move my hands, to do anything that will make it worse. I don't even hear Gregory come into the room an walk up to me.

"I will tell them to remove the needles," he says, an my head jerks up at his voice. The movement makes my hands shift, an another wave of pain rolls up my arms. "But I'm afraid that can only happen when you cooperate."

"Cunt," I manage to choke, which as insults go is not up to my usual, but my head is too sore to think straight. There's iron in my blood, an it's making the shivers worse. Even my teeth are clacking in my head now. Every shiver moves my fingers an I'm pretty sure I'm crying. Fuck.

This is what the Mekekana will do to us, what they will do to Sel, an the other wrays, the Lammers. Oncle, if he's still alive. They will hurt my family, destroy them.

He taps his hand against his thigh again, slap slap slap, like he's thinking. Wondering what he's going to do with me. There's a squeak of leather, then footsteps. Voices. He's talking to the guards. I close my eyes an let the cold table numb my cheek.

There's no point in them even knocking me out again; they just make me stand an prod at me until I walk, go where they want me to. Part of me is thinking I should be trying to study the place, learn something, but since I've already decided that I'm going to die, I don't bother. If I don't give them nothing, I die, an Sel dies too. But if I start speaking, if just once I open my mouth to tell them everything, then there will more deaths – the wrays in the Splinterfist, all the Lammers who'll bond with them. Everyone who the Mekekana will trample over.

Somehow I find myself back in that little cage, an I don't even remember walking there. The burning in my feet is nothing now, an I just lie on my side trying to not move. I swallow thick an wait for the guards to leave. Finally, they turn off the lights an I'm alone in the dark, my skin blistering. My hands are huge, tight. I can't see them, so I have to move extra careful-like to get hold of the first splinter with my teeth.

The pain shocks up my arm, but I bite at the end of the flat metal that's poking out from under my right thumb, an make myself pull it out, like it ain't nowt more than a splinter of wood jammed under the nail, not a wedge of burning iron that sits deep in my flesh, that blisters my mouth.

It takes me a very long time to get them all out.

Sixty-Two

A Game of Wasps

MAL LEAVES ME alone when he goes to talk to my mother, and I lie on the bed with the covers pulled up to my chin, willing the headache away. With my eyes closed, I can still feel the dull pulse of the after-effects behind my lids, like a light flashed in my face. The minutes swim together, and I manage to sleep a little, drifting in and out of a pain that must rival one of Mother's infamous heads.

A door clicks. Mal comes into view. He walks so very quietly, it's unnatural.

"Seems the crowd wasn't out for you," he says, voice lowered, and sits on the end of the bed. I crane my neck to get a better look at him and feel the muscles tense in protest. He looks tired, even pastier, if that's possible, and his eyes are dark with shadows.

"They weren't?" I'll admit I thought it odd that Mother would have made such a public fuss over my disappearance. She tries to keep all our failures and flaws under wrap. Wincing, I try sit up, and Mal hands me a pillow to lean back on. "What's happening?" Finally, I get a good look at his face. "What did she say to you?" I ask, suspicious. I wonder if she has admitted her conspiracy, her part in my choices. Has she had some new Vision that set her to manipulating me so subtly?

Mal shakes his head. "I don't think she had time to say exactly what she wanted to –" he stops and puts a hand over his eyes. "The blaas – the Mata blaas. It's gone down somewhere near the city. Someone picked it up, one of the Mata's Readers, I assume, and they're sending out search parties now, to see if there are any survivors."

Shock, sharp and clean, thrusts away the lingering pain. "Trey." I put a hand over my mouth and will him to be not dead.

Mal nods. "It shouldn't take long – they've sent out a fast coach. Your sister's gone with to hold a shield over the whole thing, in case the Mekekana attack."

"They're close to a ship?" My throat is dry, the words strangled, too tight.

"Not that the Readers can tell, but it won't do for them to take chances." He sighs. "We didn't have time to speak long, but your mother doesn't seem overly surprised about your –" He waves one hand. "Decision."

Not exactly a shock. I let my head fall back on the pillow. I want to close my eyes, to wish everything away – the loss of the scriven, the Mekekana ships waiting for us in the desert, this thing I've done. But I can't do it. I stare up at the ornate ceiling instead.

Next to me, Mal shifts. "There's more," he says.

"Do I want to hear it?"

I feel him shrug. "The little feyn that the Mata gifted your family?"

Of course I remember them. Father had to turn them over to House Guyin in order to get the bastard's cooperation. "I know of them."

"Seems they took ill – some experimental thaumaturgy gone wrong. The younger of the twins died about an hour ago. The older is set to go before the night is out."

"What!" I jerk up, forgetting the last traces of pain and my own self-pity.

Mal gives me a strange look. "I had no idea you were so close," he says drily, and there's a bitterness under it, something I can't quite understand. "Whatever magic House Guyin used to try fix them, it failed. And if one of a bonded pair – or twins, in this case – dies, then the other will follow." He folds his hands, twiddling his thumbs.

I'd forgotten reading that, that once bonded the pairs live or die together. Then it hits me – if someone kills Mal, I die too. It's a terrifying thought, and Mal must see it on my face.

"Oh no," I say.

"Yes," he hisses. "It's the one little flaw in your plan."

"And now everyone knows?"

He nods. "Most likely."

"No one is going to do this now," I say as I dig my fingernails into the wool of the over blanket. "This whole thing will have been for nothing, a waste." I want to claw my fingers into his eyes, punch him, anything. Even though, deep inside, I know this isn't his fault.

"You were expecting that the other Houses would follow in your footsteps?" he asks it carefully. "You should have known it would take more than that to make the Houses change their ways." Mal watches me, his brow furrowed. "Forgive me, but I'm not sure, was the offer to bond ever made to the Hobs?"

"No." I sigh. "Nor will it be."

"Did it ever occur to you that they might be the ones most willing to take this kind of risk? Hobs who would suddenly have status, a tap straight into magic –"

Yes, of course it did. "They can't use magic," I snap.

"They can't use scriven, you twit." He sounds exasperated, and somewhat amused. "Your brother is a Hob –"

"Half-Hob."

"And he still tapped Sel."

There it is again, a flash of guilt and sorrow. "Mal?" I say.

He watches me, his face drawn.

"I've already spoken with him. The Mata will not make the offer to the Hobs."

Mal just stares. After a while, he says. "Then why don't you?"

"I have nothing to offer them –"

He holds up one hand, silencing me. "Do you really believe that?"

He's right. It's not about the deeds to houses or the station of a War-singer or the chance to maybe earn a few of the Mata's coins. It's about power.

It's about magic.

And who will the Hobs be loyal to then? If it's an Ives who gives them this chance, who tells them exactly what House Mata has kept from them. If the Hobs are loyal to me, I'll have the Mata under my bootheel, begging for my mercy.

I smile.

We wait for my mother and the others to come back with news of Trey and the blaas crew. I write letters, drafting an offer to the Hob pack leaders of the Digs and the Wend, and another to the Heads of the three rookeries. I'll find loyal servants to read them out, if it comes to that.

Mal comes and goes; he's talking to the bats and to the Lady Pelim.

Apparently the shock of the twins' death was too much for her, and she's holed up in her manse, on bed rest. Mal says that she's a fool for trying to carry a child anyway. I never thought of that, of the twisted thing that grows inside her. Will it be more a bat than a Lammer? If it comes out looking normal, perhaps that would also encourage the Lammers and Hobs to bond. Unfortunately, the reverse holds; if it looks like a bat, that's another mark against the bond.

Faint light is seeping through the lace curtains, speckling the carpeted floor. The clouds have blown away again, leaving the sky outside a thin and pale blue. My head still feels too heavy, as if a fast turn could send it flying from my shoulders. It's been hours since my breakdown, and still I feel like this. Fear makes it hard to breathe sometimes, my lungs tight with the knowledge that I can never again indulge in any normal companionship. Mal thinks I might be able to tolerate the presence of a bonded Lammer, if his bat is with him, acting as a shield. With one stupid act, I've cut myself off from everyone.

Did my mother See this happening?

I put down my pen and stopper the glass bottle of ink.

The curtains are thin as spiderwebs under my fingers, as I bunch them up and push them aside. The light is harsh, making me blink, my eyes tearing up. Already the little drifts of snow have melted away, just a few white corners still untouched. This has been our worst winter – snow – the first snow in ten years. I crane my neck, trying to see out past the gables and spires, to the white, flapping fields of windle-silk tents – the huge domes of silk that cover and protect the irthe groves. The trees come all the way from the eastern coast past Pelimburg, and if they're not protected from the sun they wither and die. Without the irthe trees, there are no windle moths. Without them, those scraps of velvet-winged darkness, large as a songbird, we have no factories, no spinning wheels, no steam from the silk baths.

Bones Like Bridges

I'VE GROWN UP with the windle tents a constant. Like the scriven underfoot, deep veins of magic. And now, all we have left are those fields of silken tents, the groves hidden away.

Once, before House Mallen fell, there was a terrible war between magic and mundane. Between Lammer and Mekekana. No one knows how it began, but it decimated populations, destroyed fertile land. The thousands of Mekekana with their strange iron ways were too strong even for the greatest War-singers of Mallen.

And so House Mallen fell. Oh no, not because of the Mekekana, but because of the Well. They turned from scriven, and they opened the horror of the Well. Burnt the green land red, turned the lions in the fields to sphynxes, the giant horned goats into unicorns. We turned the mundane to magic.

After House Mallen was destroyed, and Mallen Erina burnt up in the first outpouring of pure magic, her immediate family were marched out and left to die in the desert.

A minor nephew managed to close the Well. And so House Mata was born. And Ives? Well, as usual, we stood on the sidelines and watched, and changed our allegiance with the turn of the wind. We're still doing it.

The door creaks, making me pull back from my dreamy contemplation. Thankfully it's Mal, and not Mother or Illy, or a servant who doesn't know better.

"What's wrong?"

He wipes his hands down his face, clearing the distraught expression away, wiping a slate clean. "It's so obvious?"

I nod.

"They got to the blaas." He catches the look on my face. "Mata Trey is safe." He grimaces. "Everyone is safe, actually, barring your brother."

Trey is safe. I lock that thought away tightly and turn to the other matter. "What's happened to Jek?"

He shrugs, throws his winter coat over the back of a chair. Already he has patched the alerion to his left lapel. "No one's certain. He's still alive, and they're convinced he's in a Mekekana ship."

"Why would the Mekekana take my brother?"

He slumps down on the unmade bed, and glances across at me, his eyes full of mist and shadows. I push myself away from the sill and walk over. It seems so natural to just sit alongside him, thigh to thigh, arm to arm. I don't even feel a glimmer of distaste. The bond must be working overtime. That, or somewhere I've accepted the fact that I'll only ever be able to spend time with him or his people. I was always practical, I suppose.

""No one knows. All that's certain is that he's still alive."

It takes me a moment to work out that last. "Sel?"

"Just hanging on." He knots his fingers together, doesn't look up, although it seems to me that he presses closer against me. "How well do you know Sel?" he asks.

Not well at all. "He's . . . strange," I venture.

The comment prompts a bitter laugh. "Strange is one way of putting it, I suppose." Mal looks up into my eyes. "He's gone completely catatonic. Isidro and Lord Guyin are taking him to their house, and then they want to come speak to you."

I've no idea if Mal is right, if I'll be able to bear the presence of a bonded Lammer, and he must see the tight spasm of fear in my face, because he lifts one hand to touch my cheek briefly then drops it again. "They'll be here soon," he says, softly. The after-shivers of magic dance between us.

"I'll be ready." I'm dismissing him, and he knows it. Mal looks at me, half-smiles, and then leaves the room to go sit in the little parlour that leads off all the private rooms in our quarters. I can hear him, the clink of glass as he pours himself a drink, the scrape of a chair on a patch of uncarpeted wood. He comes back when I've dressed in a grey robe with salmon-scale undertones. It flickers in the light when I turn, the long skirt trailing over a small bustle. I've had to forgo a corset, even though it's the current fashion. No servant will ever be able to lace one up for me, and I've no intention of asking Mal for his help.

He knocks, peering around the door just as I'm buttoning up my long black overcoat. Voices come through from the parlour. He doesn't have to tell me. I pull my hair back in a loose bun and follow him through, fear eating at my stomach, waiting for the hit of emotions.

"Miss Ives." Lord Guyin stands and dips me a quick bow. I feel a faint prickling of exhaustion and worry against my head, but nothing I can't live with. I glance across at where his bat stands – Isidro. He's watching me through lowered lashes, flicking his gaze back and forth between myself and Mal, and his expression is tight.

"Can you feel anything?" he says, and I hear the strain in his voice.

"Are you stopping it?" I ask.

"Barely."

I nod. "I feel a little, not enough to trouble me."

Isidro's face relaxes a little, and the emotion in the room trebles, battering at me. Gasping, I'm almost on my knees, and Mal is next to me, grasping my elbow to keep me upright. Isidro catches the imbalance, and his jaw clenches as he ups whatever shields he has built in Harun's head.

The emotions drop a little. Now I can feel them individually, instead of just a morass of pain. Harun's worried, worried for me, for Jek, for Sel, mostly for Isidro. He's tired and drained, although I could have seen that just by looking at his face – grey and drawn. "It's like Reading," I say. "Only more direct."

Harun turns to his bat. "We'll have to let the Mata know that we need to screen for Readers." He looks back at me. "We'll work on how much you can handle," he says. "And you'll have time enough to do it."

"What do you mean?"

"We're going back to the Mekekana ship. We're going to find Jek."

If they take me, who will navigate? How do I tap Mal? Will Harun even be able to teach me more than a rudimentary grasp of the magic? How long can the bats keep their shields up and stop me from being crushed in emotion?

Will we have time to get our messages to the Hobs?

I blurt these things out, the words tumbling over each other as my heart beats faster and faster.

Harun ignores my protests. "It's one of the biggest Meke ships, Trey says. We need every Lammer we have left."

"How soon do we leave?"

Harun smiles grimly. "Right now."

Sixty-Three

The Grinningtommy

I MUST HAVE slept through the pain. Still can't move my hands, though I've long since kicked those splinters out of the cage an heard them fall to the floor.

Something woke me.

There. A noise in the dark. And my stomach goes tight an knotted. I want to be strong, to go to my death like a Grinngtommy from the old stories, head held high an all that shite, but, honest-like, I don't know if I can. Must be the blood is thin.

My eyes slowly get used to the dark, an there's a figure there, in the grey. It comes closer, an I kick back across the cage, opening blisters on my side, make myself shriek in surprise against the pain. Making my dry lips split.

"Shh," says the figure, an I hush.

"Look," it says, although it takes me a moment to work out what the bastard is trying to say. "Water." It holds something up – a smooth handle-less cup made from the same strange white material of the table that they tortured me on.

It's too good to be true, so I just sit, watching him. Don't think I'm as stupid as I look, Meke. Finally, he pushes the mug between the bars an sets it on the cage floor. After a few minutes, I hunch my way closer to it. I can barely pick the thing up, can't bend my fingers

– they're tight an burning, the pain shooting up my arms with every move, but I want water more than I give a shite about pain.

Even though I spill half of it down my chest, it's good. Cold an almost untainted. It's been in iron at some point, but it's clean enough.

The empty mug slips from my fingers an clatters loud enough to wake a sleeping scriv-head. The man edges closer to pick it up. He's short, fattish, with a face that looks rabbity an scared.

"Thanks," I croak, an he nods, understanding.

"Not tell," he says.

"Not a word, chum."

He leaves, his face relieved, an I'm alone in the dark again.

There's no getting back to sleep now. So I sit an wait for my pal Call-me-Gregory to come back with more pain. Somehow, I feel a bit better about dying. I dream of Sel, an hope that when he goes, it's quick an quiet.

There's no way to tell time here, just the flickering light that burns on when the Mekekana come. Light means pain, means going to room 16 an having more skin burnt off, needles shoved under skin, iron an blood.

Gregory an his guards come back, bringing light with them, an well, I'm not hundreds happy to see them.

He stops in front of the cage, looking at me with eyes all sharp an bright like a crow's. "Still with us?" he says.

I don't even bother to spit this time, don't say nothing. It's not worth it.

"I'll be direct," he says. "I need to know if you Lammers have opened the Well."

This is the first I've heard of it. No one'd be stupid enough to do that again. I raise one eyebrow. The world changed, last the Well was opened – everyone from the smallest Hob to the highest Lam knows that. There are things deep in there that make even the Mekekana look like little boys playing war between the Lam-heaps.

Let him think we've opened the Well. What does it matter?

"Not going to talk?" He nods at my hands. "That's not the worst I can do." Now that the lights are on, I can see the skin, red an cracked, like my hands are burnt from the inside out. I can't flex the fingers, wouldn't even want to.

I bloody well know it's not the worst, seeing as I've had what feels like a whole night to think about what else they could do to me with iron. It's done nowt for my courage, I can tell you.

"Fine," Call-me-Gregory says. "I can put out an eye, if you'd like. Or drive needles under your skin again, yes?" He grins. "See? Once more I give you a choice." He spreads his hands, like a merchant showing his wares.

"Skin," I say. The sound is dry. Like a log popping in a fire.

He mock-bows at me, like we just started a dance. I don't even fight them, no passing out, just hobbling down that long cold passage.

There are longer needles this time, an I scream an tell them nothing.

I'm back in my cage again, an there's no way of getting these needles out. They're deep in my back, slid under the skin just too low, just too high. Even if I could reach them, I don't think I'd be able to close my fingers enough to pull them out. Perhaps I say something to Call-me-Gregory. I don't think I do, but he gives me water. He has to hold the cup for me.

It's only after I've slopped most of it down my front, an swallowed a good lot that the heavy taste hits me. The burn. They've put iron in the water, an I vomit out as much as I can. Everything is on fire. I start laughing, not that it sounds like laughing, just like weird hacking sounds like a cat throwing up in your shoes. Because my throat is on fire, an I couldn't tell them nothing even if I wanted to.

Sixty-Four

A Game of Wasps

THE LAMMERS AND their bats shield me all the way down through the Mata Palace, to where a fresh blaas is waiting, the little carriage beneath open. Just inside, I can see red and gold, heavy curtains that pull around to close off the glass windows.

The Mata family stand at a distance, Blaine white-faced, his hand on his sabre, Trey at his shoulder, not looking at me. Next to them my mother is ashen. She's aged a decade during the past few days, the lines cut deeper, her hair greyer. Everyone around me is tired, the exhaustion radiating off them. Mal has added his shielding to the others though, and it's just bearable.

By the time we're in the air, my insides have unclenched enough for me to take stock of the situation.

Isidro and Lord Guyin sit opposite me, Sel curled at Isidro's side. He didn't look up when I got on; hasn't moved or spoken. To my right, the Lady Pelim is holding herself, her arms tight around her belly. Jannik, the long-nosed bat, keeps one arm about her, and glares at the others. His thin face looks cadaverous, and over everything hangs the pall of the twins' deaths.

"We've a rough estimation from Trey of where we went down," Harun says, clearing his throat. He's looking at me. "He's told the blaas where to go and ordered it to respond to you." It's an honour I would never have been given had this war not demanded it, though it's clouded under my fear that I won't even be able to guide the blaas, that my bond with Mal is too new and untried.

Harun must read my uncertainty in my expression. "You will learn fast enough," he says.

Mal presses his fingers against my arm, and I can feel the stirring of magic. Even in its strangeness, it is familiar. I take a breath. I am an Ives, and our family is powerful.

With Mal's fingers still against my skin, I send a faint tendril of thought to the blaas. The alien mind throbs against mine, then I feel the beast lurch in answer, pulling upward. I grin for a moment – the Mata must be terrified to agree to this. Then a cold thought strikes me, makes my breath catch in my throat. I shake my head. No. Even if the Mata saw this as a way to draw attention from him, my mother will see to it that he does not open the Well. At least my father told her of my fears.

"We can be there within the next sixteen hours," Harun continues. "Until then, you'd best work at Reading and filtering."

"What happens when we get there?"

"You'll have to pinpoint the Meke's ship. Help us tear it apart, if necessary."

"That's all?" I laugh, hysterically. "I've no idea if I can do that."

"You have half a day to find out that you can." Harun is not letting me go. For once, I've found someone from whom I cannot slip away. "We've lost two," he says, and his voice is soft. "I will not add to that number."

"And you think that once I find it, you can rescue Jek? Destroy the ship?" I want to hear him admit defeat, hear his uncertainty, but he says nothing. It is Lady Pelim who speaks.

"Yes," she says, in a broken glass voice.

Sixty-Five

The Grinningtommy

IT WILL END soon. When all you can hear is your own breathing, an it's that strangled sound, well, you're not much longer for this life.

At least it seems that my chum Gregory has given up on me. Probably finally realised that I've nothing to tell him. The giant ship is rumbling an clicking, juddering under me. It's on the move again. Closer to MallenIve, closer to Sel. Isidro an his lot better tear them apart, or else I'm going to be mighty pissed. Not that I'll know, I suppose.

Fuck.

My tongue feels too big for my mouth, swollen an dead. The iron has burnt away my hair in a patch, where I'm lying, right down to my scalp. I'm trying to decide which smells worse, burnt hair or skin. I watched someone burn to death once. Didn't know it was Sel's brother at the time, an back then, I doubt I would have cared. Now all I remember is the blood at his eyes, an the way he begged for his mam. I could ask for Prue, maybe, if I could still talk.

I wonder if she'd come?

An then I slip. There's a time when I was small as a nilly foal. I was sick, got the same thing that would eventually kill Prue, lungburn, an most hoblings get it at least once. The ones that don't die, well, no one even thinks it's luck. It's just life. It burns though, guess it's why they call it that, an it makes you see an hear things. Oncle says its from all the scriv dust in the air around the mines, it's too much for Hobs. Gets the young an the weak.

Well there I was, small, not weak. An so sick I couldn't move. Every joint aching, an Prue washing my head with an old rag. Cool water on my face. Prue sang for me. She sang me every song that Hoblings learn in their cradle, an when she ran out, she made them up.

I want someone to sing me to my death.

Sixty-Six

A Game of Wasps

WE DON'T EVEN get through the first ten hours of that flight, when my brother's insane burden starts muttering to himself. For all this time, Sel's been motionless, his hands over his face like he's trying to hide from some unimaginable terror.

"Now what?" says Harun, looking over at him.

Jannik and Isidro are staring at the little bat, and next to me Mal shifts.

"Well," says Isidro, after a pause, his voice slow and full of something that sounds like memories. "Haven't heard that in a very long time."

It takes me a moment to realise there's a cadence, a rhythm to what Sel's saying. Then Mal starts singing softly, almost under his breath. It's not Lammic, although I catch a word here and there that I can almost understand. The two voices rise and dip, a slow lamenting croon.

"What is he saying?" Lady Pelim pulls her shawl tighter around her shoulders, shivering even though it's quite warm here in the velvet-draped interior of the small carriage.

Jannik laughs. A bitter sound, full of future loss. "It's a lullaby. A nest-song. I haven't heard one sung since. . . ." He glances at Isidro.

"For a very long time. No one speaks Lerion outside of a

rookery."

The song is quiet, soothing. Mal stumbles over some of the words then stops. "It's normally feyn that sing it," he explains. "I never really learnt it."

Then the blaas lurches; Mal must have dropped his shield inside my head, because something huge swamps my consciousness, something black and burning with a cold pain. "The Meke ship – it's here. Below us." My breath comes in gasping pants; the thing is huge, and I have no idea how we are supposed to destroy it.

The only advantage I have is a natural grasp of magic. I have to hope that it is enough, that between Harun's considerable strength and what little I've been told of Lady Pelim's mastery, it will be enough.

I struggle to my feet and do what they've told me to – send my thoughts out to the alien consciousness of the blaas, mentally stroking it. The beast shudders, making the carriage rock, but eventually its flight smooths, and we glide down towards the waiting ship. Harun has thrown open one curtain. Outside the desert is black. The stars are obscured by cloud, and there are no city lights to bathe the sky orange. Even so, the ship is clear, a few small blue lights demarcating the edges.

"Can you read past the iron?" Harun's face is drawn.

I don't actually know for certain, but I will try. One deep breath to calm me, then I nod and close my eyes, feel the tug of Mal's swirling magic. He's moved closer, holding my hand so that the touch will help me focus. I push my mind through layers of burning iron, through a touch that makes my skin sweaty and cold, that makes me wish I hadn't eaten on the journey.

There.

A pale spark, like a mercury fly on a midsummer night. Then I lose it, and everything is cold and oily. I'm deep inside the ship, inside the aura of antimagic, and I'm drowning, my lungs crushed. Something tugs at my hand, and somehow, I'm swimming again, looking for that little silver beacon.

Again. Once. And before it's gone, I've pinpointed it.

I surface, gasping. "Back." Mal's hand is white around mine, so tight that I've lost feeling in my fingers.

"You saw him?"

All I can do is nod. When I'm able to speak again, I tell them what areas to avoid, as best I can describe what I understood of the ship. It will have to be enough.

The blaas circles, and the others stand, readiness in every angle of their postures. Harun swings open the carriage door. Cold wind buffets us, tugging my hair loose, making it swirl about my face.

I feel Lady Pelim tap Jannik's magic. It's as unexpected as a blow to the face. I had no idea how strong it could be.

I've seen Harun and Isidro work this magic before when they bested the Mata Blaine before the Lammer jury, but it was almost nothing. Now I understand why Harun believed they could take on the ship. Lady Pelim and Jannik are a whirlwind of power; it envelops all of us. I can feel my own tap on Mal sucked into that swirling vortex.

Beneath us, the Mekekana ship is tearing apart, in slow motion. Girders snap and iron peels back as easily as a fruit skin.

It's like nothing I would have ever imagined. That raw surge, so sweet and primal. I manage to move my head, to glance across at the white-faced lady. Jannik is holding her upright, and I can see the power dance between them, even as blood soaks through her skirt, black on black.

She collapses, screaming, bent over her stomach, and the flow of magic dies.

I stare at her, my mouth open. Even with Mal holding shields as high as he can, I felt that pain tearing through my stomach, felt the burst of blood and uterine fluid on my legs. I look down, involuntarily, but there is nothing on my skirts.

Jannik holds her tighter.

The pain stops suddenly, and Mal's face turns almost grey with the effort. "Sorry," he says. "Knew it was coming, but. . . ." He didn't expect it to be that bad.

The metal ship is a stinking, smoking ruin. Already Harun and Isidro are systematically picking off the survivors, slicing through their screams with a frightening intensity.

Carefully, with Mal blocking Felicita's pain from me as best he can, I send a tendril of magic back out to the ruined ship. Now that the iron is dying, I can feel Jek's aura clearly.

It's sick, distorted, and as I watch, it's dimming, turning in on itself like a snake eating its own tail.

"Harun!"

He turns to me just as Isidro's magic cuts a man's legs out from under him. The Mekekana are firing up at the blaas now, red light and hard sound, alien. A wind picks up, tearing the thin clouds apart, and starlight silvers the blood, the broken bodies. I sway, vomit threading up my throat in a line of searing revulsion. Around me everything swims, pulsing from monochrome nightmare to bright sickening colour – the reds too intense, the yellows like streaks of urine. Around me the stars whirl drunken-dizzy.

My head is collapsing inwards, the bones of my skull cracking. I press my hands to my head as though that will hold me together, and I grit my teeth, feel the pain bright at a bit in my mouth. I snatch on to a moment of clarity, focusing on one thing and one thing only. The spark we are here for. I let it pull me like a firefly through the dark, a zig-zagging madness that is still saner than the maelstrom around us.

Talking seems impossible. I'm scared that if I move my mouth my teeth will shatter, exploding my skull. I have to be rational. That will not happen, I tell myself. Communicate. Or Jek will die.

I think of Sel, and his brittle little song that Mal knew, that Isidro knew. I think of him snuffed out. Why should I care, the part of me that is cold and merciless sneers. But I am through with that Calissa. She's brought me only hurt and loss. Open your mouth and speak.

"Jek," I say. "You need to get to him quickly." I can feel the taint of iron in his aura, can't articulate it, but Harun must see the depth of it on my face, and he turns back to the fray with a clinical determination and soon the slamming sound of the Mekekana's weapons falters and dies.

"There are others," I say. I can feel them, trembling, crowded around Jek's dying aura.

Sixty-Seven

The Grinningtommy

THE SHIP IS rumbling, making the cage shake. I lift my head a little, leaving skin an meat behind. Gregory is in the room, hands scrabbling at the walls, but no light comes flooding, just cool air that smells of sand, of stars.

There are stars. Above me the roof is pulled back, a twisted mess of iron. Magic. Has to be. But I can't hardly feel it. An I should, especially when it's ripping up the Meke ship like it weren't nothing more than a folded paper toy. Another jolt sends me skidding into the bars. Gregory is shouting commands at his two lackeys, an they bound over to my cage, unlocking it an pulling me out. The pain wrenches through me, the iron at my neck pressed into the raw flesh. His fingers fumble, an then the iron falls away.

It takes me a moment, a small still second, to realise there are only the iron needles in my back between me an Sel's magic. An Sel is close. I know it, as certain as I know my own name. I can feel him in my head, sweet as anything. There is power, an not even these little slivers under my skin can stop it coming for me.

Magic digs straight into my dead throat an comes pouring out, from wherever Sel is hidden, through me, straight into Old Gregory's face, splattering him like an over-ripe melon. Next to him, in the same instant, his two guards burst, blood raining down like leaves from an irthe tree when the seasons turn. Between the blood an bone comes rage, a rage so big it scares me, it shakes the whole ship.

An Sel is in my head. White light. Clean an clear an sharp an not broken at all.

Sixty-Eight

Singing for the Dead

IRON FALLS AWAY from Jek. The bond is back, and I stop singing the songs you sing for babies and the dying.

Everything is back.

I smooth down Jek's pain, wipe it away as best I can. The Alerion gave me more than just her sin, some of what is good about her slipped in too.

It's a mistake on her part, but one that I can use. I pull that little bit of healing from myself, pour it into Jek. It's not much, but it's still better than nothing.

Hush, I say in Jek's head. *We are here. We are coming.*

It's almost distracting, having the words come to me in neat easy parcels, full of meaning. There's truth under the clamour, under the screaming.

My mother's voice, the Alerion's voice, they're all still in my head, and somehow I don't think they'll ever leave, but I can build a wall to keep them from talking over my thoughts. A wall like glass and silver, so I can just barely see them. I just need something to block out their voices.

My mind is a city. All I have to do is walk from the dark parts to the light. Past stone-cold houses filled with unopened memories. I'll come back to them another day.

It's a city I have never seen, but there is no time to breathe in its salty air, instead I run down the empty rain-wet streets, looking for the place I have to be.

I stop before a narrow blue house with a squat round turret made of coloured windows; a strange old building that looks over chalk cliffs into a vast swirling water.

Here. This is where Jek lives.

Sixty-Nine

A Game of Wasps

BELOW US THE ship is so much scattered metal. Jek must be dead.

"He's alive." The voice is gravelly, and it takes me a moment to place it.

I turn to see Sel standing, the third eyelid covering the iris so that he looks stranger than ever. "Mallen," he says, and Mal looks at him with a white face, his lips parted. "Jek is going to die, unless we get to him now. There's iron under his skin." He speaks calmly, but the covered eyes give him away. "Help me get to him."

When did Sel pull himself together?

"Bring the blaas down," he tells me, and I obey instinctively. The blaas banks, wheels down, and the carriage hits sand with an audible thud that knocks me to my hands and knees. From here, I can see Pelim's face set in lines of pain, the blood matting her skirts. Jannik is holding her tight, the Mekekana forgotten. The smell of blood is thick in the air, and I can feel it setting all the vamps on edge, like razors held to throats.

Harun, Isidro and Sel are already out of the carriage, and I struggle to my feet, letting Mal help me up so that we can follow them across the starlit sands. We dodge limbs, mangled corpses, smoking chunks of iron, and race across the hard-packed dirt to the rear of the ship.

Sel leads unerringly, like a dragon-hound on a scent. He flits through the labyrinthine interior of the ship. There is iron on every side, but Sel seems to barely notice.

We've caught up with Harun and Isidro. Harun has slowed to a walk, and I can see the drain has hit him, the post-tap exhaustion.

"Go back to Lady Pelim," I say, gritting my teeth against the black despair and tiredness that roils off him. He doesn't answer, can barely lift his head, but I meet Isidro's gaze, and the bat nods, before turning back.

Sel has already disappeared behind a turn up ahead. Mal and I set off after him, and just then I pick up on Jek again, a powder burst of pain and magic annihilates every living thing in his vicinity.

Mal must have felt something of it too, because he gasps and presses one hand to his ribs.

Jek's close. I slow to a walk, peer around the jagged corner of the passage and into a room that is opened to the sky.

There are bodies everywhere, or parts of them. The drip of blood is loud, clear. It reminds me of frost melting in the eaves. There in the middle of this carnage, Sel is crouched over a figure. I catch a glimpse of torn skin, of dark-blond hair, matted with sweat and filth. Over the reek of blood and faeces, I smell burnt skin. Burnt hair.

In the sudden stillness, I notice how the heat is burning off the iron, beating at my skin like a live thing.

The world goes silent, and we walk forward, until I can hear Sel singing.

Seventy

The Grinningtommy

SEL IS HERE. Crazy as that is. He's pulling the splinters from my back, singing something I don't right understand. I try to tell him about Prue, to tell him that I'm about as glad as you can be to see him. But I forgot my voice is gone.

"Shh," says Sel. "I know." He pulls the last iron splinter out of my back, and it's like my skin is my own again; my hands an feet an side have gone numb, but all around it the pain flares. I might be hurting, but it's my own pain; it's something that can be dressed, made better.

Then I see my face, the lips chapped and broken, the blisters, the raw flesh, the skin mottled black an red an white, seeping with clear stuff. I'm in Sel's head, watching myself shake.

"It's very straight-like in here," Sel says. My words, his voice. His head is clear, clean as a ringing bell. I'm the one that's shattered now.

Sel turns his head, an there's Calissa. Confusion an pain cloud together. I want to ask Sel what the fuck that frowsy bitch is doing here, an haven't I been through more than enough? Why now do I still have to deal with her?

"Shhh," he says again, in his own voice.

There's a vamp I ain't seen before standing next to my sister. Sel looks down at their hands, tight held.

"Fuck me," he says for me. "What have you gone an done?"

It's all there in Sel's head, an if I could laugh I would. Never thought a day would come when I'd be glad to see her.

"Jek," says Calissa. She don't want to look at me, I can tell. "We need to move him, soon. There are doctors in MallenIve who can do something for him."

"No need to stand about gabbing," Sel says for me. "I'll be gone dead if I have to listen to idle chat."

"Gris, sometimes I wonder how anyone can stand Hobs," she says. "Mal, can you get that jacket off the Meke?"

'Fore I know it, they've got me cradled in a torn coat, like a babe Hobling in a sling, an the blood from some dead bastard is soaking through my trousers. They lift me like that, an I watch the stars swinging overhead as they carry me out the ship.

I catch glimpses of their faces – Sel's, my sister's, that strange new vamp. She did that. She might've not gone an done it for me exactly, but it almost feels like it. It hurts like fuck, but I lift one hand to touch her fingers, where they're gripped tight on the coat-sling.

"Don't," she says. "Please."

"He says thank you," says Sel.

Calissa bites her lip an don't look at me, then she nods so slight I'd almost miss it, if I weren't watching her. "You're welcome," she says, all stiff-like. "Jek."

With Sel so close, his magic muffling the pain, I can almost think straight.

Almost.

"There's a house you can go to," says Sel. "Where you'll be safe."

I've no idea what he means, until he opens his mind to me an I smell wet air, briny. A sharp clean wind blows around me, pushing me forward. It's tugging at me, an finally I step the way it wants me to. There's no pain in here. I look down at my hands as I walk an there's nothing – not a flaw, not a blister.

The wind leads me to a blue house, with hundreds of small square windows in a round turret. Inside the light flickers blue through the coloured glass, an I go up the winding stairs until I reach the highest part of the house.

At the top of the spiral steps is a room, a little round room with a clean-made bed, crisp cotton, cool an inviting.

"Go to sleep," says Sel's voice in my head.

Seventy-One

A Game of Wasps

SOMEHOW, SOMEHOW, GRIS alone knows, we get Jek back to the blaas. He passed out while we were carrying him, and he's still asleep, Sel sitting next to him, head bent over him as he whispers something to my half-brother. The Hob is so motionless that if Sel weren't still alive I'd be certain Jek was a corpse.

The Mekekana ship burns below us, turning the desert into a roaring inferno, a mess of flame. Smoke and heat coil up into the chill night air. I don't even want to know what kind of power Felicita and Jannik poured into that metal to set it alight. The thought makes me shiver.

Felicita is pale now, a bundled cloth between her legs to still the bleeding, Jannik holding her hand so tightly that it's almost blue.

"How?" I finally say. Everyone is shielding so strongly against the pain and the smell of blood that the air around me feels flat and stale.

Jannik glances away from Felicita for just a moment. He snorts, like someone trying to turn tears into a harsh laugh. "I'm a Sandwalker," he says.

I've heard the name, but my mind is drawing a blank.

Mal leans in and says to me, "House Sandwalker, the most powerful line – it's where the Alerion comes from."

"She's that powerful?"

"She wouldn't be the Alerion otherwise," Jannik says, eyes still on Felicita's paling face. "My great-grandmother is her great-aunt. She left Urlin, no one ever knew why, and so another Sandwalker branch ruled in Pelimburg."

"I wouldn't say ruled," Felicita says with a cough. "Although you were certainly notorious enough."

He manages a weak smile. "In Pelimburg, the vampires are supposed to have equal status to Lammers. In practice." He gives an awkward, one-shoulder shrug. "Suffice it to say that my family was powerful and rich enough to influence many of the ruling Lammer House's decisions."

"So we might be distant cousins," says Sel.

Although his voice is tight with fear, he sounds so normal that we all of us turn to look at him. Next to Sel, Harun is carefully covering my brother with a loose sheet. I saw the burns, and I'm glad I can't see them now. To be honest, I don't believe he will make it to MallenIve, that we've wasted power and time.

"Cousins? How so?" Jannik's voice is flat, dead. He's talking so he doesn't have to think. I know the feeling.

Sel shifts to let Harun past to dress the burns on Jek's hands as best he can. They've woken him once and tried to give him a little water, but he started shaking, so we've left it. Hopefully when we're in Harun's house, with access to chirurgeons and medical supplies, we will be able to do something for him.

"My mother was a Sandwalker, although I've no idea what House my father came from." Sel carefully slicks a sweat-damp lock of hair back from Jek's eyes and winces.

Jannik nods. "Explains your power. Why did you never have access to it before?"

"Someone had to unlock it," he says. "Someone had to give me back my mind." He shrugs. "And the Alerion did."

Jek shifts, awake again, his eyes wide. The only sound that comes from his throat is a pained whine. It hurts my ears to hear it.

Sel looks up at me. "How long before the blaas gets back to the city?"

I'm doing my best to touch the blaas's mind, but the animal is panicked by the flames. I give it a mental prod, easing it away from the inferno. "She'll go fast," I answer, "she wants to get away from the fire."

"Jek wants to know what the fuck you're doing here," says Sel. "Not that he's complaining, mind."

I twist to get a good look at Jek's face. The side of his cheek is burned, and there's a patch of bald scalp – also burned. But in that ruined face, the eyes are still Jek's – aware, bright with pain; it's definitely my half-brother. He hasn't lost his mind, despite whatever happened to him in there.

"Someone told me to make my own choices." I fold my hands in my lap, anything to still the need in me that makes me want to reach out to take Mal's hand. "So I did."

Felicita groans and leans back against Jannik's chest. "I need to eat something," she whispers.

At her words, Isidro lurches up from where he has been sitting head in hands, and goes through to the little fore cabin. He's back moments later with food for all of us – stale pastries, water that tastes old and musty, milk on the verge of turning. It's better than nothing, and I eat.

"Ever the practical one," says Harun. "Thank you."

The shock of Jek's rescue is wearing off, and a tiredness so heavy and deep is sinking into my bones. I need to sleep – we all need to sleep – and I can only hope that most of us are still alive when I wake.

The world shudders, and it's the blaas's fear that wakes me seconds before the pain hits. Unrelenting agony that lances down my side and makes me scream. In my head, all I can feel is fear and anger and a mangled, guilty relief. It's too fast for me to separate the tangle of emotions, to try and pluck one thread clear and follow it to its source.

Mal is awake, instantly, and he snaps his magic back into my head. The pain stops. Just like that.

"Shit," he says. I sit up and hold my head gingerly. Across from me, Jek is staring, mutely. He's wide awake. In fact, so is everyone else in the carriage. I don't think anyone could have slept through that noise.

"I fell asleep," says Mal. "I'm sorry." His face is white, tight lines about his mouth.

Sel nods. "So did I – we were supposed to take turns, so that one of us would always be shielding you from the worst."

It was Jek's horror and pain, drilled straight into my head. I put my hand to my mouth, wanting to throw up, but I make myself swallow it down, and the taste of sour bile stings my throat. A reminder, because Jek's stings worse. I felt it. I make myself look at him, face the reality of what I just felt.

He's still staring at me, and I can almost hear his voice in my head, mocking me. *Still want what I got now, Ives?* he'd be saying.

We have an understanding, I think.

There was something else. "The blaas."

"What about it?" Jannik looks up. He's curled against Felicita, who seems less pale now.

Harun is already at the windows, drawing back the curtains with a sweep. Outside, it's daylight, and the world is on fire. A desert wind is blowing the smoke southward, away from us, otherwise we would have smelled it, ash and acrid death.

MallenIve is in flames, and far below us, the great Mekekana ships are gathering at her carcass like the big black flies that lay their eggs in the dead.

"Oh." It's all I can say. We are too late. My mother, Iliana. Trey.

A million lives. The Hobs in the Digs and Wend, all the Lammers from the outer and inner cities. How many could the palace have truly managed to protect? The idea that everyone I have ever known, than an entire city could be lying dead is so immense a thought I can't even contemplate it. Trying to grasp the enormity is like climbing a hill of smooth marble. I do not even know where to begin. I stare blankly instead and concentrate on nothing more than the sound of my thrumming blood. On the pulse of my living body.

"How long before we can land?" Harun is still staring at the destruction. The windle-silk tents are burnt away, and I can clearly see the groves of trees on fire, flaming like spring came a few months early and they are unfolding the first red leaves.

"You want us to fly into that?" My voice comes raspy with disbelief.

Everyone stills, Isidro bows his head, and does not look at Harun. Jek tries to sit up, and Sel hushes him, but makes no move to touch him.

"Yes," says Harun. "What else would you have us do – run?"

Well, yes. But then Felicita speaks, and although her voice is ragged with tiredness and loss, everyone listens. "I will not run," she says. "I have slept. The pain is less. We can still fight."

Mal and I cannot match the combined power of Jannik and Felicita, but it feels churlish to want to flee when Felicita will not. I sigh. Mal glances across at me, nods. "We will fight too," I say. After all, where would we run to? I alone know that Pelimburg is gone.

The blaas dips, begins to slow. I touch its mind and urge it on. We drift over the beetle-black backs of the Mekekana ships, too high for them to bring us down with their strange weapons. We float towards the heart of MallenIve, over the burning fields, the burning roofs, to where the Mata Palace rises like a garnet from the flames.

We're close enough that I can see tiny figures crawling in the wreckage below.

The centre of the city, a tight circle of untouched houses, comes into view, and my ears pop as we cross the last tiny bubble of the shield. So small – is that all we can hold? People have clambered on the roof tops, faces ash-smeared, tear-stained. They are waiting to die. Women with babes held close, Hob and Lammer side by side, waiting for the iron army to tear them apart. After seeing what Jek looks like, I know they have every right to be scared.

We coast lower, over their heads, and the faces turn up to us, some full of hope, others snarling at the blaas, the symbol of Mata untouchables. Here and there a bone face – a bat.

We should never have all left. I grit my teeth and bite back a dry-eyed sob. There was no sign of the Mekekana when we left; they were still coming up from Pelimburg. If we'd known they could move this fast... No, Harun would still have gone, and most likely Felicita. They care more for one of their own than for all of MallenIve. And whose fault is that?

The blaas, knowing she's home, swoops down to a small courtyard at the heart of the palace. There's a direct route here to the War-singers' chambers. As we land, I feel the last of the War-singers' shields fall.

Iron presses on the city from all sides.

"Run," says Mal.

THE PALACE IS disturbingly empty

Where the War-singers should be – there is nothing. Overturned chairs, scraps of paper, empty scriven bowls. One of them is cracked in two. On the tiles it sits, two accusatory halves. But of my sister and the others with their power, there is not a sign. The scriv is gone. There is only one thing that the Mata can do now.

"The Well," I say. "We need to get to the Well." And we need to protect the city from the Mekekana, but I cannot think which threat is greater now. "We need to go," I say. "There's a passage in the eastern part of the castle, blocked with stone, ten foot thick –"

Harun is already paling as I speak; how could I forget? He probably knows these halls better than I do. "No," he says, but even I can hear the weakness in his protest. He doesn't believe that anyone would go down there, would do as Mallen Erina had. Does he too know what became of House Mallen?

"Go," says Felicita. "Jannik and I will hold the Meke off."

"Can you?" The blood has mostly dried on her dress, but she's still shaking and pale.

She shrugs. "We will have to."

Sel raises his head. "I'll wake Jek," he says. "We can help Lady Pelim."

I can't imagine what good Jek is going to be in his current state, but there's no time to waste on wondering. I nod.

Harun knows the way to the stone-closed passage. Isidro, Mal and I follow him.

The stones here haven't been touched for six hundred years. If the histories are right, these walls are more than ten feet thick. They seal the second tunnel down into the catacombs that lead to the Folly.

Harun taps Isidro's magic, and between them the rocks shatter into dust, making me choke. Mal has my hand, and I don't bother trying to pull free. Somewhere, down there, is what's left of the High Houses. The dust settles, coating us in grey.

A series of steps leads down to an unlit tunnel. The blackness is solid, impenetrable. I use my free hand to feel along the wall, still holding tight to Mal.

We edge down the steps, carefully sliding our feet forward. The steps are barely worn, only the dust making footing risky.

Seventy-Two

The Grinningtommy

SEL WAKES ME, pulls me up out of that dreaming blue house and brings me back to the pain. *Sorry,* he says in my head. *The scriven's run out.*

"We need to move to a high point," says Felicita. "Jannik?"

He nods an takes her arm, helps her stand. "I'll have to give Sel a hand..." Jannik means with me. There ain't no way I'm walking nowhere. I swing up, Sel an Jannik hauling me between them on the dead Meke's coat. The pain's gone all dull as an old mirror now, an I think that Sel has his hand in that.

Of course. He half-smiles. Best I can do in the circumstances. Just stay awake, that's all I'm asking.

We jolt our way up a set of round tower stairs, all the way to a greeny-black glass balcony high above the city. Being this high up make me want to vomit, but there ain't a scrap of nothing left inside me.

Fires and smoke are all over the city, and I can see the Meke ships, hundreds of them, circling MallenIve.

There's no way we can hold them.

"Hush," says Sel. "You forget what House stands with you."

An I see it clear now, all that dark power in Sel, how it's seething all around him. Using Sel's magic will be like nothing else in this world, though there's bound to be a sharp down-side after we take on the Meke. Gris. I'll be lucky if I ever see straight again after all this.

"Now," says Felicita, an pulls the magic straight out of Jannik, sending it dancing dangerous over to the ships. One explodes, spraying metal and fiery lumps all over the sky.

"One," says Jannik. "One. We'll never bring them all down."

No one answers him, 'cause it's true, an the thought hurts. I struggle up to sit, an willing everything I have, I tap the magic that's curling about Sel like a red-black cloud. It hurts, but Sel pushes that magic through me, channels it. An there's so much, so much more than I realised.

Meke ships pop like little Hob-crackers set off on Long Night. None of it feels real. The bug ships crackle up, making a noise like ironnuts thrown on a fire. Over on the rooftops, people are all scrabbling about like ants, trying to hide from the fire and the raining metal.

Just when I think we're gonna make it, we're gonna burn these Meke fuckers alive, an for a moment the thought is so sweet that I almost forget how much I hurt, something breaks free from the Mata palace, and sends glass an ivory up in a fountain.

The balcony shatters, long cracks spreading out all around. The edges of the balcony start falling, raining glass down on the winter gardens.

A sudden blast of something strange, something dangerous an terrible rips into us. Liquid fire runs along my arms an I try scream, but my throat is dead.

"No!" Felicita shouts, an somehow, I manage to focus through the needlefangs of pure wild magic.

My stomach is all empty as a hole.

"Blaine's opened the Well. He's opened the fucking Well." Felicita screams, an all around us wild magic skitters; across my skin, claws catching in my blisters, then, like it found sweeter meat, drops away. My back scrapes along the balcony, as Sel an Jannik pull me back to the safety of the tower.

The last of the balcony collapses, an we watch through the burst-open tower door, over the jagged remains.

I'm back in my head again, an Sel is hushing me an watching out over the city. I see it all through his eyes. It's all murky and blurred, an it takes a moment 'fore I realise he has the third lids down.

The wild magic is racing for the Meke ships – but once it's eaten itself fat on them, it will come for us.

A smoke-stack of magic so thick and dark that it is solid as wood, is twisting in the air as it hunts.

"The Mekekana," Jannik says, as the solid tentacle of magic turns this way and that, groping about for a target. "It knows they're there. Magic to unmagic."

He's right. It's hunting them. Then, like a little desert wyrm, it strikes, splitting into more an more long fingers, each heading straight for one of the shiny Mekeships. I feel the magic falter and die as it connects.

The city turns into a storm-mess of iron shards and globs of magic that burn the dead fields around MallenIve in wide black scars.

There's something we need to do, Sel says.

Then aloud. "Jannik? Lady Pelim?"

I can feel them nodding, feel them saying yes to what Sel's asking.

Seventy-Three

A Game of Wasps

WE DON'T EVEN get a hundred steps down when I hear the screaming.

"Oh Gris," I say and lunge forward, but Mal stops me. "What are you doing?" He pulls me back with one hand on my wrist. "Are you insane?"

"What? There are people dying, my mother, Trey, Illy –"

"And what would you do?" he asks softly. "Take on all their pain?"

The realisation hits me; around so many people, in fear, in pain, in magic-induced frenzy I would be next to useless. Worse, I would be a burden. There's no way for Mal to shield me from so many. The tears that have burned hot behind my lids come searing down my cheeks.

"Why?" I say through a throat choked tight. "Why couldn't it just have been simple?" Hate lashes through me, a self-pity, and I'm blaming Mal, even though deep within I know it's not his fault.

He pulls back, frowning. "It's not yours either. You didn't want to believe the Mata would go this far, even though he killed your father."

"You read my mind." My mouth drops open.

"Side effect," Isidro says, from where he's standing up ahead, next to Guyin. "We all do it."

I shudder. "If you and Mal both shield me, can you take me down there?"

The screaming has turned high and broken – so many voices shrieking in unison. I close my eyes and wait for an answer.

"Yes," says Isidro, but his voice is tired, and I hear the subtle shake of it. He's not convinced. And I don't care.

The four of us walk on, down deep into the belly of the palace Underground, towards where the wild magic is seething and crawling along the walls. It brushes against my skin. It's weaker now, most of its energy concentrated on the mundane of the Mekekana. I hope.

"We're going to change," I whisper. No one answers, but the terror rises in me. Am I going to become like Mal, my skin turning wax pale, my eyes darkening? Am I going to suffer in the sunlight, blister if I stay out too long or is it only the War-singers who are trapped below us who will suffer the full effect of the Well?

Finally, we come out into the small circular room of the Well. The figures of the War-singers are black shadows against the walls, and I can make out not a single individual. Everything is overwhelmed by the raging pillar of wild magic streaming from a black pit in the centre of the room.

There's a body – no, two – on the lip of the Well. Neither of them is moving.

"Isidro," I say. "You need to drop shields and let Harun help me seal the Well." It's going to hurt, but I think of Felicita, and know that Ives has as much honour as Pelim, and that I will do this as best I can.

"You're not trained," he says, but he is tired and full of pain, and that's as much argument as he gives me. While I've not learned how to tap Mal, I know magic, and I've seen enough from Felicita and Jannik to know that I can do this.

"I will not be good," I say. "But we don't have time for good."

"I'll lead her once she has the connection open," Harun says to Isidro. "I can do that much. Let her help."

The shields drop instantly, and with only Mal's magic buffering me from the pain of the people all around me, I drop to my knees.

The pain is intense, running down through my skull, sending pathways of molten fire through the marrow of every bone in my body. My skin is not my own, and I have to claw my way through the terror and hurt of so many people before I can focus on Mal's magic.

"Now." I pull the magic into me and send it towards the broken seal of the Well. It's like drawing on scriv but instead of giving me the secret knowledge of human emotion, the whole world is a vibrating living creature, and all I need to do is push it to my bidding. Mal's magic is like him – smooth and withdrawn, and full of shadows and secrets, but it flows through me and towards the well, tearing at my body like a raging storm that has passed right through me as though I were no more substantial than a ghost. It feels less like I direct it, than that is knows what I want it to do.

Magic. Real magic.

Ahead of us, Harun and Isidro are doing the same.

I'm caught up in the magic, and it burns down every nerve, spills from my pores like sweat-slick heat. Isidro's and Mal's magic meet, twine together, and then Harun is in my head, guiding me. His exhaustion trembles against my mind, and a sudden wave of nausea sweeps through me as we are so intimately connected. Isidro to Harun to Mal to me. There is no secret thought or dream that is not known to all four of us.

Ignore it. Harun's voice. *Concentrate.*

I push away all the embarrassment and anger and fear, and do as he says, forcing Mal's magic to do my bidding. The clouds of dark bat magic blend seamlessly together under Harun's expertise. Finally, as much as I hate losing control, I let him take over, and do nothing more than feed our power to his.

He builds a net of magic, looping it around the power spilling from the Well.

It's not enough, and the wild magic bucks and shudders under our yoke.

Not enough.

I don't even know whose thought it is. We're ready to give up, all of us, there is nothing we can do, and the wild magic is going to tear MallenIve from end to end, destroying what the Mekekana haven't.

Hush.

Unbelievable force barrels through our connection, black and implacable as a night worm. Even Harun is staggered by the sheer force passing through us, gathering our power in its wake, almost as an afterthought. In my head, four more consciousnesses intrude: Jek, so full of pain that he's barely coherent; Felicita dead and numb and just moving because she can see no other choice; Jannik is anger, tired and bitter. And over them all, reflecting, amplifying them, is Sel, a cold glass knife.

There's no finesse to it, not like what Harun was attempting. The new magic just pounds down at the Well, like an iron sledgehammer, beating the wild magic into submission, and pouring stones and power and bodies into the neck of the Well, plugging it.

There now, says Sel as the room falls silent. We're on our way. Magic residue drops down all around us, soft as ash.

Thirst crawls up my throat, and I'm about to start screaming when Mal snaps the shields higher. The fear still ricochets at me, forcing me to bend double for a moment, to catch my breath. Then it stills, as Isidro adds his strength to Mal's.

Done. It's done.

I look up. What in Gris's damned name are Sel and Jannik, that they could do what they did?

Two figures are making their way towards us. They come out of the gloom, and I recognise my mother, vacantly staring, held upright by my sister.

She doesn't see me, because her eyes are rolled back in her head, the whites like pits of marble in the gloom. A Vision has her, deep enough that she's not even walking this world, but another, where the future is spread out in a map of possibility. Iliana guides her forward with shuffling steps.

"Calla?" Iliana says. Shock makes her voice small.

"You sealed the Well." Iliana lunges forward to grab my hand, but Mal pulls me back. "Mother said you would, that's why you had to bond with a bat, but I didn't understand how..."

"Yes." I catch my breath, swallow down the nausea. "We sealed it." I ask the question that burns in my chest. "Trey?"

"Dead," says Illy.

No. There is no truth to that, I will not let it be. My eyes burn, and my chest is so tight that it hurts to breathe.

Illy looks at Mother, then back to me, and I can see the tracks of tears through the dust on her cheeks. All she does is nod.

"And the other Lammers?" Harun asks.

"Dead. Mostly," she says. "Trey tried to stop him – the Mata."

"And now he's dead. Good for him." I don't choke on the words. I turn and start back up the steps.

"You think I didn't feel anything for him?" There are no footsteps, none of them are moving to follow me. "The wild magic turned him inside out. I watched him die, Calissa!"

"Stop talking!" I scream, because Mal's shields are buckling, and everything is pressing on me, so that I feel like I'm about to be buried alive in a sandstorm. "I don't want to hear any of this."

"Will you stop shouting," Mal hisses through gritted teeth. "Calm down before you make this any harder than it already is."

I chill, my skin prickling into goose bumps. "Please tell me you can still hold it."

Mal's face is slick with sweat. He peers at me through damp hair and grins. It's ugly. I'd almost forgotten how sharp his teeth are. "I can hold it if you'll just shut up and walk. The sooner we get to other vamps the better."

I'm still not moving. "Why?"

"Because, you idiot girl. I really need to feed."

That gets me moving. I'd pushed all thought of feeding and blood from my head. Perhaps I was hoping that if I didn't acknowledge it, it would go away. No such luck.

"I can't believe you actually did it," Illy says as we move forward. "Mother thought you wouldn't dare to walk that path."

"You knew all the time – both of you." And they kept it from me – Gris how they must have pitied me as they made their plans, as they justified themselves.

"Stop talking!" Mal's shouting now, and the headache that was pinching at the base of my skull is spreading.

Thankfully Illy falls quiet, and there, up ahead, pale buttery light spills down into the tunnel.

"Oh," says my mother. "So that's where it is." She's talking to herself, her tone light and conversational, but her eyes are still rolled back into her head.

"Where what is, Mama?" I haven't heard Illy call her that for years. She's gentle, her voice like a soothing hand on a child's brow.

"Why, the scriven, of course."

She sounds like she's talking about a mislaid pen, rather than the very bones of Lammic society.

Trust my mother to finally have a Vision worthy of Gris himself now that MallenIve is in ruins.

Father is dead. Trey is dead. Let my mother have her Visions, let the Lammers rejoice. I will not forget to mourn.

Seventy-Four

The Grinningtommy

THERE'S A STICKINESS in the air up here. The Well is closed now, but magic is still shivering up my bones in a way I don't right like.

Sel's here though, in my head. Lucky that. He's talking for me, asking Felicita questions, an even making them sound halfway clever. Never knew Sel was that bright.

He laughs. I surprise it out of him.

What's it gonna be like now, if I live?

Of course you'll live, he says in my head. *You're too damn stupid to know when to give up*.

Well, he's probably right about that. I never could just take no as an answer.

It will be fine.

An if the damn vamp believes that then I'm a Wend Hobling that's just learned to crawl. Nothing will ever be right again. Sel's all straight an fine, and I'm so fucked I can't even sit up straight. Add to that, Sel is a right smart little bugger, smarter than I ever credited him.

"You're not as dumb as you look either, Jek," he says it out loud. "We'll work it out."

I realise his fingers are just brushing the top of my left hand, careful an light as a moth's touch.

MallenIve ain't nothing more than a mess of burnt-out shite. The irthe orchards gone an turned to ash, an with them the moths an the money.

There are still irthe orchards in Pelimburg. We could go to the coast. Jannik says vampires are free there.

I'll go wherever Sel wants, an he knows that.

"I want to go back home," Felicita says. "I hate this city." She's on her knees, fingers splayed out on the tower floor, watching what's left of MallenIve burn.

I've been inside her head. Me an Sel, we know everything about her, about Jannik an Harun and Isidro. About Callisa an Mal. How the fuck did Sel go an do that?

She was thinking the same thing. Just before we pushed the Well shut.

I look out at where she's staring, at the smoke an the people all ant-like in the streets. Iron Meke ships are burning on the edges of the city. There's nothing out there worth saving.

Lammers will rebuild the city I suppose. On the backs of the Hobs, grind them into the dirt. Maybe the vamps will be better off now that the Lammers will find them useful. Right now, I don't care enough. Whatever happens, the Lammers will come out of it smelling fresh, an everyone else will just get trampled back into the dirt.

An fuck me, but I hurt.

Sel hears me, or thinks me, or something, because he brushes over me with that Alerion touch, and the pain throbs down to a level I can deal with.

"Go to sleep, Jek," he says, and his voice is all quiet an thoughtful an sad.

I CAN'T HOLD nothing right.

Sel is sitting on the edge of my bed, knees tucked up under him, and he's holding the cup for me. I feel like a fucking Hobling, but I can't complain. If I tried to do this myself, there'd be tea all over the fancy Ives bedspread, an none in my damn mouth.

"Here," says Sel. "I found this in what was left of the Ives house." He hands me a little sweet-wood box. I don't have to open it to know what's inside. The millions of tiny eggs the moppet laid 'fore she died.

"I don't want it none."

He shrugs, an sets the box down on the bed-covers.

Most of what happened after Isidro came for us is a blur. Sel tells me I passed out, just fell asleep like a milk-fed brat an didn't wake for two weeks.

Turns out everyone's taken turns at playing nurse for me. Ain't that just peaches.

Now they've got me propped up with pillows, an there's thin sun coming through the windows, dappling the dark blue covers. There's new bandages over the burns an the pain is bearable. Uncomfortable, for sure, an I keep wanting to go drown myself in a vat of ice water, but it's nothing compared to my time in the Mekekana ship.

Mekekana. The wild magic ate through what was left of them, turning the last iron ships into traps, fiery cages that burned the crew alive before the survivors fled out into the red desert. Gris only knows what will become of them, how they'll be magic-touched.

How much has changed, I wanted to know, but no one would tell me. Today, Harun says, they'll take me out to see the city. So here now, I'm drinking sweet tea for healing an getting ready to see if I can stand. Sel says I'm an idiot, an my feet are too fucked to walk on at the moment. He keeps glancing over at this chair they've rigged up to carry me in, with two poles bound along the arms. It's foolishness; there's no way I'm being hauled around in that.

"You're determined to try?" That's one good thing that's come out of this whole fucked-up mess; that Sel is sane an together as I've never seen him. He gets a bit flinchy when there are others around, like he's scared they're going to try touch him, but when I asked him about it he said, "It'll pass," an that was that. Now he won't say nothing if I bring it up, an I'm not stupid enough to carry on about it.

"You want to hang on to me when you try this great experiment of yours?" he says all dry-like. The boy's been spending too much time with Harun.

"Yeah," I croak, 'cept I've got this sinking feeling in my gut that even with Sel's help I'm not going to get far at all.

He sets the tea down on the side table an sweeps the blankets off my legs.

My feet are bound in white bandages.

"Come on then." Sel's got his hand out.

"I'm not asking you for a dance," I says. "Just bloody help me up." My voice is all throaty an raw, barely sounds like me at all. I'll have to learn to just keep quiet. That's going to be difficult.

The moment my feet touch the ground though, I know Sel's right. To save face I hobble over to the chair myself anyway, an take a seat like it's what I intended all along. Sel shakes his head. "I'll be right back," he says as he slips from the room.

While he's gone, I stare at my hands on my lap. There are no bandages, but my nails are gone. Sel told me they turned black an dropped off. Honest, I'm glad I wasn't awake to see that. I raise my right hand, an press it 'gainst the wood of the chair's arm. Nothing. I should be able to feel something, but the best I get is a kind of far-way pressure that I can't even tell is real or just me hoping to feel something. Fuck. Least I got my voice back, sort of. It's something. That, an Sel knows when I don't feel like talking an just says what needs to be said.

I drop my hand back to my lap as footsteps drum on the carpeted wood floor outside.Sel's brought Mal, Jannik an Harun to help carry this damn stupid chair around.

Calissa, it turns out, can barely go near people without being drowned with all their thoughts an emotions. I heard it's not so bad seeing as how most of the city is dead, but she still gets some bad heads, an she needs to lie down in a dark room as far away from everyone as she can. Not a life I'd want, for sure.

"How are you feeling?" Mal asks. An there's another little bit of a tale, that Calissa went an bonded with him. I don't know Mal at all, but he seems friendly enough. Sel seems to think they'll be fine, an there's a spot of hero-worship in his voice when he talks about Mal. If I could be bothered, I'd think I should be jealous, but if there is anything there, Mal pretends like he don't notice it.

"Brilliant. Like I could take on a wild sphynx wearing a blindfold then walk across the desert barefoot." An fuck me, it hurts. Keep your damn mouth shut, Jek old boy.

"Ignore him," says Sel. "He thinks he's being clever."

"Are you sure you want to come with us?" Mal asks.

'Course I'm sure. Sounds like the whole of bloody MallenIve is packing their bags an leaving the ruined city for some fabled scriven ground my step-mother saw in a Vision. Who am I to argue? "Let me see the city first," I let Sel say for me. "Harun says the irthe trees are gone. Can you take me that far?"

I have to see that for myself, the dead orchards, the empty Low Walk, an then I can be sure that there is nothing left to keep me here.

Sel puts the sweet-wood box on my lap when we leave, even though I din't ask out loud for him to do it.

The irthe trees look bad; worse even than I'd thought they could. Harun thinks a few might still sprout come spring.

"Without the tents, they're fucked anyway," I says.

Harun smiles. "There are already spinningjennies weaving new ones. There are windle-moth eggs ready for hatching. Not everyone is leaving."

"What's the point in staying?"

"Because it's their home," he says all mild-like back at me. Then he looks away from the ruin of the Low Walk, and the dead trees. "Pelimburg still has orchards standing, since you're so keen on trees," he says.

It's not about the damn trees, 'course, but no explaining that to him. I look down on the blackened mess, past the orchards to where the Wend an Digs once stood. It's a mess, the Lam-heaps steaming in the rising sun. I can smell the shit an rot an flame-licked skin even from here. A few Hobs still toil; they're the ones that decided not to leave. Marlon could be in there among them, not that I'm right keen on finding that out.

There's the little hill where Oncle's lean-to stood. The conetree is black an ragged, an the hut is gone. I hope he's somewhere in that train of scriv-heads marching after my step-mother's Visions. That's better than the thought of him under all that muck, burnt up like an old stick.

I don't need to say nothing out loud. Can't really.

So I just thinks it in my head. Thank him for giving me Prue's two bits, at least.

Sel hears it all, but I'm getting used to that.

"Okay," Sel says for me. "We can get on that floating table those Pelimburg fools call a barge."

Seventy-Five

A Game of Wasps

THE FIRST BARGE came from Pelimburg three days ago.

We saw them from what was left of the Ives family house, flags drooping as they struggled upriver.

I don't think I've run as fast before or since, Mal at my heels.

Now that we know Pelimburg still stands, in a way, Felicita is convinced that this is a sign that she must move back to her city.

Most of MallenIve is destroyed. The houses still standing are in need of so much repair that it would be easier to just raze them to the ground and start over. The streets are slowly emptying as the last of hangers-on load their barrows and nillies, and trail off into the desert, past the hulking corpses of the Mekeships.

My mother, it appears, is being lauded as the new Gris. She caught a powerful backlash of magic, and while it has blinded her permanently, it seems she sees other paths now.

I wonder if she sees the future where she and any other Lammer close enough to that blast is going to slowly start turning into a vamp. She hasn't mentioned it, but then again, these last days I needed an appointment just to see her.

Now she's gone, Illy with her, and a host of Houses and Hob servants and scriven-miners and all the dross that makes a city what it is.

Not everyone, though. While the people who've elected to stay are skirting MallenIve, spreading rumours about ghosts and magical-fallout, the Hob township that circles the city is slowly being rebuilt. And from what Mal tells me it's not just Hobs hard at work, but Lammers, mostly low, but here and there a High House, here and there a freed bat: bonded pairs slowly learning just what the rest of their life holds.

"I find it hard to believe that Pelimburg looks worse than MallenIve," Felicita says. She's wearing a thin shawl, but the weather is changing, and I can feel the faint stirring of spring. Jannik links his arm in hers.

"Some of it will still be standing." Jannik doesn't sound as if he believes it himself, although the wherrymen have assured us that Pelimburg, battered though she is, has raised her proud head and begun the mammoth task of rebuilding.

Of course, Pelimburg has been without scriven for longer than we have; they've made their own adaptations. A society that runs purely on wealth and power, rather than who has the most magic.

We will change that, even if we don't mean to. The strong will rise, and we, with our bonds, will be the most powerful force Pelimburg has seen in decades. I smile.

For the past few weeks, while the city licked its wounds like a cat, and Jek slept, I've spent most of my time with Jannik and Felicita. She's bitter and angry, blaming Harun for her lost child. Blaming herself for the deaths of the twins. The first fell with fever the night she stood in the Mata Palace, trying to convince the Houses to bond.

"She will come around," Jannik says to me one night, over a pot of tea. "She's prone to temper, and used to getting her own way, but she doesn't hold on long to her hate."

"Do you think it will be better in Pelimburg?"

"Perhaps."

"What's it like?"

"Like itself." He grins. "I don't care how bad she might have been hit, Pelimburg will rise. She's like that, full of sea-strength."

"You miss living there?"

Jannik shrugs then poured me more tea. "Always." He grins at Mal. "You've never lived in a city where we are accepted."

I wonder then if his family are even still alive. Here we are, leaving our ghosts, only to trade them in for Jannik's and Felicita's.

"Have you had word from your family?"

He looks down then and says nothing.

A candle flickers out, blown by a desert wind. "The Pelim House will have fallen," he says. "It would have been a target." He buries his head in his hands. "I do not think we will go to Eastern Pelimburg, to see the carcasses of our families."

"But perhaps we will walk on the promenade," says Felicita. I jump. None of us heard her come down the stairs. "And we will stand in the rain, and pretend we have just met, and are hiding under an umbrella, hoping that my brother didn't see us almost kiss."

Jannik even manages a smile. "A good memory."

"Was it?" She sits down and pulls a cup towards her, smiles faintly. "Oh," she says in mock-surprise. "You may be right. Certainly a memory worth repeating."

I realise then, in that moment, what is possible – the way that Jannik and Felicita can just be people undefined by caste, or magic, or society's rules. I look across at Mal, and wonder if he's seen it too.

How strange to think that I hope he has.

"Here comes our invalid," says Jannik. He's shading his eyes from the sun, and when I do the same, I can see the four figures and the burden they carry.

Mal sees me and waves. I raise one hand, drop it quickly. I'm still unused to his easiness, the way he doesn't layer truths like Trey did. We've even managed to work out the worst of the feeding issues, straight-forward, compromises. No games.

Strange. I sit down on my packed trunk and wait for them to come closer.

MallenIve fades. The last thing I see is the smoke-damaged finger of the Chalice pointing up into the sky. Clouds are billowing up behind it, the first sign that the seasons are changing. They're dark blue, heavy with rain, and maybe they will wash MallenIve clean of all her histories. A ghost city.

Pelimburg is waiting for us. Felicita calls it a city of dreams and salt-spray, and very bad poetry. Her words make Jannik smile. Even Harun looks almost relaxed, the thin constant frown that plagues his brows smoothed out. Next to him, Isidro is the only one of the vamps looking back at MallenIve. Mal told me that he remembers hearing stories about Isidro from the Splinterfist rookery; that he was the first vamp sold out of Riam's house. Perhaps he has better memories of MallenIve than the rest of us. He was the only one who argued for us to stay.

Isidro sighs and looks away from the skeleton city. He's wearing a navy coat that ends at his thighs: unfashionable, but it was one of the few salvageable pieces from what was left of the Guyin House. There's a dark patch on the left collar, a blurry indistinct shape where once something was pinned.

I turn closer to Mal, sinking into the protective layer of shields. He's also bundled up in his great-coat, but he's not looking back. With careful fingers, I reach out and tear the weak stitches that still hold that stupid alerion crest to his collar. Mal starts, but lets me pull it free, and keeps his head lowered even as I throw the embroidered scrap into the silted muddy water churning into froth under the paddles.

I look up, and Jek is grinning at me.

"It's just a fucking bird," says Sel.

End

Acknowledgements

There are so many people to thank, and there is no way my thank-yous will be enough.

Novels are not made in vacuums, and it is only with the support of friends, peers, and family that I was able to write Bones Like Bridges.

Bones first began life before When the Sea is Rising Red came out, and I was still a regular on the AbsoluteWrite forums. Back then Bones had another name, but that opening line never changed. It was on those forums that I met a group of writers who have been invaluable friends: the Musers. Thank you to all of them for their help, but special thanks to Elissa Hoole, Brianna Privett, Micheal Strother, and Amy Ross. Other writers and readers have had their hand in helping shape this novel, particularly those from my writers' co-op Skolion. A huge thank you to Nerine Dorman, Tallulah Lucy, Suzanne van Rooyen and all those at Skolion.

And last but definitely not least, thank you to my family and friends, to the readers who wanted more, and to the writers in Scotland who kept me sane and told me to keep working.

Thank you,
Cat.

About the Author

Cat Hellisen is a South African-born writer living in Scotland, where they survive on blackberries and pakora.

You can follow them on twitter @cat_hellisen

Previous works include

When the Sea is Rising Red
House of Sand and Secrets
Empty Monsters

Beastkeeper
Charm

CPSIA information can be obtained
at www.ICGtesting.com
Printed in the USA
LVHW051711161220
674342LV00006B/1268